ALSO BY E.E. HOLMES

SOUL OF THE SENTINEL

SOUL OF THE SENTINEL

The Gateway Trackers Book 6

E.E. HOLMES

Lily Faire Publishing

Lily Faire Publishing
Townsend, MA

www.lilyfairepublishing.com
www.eeholmes.com

ISBN 978-1-7339352-1-0 (Print edition)
ISBN 978-1-7339352-0-3 (Digital edition)

Publisher's note: This is a work of fiction. Names, characters, places and incidents are either the product of the author's imagination or are used fictitiously.

Cover design by James T. Egan of Bookfly Design LLC
Author photography by Cydney Scott Photography

To any girl anywhere who turned a "no" into a "yes" with the sheer force of her spirit, I see you. This one's for you.

"For boys and girls who will not mind,

Who trouble court and mischief find,

The Tansy Hag, she lies in wait

To leave her mark upon your gate."

– Durupinen Children's Tale

CONTENTS

PROLOGUE

T HE MOMENT HAD COME.

She had read all the signs, interpreted every sprawling pattern, and every tiny detail. She could be left in no more doubt. It had to be tonight.

She sent up a silent prayer—it seemed the prudent thing to do, in case anyone was actually listening—and set to work. She had never performed this Casting before. *No one* had ever performed this Casting before. She had, after all, just invented it. She clenched and unclenched her shaking hands. Every Casting had once been performed for the first time, she reasoned. Every Casting was once nothing more than a whispered prayer and a leap of faith.

And she had to leap. She had no choice.

She had extinguished all the candles and drawn the curtains on the tower windows. The fire was burning brightly now, but there was nothing to be done about that—it was essential to the Casting. She would just have to hope that no one spotted it before she could extinguish it.

The full moon was so big and so bright, that she could see the swollen, glowing shape of it through the curtains, anointing her secret work with its light.

The herbs had been drying in bunches by the hearth for weeks. No one had asked about the widow's weed or the feverfew, because they could be used in many Castings. But she had had to be cautious in concealing the rue and the mandrake and the foxglove, tying them into much smaller bunches and hanging them behind larger, more fragrant herbs to mask their scent. Naught but mischief dwelt in the purple bells of the foxglove, all Durupinen knew that.

Well, she thought to herself, this was mischief of a sort, wasn't it?

She worked quickly and silently, stripping and crushing the leaves and flowers, grinding them into a fine powder with her mortar and pestle, just as the old Traveler woman had shown her. She measured and remeasured, knowing that she could not afford to make a single mistake. She would get only one chance—one chance to set this in motion.

She carefully tipped the crushed herbs into a bowl and set it on the hearthstones in front of the leaping fire. Then she pushed back the sleeve of her nightdress to reveal the bandaged length of her forearm. She untied the end of the bandage near the crook of her elbow and unwound it carefully, revealing, inch by inch, an elaborate design of runes and florals that had been painted onto her skin. She breathed a sigh of relief to see that the old Traveler woman had been right—the paint had not smudged or faded, even after three days of being bandaged so.

This artwork had been, perhaps, the most difficult part of her plan to conceal. She had neither the skill nor the knowledge required to paint the intricate artwork herself, but the Casting would not work without it. After much argument and discussion, they had decided that the Traveler woman would apply the paint for her, and that they would obscure it beneath bandages until it was time to perform the Casting. If anyone asked about it, she could say that she had cut or burned herself. Fortunately, the sleeves of her gowns and ceremonial robes had kept the bandages well-concealed, and not a soul, living or dead, had uttered a single word about them.

The light of the fire glinted off the swirling patterns, and the woman allowed herself a moment to admire the intricacy of the artwork before focusing her mind once again on the task at hand. Very carefully, she used a metal spoon to scoop a small pile of glowing embers from the heart of the fire. She could feel the heat singeing the tiny fair hairs on her arm, but she did not care. It made her feel alive—connected to her body. She needed that connection to be as strong as it had ever been, if this Casting was to work. And it had to work.

Taking a moment to steady her hand, which seemed hellbent on trembling, she held the embers beneath the bowl of herbs. Sweet, cloying tendrils of smoke began to rise from it, and she leaned forward, inhaling deeply. Almost at once the inside of her head felt as light and sinuous as the smoke, and as free to roam.

Create the door, she told herself. *Create the door and she will find me—across time, across space, across the wide and mysterious expanses of the spirit world. And then this greatest of all wrongs will be righted at last, before it is too late.*

"Create the door," she whispered, before falling at last into the depths of the Rifting.

2

THE GIRL IN THE FLOWERS

"Smile."

"I am smiling."

"Sweetness, I hate to have to break this to you, but you clearly missed that day in 'How to be a Human' training because no one else in the world has ever made that expression and called it a smile."

"Would you just hurry up and take the damn picture already? My face hurts."

The sun beat down on my head and my armpit itched. I felt a single droplet of sweat slithering down the back of my neck and longed to wipe it away. The lace dress into which I had been stuffed was corset-tight, and I was ravenous. My stomach began loudly protesting my continued torture, but I ignored it. The truth was that I had signed up for this cruel and unusual punishment, because when your Spirit Guide is also a world-class fashion designer, you resign yourself to making certain sacrifices.

"This is beautiful," my sister Hannah said, clicking her camera and then gazing happily around the Fairhaven gardens and breathing a sigh of contentment. "I can't believe we never thought to take your photos out here before."

"Right, okay, one last pose, just toss your hair back and close your eyes, like you're imagining something," Milo said, cocking his head to one side and eyeing me critically.

I obeyed his order, casting my face up toward the sun and closing my eyes. "I am imagining setting this dress on fire and dancing around the flames in my sweatpants," I said dreamily.

"See, *that's* a smile," Milo said, clapping his hands together. "Okay, you're done. Thank you."

"You're welcome," I said grudgingly, raising myself carefully from the flowerbed in which I had been lounging and trying not to trod on the hem. "When are you planning to post these?"

"As soon as Alice finishes up with the alterations on the last order," Milo said, his eyes shining. "So, Saturday, hopefully? And I had a request to have a design lent out to a runway show in London next month, so I want to get that shipped out first."

My face broke into a real smile this time. Since Hannah and I had created a fashion blog for Milo as a Christmas gift, his longtime goal to become a famous fashion designer had transformed from unattainable dream to a very tangible possibility. At this point, our biggest challenge was stopping him from becoming *too* famous. After all, ghosts may have been a daily reality in the Durupinen world, but I didn't think the Hollywood red carpet scene was *quite* ready for it.

Hannah looked down at her watch and frowned. "Do you think you've got what you need, Milo? I'm sorry, but I have to get back to the library. Karen is meeting me with more research materials, and I still have several pages of revisions to make."

"Yeah, this should be fine," Milo said, floating up behind Hannah so that he could watch the camera's tiny screen as she clicked back through the photos. "We can head in. It looks like some of those clouds heading in are full of rain anyway."

We trudged back up to the castle, and as much as I'd grumbled and complained about being forced into haute couture so early in the morning, I found myself wishing we could linger in the garden a little longer. Returning to the castle meant returning to some aspects of reality I wished I could forget. I had a newfound understanding for people who liked to lose themselves in the simple beauty of a fashion magazine—if I could have spent a little more time as that carefree, airbrushed girl in the lovely dress, soaking up the sun like a flower, and a little less time as myself, I wouldn't have complained. Being myself at the moment was... well, complicated.

It had only been a few weeks since the attempted coup at Skye Príosún, where our own Caomhnóir guardians had nearly been suborned into service of the Necromancers. And though we had managed to thwart the attempt, the fallout had been severe, and we were still trying to assess the damage. The tense relations between the Durupinen and the Caomhnóir which had proved to be an exploitable weakness, were more strained than ever. The Trackers were scrambling to sort through the aftermath, to determine the traitors and the victims, and to track down those who had escaped, including Charlie Wright and my former Caomhnóir Ambrose, who had taken over in Finn's absence and then betrayed us all by joining with the Necromancers voluntarily. And on top of all of that, Fiona's injuries from our escape had left her nearly blind, and Hannah was only a few days away from presenting a policy proposal to the Council that would completely overhaul how Caomhnóir and Durupinen were permitted to interact. If the proposal failed, Finn and I would find ourselves once again in limbo, our relationship elicit and our future in the Durupinen world uncertain.

So, in conclusion, yes, could I just go lay in the flowers and be pretty some more, please?

Everyone stared at me as we entered the castle—unsurprising, seeing as I looked like I was headed to the prom at nine o'clock on a Tuesday morning. Luckily, I was so used to being the subject of curious stares in this castle that I hardly registered them as I crossed the dining room to grab a cup of coffee and a croissant from the breakfast buffet.

"Jess, I think you need to wear your shoes in here," Hannah whispered as we passed yet another table of judgmental glares.

"The first person to tell me to put these shoes back on gets them duct taped to their feet for the rest of the day," I said with my mouth full of pastry.

"They're staring because they wish they looked this fierce!" Milo sang, not troubling to keep his voice down. Several Apprentices at a nearby table quickly dropped their blushing faces to their plates. I snorted. Well, we might still be spectacles around this castle, but at least we owned it now.

Hannah looked at her watch again and groaned. "You guys, I really need to go meet Karen. I'm sorry. Can you take the camera back up to the room?"

"Um, sure," I told her, cramming the rest of the croissant into my mouth, tucking my shoes under my arm, and holding out my coffee-free hand to take the camera from her. "Don't worry about it; go. I'll see you there later, after I meet with Catriona."

Hannah gave me a sympathetic pat on the shoulder. "Oh, that's right! Good luck!"

"Thanks," I replied. "I'm going to need it."

5

Milo and I rounded the corner at the top of the entrance hall staircase and nearly walked right into Finn.

"Gah!" I cried, fumbling everything I was holding in an effort not to fall over. Milo let out a shriek that echoed into the rafters over the fate of his latest sartorial creation, but thankfully I managed to slop my coffee down onto the rug rather than the dress.

"Jess! I was just looking for... I... bloody hell!" Finn breathed, really taking me in for the first time. "That is... my God, you look positively stunning!"

I felt the color creep up my cheeks and the beginnings of a goofy smile on my lips, which I quickly smothered. "Thanks. It's Milo's fault. We had a photo shoot for his next blog post this morning, and I was the sacrificial lamb this time around."

Finn turned to Milo and inclined his head. "She's a vision. Well done, you."

Milo tossed his head. "I know, you can say it. I'm an undiscovered genius."

"I think we can all agree you're a pretty well-discovered genius at this point," I told him, before turning back to Finn and bestowing a quick kiss on him. "I don't suppose you could do me a favor and carry this, could you? Hannah abandoned us for the library, and Milo is completely useless in these types of corporeal situations."

Finn chuckled. "Of course," and held out his hands for the camera.

"Why were you looking for me?" I asked as we made our way down the corridor that led to my room and the sweet, sweet release of normal clothes.

"I wanted to tell you that I've finished all the measurements in Fiona's studio," Finn said. He pulled a small notebook from his back pocket and waved it at me. "And I think I've calculated what we'll need for supplies, but I'll want you to look at the sketch before I go ahead and order everything."

"Perfect. I'll have a look as soon as I get changed. Thank you so much for helping me with this," I said.

"You are most welcome, love, although... do you think you might be biting off more than you can chew?"

"What do you mean?" I asked. We had reached the door to my room, and I dropped my shoes to the floor as I fumbled with the key in the lock.

"Well, I must admit, I've never been inside Fiona's tower before and it's... well..."

"Disorganized?" I suggested.

"A bloody disaster, actually," Finn said, shaking his head. "I know she's eccentric, but that was a nightmare! I can't understand how you're going to get it all done in just a week."

"Well, I've got to try," I said and then, when I was sure I had my voice under control I added, "She would do it for me."

Finn smiled at me. "Yes. Yes, she would." He planted a kiss on my forehead and handed me the little notebook. "Have a look at that and let me know what you think. I'm due down at the barracks, but I'll see you this afternoon. And don't let Catriona bully you!"

I laughed with slightly more bravado than I felt. "Don't worry about Catriona," I said. "I can handle her."

§

The Tracker office had never been so busy. In fact, the Tracker office was now the Tracker offices, two additional classrooms nearby having been taken over to accommodate all the additional staffing and workload that the recent uprising at Skye Príosún had necessitated. Not only had nearly every Northern Clan Tracker been pulled off their regular caseloads in order to help with the investigation, but Clans from other parts of the world had actually loaned out some of their own Trackers to aid in the process, which Durupinen everywhere could agree was of utmost importance.

I had never met a Tracker—or indeed any Durupinen—who wasn't descended from the Northern Clans. Well, unless you counted the Travelers, but they prided themselves thoroughly on being disconnected from any country at all. Walking into the Tracker office now was like walking into the UN or something—at any given moment, there were four or five different languages being spoken as the Durupinen tried to come together in the service of a single, unified task: wiping the remaining Necromancers from the face of the earth. Given the importance and intensity of the work being done, I was sincerely dreading telling Catriona what I had come there to say.

"Is that your report? Let's have it, then," Catriona said by way of a greeting. She held a hand out and snapped her fingers impatiently at me as I extracted the papers from a folder. She flipped through them, her eyes rapidly scanning the pages for glaring omissions. "Right. That looks in order. If you can hang tight for a minute, Elin should be here in a tick. She's got some things for you to sign."

"Yeah, sure," I said. "But I need to talk to you about something."

Catriona had already pulled a highlighter from thin air and was busily marking-up my report. "Talk, then. Who's stopping you?"

I took a deep breath, steeling myself. "I need to ask for some time away from the Trackers."

"Time away, what the hell does that mean?" Catriona grumbled, still deep in her read-through of my work.

"I'm not sure what to call it," I said, shrugging. "A leave of absence, I guess?"

Catriona's head shot up suddenly, as though my words had only just penetrated her concentration. "Are you telling me you're quitting?" she asked in a voice that snarled with contempt. "Now? With everything that's happening?"

"I'm not quitting," I said, trying to counter her anger with some calmness. "I just need to take a step back for a bit."

"I don't need people to step back, I need them to step *up!*" Catriona cried, snatching a paperweight from on top of her desk and hurling it to the ground in frustration. "It's utter madness here, Jess, in case you hadn't noticed!"

"Yes, I have noticed. I've just barely arrived back from the most dangerous Tracker mission you've ever sent me on, remember?"

"Yes! And I'd think, given its importance, that you'd bloody well like to finish it!" Catriona shouted. Over her shoulder, a Tracker who had been about to enter the office from an adjoining room turned right around on her heel and walked back out again.

"I do want to finish it," I said. "Truly, I do. But there's something else I need to do first."

"Are you going soft on me?" she demanded. "That mission into the *príosún*, was that too much for you? You might as well come out with it now, if that's what this is about. I'm not in the business of coddling and hand-holding, and I can't have Trackers on my team who can't handle a simple undercover—"

"Okay, first of all, there was nothing simple about that mission, and you damn well know it," I said, firing up despite my best efforts to remain calm. "Secondly, I'm not going soft. I haven't been scared off, if that's what you're thinking. But there is something really

SOUL OF THE SENTINEL

important I need to do here at Fairhaven, and I think it's going to be incredibly time-consuming at first."

"And what is that, then?" Catriona sneered. "What could be so vital that you want to abandon the Trackers at the very moment when some of the most dangerous Necromancers in the world have scattered to the four winds and our own Caomhnóir have been breached and compromised? Not enough time to snog your boy toy now that he's back from exile?"

I could have reached across the table and slapped her, but I managed to swallow the impulse, which I must admit was uncharacteristically mature for me. Instead, I took a deep breath and replied. "It has nothing to do with me, or with Finn either. It has to do with Fiona."

This pulled Catriona up short. She pressed her lips together for a moment before replying, curtly, "What about Fiona?"

"Have you been getting updated? About her condition?"

"Not since she got back," Catriona said, her tone a bit defensive. "I've had a lot going on. She was burned quite badly, wasn't she? On her face?"

"Yes," I said, taking advantage of the temporary ebb of her rage to continue explaining. "I've been to see her every day, and she's... well, the burns have affected her eyesight."

"How badly?" Catriona asked quietly.

"Very badly," I told her. "She's not completely blind, but she's close to it."

Catriona stared at me for a moment as though I had been speaking in tongues. Then she replied, curtly, "I had no idea."

"I know. That's why I'm telling you."

"I haven't even been down there to see her. Once I knew she wasn't in danger of... I just didn't bother to..."

"You said it yourself, it's been pandemonium up here these last few days."

"That's not a proper excuse."

"Maybe not, but it's an explanation. No one's faulting you here, Catriona. This isn't an accusation. I'm just filling you in."

"Blast it all to hell," Catriona muttered, collapsing into her chair. She rubbed a hand wearily over her face, letting the information sink in. "That'll devastate her, that will. She's an artist, for Christ's sake. How is she going to... *blast it all to hell.*"

"Yeah, it's going to suck, no doubt about it. That's why I came to

9

you. I think there might be some things I can do to make it easier on her, but it's going to take some serious time and energy, and I've only got maybe a week until she's out of the hospital ward."

"Let's have it, then," Catriona sighed. "What's your plan?"

I explained what I wanted to do. Catriona listened intently until I had finished, and then frowned. "Will I still be able to get a hold of you if I need you?"

"Catriona, I probably won't be able to leave the castle for the next week. Unless I'm sleeping, eating, or peeing, you will find me in Fiona's tower," I said.

Catriona nodded grudgingly. "Right, then. Well, do what you need to do, then. I'll rearrange some people to cover the offsite work I was going to assign to you."

"Thank you," I said fervently. "It means a lot to me to be able to—"

The office door burst open behind me, and Lucida stood framed in sunlight streaming in from the window across the hall. "I need to talk to you, Cat," she hissed.

I had seen Lucida around the castle several times since we had arrived back at Fairhaven, but the shock of seeing her freely roaming the halls didn't seem to wear off. I'd grown so used to the idea of her being a convicted traitor locked behind bars that every sighting of her at liberty was like a punch to the gut.

The weirdest thing about it was that I wasn't even convinced she should be back behind bars. Lucida had been instrumental in my escape from Skye Príosún. Not only had she freed Fiona and me from our cells, but she had helped to rescue Fiona's mother as well, and even used her Caller abilities to save Finn and the rest of the Caomhnóir from a legion of spirits who had been weaponized as Blind Summoners. Watching her and Hannah work together to overcome the Necromancers had been at once surreal and cathartic. It had felt like the beginning of something—like a door that had been opened just a crack, revealing a glimpse of light beyond it. I had no idea if Lucida intended to open that door wide, or slam it shut again, and I think it was the not-knowing that left me so unsettled in her presence.

"Can't it wait, Lucida? I'm up to my eyeballs in it, here," Catriona said wearily.

Lucida did not even spare me a glance. "If it could wait, I would have damn well waited."

"Well, what is it, then?" Catriona huffed. "What could be so pressing that—"

"Why didn't you tell me they were coming here?" Lucida cut in, her voice raw with what sounded like fear. Catriona heard it too, and it pulled her up short.

"Who are you talking about?" she asked, her voice a cool and rational counterpoint to Lucida's slightly frantic one.

"You know full bloody well who I'm talking about!" Lucida snapped, but when Catriona continued to look bemused, she added, "The Caomhnóir! The Caomhnóir and the Necromancers from the *príosún*, the ones facing charges!"

Catriona still looked utterly bewildered that a handful of shackled prisoners should cause her cousin such distress. "Yes, of course they're coming here! You were a Tracker, Lucida, you know how it works. If a prisoner has to face the Council for questioning or sentencing, they stand before them here at Fairhaven. I know you've been in prison for a stretch, but surely you haven't forgotten the bare basics of our judicial system. I mean, you went through it yourself, for God's sake!"

But Lucida seemed barely to have heard a word of what Catriona had said beyond that first "yes." She began pacing the room like a caged jungle cat, clutching at her hair. "I can't be here," she muttered to herself several times before rounding on Catriona and repeating it. "I can't be here! You've got to get me out of here when they come!"

Catriona threw me an anxious glance before replying, "I can't do that, you know I can't. You're under house arrest, Lucida. You can't leave the grounds unless you're cleared at your hearing, and that's not for another two weeks."

"Well, talk to someone, then!" Lucida shouted. "You're on the bleeding Council! Appeal to the other members! Get it moved up!"

"Do you really think the Council will be inclined to change their schedule to suit the whim of a convicted traitor?" Catriona shot back, getting heated herself now. "If you ask me, it's a miracle they're giving you a hearing at all. If it weren't for Hannah Ballard—"

"What about Hannah?" I said, speaking for the first time and breaking a sort of spell that Lucida's fear had cast over the room. Both she and Catriona stared at me as though I had just materialized out of thin air into my chair.

"She lobbied for Lucida's hearing," Catriona said. "She was quite impassioned. Seemed determined that you should have a chance to be heard, even after everything you put the poor girl through."

I stared at Catriona. "Hannah lobbied for her? *Hannah?*"

"Catriona this isn't just some whim," Lucida growled through gritted teeth. "I'm telling you now, it will not be safe for me here. You can't let them do this, you can't let them in the castle while I'm here."

"Lucida, just explain what you're on about!" Catriona cried.

"They'll know I'm here! They'll know, and they aren't going to miss an opportunity to take me out of this equation," Lucida said. She was pacing again, twisting her fingers together.

"They won't be able to touch you! Every one of them will be under lock and key, guarded twenty-four hours a day under the strictest of security protocols!"

"Protocols they all know like the back of their hands because they used to execute them as part of their jobs," Lucida said. "I'm telling you right now, Cat, I am not safe here!"

Catriona was looking at Lucida in frank alarm now. "Lucida tell me what's going on. You were in the *príosún*, holed up with the Necromancers for years. If they wanted to remove you as a threat, they would have done it then. No doubt they had ample opportunity, especially if they were turning the guards."

"I wasn't out then!" Lucida cried. "And who would have listened to me anyway, to the mad ravings of just another prisoner desperate to get out. But now that I'm here, now that there's a chance I might have the Council's ear again..."

"But what are they so afraid you're going to tell us that you couldn't have told us years ago when you were first tried before the Council?" Catriona asked. She went still, and her eyes narrowed. "Lucida? What do they think you know?"

Lucida met Catriona's eye, and the look upon her face was... arresting. Devastated. She shook her head, her lips trembling. "Keep me safe, Cat," she whispered, and slipped back out of the door.

The intensity of her words left both of us unable to speak for a few moments after she disappeared through the doorway. Finally, I broke the spell by turning to Catriona and murmuring, "What the hell was that about?"

Catriona shook her head. "I have no idea. She's never... I've never seen Lucida afraid like that, not even when... well, I've never seen her afraid like that," she finished. Then she turned her gaze fiercely onto me, making me feel as though I were being x-rayed. "Did she say anything to you in the *príosún*? Anything that might make you think that she was scared of something?"

I tried to recall our conversations during that frantic escape, but most of it was an adrenaline-fueled blur of terror. "I can't... I honestly can't think of anything specific. She just really wanted to get out of there. She... talked a lot about how the Necromancers didn't need her anymore—that they'd cast her off as worthless. And she also mentioned that, because they'd basically forgotten all about her, they weren't careful about what they said in front of her anymore. That's how she knew that they were planning to overtake the rest of the Caomhnóir."

"So then, it's possible that she overheard something more than just the plan to overtake the *príosún*," Catriona said, more to herself than to me.

"Like what?" I asked.

"Jess, let me ask you something. What is the point of taking over a fortress?" Catriona asked.

"The... the point?" I asked. "I... I don't know. To have somewhere to fight from?"

"Ah, yes," Catriona said. "But to need somewhere to fight *from*, you first need something to fight *for*."

I blinked. "I'm... not following you."

"Oh, come on, Jess, this isn't rocket science. If all you want to do is escape, you don't take over a fortress. You don't create an army. There had to be another end game, a reason they wanted to take that location, and hold it. It's the missing piece to this whole puzzle!"

I felt like an idiot for admitting it, but I hadn't realized there was a missing piece to the puzzle. I never questioned why the Necromancers were trying to take over the *príosún*. They were forever looking for ways to take what was ours, to undermine our abilities to protect ourselves and our gifts. Taking control of one of our most impenetrable sites and enlisting our guardians as soldiers was just another attempt to do that... wasn't it?

"You... you mentioned the archive there. We ran through it when we were escaping the *príosún*. You said before that you thought they might be interested in something that we stored down there—some artifact or piece of information?"

Catriona bit her lip. "Yes, and we've been combing the archive ever since we took back the *príosún*. As far as we've been able to tell so far, nothing is missing."

"So then, you think they might have wanted to secure the *príosún* for another reason? Something we haven't thought of yet?"

"It's possible," Catriona said.

"And maybe Lucida knows something about it?" I pressed.

"Also possible." Catriona sunk into her chair. "Blimey, what a clusterfuck this all is."

"What are you going to do?" I asked. "About Lucida, I mean."

Catriona gave a long, weary sigh. "What can I do? When all is said and done, she's my blood and she's asked me to protect her. I'm going to walk into the Council Room and make a complete arse of myself by putting forward her request. And then, when they all laugh in my face and tell me to sod off, I'm going to have to think of some other way to make her feel safe."

"Do you really think she's in danger?"

"I don't know," Catriona said. "I honestly can't see how. But I do know this. The toughest most ruthless criminals I've ever seen in my life were broken within months of entering Skye Príosún. Lucida might be battered, but that place has not broken her. I've never seen her scared like that. If she says there's something to be scared of, she may bloody well be right."

"Is... does this change anything? Is it still okay with you if I help Fiona out for a few weeks?"

Catriona had sunk down so deeply into contemplation of the conversation with Lucida that it took a few seconds of staring blankly at me before she realized what I was even talking about. "No, no, do what you need to do for Fiona, but... just do it as quickly as you can, alright? And I still need you on call for an emergency."

"Thanks, Catriona," I said. "It means a lot to me to be able to—"

"Put it in a letter, duck, I'm drowning in it here," snapped Catriona. She had already returned to her paperwork and was waving me impatiently out the door.

2

A NEW ALLY

I COULD HEAR MILO's disappointed sigh from all the way across the main library reading room as I approached the table where Hannah, Karen, and Savvy were working.

"Did you have to take all the make-up off, too?" he grumbled. "All that hard work. That smoky eye was flawless."

"Milo, who the hell gets contoured to go sit in a library?" I snapped. "Besides, those false eyelashes were making my eyes water."

Milo muttered something about libraries needing "more glamour," but I ignored him, turning to the others instead.

"So! How's it going?"

Hannah barely looked up from the paper she was highlighting, her nose only a couple of inches from the page. "It's going," she replied vaguely.

Savvy gave a low whistle, and ran a hand through her newly-shortened hair. "Mate, don't ask me. I can't make heads or tails of most of this lawyer-speak."

"It's coming together very nicely," Karen added. "Hannah is being too hard on herself."

"I don't want it to come together nicely. I want it to be unassailable," Hannah mumbled, still not looking up.

"Well, that's why I'm here, isn't it?" Karen said with a wink.

Karen had transferred to the new London office of her Boston-based law firm so that she could be closer to us. It seemed we had scared the hell out of her one too many times by getting into life-or-death situations and then neglecting to tell her about them. We'd meant to protect her—to keep her from worrying—but she'd only worried more when she realized what kinds of shenanigans we'd managed to stumble into without her knowledge. I still felt little pangs of guilt every time I saw her within the walls of

Fairhaven, a place she'd sworn she'd never stay again, because I knew that she was only here for us. But that guilt was always swallowed up by a deep gratefulness to finally have an adult in our lives who was so dependably present.

"Can I do anything to help?" I asked, dropping into a seat and gazing, rather unenthusiastically, I'll admit, at the stacks of books, papers, and scrolls.

"Here, proofread this," Hannah said, tossing a packet at me. "Mark any typos you find with the pink highlighter."

"Yes, ma'am," I said with a little salute.

"Also, don't tell me how many typos you find, because I've proofread it about twenty times, and if it's still full of mistakes, I'll probably burst into tears," Hannah added in a slightly hysterical voice.

I opened my mouth to reply, but then caught Milo's gaze, who gave his head a tiny shake as if to say, "Don't poke the bear." Obediently, I dropped my gaze to the document. It was really for me and Finn that Hannah was doing all of this work in the first place, so honestly, I should probably just shut up and edit, if I knew what was good for me.

"And when you're done with that, maybe look over this part I've been working on, because I don't think editing is my calling," Savvy said with a laugh. "I'm doin' me best, though, cross my heart," she added hastily when she saw Hannah's tense expression.

"How many days have we got left?" I asked tentatively a few minutes later.

"Fourteen. We have fourteen days to get this done," Hannah replied sharply.

"And greater feats have been achieved in less time," Karen said calmly. "You are in excellent shape here, Hannah. I know you have a hard time believing that, but I'm going to pull the lawyer card here. If one of my legal briefs was this far along two weeks out from the court deadline, I would be very pleased indeed."

Hannah looked up at Karen. Her face twitched into something resembling a smile, although it was fleeting. "I could probably spend another year on this and still feel like I'm rushing things," she admitted. "There's just so much riding on it."

"Which is why all of us are helping you. And I promise you, if this legislation fails, it won't be because you didn't try hard enough," Karen said firmly. "You are attempting to overhaul hundreds of years of policy. This battle isn't so much an uphill climb as it is trying to build a homemade rocket to the moon." Karen stood up. "I'm going to see if the Scribe has made any progress with our call slips from this morning," she added, and walked off toward the circulation desk.

"Hannah, you seem more stressed out than when I left you this morning," I said, setting my highlighter down. "Is something else bothering you?"

Hannah sighed, mirroring my movement by dropping her own pen. "I'm sorry. I'm finding it hard to concentrate today."

"Why?" I asked.

"I think I've got a hunch," Milo said, and cocked his head toward the far corner of the library, where a familiar head full of tight black curls was protruding above the privacy walls of a study carrell.

"Is that Lucida?" I asked in surprise. "What's she doing here?"

"You mean besides distracting me?" Hannah asked with a sigh. "I'm not sure. Reading, I suppose."

"She hasn't been here long. Arrived maybe ten minutes before you did, mate," Savvy added. "Bit weird, seeing her just walking around wherever she pleases as if she owns the place."

"I still think we should ask her to leave," Milo said.

"On what grounds?" Hannah asked, putting her pencil down with a resigned sigh. "She's perfectly within her rights to sit in the library."

"On the grounds that she's a convicted traitor and I don't trust her!" Milo hissed, loudly enough that Hannah shushed him with a frantic flapping of her hands. He went on, undeterred. "Look, I'm not going to apologize for looking out for you. It's literally my purpose in life—well, *after*life—and even if I wasn't Bound to do it, I'd be doing it anyway! I don't trust that woman and I never will."

"You don't have to trust Lucida, just don't cause a scene that gets us kicked out of the library! She's not worth it," Hannah pleaded.

"Fine," Milo said, his tone very dignified. "But I will continue to glare at her, and if she so much as approaches the table, I'm going to let the full power of my scene-making ability rain down upon this place, so keep your umbrella at the ready, sweetness."

Hannah managed not to roll her eyes, but it was a close call. "Fine. Consider me braced for the downpour. Can we just get back to work, please?"

Despite Milo's dire prediction of inclement weather, nothing happened. Lucida appeared to be much too absorbed in her own work to pay even the slightest attention to anyone at our table. In fact, the only time she raised her head from the book in front of her was when she was replacing it with a new book. I tried to remember if I'd seen Lucida in the library even once during my time as an Apprentice but couldn't think of a single instance. When had she become so studious, or was she simply making up for years locked away behind bars? There wasn't much to do in prison after all; maybe she'd discovered a new passion for reading. I tried to return to the task Hannah had set me, mildly annoyed at Lucida for having sufficiently distracted me just by existing.

"Catriona told me that you lobbied for her," I said suddenly, though I was unaware of having made the decision to speak the thought aloud.

Hannah looked up, frowning. "What?"

"Catriona told me that you lobbied for her to be able to stay out of prison."

"Blimey!" Savvy whispered.

"You did?!" Milo gasped. "You never told me that!"

Hannah leaned away from Milo, whose expression was suddenly quite fierce. "I... it didn't really feel like something I needed to tell you."

Milo snorted. "In what universe?"

Hannah shrugged. "It wasn't a big deal."

"You kept her out of prison and in this castle," I said quietly. "You must have known the Council would listen to you, given your history with Lucida. That feels like a big deal to me. Why did you do it?"

Hannah sighed and put down her highlighter. "I don't know."

Milo made an incredulous noise, but Hannah cut him off before he could launch into a rant. "I'm serious! I wasn't even planning to! But they brought her in, and I just... I think she deserves a chance to be heard out, that's all. She... she saved Jess' life, and I wouldn't have been able to Call all those spirits without her help."

"Yeah, but that doesn't just, like, erase all the evil, twisted shit she put you through!" Milo replied, his voice nothing more than an indignant squeak at this point. "What she put all of us through!"

"I'm not saying it does. And I'm recusing myself from the rest of the process," Hannah said. "But I think she should have the chance to plead her case, just like anyone else. I don't want to talk about it anymore."

She returned determinedly to her work and refused to discuss the matter again. Savvy shrugged and returned to her packet. It was my turn now to silently reprimand Milo to let the matter go and let Hannah focus. We all attempted to settle back to work, but Milo kept sighing huffily and I'd only completed a few more lines of editing when a woman's voice called out in the quiet space.

"Hannah."

I looked up, expecting to see Karen coming back up toward us, perhaps in search of another text to add to her pile, but instead, I saw Keira striding between the stacks, accompanied by a young man I was sure I'd never seen before, and yet something about him looked familiar. He was tall and slenderly built, with a square jaw, warm brown eyes behind wire-rimmed glasses, and a deep brown complexion that made his bright, friendly smile seem even brighter. He followed Keira to our table and regarded us and our teetering piles of research with mild-mannered curiosity, waiting to be introduced.

"Well, this looks... ambitious. How is it all going?" Keira asked, gesturing to the stacks of books and documents.

"Well, I think," Hannah said with an edge of defensiveness in her voice. "I'm just trying to be as thorough as I can be."

Keira nodded solemnly. "Yes, you are going to need every ounce of research you can possibly muster to help this bill hold up in front of the Council. They will surely attack it with everything they've got, as will many of the Caomhnóir. To this end, I've brought you a secret weapon."

Keira gestured to the young man beside her, who looked taken aback before smiling sheepishly. "Well, I must confess, that's the first time I've ever been introduced in such a manner. Kiernan Worthington. I'm a Caomhnóir here at Fairhaven, assigned to Scribe security."

He held out his hand first to Hannah, who hesitated a moment before taking it and stammering, "Hi. N-nice to meet you, Kiernan. My name is Hannah Ballard."

"Oh, yes, I know who you are," Kiernan said. "Everyone knows the Ballard sisters."

Hannah flushed, and Kiernan looked abashed. "I'm terribly sorry," he said at once. "I only meant... well, that is to say—my own clan is fairly infamous now, as well." He dropped his gaze to his feet.

I thrust my hand out toward Kiernan, smiling broadly. "No need to apologize, Kiernan. We're well aware by now that our reputation precedes us. I'm Jess Ballard."

Kiernan took my hand and shook it. His fingers were long and slender, like he ought to have been a concert pianist rather than a Caomhnóir. I smiled at him sympathetically, because I had just realized why he looked familiar, and also why he was subject to the worst kind of reflected infamy.

Hannah had mentioned Kiernan to me before. Just a couple of years ago, he had been a Novitiate, finishing his training, and had petitioned the Council to become a Scribe instead of a Caomhnóir. His unusual request had been denied, but not before he had put together an impressively researched presentation supporting his petition. Keira had thought that he would be a good resource to help Hannah with her upcoming legislation.

But all of this had nothing to do with why he looked familiar. No, it was a family resemblance that had caught my eye, and a striking one at that. Kiernan had the same almond-shaped eyes, the same aristocratic cheekbones, and the same graceful confidence as his aunt, the one and only Lucida Worthington, currently sitting in the very same library. Incidentally, she was also the reason he was walking around saddled with the heavy baggage that only a clan scandal could produce, given all of her past misdeeds. Though Lucida's status was still in question, the fact that she had been allowed back within the castle walls sans handcuffs was an indicator that redemption might just be within reach. Her recent actions did not erase past betrayals, however, and Kiernan had no doubt suffered a great deal of negativity—a sort of inherited guilt by association—just as we had when we arrived at Fairhaven for the first time. I suddenly found my curiosity about him tinged with pity. Milo seemed to have made the same connection as well—he kept glancing back and forth over his shoulder between Lucida and Kiernan, his mouth hanging open. I shot a little zing of energy through our connection to get his attention and widened my eyes at him. "Stop staring! And close your mouth!"

He did as he was told, but it was clear his interest was piqued to the point of excitement. Milo could smell a juicy backstory a mile away, and it was clear he would be very eager to get Kiernan's.

Savvy had definitely taken more than a passing notice of Kiernan as well, shaking his hand and looking him over with an appraising eye that I knew all too well from when I'd seen her on the prowl. I kicked her in the ankle under the table, and she let go of his hand, trying to arrange her face into a more indifferent expression.

"I'll let you two talk it over then, shall I?" Keira was saying, looking between Hannah and Kiernan. "If it seems like something you might be interested in assisting with, Kiernan, I can amend the agenda for the next Council meeting and have you formally added to the presentation."

"Thank you," Kiernan said, nodding deferentially toward Hannah. "I leave it up to Hannah, of course, whether or not she would like my assistance. I am pleased to offer my help, but I certainly won't force it upon you."

Hannah flushed a little, and then gestured to an open chair at the end of the table. "Why don't you sit down, Kiernan. I can fill you in on what we've been working on."

"Excellent," Kiernan said, looking frankly relieved that Hannah had invited him to join us, and dropping into the chair at once, looking eager. Savvy shifted a pile of books so that he would have some room.

"I'll leave you to it," Keira said and, with a last nod to all of us, left us to our work.

Hannah did not speak at first. She seemed somewhat flustered about where to begin. As she fumbled through her stacks of papers, I jumped in.

"So, Kiernan, we heard that you wanted to be a Scribe. Is that true?"

Kiernan nodded. "That's right. I've always been a bit... well, bookish, I guess you might say. From childhood, I was much more interested in the history of combat, say, than in actually learning to fight myself. I don't think Seamus quite knew what to do with me when I arrived for Caomhnóir training." He crooked his mouth into a half-smile, as though the memory amused him.

"Yeah, I'll bet," I said, returning the smile. "It's a bit like joining the military down in the barracks, isn't it?"

"Indeed," Kiernan said. "I knew I was ill-suited for it, but that didn't mean I didn't feel a sense of duty, to my clan and to the spirits we serve. I simply felt that I could contribute more—have more to offer—if I was permitted to use my talents."

"And what are your talents?" Milo asked, leaning across the table and resting his chin in his hand. I smirked at him. It was evident he was enjoying the view.

Kiernan looked embarrassed. "Not hand-to-hand combat, that's for certain," he said with a shrug. "But I've always had an excellent memory for facts and figures, and I have a real interest in historical research—especially the development of our Castings. It's truly remarkable, the way we've experimented and built up our cache of knowledge in that regard. And there's so much still to discover."

His face was alight with excitement. Hannah had stopped rifling through her papers and was watching him. It was hard not to watch him—his enthusiasm was contagious.

"The first time I set foot in here," Kiernan went on, gesturing around the vast library with an awed look in his eye, "I knew that this was where I wanted to be. I began volunteering with the Scribes, learning about all the different types of collections here, and how to care for them. And this room is only the tip of the iceberg!" he added. "We have archives in London and Dublin and Edinburgh, and of course the catacomb archives at Skye are remarkable, too."

"Yeah, I've been in there," I said, and Kiernan gaped at me. "Well, briefly," I clarified. "Like, not to do research, or anything. Just sort of ran through it in a blind panic when I was fleeing for my life, that kind of thing."

Kiernan continued to stare. Hannah cleared her throat. "Who did you speak to first? About becoming a Scribe?"

Kiernan tore his eyes from me and turned to answer Hannah. "The Scribes themselves, actually. I'd gotten to know them so well, after all. They were the staff here at the castle I was closest to. But they all said the same thing: only Durupinen were permitted to become Scribes. That was the way it had always been."

"Yeah, we hear that sort of thing a lot around here," Hannah said with a rueful smile. "It seems to be the go-to answer anytime we dare question anything."

"You're right about that," Kiernan agreed. "I heard it over and over again, first from the Scribes, then from the Caomhnóir leadership, then from my Durupinen teachers. Finally, it was the High Priestess herself who suggested I submit my request to the Council in the form of an amendment."

"The High Priestess?" I asked. "You mean Finvarra?"

Kiernan shook his head. "No, I meant Celeste. She wasn't the High Priestess at the time, of course. She was still the Deputy High Priestess, but I knew her primarily as my History and Lore instructor. She had experienced my love of history and research firsthand, having had to grade my papers for her class, which were generally twice as long as required, with an indecent number of footnotes," he chuckled.

"So, what happened?" Savvy asked, looking rapt now, resting her face on her hand. "When you went before the Council?"

"I did everything I could to prepare. I compiled an extensive compendium of examples from our history, in which Caomhnóir helped in untraditional roles. I also included the many regrettable instances where Caomhnóir were ill-suited to their duties or rebelled against them. I thought perhaps a detailed history of the unrest might persuade them that a broadening of roles would be in everyone's best interest."

"Gee, you think?" I said, unable to even slightly reign in my sarcasm. "Just look at what happened at the *príosún*, for God's sake."

"Precisely," said Kiernan solemnly. "I had no such recent event to cite, but was still hopeful that my historical precedent would be compelling."

"And was it?" Hannah asked.

"Not in the way that I had hoped," Kiernan said with a sigh. "They found the pattern disturbing, to be sure, but some of the Council members misconstrued my intentions. They seemed to look at my citation of Caomhnóir unrest as some sort of veiled threat. As though I were suggesting that I, too, would rebel if I were not granted my request."

"That's ridiculous," I said. "Who creates a formal presentation announcing their rebellion to the very people they're going to rebel against?"

"Total bollocks," Savvy agreed.

Kiernan laughed. "A few of the Council members attempted to make a similar point in my defense, but it was not enough to turn the tide for me. In the end, they denied my request. Celeste was able to speak to Seamus, however, and that's how I ended up on Scribe security."

"Isn't that worse, having to be around the Scribes all the time, watching them do the work you wish you could be doing?" Hannah asked quietly.

"Perhaps at first," Kiernan said. "But bitterness is only unpleasant to the one who tastes it, as my grandmother used to say. I decided to make the best of a less-than-ideal situation. And the Scribes still let me assist, when my duties and schedule permit, so that's some consolation."

"It's not the same as being a Scribe, though," Hannah said.

"No, it's not," Kiernan said, and then he looked around at us, looking a bit embarrassed at how long he'd gone on talking. "So, that's why I'm here, I suppose. And I'm very interested to hear about what you've been working on. Would you tell me more about it?"

It was Hannah's turn to look embarrassed, but she obliged. "Well, I'm not sure how much Keira's told you, but we're trying to get the Code of Conduct amended. Here's the introduction to my presentation. It sums it up fairly well, I think."

Kiernan took the paper from Hannah's outstretched hand and began to read it. His eyes moved very quickly over the words, and his eyebrows drew together in his concentration. He began nodding along, and by the time he had reached the bottom of the page, he was smiling slightly.

"Well," he said, at last, looking up to meet Hannah's eye as she watched him anxiously. "You're quite determined to leave not a stone standing of this old law, aren't you?"

"I... well..." Hannah stammered, unsure of how to respond.

"Not a pebble," I said firmly. "I'm sure, as a result of our previously mentioned infamy, that you understand why we'd have a vested interest in seeing this whole thing overhauled."

Kiernan laughed. "I think I remember hearing a thing or two. Something about a Prophecy, wasn't it?"

He kept his tone light, but I could hear the strain in his voice nonetheless. The Prophecy had destroyed his family as thoroughly as it had destroyed ours, or nearly so. Certainly, he probably got as many suspicious looks as we did, thanks to Lucida.

"And of course, I've got my own selfish reasons for wanting the code changed, too," I added. I watched as Kiernan's eyes widened and his mouth opened and closed several times before he managed to answer.

"I... I don't know what you..."

24

I grinned at him. "It's okay, Kiernan. Finn's your superior now that Seamus is away. I'm sure the entire barracks is buzzing like a beehive with the gossip about the new boss and his illegal relationship with a Durupinen."

"I... well, you're not wrong," Kiernan said with a bit of a sheepish grin on his face.

"We're prepared for it," I said with a resigned shrug. "We hid it for a long time. We're done hiding."

"And you shouldn't have to hide anything, not after everything that's just happened," Hannah chimed in, her face glowing with indignation on my behalf. "If the events at the *príosún* taught us anything, it's that things cannot continue the way they are between Durupinen and Caomhnóir. Something has to change—a lot of things, in fact. And we're starting here." She tapped her finger on her proposal, looking uncharacteristically fierce.

"It's not just about the rebellion and the Prophecy," Savvy added, looking very serious. "It's like you said, about letting people use their talents, and not just forcing them into jobs they've got no business doing. I suppose you knew my Caomhnóir Bertie?"

Kiernan's expression grew sober at once. "Yes, indeed, I did. Terrible, what happened to him."

"Yeah, it bloody well was," Savvy said. "Because he was doing a job he wasn't equipped for. I imagine if your request had passed, Seamus might have let the poor bastard off the hook and given him a desk job or some tosh like that."

"That was my goal," Kiernan said. "We aren't all made in the image of soldiers. We should all be free to serve the spirit world in our own way."

"That's right. That's exactly right, mate," Savvy said, nodding her head thoughtfully.

"So, anyway, that's why I'm here, and I'm exceedingly glad that Keira thought to ask me," Kiernan said, turning back to Hannah. "I'd really like to help you with this, if you'd have me. Including a Caomhnóir in the drafting will go a long way in helping get other Caomhnóir to support it. We aren't often consulted in this process, and it's a sore spot."

Hannah smiled back. "We'd love to have you. We need all the help we can get."

Kiernan knocked on the table. "Cheers," he said, and reached into his bag. "I've got several copies of my proposal here. There's quite a lot of research I've already done that I think you'll find useful."

"Could I have a look at one of those, mate?" Savvy asked, holding out a hand.

"Certainly," Kiernan said, handing one to her. "And what about you, Hannah? Could I show it to you?"

"Please!" Hannah said eagerly and slid over on her bench to make room for him beside her. "Let's get started!"

3

SENSES

WITH KIERNAN ON BOARD, our scrappy little band of researchers found new enthusiasm for our project, which was good, because I was nursing a guilty conscience about how little I would able to be there to help over the final two weeks. Hannah continuously assured me that my project for Fiona was important too, but it did little to ease the boiling shame in the pit of my stomach.

"You're doing all of this for me, and I'm abandoning you in the eleventh hour!" I cried, arriving home aching and exhausted from a long day working in Fiona's studio.

"I'm doing it for everyone, not just you, and you've given me lots of help already," Hannah insisted. "Fiona is the one who really needs you now, so keep your focus on her, please. I've got plenty of help proofreading and copying. Besides, I really think Kiernan was the element we were missing. I'm feeling more and more confident about where the legislation is now."

And it was true, thank goodness. Hannah was so thrilled with the material she was able to pull from Kiernan's proposal that some of her panic and doubt started ebbing away. It was as though the addition of a Caomhnóir's perspective had opened up an entirely new dimension to her argument, and there was no denying it was a powerful one. Even Savvy, whose participation had been half-hearted at best, suddenly began spending more time in the library, even when the others had called it quits for the day. In fact, she was spending so much time there, that it was the first place I attempted to find her a week later.

"Hey there, bookworm," I said, dropping into the chair beside her.

She shoved her papers into her book, slammed it shut, and scowled at me. "How very dare you, you cheeky monkey! The sixth

27

form skive off champion will not be addressed in such a manner, thank you very much."

"What are you doing here so early?" I asked her.

"Oh, you know. Celeste told me to get involved, so here I am, making a right lifestyle out of it," she replied. "What about you, then? What are you up so bloody early for?"

"I set an alarm so I could call Tia and wish her luck on her exam today. I would have called her last night, but it was after nine o'clock by the time I remembered, and she would have skinned me alive if I called her after 8 PM on the eve of a test."

Savvy chuckled. "How is old Tia, then?"

"She's good! Modest as usual, but she's been asked to present a paper at yet another fancy medical conference, and based on her general lack of hyperventilating, she's at the top of her class right now. She's decided to stay on campus for the time being. I think she likes being surrounded by science nerds 24/7 instead of ghosts."

"Ah, good on 'er! I worried about her after... after everything that happened." Savvy's voice faded. She looked back down at her hands, which now looked in danger of snapping the pencil she was holding right in half. I plowed on awkwardly, knowing that talking about Charlie Wright would only send Savvy into an emotional downward spiral.

"Yeah, so anyway, she's good. But I had to be up early to catch her, so once I was up, I... Finn?"

Finn had just emerged from the stacks, carrying two books under his arm.

"Jess! I didn't expect to see you up so early!" he said, looking surprised but pleased to see me.

"What are you doing here?" I asked him.

"Taking out a couple of books," Finn said with a chuckle. "It is a library, after all."

"No, I know that, it's just... I wasn't expecting to see you," I said. "I feel like everyone I know has permanently relocated to the library."

"Not permanently, I assure you," Finn said, placing his books down upon the table so that he could kiss me. "A pleasant surprise to see you, love."

"What books are you taking out?"

"Some training manuals for Novitiates," Finn explained, holding them up. "You aren't the only one embarking on a new venture this week, remember?"

"Of course!" I said. There was so much going on that I'd nearly forgotten that the next day, Finn was taking up his new assignment to oversee Novitiate training. Some girlfriend I was. "You must be just about as nervous as I am."

"Nearly, I imagine. What brings you to the library?"

"I thought Hannah might be down here. She was already gone when I got up. Have you seen her?" I asked.

"I saw her up at breakfast with Kiernan, going over notes," Savvy offered up. "I expect they'll be along soon."

I looked at my watch and groaned. "I don't think I've got time to go all the way back down there now. I've got to get up to the hospital wing," I said.

"What for?" Savvy asked.

"I promised to help get Fiona back to her tower. Mrs. Mistlemoore is discharging her today."

"Already?" Savvy asked.

"I don't think they had much of a choice, to be honest," I said. "I mean, imagine if you were the one telling Fiona that she couldn't go and do exactly as she pleased. How long do you think you'd last before you kicked her out, just to save your own sanity?"

"Fair point, mate," Savvy said, eyes wide. "I don't reckon I'd have lasted a day, do you?"

"Well, I'm about to find out," I said with a grimace. "I've agreed to be her assistant."

"What?" Savvy asked, looking utterly horrified. "What do you mean?"

"I mean she needs someone to help her with her work here at that castle while she's healing. And, in what can only be described as a moment of temporary insanity, I volunteered myself for the job."

"Blimey," Savvy whispered.

"Yeah," I agreed. "Wish me luck. I'm going to need it."

"Good luck, mate," Savvy said, shaking her head. "You're a braver woman than me."

"Very brave, indeed," Finn agreed. "Is everything ready in the studio?"

"I think so," I said. "I'm not sure whether she's going to thank me or murder me."

"Well, if she murders you, I know a few people who can help you Cross," Finn said in the most practical of tones.

"Thanks," I grumbled. "I'll keep that in mind."

§

When I arrived at the hospital ward a few minutes later, I found Fiona sitting in a chair beside her bed, her arms folded tightly across her chest and a truculent expression on her face. Her eyes were still bandaged. Mrs. Mistlemoore stood beside her, looking exasperated.

"Fiona, you have to wait until someone gets here to—"

"Gets here to what? Gets here to *what*, exactly?" Fiona was shouting. "Carry me over their shoulder? Lead me around like a lost little lamb? Walk in front of me with a bloody rib roast so I can follow the smell?"

"Oh, shit, I left all my rib roasts back in my bedroom. Should I go grab a couple?" I asked as I approached the bedspace. Mrs. Mistlemoore looked up, looking frankly relieved, but Fiona gave a dismissive snort.

"That you, then, Jess? Have you been appointed my nanny?" Fiona asked, her voice caustic.

"Rib roasts? Nannying? Your expectations are pretty high, Fiona. All I did was offer to walk you up to the tower, not feed and entertain you," I said, coming to stop beside Mrs. Mistlemoore.

"Well, you're just a barrel of laughs today, aren't you?" Fiona grumbled.

"I'm a barrel of laughs every day, and you know it," I replied, before turning to Mrs. Mistlemoore. "So, what are my instructions?"

"She's got to apply this cream with a clean swab once every three hours," Mrs. Mistlemoore told me, handing me a large tube of ointment and a paper bag of bandages. "The bandages should stay off for twenty minutes after the application, and then she can put fresh bandages on. There's medical tape in there, along with the bandages. If she's got any questions..."

"If she's got any questions, she can bloody well ask you herself, seeing as she's right here!" Fiona barked. "And she'd quite like it if you didn't talk about her like she was a half-wit who can't understand simple instructions."

Mrs. Mistlemoore closed her eyes and pressed her lips together, probably to prevent herself from calling Fiona something rather more offensive than "half-wit." When she opened her eyes again, she kept them focused on me. "You're quite sure you're up to this?" she asked, hoisting one skeptical eyebrow.

"Oh, sure," I said, waving a casual hand. "We're going to be just fine. I already drive her crazy, so that's nothing new. Besides, you could probably use a break. I'm sure she's been a delight."

Mrs. Mistlemoore tried not to smirk, but couldn't quite smother it. "I have repeatedly told Fiona that I am happy to keep her here with me in the hospital ward until she is more fully healed."

"And Fiona has told you repeatedly that she would rather gouge out what's left of her eyes than have to spend another day cooped up in this place," Fiona snapped. "So, are we going, or aren't we?"

"Sure, if you're ready," I said calmly, refusing to rise to Fiona's bait. She wanted a fight, and I wasn't going to give her one, at least not until we were safely back up in her tower. If she wanted to rage and storm, she could do it up there, where she'd already destroyed half her possessions anyway.

Fiona rose from her chair, and I hurried over to stand beside her. "How do you want to do this?" I asked her.

I expected a snide reply, but now that she was faced with the reality of walking through the castle without the aid of her eyes, she looked suddenly small and frightened. "I don't reckon I know..." she muttered, unable to control the quaver in her voice. "Maybe... just give me your arm, I suppose."

I took Fiona's hand and tucked it around my arm, and then pulled my elbow in against my side in an effort to help her feel snug and secure beside me. Her fingers dug sharply into the skin on the top of my forearm, but I tried to ignore it.

"Just let me know if I'm going too fast, okay?" I told her, and she nodded once, curtly.

"Don't hesitate to call me if you need anything," Mrs. Mistlemoore called after us as we left.

Fairhaven was sprawling and cavernous, but it had never seemed bigger than it did on that first walk back to Fiona's tower. Every hallway seemed to stretch on forever. Every staircase felt needlessly, endlessly long. Fiona shuffled along at first, as though she were afraid to let her feet part company with the floor. This strategy to orient herself backfired, however; the stones of the castle floors were too uneven, and she kept stumbling. Finally, after catching her for the tenth time, I convinced her to lift her feet and set them down just as she normally would have done, and our progress became slightly smoother.

"Why don't you put your other hand out along the wall?" I suggested, once we emerged from the hospital ward corridor and into a second, wider hallway.

"What in the devil's name for?" Fiona grumbled.

"You'll be able to feel for clues that will help you know where you are," I replied.

"I know where I am. I'm in the seventh circle of hell, that's where I bloody am," Fiona said.

"Okay, fair enough, but let's learn to navigate the seventh circle of hell, then," I suggested.

Fiona sighed and reached out her right hand, so that her fingertips brushed along the wall. At first, she seemed to be doing it only to humor me, but after a few minutes, I noticed her feeling around, taking note of windowsills and counting doorways.

"So, that was five doorways and three windows along that corridor, and now we've reached the first flight of stairs," I said encouragingly.

"I can count, thank you very much," Fiona replied, though with less snap in her voice than I had expected.

We ascended the steps, each of us counting them silently, trying to commit as many details as possible to memory. It was rather alarming to me how many details of the castle I had never noticed before, now that I was making a concerted effort to pay attention—as though I had been walking around the place for the last few years seeing as little as Fiona could see now. This stairway had a niche window halfway up, with a stained-glass window, and a faded, grimy portrait of a long-dead Caomhnóir standing at attention before the Geatgrima. We emerged into a wide hallway of classrooms, skirting the righthand wall so that we could count how many of them we would need to pass before we turned again. Classes were in session, and I caught glimpses of Apprentices, their heads bowed over notebooks, and a room full of Novitiates, all staring attentively at a fellow student giving some sort of presentation. I remembered how Mackie had walked me along this very hallway on my first day, guiding me through the unfamiliar passages, to meet for the first time the woman now clinging to my arm like a lost child. I had to swallow the memory along with a sudden and violent urge to burst into tears.

We turned along another corridor and found ourselves in the Gallery of High Priestesses, a collection of tapestries and paintings and portraits that documented the history of Durupinen leadership going back centuries.

"We're in the gallery now," I said to Fiona, who snorted.

"No need to tell me that," she said. "I could feel their eyes on me the moment we turned the corner. Always have, from the first time I set foot up here. Gives me the absolute willies."

I glanced at her, surprised to hear her talk like that. "Are you serious? The amount of time you spend around ghosts and old paintings, and this place freaks you out?"

Fiona shrugged. "Can't explain any better now than I could the first time I walked this hall. There's just this feeling—like they've just asked a question I couldn't hear, but they're all waiting for me to answer it. Let's keep moving, there's a good lass."

I picked up the pace slightly, pausing only once more, as the serene countenance of Agnes Isherwood gazed down upon me from her tapestry. Mackie had told me that she was a High Priestess from my own clan, the Clan Sassanaigh. She had meant the information to be comforting—Hannah and I had not exactly received a warm welcome and were feeling distinctly like outsiders. The presence of Agnes' likeness in this hallway proved that we belonged within the walls of Fairhaven—that the gift in our blood was ancient, powerful, and wholly our own. It wasn't until later that I discovered that Agnes Isherwood was the one who had made the Prophecy that had shaped my entire life and nearly ended it. Since then, I'd regarded my connection with the long-gone priestess with a combination of pride and fear. I looked up into her face, a face that, for all the age and wear on the fibers, still resembled mine. It was a curious expression on her face—as though she were forever about to open her mouth and tell me a great secret—as though the very fibers of the tapestry knew things it dared not speak. I found myself shuddering from head to foot with my own case of the "willies" and though I dropped my eyes and focused again on guiding Fiona down the hallway, I felt the eyes of Agnes Isherwood on me until we had turned the corner.

We took our time mounting the staircase, which suited me fine, seeing how long and arduous the climb was. We took note along the way of how many stairs led to each landing, and where the gaps in the railings were. We paid heed to the step with a missing chunk of stone at the edge, and another which seemed to be at least an inch higher than the others. At last we arrived at the door to Fiona's studio.

"Okay, before we go in, I have something I need to tell you," I said to Fiona, who was struggling to catch her breath despite the slow pace.

Her head snapped up, and even through the bandages I felt her eyes attempting to penetrate me like lasers. "What is it, then?"

"Don't worry, it's not bad," I told her quickly. "Well... okay, you might not love it at first, but I think in the long run, you'll see it's a good—"

"Are you going to tell me, or are you just going to babble nonsense at me?" Fiona barked.

"I... sort of... took it upon myself to reorganize your studio."

Complete silence met my words. Fiona didn't move. I'm pretty sure she stopped breathing. It was as though my words had been an incantation that had turned her to stone. I waited a solid ten seconds, but she did not reply, so I ventured to speak.

"Fiona? Did you hear what I said?"

Her nostrils flared. "My ears are one part of me that *are* working entirely properly, thank you," she hissed through tightly clenched teeth.

"I knew you would be pissed," I began.

"Seems to me that might have been a good reason to leave my space bloody well alone," Fiona mumbled. Her face still wasn't moving. Maybe she thought if she released even a single facial muscle, she'd explode. It certainly seemed that way.

"If I overstepped, I'm sorry," I said, and then stopped myself. "No. Okay. There's no 'if' involved here. I overstepped. I'm sorry. But the fact is that you couldn't live in here, not the way it was. I know it was the way you preferred it, although I can't for the life of me understand why. But we're beyond preferences now. You'd prefer to have your space—and your sight—the way it used to be. That's not reality. Reality is that if you tried to live in your old studio, you would hurt yourself. You'd never find what you needed. You'd never make art again."

"I'll never make art again anyway, couldn't you at least leave me my space?" Fiona muttered.

34

"That's not true. It's *not true, Fiona!*" I was shouting now, which was not at all what I intended, but anger was boiling up inside of me. It wasn't anger at Fiona, not even a little. It was anger at—I don't know, the world? Fate? Karma? Whatever forces of the universe that came together, wittingly or unwittingly, and had left Fiona in this state. I took a deep breath and tried to bring my voice down to a reasonable volume, but it shook nonetheless. "I've seen you make art," I said. "I've seen the way it takes over everything—your body, your mind, your will, your fucking common sense. I've seen you work for days without sleep. I've seen you forget to eat. I've seen you create until your hands are cramped and bleeding. It's not a choice, Fiona. It's a calling, and a damn stronger one than any pull that the spirit world might have on you. You couldn't stop making art even if you tried—the universe wouldn't let you. *You* wouldn't let you. And fuck it, *I* won't let you. But it won't be the same. You are going to have to adapt. You are going to have to adjust and change the way you've always worked. That's going to suck for a while. It's going to be frustrating and it's going to feel like moving backwards at first, but not forever. Soon your gift is going to find new paths to help you create, and if you are open to them, Fiona, you might just make the best art of your life."

Fiona still hadn't moved, but now the muscles in her face were twitching and spasming against emotions too unwieldy to deal with. I waited patiently as she fought with them, conquered them, and swallowed them. It probably would have been healthier to let them out and deal with them, but hey, who was I to judge? She didn't owe me any vulnerability, not now, not ever.

"Let's get this over with, then," Fiona mumbled at last. "The sooner I see how badly you've cocked this all up, the sooner I can fix it."

I suppressed a smile that she couldn't have seen anyway, and stepped forward to open the door. Then I turned, took her arm, and guided her through. We started a slow trip around the room, and I guided her hands to each element as I described it, so that she could experience it for herself.

"Okay, well, the first thing you'll notice is that the floor is clean. Yes, the whole thing," I added, as Fiona opened her mouth with a skeptical expression. "I had to use a shovel to uncover the floorboards in some places, but I found them. So, there's nothing anywhere lying around for you to trip on. That's probably the most important thing, as far as your safety goes."

"My safety," she snorted. "You talk like I'm a wee baby who's going to eat the paints if I'm left unattended."

"The easier this place is to navigate, the less time people like me have to spend up here pissing you off," I pointed out. "And the quicker you can return to your traditional role of curmudgeonly misanthrope of the tower."

Fiona snorted dismissively, but I thought I detected a hint of a smile. I felt my heart lift just a bit and went on with more confidence. "I spoke to the Caomhnóir and got them to bring a bunch of shelving up here from other places in the castle where it was just sitting around empty—unused classrooms and some stuff from the basement. Then Finn helped me build a couple of custom pieces to store canvases and stuff. I've got it arranged around the perimeter of the room, and everything is organized in them, so you can always find exactly what you need."

We approached the first row of shelves, and I took Fiona's hand lifting it to the edge and running it over a metal letter "A" and, beside it, a number "1." "The shelves are labeled with letters and numbers along the left side, feel it? Think of it as a Dewy Decimal System for your crap. Each shelving unit has a letter, and each shelf on that unit has a number, starting with the top and working down. So, this first one up here is 'A1.' Got it?"

Fiona traced the letter and number with her forefinger, and nodded once, curtly. "Got it. Go on."

We went on. And on and on. Through twenty-four sets of shelves full of everything from paints to brushes, from potter's tools to embroidery thread, from glues and scissors, to everything she needed to make a good cup of tea. Finally, we sank exhausted onto the newly cleaned and arranged sofa. Then, Fiona, who had been silent through the entire tour except for the occasional grunt of annoyance or assent, spoke.

"How am I ever going to remember it all?" she sighed with a helpless gesture.

"You won't," I said. "Not at first. But over time, it will become like second nature. And it doesn't have to stay exactly like this. If you prefer the pastels next to the watercolors, we move them. If having clay near canvases throws you off, we change it. None of this is set in stone, the whole point is that it works for you. And in the meantime, I've made a chart of what goes where."

"And what good is a bloody chart if I can't see it?" Fiona asked.

"It's not for you, it's for me, and the Caomhnóir who've been assigned temporary duty. If you need help locating something, have one of them, or me, consult the chart. As time goes on, it will become like second nature, and then you can tell us and our chart to fuck off at last."

"What a happy day that will be," Fiona said.

"Indeed," I agreed.

We sat together, in a silence that was somehow both empty and full at the same time. I decided that it wasn't mine to break. I'd made too many decisions for her in the last few days. It was time for her to make them now.

"You didn't have to—"

"I know."

"I'll probably just undo it all, in the end."

"I know."

"I'm still going to throw shit around here."

"I'm counting on it."

Her rough and callused hand groped around until it found mine, and gave it a squeeze.

"Thank you."

"You're welcome."

4

JITTERS

I ARRIVED BACK IN MY ROOM around two o'clock in the afternoon, utterly exhausted. Once Fiona had gotten over her initial anger and then gratitude for what I had done to her studio, she had become possessed with an almost manic need to understand it all. So, after we applied her ointment and changed her bandages, we went over the shelving system again. And again. And again. She was all for doing it a fifth time when I finally waved the white flag.

"Fine, abandon me," Fiona said as I briefed the Caomhnóir who was taking over at the door. "But if I mistake my paint thinner for my tea and poison myself, that'll be on your conscience."

"If you mistake paint thinner for tea, there's something wrong with more than your eyes, you mad old bat," I shouted, and Fiona snorted with laughter. "Someone from the hospital ward will be up at dinner time to take you down to eat and help you get ready for bed, and I'll be back first thing in the morning, alright?"

"Eh, just be gone already if you're going," she said by way of affectionate send-off.

I hit my bed like a ton of bricks and slept right through dinner. By the time I woke up, darkness had fallen outside the windows and my stomach was rumbling so loudly that at first I stared around in confusion, wondering where the noise was coming from.

"I've got a cure for that," said a laughing voice, and I turned to find Milo at my desk, examining photos on my laptop. He gestured over to the coffee table by the fire, where a plate heaped with steak and ale pie, mashed potatoes, and hot buttered rolls was waiting for me.

"Oh my God, I love you so much right now," I groaned, sliding out of the bed and plopping myself onto the sofa in front of the glorious calorie-fest. I picked up a roll. "It's still warm!"

"You may love me all you like, but thank Finn for the food. He didn't want to wake you, but he knew you'd be hungry so when you didn't turn up for dinner, he made a special delivery. He said to text him when you got up."

"This is literally the best thing they make down in that dining room," I professed, stuffing my face.

Milo laughed. "I'll have to take your word for it."

"How's the blog coming?" I asked him between spectacularly unladylike mouthfuls.

"Fabulously," he declared. "I've already had three runway requests for the dress you wore in those garden photos."

"Nice," I said. "Make sure to tell them it's itchy as fuck."

"I'll be sure to add that to the garment description," Milo said, rolling his eyes.

"Where's Hannah?" I asked, looking around and then checking my watch. It was after seven o'clock. "She's not still at dinner, is she?"

"Where else would she be?" Milo sighed. "Down in the library, of course."

I shook my head. "She needs an intervention. There can't possibly still be this much work to do on the proposal. Karen said it was Council-ready three days ago."

"Oh, I don't think it has all that much to do with work anymore. In fact, she's left her whole bag of documents here."

I dug into my pie. "What do you mean, it's not about work? Why else would she go?"

"Let's just say the library has a bit more allure these days than it used to," Milo said, smirking to himself.

I started in on my mashed potatoes, which were now swimming in rich brown gravy from my half-demolished pie. "You know, just because you're a ghost doesn't mean you have to be so damn cryptic all the time. Just tell me what you're talking about!" I said.

The look that Milo bestowed upon me was almost pitying. "Oh, sweetness. Come on. Don't tell me you haven't noticed."

"Noticed what?" I asked defensively.

Milo gave a deep, long-suffering sigh. "I swear to Versace, if I wasn't here, you Ballard sisters would just walk around the world obliviously bumping into men with your eyes closed, wouldn't you?"

"What men? Milo, either tell me what you're talking about, or

SOUL OF THE SENTINEL

shut up about it already! You're interrupting time I could otherwise be spending stuffing my face."

Milo flung his hands up in exasperation. "I'm talking about Kiernan!"

I blinked. "Kiernan?"

"The Caomhnóir! The one who is helping Hannah with her proposal!" Milo practically shrieked.

I leaned back from him as his frustration blasted out from him in a wave of cold energy that made my teeth chatter. "Oh, right. Him. What about—wait," I put my fork down reluctantly and gave him my full attention. "You don't think that Hannah has a thing for Kiernan, do you?"

Milo arched an eyebrow in reply. Seriously, he could say more with the twitch of a single spectral facial muscle than most people could say with a word processor and a thesaurus.

"Oh, come on!" I laughed. "Hannah's not interested in him. She's too..."

"What?" Milo prompted. "She's too what?"

I hesitated, flustered. Honestly, my first thought, the word that had almost escaped my mouth before I'd considered it, was "young," which was completely ridiculous, given that Hannah and I were the same age, and our peers were already getting married. Maybe it was because she was so tiny, or because only a few short years ago she had had to be handled with the same delicate care as a soap bubble. Maybe it was the fact that I was still so protective of her that I felt more like a mother or an older sister than I did her twin. Maybe it was the fact that she'd never shown even the slightest interest in dating anyone. But regardless of why, I realized in that moment that I'd never once thought of Hannah as a woman who might enter into a relationship with another adult. There was probably quite a bit to unpack there, and I wasn't exactly up for that level of self-analysis when my stomach was still growling at me.

"I don't know," I answered Milo. "Too sensible. Too work-driven. Too independent. Too something, okay? I just... I don't see it."

"I know you don't, sweetness," Milo said, reaching out and patting my hand in a gesture that was both sympathetic and pitying. "That's why you have me."

"Why do you think she's interested in Kiernan?" I asked.

"I'm not sure she realizes she is," Milo said slowly. "But he is absolutely interested in her."

41

"How do you know?"

Milo pointed to his eyes. "These aren't used exclusively for rolling, honey."

"Wow, well... that would be... um, great," I said dazedly.

"Oh girl, that was pathetic. Seriously, don't ever let anyone talk you into playing a game of poker unless you just enjoy giving your money away."

"No, it's not like that. I think it would be great for Hannah to find someone, I just... a relationship with Kiernan would be... complicated, don't you think?"

Despite his previous assertion, Milo gave his eyes a vigorous roll. "All relationships are complicated. I'm pretty sure the word 'relationship' is, like, Latin for 'complicated,' or something."

"Yeah, but this would be particularly complicated," I pointed out.

Milo frowned, and I knew he had to admit I had a point. Kiernan was a Caomhnóir, so there was the initial hurdle of a relationship between the two of them being technically forbidden, although that may be about to change. But beyond that, there was the awkward detail of Kiernan being Lucida's nephew. Milo, of all people, who harbored an undying mistrust and hatred for Lucida, had to see the pitfalls. It was possible that Kiernan was the one person at Fairhaven whose relationship with Lucida was even more complicated than her own. Could she really overlook that in a boyfriend?

"Look, I know you've been distracted getting everything ready for Fiona, but just... see if you notice it, now that I've put it on your radar, okay?" Milo said. "How did that go, by the way? I see you don't have any pieces of occasional furniture embedded in your body, so that's a good sign."

I nodded. "It went better than I thought. It's going to take some adjustment, but I think it's going to work out really well for her."

"Good, I'm glad," Milo said.

"Me, too," I agreed. "This situation is shitty enough without Fiona having to give up life in her tower. How could she sufficiently shun polite society if she couldn't lock herself away?"

I pulled out my phone to text Finn and found that I already had a message waiting from him.

Come to our secret spot. I'll be waiting for you.

I smiled. My desire to see him gave me another reason to eat with impolite haste.

42

Half an hour later, I knocked softly upon the door of the little ramshackle cottage in the Fairhaven grove. Finn poked his head out and narrowed his eyes at me.

"Password?" he demanded.

"The Council can take their Code of Conduct and shove it?" I suggested.

"Hmm, that's technically a passphrase, but I'll allow it," he said, and pulled the door wide to admit me.

He had already lit the fire in the wood stove and it crackled merrily, bathing the room in dancing golden light. The tiny cabin had been ready to fall over when Finn had found it years ago, but in the time since, he had made repairs and turned it into a clandestine retreat. Once he had come simply to be alone with his thoughts and his poetry. Now, it was a place the two of us could come together.

"Doing some last minute cramming?" I asked, noticing the books from the library on a stool next to the makeshift bed.

"Yes, just... brushing up," he said. "How was your dinner?"

"Wonderful, thank you. I was just so exhausted," I sighed. I sunk down onto the heap of pillows and cushions and blankets and gave a sigh. Finn crossed over and lay down beside me, and lay my head on his chest.

"I've been thinking about you all day. Tell me about your day with Fiona. How did it go."

And I told him. Well... I definitely started to tell him. But the fire was so warm, and the bed was so comfortable, and my body was still so tired from a week's worth of manual labor and worry and stress. I didn't remember falling asleep, but suddenly I found myself waking up.

I felt the absence of warmth first—a cool, breezy emptiness where Finn's body used to be. My fingers ventured out from under the pillow, searching the indentation in the rumpled bedclothes, but were not rewarded with the feel of him. I rolled over and forced my sleepy eyes open, squinting through the darkness until I saw him, silhouetted against the moonlight in the window by the dying remains of the fire.

I didn't call out to him at first. Instead, I watched him for a few moments, the way the light of the full moon highlighted his cheekbones and glimmered in the hair that fell to his shoulders. As I took him in, he lifted a pencil to the little black book resting on his knees, held it suspended over the page for a moment, then brought it to his mouth and began chewing on it pensively. My own mouth curled into a smile.

"Finn?" Though I whispered his name, he jumped as if I had shouted at him, and his pencil clattered to the floor. He bent to retrieve it.

"Sorry," I said, slipping from the bed and shuffling across the room to join him, shivering as though I had stepped outside. The cabin walls were thin, and the wind whistled its way in around the windows and doors.

"No, love, *I'm* sorry," Finn replied, tucking the pencil behind his ear and shifting over on the threadbare wingchair to make room for me to tuck in beside him. "Did I wake you? I tried to be quiet."

"No, you didn't wake me," I told him, sliding my chilly feet under his legs. "I didn't mean to fall asleep on you. I guess I was still really tired."

"You certainly were. That was some world-class snoring you were doing."

I smacked him on the arm. "What are you doing up?"

"Couldn't sleep," Finn replied.

"Yes, I figured that much out for myself," I said with a playful nudge of my toe. "I meant, why couldn't you sleep? I hope it wasn't just my snoring."

"Nervous, I suppose," Finn replied.

"About tomorrow?"

"Yes," he said with a long sigh. "Foolish, I know."

"It's not foolish," I said. "You're starting a new job. It's a lot of responsibility. I'd be nervous, too."

"It's not the responsibility I'm worried about," Finn said with a dismissive wave of his hand. "You know me, I've always wanted the chance to prove myself. I've been eager for more responsibility, it's just... I'm more nervous about my reception."

"Your reception?"

"By the other Caomhnóir. The ones I'm supposed to be training."

I frowned. "I'm not sure I understand. Are you saying you're afraid they won't like you or something?"

Finn chuckled. "I am utterly unconcerned about whether or not they like me. Liking me is irrelevant. I'm there to be their instructor, not their drinking mate. What I mean to say is... I'm concerned that they won't take me seriously as a leader."

This was not at all what I expected him to say; Finn had always

44

been so sure of himself in his Caomhnóir role. "But why wouldn't they? You're a natural-born leader, Finn. You take charge in every situation, even when I'd rather you didn't."

He smiled at my feeble joke. "It's not a question of my confidence or abilities. It's a question of whether they can respect me, knowing what they all know."

"I'm still not following you. What is it you think they know about you that's going to make it impossible for them to respect you?"

Finn gave a shrug. "Us. They know about us."

I blinked. "You ... you think *I'm* the reason none of the Novitiates will respect you?"

"No," Finn said firmly. "I didn't say 'you,' did I? I said 'us'—our relationship. It flies in the face of centuries worth of traditions and rules."

"I thought we decided those centuries worth of traditions and rules are bullshit," I pointed out, attempting to sound reasonable rather than like a hurt child, which was how I felt.

"We did," Finn said, and his expression made it clear that I was not fooling him in the least with my pathetic impression of "reasonable." He reached out and pulled me by the hand, so that I was curled up against his chest. "And I'm not doubting that assessment, not for a moment. I choose you over every one of those rules and traditions, and I'll never stop choosing you—choosing *us*. But just because we've rejected the status quo doesn't mean that others will do the same. Most of those Novitiates grew up just as I did, their heads crammed full of Caomhnóir propaganda about Durupinen and duty and honor and codes until there was no room left to think properly for themselves. You remember how I behaved when we first met—what a daft prick I was."

"Oh, come on, you weren't daft. I mean, okay, you were kind of a prick, but…"

I felt the laugh rumble in his chest, and the sound of it filled me with contentment. When he spoke again, though, he still sounded troubled.

"What I'm trying to say is, why would they bother following orders from someone who spat on everything they believe in? How can I be the one to enforce the rules and regulations when I've proven I don't give a damn about them myself?"

I lifted my head from his chest and tugged on his chin until he was forced to look at me. "You are the bravest, most selfless man I've ever met," I told him. "You have risked everything you have—body and soul—for me and for the spirit world. You've faced dangers most of those boys can't even conceive of. You are the absolute epitome of what a Caomhnóir should be, and if they can't see that, then they don't deserve to be here, because they don't understand the first thing about honor, duty, or courage. If a single one of those little shits gives you attitude tomorrow, you just remind them who put you in charge of them in the first place. The High Priestess herself hand-picked you for this job. If they question your fitness, they question hers. That's all the legitimacy you need, and don't let them forget it."

Finn smiled, and then leaned forward to kiss me. When he pulled away again—*entirely* too soon, in my opinion—he said, "What did I do to deserve you?"

"No idea," I said, planting another quick kiss on his chin. "Just lucky, I guess."

"Lucky, indeed," he agreed. "Thank you, love. You're right. I've got to get out of my own head."

"Were you trying to distract yourself with some writing?" I asked, tapping on the book in his hand. It was then I realized exactly which book it was. "Hey! That's the book I gave you for Christmas! Where—how did you get it back?"

"I found it waiting for me on my desk in the barracks today, when I went in to prepare for tomorrow's drills," Finn said, flipping through the pages. I watched my own artwork flash past as page after page sped through his fingers.

"I thought Celeste still had it!" I whispered.

"I guess she thought it was time for me to have it back."

I smiled down at the book. Giving it back to Finn was not just a matter of course—a simple return of someone's property because it rightfully belonged to them. It was a sign of solidarity—a symbol of her support for the two of us, a way to say that she was sorry for what she had put us through, and that she would stand by us through the struggle that was yet to come. It had once seemed impossible to me that I could ever forgive Celeste for what she had put us through—for the way that she had torn our lives apart by tearing *us* apart—but looking down at that book, knowing that she would use her considerable power to help us—I realized that I had already begun to forgive her.

"Did you write anything when we were—when you were at Skye Príosún?"

Finn shook his head. "Nothing that I didn't immediately toss in the bin. I tried, but..." He shrugged, and the movement held such echoes of sadness that I felt a lump in my throat at the sight of it.

"I know what you mean. I hardly drew a thing the whole time you were gone," I told him.

"There's something about that place," Finn said, stroking my hair absently and looking back out the window, as though he could still see the hulking outline of the great fortress hanging in the stars. "There's such a deep despair there, it's like a disease. It infects everyone and everything. You can't fight it off, even if you're the one on the right side of the bars. Honestly, those of us who guarded the place were just as trapped as those we were forced to guard."

"I can't imagine," I whispered. "I couldn't wait to leave the place, and I was barely there for a day."

"It's like time stands still out there," Finn said, looking at the moon, whose round face seemed to be listening intently. "It's so isolated—so remote, and there's nothing but anger and sadness and barely contained chaos all the time. Sometimes on my breaks, I would leave the castle entirely and walk the cliffs instead, just to get away, but it wasn't any better out there. Watching the waves batter themselves repeatedly and relentlessly against the rocks—it felt like a metaphor, and not one I wanted to even think about, let alone one that might inspire a line of poetry."

"I'm so sorry, Finn," I whispered, and I felt the familiar guilt begin to batter against me as though it had taken lessons from those waves on the cliffs.

"Don't you dare apologize to me," Finn said, so sharply that I looked up in surprise. "You were the difference, don't you understand?"

I shook my head.

"The difference between me and the rest of those sorry, miserable bastards out on that godforsaken rock," he said, running his fingers through my hair. "They had nothing to moor themselves to, don't you see? There was nothing to stop them from letting their despair eat them alive, but me? I was the lucky one, just as you said. I had you."

"But you didn't have me," I said. "Finn, we were hundreds of miles apart."

47

"What does distance matter when I knew how we felt about each other? I knew you loved me just as deeply and completely as when you lay right here beside me. And the ache of missing you only made me surer of that love. That pain was an anchor. Don't get me wrong, I was a miserable bastard, and no mistake, but I was anchored in my pain. It kept me thinking clearly. It reminded me of what mattered, so that when the others fell, one by one, to the dark thoughts and suggestions the Necromancers would whisper from the dark corners of their cells, I could turn and walk away. So many of those Caomhnóir had nothing left to fight for. I had you to fight for. I'm just sorry it took me so long to figure that out."

I didn't know what to say. I was afraid if I opened my mouth, I would burst into tears. Finn wasn't done talking, however.

"I need to apologize to you. You were right all along. We couldn't hide what was between us. Our feelings weren't going to change and so we needed to change the rules instead. I was just scared, Jess. Scared of... well, of exactly what happened to us."

I mastered my emotions long enough to reply coherently. "You had every reason to be scared. We both did."

"But if we'd just taken the risk and tried to change the law, we might have avoided all of that pain. But we couldn't know that. We couldn't know for sure, and—"

"Who knows anything for sure?" I asked. "What situation ever in life have we known for sure exactly what was going to happen?"

"I'm a Guardian, Jess," Finn said. "It's my nature and my job to always choose the path with the least amount of risk—at least when it comes to *you*. I thought that was what we were doing, keeping our relationship secret. I couldn't have been more wrong."

"Finn, we can't look back," I said, and to my surprise, all the feelings welling up inside me served to steel my voice rather than weaken it. "We spend our entire lives trying to help people stuck in their pasts, in a world they don't belong to anymore. We encourage them—and sometimes force them—to step away from the past and into the future, even if that future terrifies them. Even though that future lies somewhere they can never return from. It's our job to encourage others to take that risk, to leap into the unknown because that's where they're meant to be. And it was what we should have done for ourselves all along."

Finn blinked, his expression utterly blank. At last, he whispered,

"I... never thought of it that way before, but you are absolutely right."

"I'm not sure I ever really thought about it that way before either," I admitted. "But it seems logical to me. Sometimes we take the greatest risks for the greatest rewards, and this?" I took his hand and intertwined our fingers. "This is the greatest reward I can think of."

He lifted our interlocked hands to his lips and planted a kiss on the sensitive underside of my wrist.

"Yes, love," he whispered. "The greatest reward."

I closed my eyes and reveled in the tingling sensation his lips left on my skin until it faded away. Then I sighed, opened my eyes, and found Finn's gaze. "So, what do we do now?"

He shrugged. "We wait. We wait for Hannah to make our case, and hope that the Council will agree."

"And what if they don't?" I asked.

"Let's cross that bridge when we get to it," Finn said, his face folding in on itself into one of his surliest frowns. It was the kind of expression that, in the first days of knowing him, would have convinced me not to attempt conversation. Now, however, knowing him the way I did, I knew his stormy expression was one of worry, not anger, and I knew the clouds wouldn't lift unless we talked through what worried him—what worried both of us.

"Let's cross that bridge now," I said, and as Finn opened his mouth to protest, I raised a hand to silence him. "Finn, we can't do this again. We can't be passive bystanders in our own lives and we can't wait for someone else to make our decisions for us. We waited for the bridge last time, and by the time we reached it, Ileana had taken a torch to it and stranded us on opposite sides of the chasm. We need to decide, and we need to do it together: if the Council votes against us, what will we do?"

"We walk away," he said quietly.

"From each other?" I asked, my voice a breathless whisper.

"No," he replied. "From this." And he took the golden pin upon his vest, the one that signified his role as Clan Caomhnóir, and placed it on the window seat between us.

I stared down at the pin, trying to decipher the full meaning of the gesture. I looked up at Finn, and saw that his eyes were bright.

"I know that you have no choice but to be a Gateway," Finn said.

49

"I know what happened to your mother when she tried to give it up. You have no choice. But I do."

"Finn, I can't ask you to—"

"You aren't asking me to. This is my decision. I will always be connected to the spirit world—that can never and will never change. But if I must walk away from my role as a Guardian, then I will do it. I had the opportunity to choose you once before, and I failed that test. I'm not sure I'll ever forgive myself for that failure."

"There's nothing to forgive, Finn," I said. "There was no way to know what was going to happen. Only one of us can see into the future, remember?"

He nearly smiled. Nearly. "Well, the future is all I'm focusing on now—*our* future. And I won't hesitate again, I promise you that."

"Neither will I," I told him. "Let's hope the Council also feels compelled to look forward instead of backward."

"That would be a first," Finn said with a smirk.

5

FOR YOUR CONSIDERATION

F INN WAS GONE WITH THE SUNRISE to begin his training duties, and by the time the sun went down, his worries had sunk over the horizon with it.

"You were right," he told me when he met me for dinner that night.

"Obviously," I said as he pulled a chair out for me. It was one of those antiquated gestures he did without even thinking—entirely unnecessary and yet somehow adorable. "But about what specifically, this time?"

"I needn't have worried about the Novitiates respecting me," Finn replied, dropping into the chair across from me and pulling a soup bowl toward himself. He tucked in hungrily, taking two enormous swallows before he went on. "In fact, I think you may have done me a favor."

"What favor," I asked, handing him a napkin.

"Well, I can't be sure, of course, because they would never say such a thing out loud to a superior, but I think my reputation may have preceded me."

"Explain," I said, grinning.

"Well, I arrived at the barracks extremely early, as you know, and went straight to my office, and I could hear them trading stories as they got dressed—rumors they'd heard about me, and so forth. And as it turns out, many of them seem to regard me as what you Americans might refer to as a badass."

I threw back my head and laughed, causing several people to pause in their eating so that they could turn and stare at me.

Finn shrugged, unable to stifle a smile. "They were rather eager to listen to me. At one point, one of them asked me if I'd really led the charge against the Necromancers in battle not once, but twice. I confirmed that to be the case. That confirmation seemed to seal me some sort of respect from the ranks. I had not a spot of trouble from them all day. Didn't have to hand down a single demerit."

"That's fantastic, Finn. You see? I told you they were lucky to learn from you. I'm glad to hear that they know it."

"Well, I'm not sure about that," Finn said modestly. "But if it means they're going to give me an easy time of it, I'll not disagree with them."

"Finn?"

We both turned to see Savvy standing in the doorway of the dining room. She looked pale and drawn, like she needed a good night's sleep.

Finn looked down at his watch and swore under his breath. "I'm sorry, Savvy, I've only just sat down. I'm running a bit behind. It took me rather longer than I expected to oversee the proper locking away of all the weaponry at the end of drills. Can I meet you in about fifteen minutes? I've just got to bolt something down here."

"Cheers, mate," Savvy said, looking relieved. "I'll see you in the library, then. Oi, Jess."

She threw a cursory smile and wave my way, turned around, and walked right back out of the dining room again.

"What's that all about?" I asked Finn.

"Oh, she asked for my help with something she's working on," Finn said, settling back to shoveling soup into his mouth. "I was so preoccupied with training today that it nearly slipped my mind."

"Something she's working on?" I asked. "You mean for Hannah's proposal?"

"Well, not exactly, but it's... related," Finn said, seeming to choose his words carefully. "I think I ought to let her explain it to you."

"I... okay," I said, mystified, but deciding to let it go. Whatever Savvy had found to keep her occupied, I was glad for it. She had spent so many weeks moping in her bedroom, skipping meals, and avoiding social situations. Spending time in the library wasn't exactly partying, but at least she was motivated to do something besides wallow. I considered it a step in the right direction. I knew when she was ready to share... whatever it was she was doing, she would share it. I had enough confidence in our friendship and enough respect for her grieving process to mind my own damn business.

But she didn't share, and I was far too preoccupied for the rest of the week to give it another thought. Hannah's proposal day loomed, casting a long, dark shadow over everything and filling us all with a sense of dread and anxiousness that we could not shake, despite the knowledge that she was, perhaps, more prepared than any person ever to propose anything in that Grand Council Room. On the eve of the big day, the rug in front of the fire was covered with twenty perfectly stacked policy proposals, each one neatly bound and marked with color-coded tabs that organized the content into sections. Hannah sat in the middle of them, having just finished sliding cover pages into the clear plastic covers, and sighed, looking at each packet as though it were advancing to attack her.

"That's it, then," she said. "I've done everything I can do."

"Then why do you sound so defeated?" I asked her, finding an unoccupied corner of the rug to sit on.

"I'm not feeling defeated," Hannah said. "Not exactly. I guess I'm just feeling... well, haunted by the idea that all this work might have absolutely no impact at all. As though I could have just skipped all of it and achieved the same result."

I shook my head. "I understand why you're nervous. I'm nervous, too. But there's not a single person on that Council who won't be mightily impressed with what you've done here, even if they don't want to vote for it. You've made arguments here that can't be dismissed, and you are going to make a lot of people question things they've never even thought to question. This might be a longer road than we want it to be, but you are setting people on the journey, and that is something to be proud of no matter what."

Hannah smiled. "Thanks. I wish that sentiment made me feel even a tiny bit less nauseous right now."

I laughed. "Sorry. I don't think we're going to talk ourselves out of being nervous."

It was possible that Hannah sat on that rug all night. I couldn't be sure. It was a very restless night, full of tossing and turning and bizarre dreams chasing themselves through my brain at a faster and faster pace so that, by the time my alarm went off, I woke up feeling disoriented and dizzy and like I'd barely slept at all.

Hannah was in the bathroom brushing her teeth. She was already showered and dressed. She had even allowed Milo to advise her on her hair and make-up. As I shuffled in behind her to take my turn in the shower, she gave herself a satisfied nod in the mirror and turned briskly to me. "I'm headed down to the Council Room to put the proposals at all of the Council members' seats. Then I think I'm going to run through my speech a few times. Karen and Milo are going to come down to help me."

"Oh, okay," I said, a little startled at how calm and put-together she seemed. "Do you want me to come? I have to get up to Fiona's tower to get her ready for the Council meeting, but I could—"

Hannah cut me off with a raised hand. "Nope. Go take care of Fiona. I've got this."

Behind her, Milo made a face that seemed to say, "What's gotten into her?" Then he shooed her out of the bathroom. "Madame Councilwoman has spoken. Do your thing, sweetness. We'll see you down in the Grand Council Room at nine."

Getting Fiona ready for a Council meeting was very much what I imagined it would be like to get a truculent, tantrumming toddler out the door when she'd skipped her nap. She whined. She moaned. She complained about everything from the clothes I insist she wear ("I don't give a damn if I've been wearing them for three days or if they're covered in plaster! They're bloody comfortable, so the rest of the Council can get well and truly stuffed.") to the food I brought up from the dining room. ("How do you expect a woman to eat scones without Devonshire cream? What kind of a monster are you?"). By the time I'd settled her in her place on the Council benches and offered to read Hannah's proposal out loud to her before the meeting started, ("Oh, yes, please read me a bloody bedtime story, seeing as I'm about to doze off from sheer boredom in this interminable meeting.") I was more than pleased to get the hell away from her. I was glad that she was starting to feel back to her typically irascible self, but not glad enough to put up with it a minute longer than was necessary.

Within a few minutes, the hall began to fill with spectators, far more than would attend a typical Council meeting, which was always open to anyone in the clans who wanted to attend, though most people rarely did. I supposed word must have spread about what Hannah had planned to present that morning. I turned to find her where she already sat in the benches, worried that the large crowd might intimidate her, but her face, as she observed the people coming in, was completely impassive. She'd probably expected this, I reasoned. After all, she was prepared for absolutely everything else, so why wouldn't she be prepared for this as well?

I lingered awkwardly near the back of the hall, watching dozens of Durupinen file in, until I spotted Savvy and Finn enter, and waved them over to me. "What took you so long?" I asked Finn, glancing at my watch. "You're cutting it very close. I was starting to think you'd forgotten."

"Not the case, I assure you," Finn said, looking a bit frazzled, but taking my hand and smiling stoutly at me. "It's the big day. I haven't forgotten, I promise."

"Karen is sitting in our clan seats up front," I said, gesturing toward the front of the room. "Let's go sit up there with her." Not that I wanted to put us on display for the general public to gawk at, but let's face it, we would have been gawked at no matter where we sat, and in the clan seats, Hannah would have a good view of us, which might come in handy if she fell victim to nerves. I wanted her to be able to focus on friendly faces in the sea of potentially hostile ones.

"I knew this meeting might get crowded, but even I hadn't expected this," Karen whispered to me as I sat down. "I hope Hannah can hold it together."

"She seems to be doing alright so far," I replied. "She already had to stand before the entirety of the Northern Clans to run for her seat. It's hard to intimidate her after an experience like that."

When at last the Caomhnóir closed the Grand Council Room doors, nearly every seat in the place was filled. Among the crowd, I saw Róisín and Riley Lightfoot, the first of whom gave me a friendly wave when she spotted me, and Finn's sister Olivia, who appeared determined not to look in my direction at all. There were other faces I recognized as well, but many were strangers, absent from Fairhaven, no doubt, since the last Airechtas. There was also a much larger percentage of men than I'd ever seen in this space before—the crowd was dotted with the weathered faces of older men, retired Caomhnóir, most likely, who had come to see what mischief was being stirred up by the young upstarts of the next generation. But even their deep murmurs died away when Celeste swept up to the podium.

"Welcome, everyone. I am pleased to see so many of our esteemed clan members here to participate in the legislative process," she said with a wry smile. "Of course, the invitation is always open—I hope such robust interest will continue into future meetings, even when our agenda is a bit less... interesting."

There was a general squirming and murmuring. I smirked. At the very least, it seemed that Celeste was not going to let anyone get away with any bullshit.

Siobhán went through the typical start of meeting business, taking roll call, submitting requests and petitions for the public record, and reporting on several rulings handed down from the International High Council. Then Catriona stood to give an update on the Tracker investigation into the events at Skye Príosún, though she had to redact many details that were still under active inquiry. It was clear that there was still much to be uncovered regarding the Caomhnóir participation, and the tension among their ranks was palpable. It couldn't have been easy, having their integrity called into question by the actions of their brothers.

At last, the time came for new business, otherwise known as the moment that Hannah would throw a live grenade into the proceedings. My heart was thumping so loudly that I was sure people in the surrounding seats could hear it. Beside me, Finn reached over and gave my hand a surreptitious squeeze. I began to feel the heat of what seemed to be a hundred pairs of eyes burning into the back of my head. Imagined or not, it made my palms sweat.

Siobhán called Hannah and Kiernan to the podium. It caused a buzz of interest in the assembled crowd, to see a Durupinen and a Caomhnóir standing side by side, which honestly should have been signal enough that something was deeply wrong. Kiernan stood to the side and gestured Hannah toward the lectern, and she took her place with every appearance of calm and professionalism. I had a weird, maternal moment watching her there, wondering when the hell she'd grown up.

"Good morning," she began. Her tone was strong and clear—it was also slightly higher than usual, which I only noticed because I knew her so well, and was the only indication whatsoever that she was, indeed, nervous.

"I want to thank the Council for giving me the opportunity to speak today, to introduce a piece of proposed legislation that I believe is both timely and long overdue. To many of the people in this room, I will only ever be the Caller that brought about the Prophecy. I am not happy about that fact, but I have come to appreciate it. I understand that, for many people, the Prophecy—and my role in it—will always define me. But I am more than just a Caller, and more than just a figure populating a long and complicated mythology. I am also a sister who was separated from her twin for eighteen years. I am also a daughter to a mother I will never know because the Prophecy destroyed her. And I am also a woman, just a flawed human being, wondering how best to pick up the pieces, arrange them again into some semblance of a life, and move forward. Because our only option, if we are to survive, is to move forward.

"To remain stuck in the past—a past haunted by the ghosts of prophecies yet to come—is no way to heal. We spent centuries carefully walling ourselves in, desperate to prevent a future that came precisely because we tried to prevent it. And even now, with the Prophecy well behind us, still we allow the decisions of the past to direct the trajectory of our future. I am speaking, of course, of the Code of Conduct. For hundreds and hundreds of years, the Code of Conduct has kept Durupinen and Caomhnóir in a strange state of disconnect. We work together to protect the spirit world, but we do it nearly as strangers, living side by side and yet mistrustful of each other. Our training teaches us the importance of our own work, but fails to value the contributions of the others. It drives a wedge between us, making it difficult to fully trust and support each other."

Here, Hannah paused to look at Kiernan, who nodded his approval of her words and gestured for her to go on.

"The Necromancers realized something that we failed to recognize about ourselves; that our Code has caused rifts between us that could be exploited. They saw an opportunity and they took it, and it very nearly destroyed the clans as we know them. Even now, the pain and consequences of the betrayal are echoing through our ranks, tearing clans apart from the inside. Our mistrust and sometimes downright hostility toward each other have rendered us an easy mark for future infiltration and attack. I believe it is time for this to change. And I know, after the events at Skye Príosún, that I am not alone."

She allowed these words to ripple through the crowd, like a stone tossed into a mirror-smooth pond. People threw each other cautious looks, afraid, it seemed, to be the first to agree with her. And yet, the energy in the room was not hostile—hesitant, even fearful, but not hostile. Hannah seemed to take heart even from this, and went on more confidently.

"As you all know, our current Code of Conduct was developed with a single goal in mind: prevent Durupinen and Caomhnóir relationships so that the subjects of the Prophecy would never be born. As you can see by the fact that my sister and I exist, the Code of Conduct did not work as intended."

Fiona let out a bark of a laugh. It was met here and there with a nervous titter, as though the audience could not believe that Hannah would mention anything so illicit as her parents' relationship.

"And now here we are. The Prophecy came to pass anyway, and we still live under an antiquated and completely ineffective set of rules that govern our relationships. The Code of Conduct didn't work then, and it doesn't work now. It is time for change. Time for a new beginning in which Durupinen and Caomhnóir can not only coexist peacefully, but develop their bonds wherever they naturally may lead."

A woman in the third row stood up. "I understand," she said in a bold voice, "that your own sister has broken the Code of Conduct and has entered into a relationship with your former Caomhnóir. What do you say to the accusations that you only want to change this law to benefit your own sister's happiness?"

Beside me, Finn's hands tightened into fists. On my other side, Karen seemed to have stopped breathing and her flared nostrils were white around the edges. Milo was flickering with anger, and I could feel the gist of the response he longed to hurl at the woman, none of which was suitable in polite company, and every word of which would likely get him banned from the Grand Council Room for the rest of the meeting.

Hannah, however, seemed to have expected nothing less. Without missing a beat, she pulled a sheet of paper out from under her notes and said, "What is your name, please?"

The woman looked taken aback to have been asked a question in return, but cleared her throat and replied, "Aileen Donnolly of the Clan Beith."

Hannah consulted her list for a moment and then looked up sharply. "Are you aware, Aileen Donnolly of the Clan Beith, that two of your clansmen are amongst those arrested for having cooperated freely with the attempted coup at Skye?"

A collective gasp ran through the crowd. Beside me, Milo muttered, "Oh, shit she went there!" And behind us in the third row, Aileen Donnolly's face went scarlet.

"I know it," she answered at last.

"Are you aware, then, that there is hardly a clan untouched by this scandal? That you could have given me any name, and I could likely have shown a link between you and the poison that has infiltrated our system?"

Aileen did not answer. The others around her had gone quiet, no doubt wondering whether Hannah was going to start going down her list and publicly humiliate each of them one by one. But Hannah slid the paper back under her notes and went on, her voice kinder.

"I don't say this to shame anyone. The fact that two members of Clan Beith are amongst those charged is not a reflection on Aileen, or the rest of her clan, it is a reflection on all of us. Our system is battered. It is broken. But it is not beyond repair. If we are clear-eyed enough to recognize the changes that need to be made, and brave enough to weather them, then I believe that we can emerge from the events at Skye stronger and more united than we have ever been."

At these words Kiernan stepped forward and stood beside Hannah. She took a step to the side, so that she was sharing the lectern with him. "If I may be recognized, High Priestess?"

"The Council recognizes Caomhnóir Worthington," Celeste replied, inclining her head graciously.

"I am Guardian Kiernan Worthington, and I am a co-sponsor on this proposal. I want to say that this is not just about one relationship or one clan. I, too, have long believed that the restrictions upon the roles of Guardians and Durupinen alike have held many of us back from our true potential and stunted the value of the contributions that we could make to our community. Several years ago, I put forth a proposal of my own, to request that I be allowed to forgo the traditional role of Caomhnóir in favor of the role of Scribe, a position that has never been held by anyone other than a Durupinen. The proposal, which was not approved at the time, was supported by much of the same evidence and observations as the proposal before you today. I stand beside Hannah in support of this legislation because I believe it is important to know that both Durupinen and Caomhnóir can recognize the chinks in our armor, and that we would all benefit from a reworking of our current Code. It is time for Caomhnóir and Durupinen to come together in a more meaningful way, to communicate more effectively and participate in roles that play to our strengths and our abilities."

"Thank you, Kiernan," Hannah said, beaming at him. "I have appreciated your support and hard work on this project." She turned to Celeste. "With the Council's permission, I would like to read the introduction to my proposal, which outlines all of the key changes that I suggest be made, and the intended outcome of each."

"Permission granted," Celeste said, giving Hannah an encouraging smile. "Council members, please refer to the copies of the proposal that have been provided to you."

Hannah threw me a quick, relieved smile. I winked at her and smiled back, then turned to my own copy of the proposal so that I could follow along.

For the next twenty minutes, Hannah guided everyone through her proposal. It was clear, as Karen had said, that many people were heartily impressed with the thoroughness of the work, even if they weren't thrilled with the content. The remnants of Marion's old clique were predictably dismissive at first, though they certainly found it harder to sniff disapprovingly as the presentation went on. Hannah's strategy of singling out Aileen Donnolly's family had been a brilliant one, as none of them seemed willing to speak out openly against the proposal lest they too be raked over the coals. I was sure they would have plenty to say behind closed doors, but for now, at least, Hannah was spared their vitriol. It was clear that many of the Caomhnóir were uncomfortable with the meeting as well. Many of them were staring at Kiernan as though he were a turncoat, but he seemed, like Hannah, to have expected nothing less, and did not flinch even once.

At last, when Hannah had finished, Celeste stood up and addressed the room at large. "Thank you, Hannah and Kiernan. I appreciate the great effort that was put into this proposal. Thank you, as well, to Kiera for co-sponsoring the legislation. I am sure that Hannah appreciated your guidance. I encourage the members of the Council to read the proposal in full over the next week, and submit your questions in written form so that Hannah can respond to them. Several copies of the proposal will be on file in the library for the public to read, and further copies can be requested through the Council office, care of Siobhán." She sighed and looked around the room. "Unless there is any other business, I would like to—"

"There is other business. That is to say, I have business."

Every head in the room turned as one to look at Savvy, whose voice had rung out sharply. Now that everyone was looking at her, though, she seemed to have frozen. Her mouth opened and closed several times, like a freshly caught fish, and then she turned to Finn, her eyes wide with sheer animal panic.

I felt Finn reach out and give my hand a brief squeeze. Then, swiftly, he rose from his chair. As he did so, Savvy mirrored his movement, as though she had been waiting, ready to spring when he made his move. However, once they were both standing, she simply continued to stare at him with wide, pleading eyes.

"Finn, what are you—" I began, but he gave his head a subtle shake as though to say, "Not now." I swallowed the rest of my question, trying not to feel slighted, and instead joined the crowd of heads now turning curiously in his direction.

"Ms. Todd and I have some further business, should it please the Council to hear it," Finn said resolutely.

"The Council recognizes Caomhnóir Finn Carey and Savannah Todd of the Clan Lunnainn," Celeste said, inclining her head toward them. It was clearly an invitation to speak, but Savvy had gone completely still. For once in her life, she seemed not to have anything to say, or at least, not the courage to say it. Finn sighed and cleared his throat.

"Ms. Todd and I have a sort of... addendum to be considered with Councilwoman Ballard's bill."

Up on the platform, Hannah's eyebrows disappeared into her bangs. She looked back and forth from Finn to Savvy, clearly bewildered. Then she cast her eyes to me and her voice shot through our connection, shrill and anxious.

"Do you know what he's talking about? What addendum?"

"I have absolutely no idea," I replied, as her nervousness zipped through my head like an electric current, making me wince. "No one told me anything about an addendum."

"Very well, and what is this addendum?" Celeste asked, looking just as puzzled as the rest of us.

"I think it best if Ms. Todd tells you herself," Finn said firmly.

Savvy's eyes went as round as coins. She clenched her jaw and, for a split second, I thought she was going to reach out and slug Finn across the face for putting her on the spot. But then she expelled a long, slow breath, and dropped her eyes to her hands, now clasped in front of her in a pose that appeared almost supplicative, but was probably just to stop them from shaking. When she raised her head and looked at the Council to speak, her voice was a little breathless.

"Right, um... well, I'm here to... to make what you might call an unusual request."

"Unusual?" Siobhán repeated.

"Yeah. Well, alright, if I'm honest it's not so much unusual as unheard of," Savvy babbled. "But then again, my situation is unheard of as well, so I suppose it makes sense, doesn't it."

"Miss Todd, kindly clarify what you are talking about," Siobhán said. Her professional tone was already cracking, probably because Savvy had driven her to the brink of insanity as a student, and she had never quite recovered from it.

"Well, it's like this, see," Savvy said, drawing another deep breath that put some more power behind her voice. "You all know that I'm the first Gateway in my clan. I've had a bugger of a time adjusting to that, and I'd really only just gotten a handle on things when it all went to shite."

"Language, please," Siobhán said, closing her eyes and pressing a weary hand to her temple.

"Oh, yeah, right," Savvy said sheepishly. "Sorry. Well, you all know by now that my Gateway has been damaged. I can't use it right now and I've been feeling a bit... lost. The High Priestess," and she inclined her head in Celeste's direction, "told me that I still had a place here, and that I would figure out what it was if I just gave it time."

"And I still believe that to be true," Celeste agreed. "Our sisterhood is deep and abiding. Lest you forget, many of us here on the Council have already passed the responsibility of our Gateways on to the next generation, but that does not mean that we have no further role to play in the protection of the spirit world."

"Yeah, well, I thought a lot about what you said," Savvy replied. "You said I might like helping Hannah with this proposal she's been working on. And I did. Had to take my mind off things, so I dove right in, headfirst. I've spent more time in the library in the last few weeks than I ever have in my life, and it was bloody miserable most of the time. But I'm not complaining because I learned some things about the way things work around here, and also about myself."

SOUL OF THE SENTINEL

Celeste was still smiling, but the smile had become rather fixed, and her tone was wary as she said, "Really? I am glad to hear it."

"I don't reckon you will be after I've said my piece," Savvy replied. "But I'm going to say it anyway, because you told me that I have a right to a place in the Durupinen world, and you're right. I've given up too much to be here. I'm not getting shut out just because some Necromancer bastard fancied himself Dr. Bloody Frankenstein and cocked everything up."

General murmurs of disapproval were rippling through the room. Finn had closed his eyes as though praying for patience, and I knew why. Whatever point Savvy was trying to make, it was likely to fall on deaf ears if she couldn't muster up some sense of basic decorum. But now that she'd started talking, she had regained a bit of her old swagger, and it seemed unlikely that she was capable of policing her own tone once she had gotten her confidence back. Meanwhile, Hannah had gone pale, as though she were watching Savvy light all of her hard work on fire right in front of her.

But to my great surprise, Savvy paused and took several deep breaths. She clenched and unclenched her hands. Then she looked back up at the Council and said, "Sorry about that. My mouth runs out ahead of me sometimes, and I don't always say things the way I should, especially when I'm riled. If you'd been through what my cousin and I have been through, I reckon your language might get pretty colorful, too."

Celeste, looking on the verge of issuing a rebuke, seemed to sag, her expression softening. "I think we can all sympathize with what you've been through, and your... uh... *passion* is understandable," she said, though the expressions of some of the Council members behind her seemed to contradict her assurances. "Please go on, Ms. Todd."

"Well, like I said, I learned a lot about the way things have been done, and it seems to me that we force a lot of people into roles that they aren't equipped to handle, just because they are born into them, like Kiernan said. Look, don't go getting your knickers in a twist," she said to the room at large, for a collective gasp had arisen from the gathered Durupinen. "I'm not blaming anyone here in this room. This is how it's always been done, and you were just carrying on like you were taught to. But I didn't grow up with all this, and I'm seeing it from an outsider's perspective. And for all your talk

63

about sisterhood and duty and belonging and all that tosh, that's still what I am. An outsider."

Celeste opened her mouth to argue, but caught my eye from beside Savvy, and closed it again. I felt a flare of defiance inside me. *That's right,* I told Celeste silently. *Don't deny that. Don't deny that some of us will always be outsiders here. You know it. We all know it, even though many of us wish it wasn't true.*

"My Caomhnóir Bertie Winworth was one of the people I'm talking about. He wasn't a fighter. For Christ's sake, the poor bugger could barely hold a weapon without injuring himself. I know he was keen to prove himself, but anyone could have seen it would have been kinder to find the bloke something quiet and safe to do. And before all you Caomhnóir start glaring daggers at me, I mean no disrespect to Bertie. He gave his life for my cousin and me. But that don't make anything I just said a lie. Bertie is dead because he had a job he couldn't handle, regardless of how devoted he was to it."

Several of the Caomhnóir around the room shifted uncomfortably as her words sank in. Finn gave a small nod of agreement, the muscles in his face tautening with suppressed emotion. Again, no one raised their voice to argue. They'd all seen Savvy at Bertie's funeral. They'd all seen her tribute to him. None dared question her.

"And then there's me. Me, with my complete lack of propriety and all the subtlety of a drunk Scotsman," Savvy went on, with a sad smile. "I ain't cut out for my job either. Just ask anyone here who had to suffer through me in the classroom. I mean, honestly, what lost and confused spirit wants to wind up with me to guide them to the afterlife? I'm likely to get 'em lost. The only thing I've ever been good at is looking out for me and my mates. I've had to take care of myself all my life. I grew up in neighborhoods most people don't even want to drive past. I'm tough, and I'm strong. I should have been the one fighting off that Necromancer twat Charlie. It should have been me." Her voice broke.

Celeste's face crumpled into a pitying expression. "Savvy, this is survivor's guilt, my dear. It wasn't your job to protect him."

"But it should have been! Don't you see? That's what I'm good at! That's what I could have done—what I *should* have done! And that's why I'm here today. You asked me to think about my place in the

Durupinen world and I have. I've made my decision and I'm dead sure about it. I want to train to be a Caomhnóir."

6

OVERRULED

"**W**ELL," I whispered. "At least I'm no longer the queen of the Council uproar."

"The Queen is hereby dethroned. Long live the Queen," Milo agreed, curtseying flamboyantly in Savvy's direction.

"Sod off, the pair of you," Savvy muttered under her breath, bouncing nervously on the balls of her feet.

We stood grouped in the antechamber to the Grand Council Room. Savvy's pronouncement had caused such an uproar that Celeste had to call for order several times and still never really managed to get control of the room again. Then Seamus shouted over the crowd, demanding a recess to confer, and Celeste granted one—not that she'd had much of a choice. Then she'd asked Savvy and Finn to meet her in the antechamber. Milo and I hadn't been invited, strictly speaking, but if Celeste thought we were going to miss this conversation, she was out of her damn mind.

At that moment, Celeste entered the room, with Siobhán right on her heels. She pulled the door shut behind her, muffling the continued hubbub from the Grand Council Room. She looked at me in mild surprise.

"Jessica? Spirit Guide Chang? What are you doing here?"

"I'm here in support of Finn and Savvy," I said.

"And I'm here in case she needs any... guiding," Milo added, thrusting his chest out in a ridiculous attempt to look official.

"I would really prefer that... you know, what? Never mind. It doesn't matter. Stay, if you like," Celeste said, her expression both weary and resigned. It seemed she knew there was a hell of a battle about to commence and she'd rather focus on that than stir up a second one.

The door that led to the entry hall flew open and Seamus came storming in. His eyes were ablaze with fury and his barrel-chest was heaving.

"What the devil is the meaning of this?" Seamus shouted, looking back and forth between Finn and Savvy and Celeste, evidently not caring which of them answered as long as he got some sort of an explanation.

Savvy looked too alarmed to speak, so Finn said, "Seamus..."

"I leave for just a few weeks and the entirety of Fairhaven has gone straight to hell in a bloody handbasket!" Seamus roared.

"Seamus, do not forget to whom you are speaking!" Celeste replied, and rarely had I heard her sound so much like a High Priestess. Her tone evoked memories of Finvarra, and perhaps it was this that shook Seamus out of his fury.

He looked slightly abashed, and made an effort to reign in his voice. "My apologies, High Priestess. I meant no disrespect to you, of course."

"I am in charge of this castle, and I assure you, I have not sunk it to the depths of hell without you here to single-handedly keep it aloft," Celeste said scathingly. "I understand your anger and concern, but express it respectfully or consider yourself censured."

"Apologies," Seamus said again, bowing his head.

"Apology accepted. Now, please say your piece," Celeste replied. "I may be the High Priestess, but matters of the Caomhnóir are largely your domain, and your opinions here matters as much as mine."

Seamus looked slightly mollified, but when he continued, there was still a tremor of anger underscoring his words. "I left Caomhnóir Carey in charge in my absence at your request, High Priestess. I had my reservations, which I expressed to you, but never would I have thought that Caomhnóir Carey would be party to an outrageous affront to the Brotherhood such as this."

"Outrageous perhaps, but hardly an affront," Finn replied, and earned a furious glare in return. "You've barely allowed Ms. Todd to explain her request."

"Because there can be no reasonable explanation for such a request!" Seamus shot back, throwing his hands up in exasperation. "It defies all logic, all precedent, and all common sense! It is ludicrous and deeply insulting to boot. I cannot fathom why you would agree to stand beside her in such a request, which is an affront to everything you have committed your life to as a member of the Brotherhood."

"With all due respect, Seamus, I do not agree with that assessment in the least," Finn said. "What Ms. Todd is proposing is very much in line with the values and purpose of the Brotherhood, which I deeply espouse."

Seamus snorted. "That's rich, given your own difficulties in heeding those same values. Need I remind everyone of the transgressions that left you banished to Skye Príosún in disgrace?"

Finn swelled with anger, but it was me who replied. "That transgression is standing right here, so if you're going to speak about me in that manner, you'd better look me in the eye and use my name," I said through clenched teeth.

Finn lay a hand on my shoulder, which conveyed in a single gesture, both his support of me and his request that I not torpedo the entire discussion with one of my trademark outbursts. For his sake, and for Savvy's, I swallowed the rest of the colorful language I had been preparing to unleash.

"I acknowledge that I have broken our code before," Finn said. "I also acknowledge that there are aspects of that code that need to be reexamined for the good of our Brotherhood and Sisterhood going forward. My stake in it may be personal, but my belief that it will be universally beneficial to our continued mutual success is not. I am glad to further illuminate those opinions at another time, but we are not here to discuss Hannah Ballard's proposed overhauls of the Code of Conduct, or my personal adherence to it. We are here to discuss Ms. Todd's request, and I ask only that we be allowed to fully explain it. If we are permitted to do so, I believe you will find that it honors everything the Brotherhood has stood for since its inception."

Seamus blinked and then looked up at Celeste, expecting to see a similar look of consternation on her face, but he was alone in his outrage. Celeste was looking, if anything, intrigued.

"Very well," she said. "This is an extraordinary request, but I doubt very much that it is being made frivolously or indeed disrespectfully. I do wish that you had come to me with some warning, as I am sure Seamus does as well, but let us sit down and hear your proposal out."

"But—" Seamus sputtered. Celeste held up a quelling hand.

"This is Ms. Todd's time to speak," Celeste said.

Savvy looked up from her feet for the first time since we'd entered the chamber. She looked even more anxious than she had when she was speaking in front of the entire Grand Council Room. Perhaps she thought she'd never get this far. Perhaps she thought the whole thing was going to be shot down the moment it was announced, and she'd never have an opportunity to explain. Her voice shook as she spoke. There was a time I wouldn't have thought she could sound so vulnerable, but that was before Bertie's sacrifice.

"Look, I'm not messing about here," Savvy said. "I'm not trying to waste anyone's time, and I'm not trying to insult anyone. It's because I admire the Caomhnóir and what you do that I'm pursuing this at all. I just... I want to be clear on that point."

"Your intentions are noted," Celeste said. "Please go on."

"Cheers. When this idea first came to me—and believe me, I had a hearty chuckle at my own expense when it did—I tried to ignore it. I tried to brush it off, but it was a persistent bugger, and it clung on, you know, as ideas sometimes do. It took root, like, and I couldn't get it out of my head. I kept thinking, why not? *Why not?* So, then I decided to go to the library and actually find out why not."

Savvy reached back and extracted a well-folded and dog-eared packet of lined paper which had been torn raggedly from a spiral-bound notebook. She unfolded it and began consulting the individual papers, and I realized that they must have been notes. Somewhere on a campus in London, Tia Vezga was hyperventilating into a paper bag at the very thought of such gross violations of note-taking etiquette.

"Okay, it's like this," Savvy said by way of formal introduction, "I read every history of the Caomhnóir I could find. I needed a load of help because my Gaelic is absolute crap, but I got there in the end. I read four different accounts of when the Caomhnóir were founded, and they all roughly translated to the same thing. 'There were many in the ancient clans who had the connection to the spirit world in their blood, but they did not possess the ability to Cross spirits. Because the Gateways were vulnerable to attack and needed protecting, it was determined that there should be formed an army of Guardians, whose connection to the spirit world would make them uniquely suited to the role of protector of the Gateways.'"

Savvy looked up from her crumpled papers. Everyone was listening intently. Seamus had crossed his arms over his chest defensively, as though he could fend off her words purely with a hostile posture, but he gave one brief nod of acknowledgment that her words were, at least, accurate.

"That is indeed why the Caomhnóir were founded, yes," Celeste said, and there was just a hint of impatience in her voice. "I covered it fairly thoroughly in my History and Lore class, which I'm sure you would have a better recollection of if you had attended it with a bit more regularity."

"I reckon that's so," Savvy said with a shrug, completely unabashed. "But I'm learning it now. Better late than never, eh? Then I found this, which was read at the very first Airechtas, at which the Caomhnóir were officially formed." She cleared her throat. "'And so, it is concluded that the Gateways, without proper protection, cannot hope to serve the spirit world unencumbered by terrible dangers. Thus, a league of Guardians, trained both in battle and the runic arts, must be formed, trained, and widely dispersed in service of the Durupinen, to aid in their protection wheresoever it is needed. These Guardians, connected by blood to the spirit world, will devote their lives to the service of the clans, and answer to the will of the Council.'"

Seamus heaved an impatient sigh. "Fascinating though this book report undoubtedly is, I am unsure why my time is being wasted having to listen to it, when any one of our Brotherhood could recite it to you by heart. What is the point of all of this?"

"My point is that, for someone who fancies himself an expert, you seem to have overlooked one enormous detail: not once does it say a Caomhnóir has to be a bloke," Savvy shot back.

Seamus blinked. He looked as though Savvy had slapped him across the face. It took him a moment to regain his powers of speech. "That's ludicrous. Of course, it does."

"Not once," Savvy said. "Not once in the original founding proposition, voted on at the very first Airechtas, is it stipulated that the Caomhnóir be men and men only."

"You've clearly overlooked something in the original text, then," Seamus said with a dismissive wave of his hand. "You yourself said that your understanding of Gaelic is unsophisticated at best."

"We thought you might say that, which is why we've brought the original text with us," Finn said, reaching into the bag by his feet and extracting a very large, extremely old folio. "I was able to persuade the Scribes to allow us to sign this out specially. It is the oldest bound copy we have of these accounts. And then there are these," he said as he extracted a black binder, which flipped open to reveal dozens of pages in plastic sheet protectors. "These are facsimile copies of the scrolls, the oldest surviving accounts of the formation of the Caomhnóir. It includes a transcript of the first Airechtas to which Savannah is referring. You can read it all for yourselves."

He offered the book and binder to Seamus, who did not look as though he intended to give them even a glance, but Celeste gestured to him to bring them over to the desk and, having no choice, he did so. Celeste seated herself behind the desk and opened the book to the page that Finn had marked. Siobhán and Seamus crowded in behind her, reading over her shoulder. When they had finished, they moved on to the binder. As they silently pored over the documents, Savvy was bouncing nervously on the balls of her feet beside me, picking tiny bits of perforated paper from the edge of her notes and letting them flutter to the ground around her like she was standing in a snow globe of anxiety. Finn, who was showing his nervousness by standing stiffly at attention, broke his posture for just a moment to glance over at me and give me a tiny wink. I tried to smile at him, but the general air of tension had affected me too, and he had looked away again before I could get my lips to cooperate. Just off my shoulder, Milo's form was vibrating and fluttering slightly at the edges, which was his way of showing nerves. I reached out into the connection to speak to him, but at that moment, Hannah burst into it with all the subtlety of a freight train.

"What is happening in there! I can't stand it! I'm flipping out!"

"Hannah, calm down!" Milo and I intoned as one as each of us was sent mentally reeling by the dramatic nature of her entrance into our collective headspace.

"Calm down? You've got to be kidding me!" Hannah scoffed. "Please, please tell me what's going on!"

"Savvy and Finn are making the case for Savvy joining the Caomhnóir. They brought some documents from the library that they're using to prove that the original concept of the Caomhnóir wasn't gender-based."

"Oh, I'm sure that's going well," Hannah replied, and the thought was thick and sticky with sarcasm.

"It's a miracle Seamus hasn't started karate chopping people," Milo confirmed.

"Don't exaggerate, Milo," I said.

Milo snorted. "Sweetness, exaggeration is my life force."

"What's going on in the Grand Council Room?" I asked.

"We're still in recess, but Keira is going through mundane stuff with us like recording the minutes from committee meetings and accepting petitions for audiences," Hannah replied, and I could practically hear her eyes rolling. "We need to have a quorum to keep going, otherwise I would have excused myself and come after you."

"It's probably better for you to be out there," Milo said. "You can probably feel the tension through the connection, but it's like being squeezed in a mental vice grip just being in here."

"Oh my God, if this ruins everything I've been working on—" Hannah began, becoming increasingly shrill.

"Don't. Don't torture yourself with speculation, Hannah," I said firmly. "It's not worth it, you'll only give yourself a panic attack over nothing."

"Nothing? *Nothing?!* Jess, you know perfectly well that—"

But at that moment, Celeste closed the binder with a sigh. I sent a quick goodbye zinging through the connection before closing it hastily to tune back in to what was happening in the room with us.

"Well, it would appear that Savannah is entirely right," Celeste said. "There is not a single reference to any gender requirement in the original concept of the Caomhnóir." Her voice was tinged with something hard to identify. Awe, maybe?

"I concede that is the case," Seamus said. "But even if gender does not arise in the original proposition, it became the reality of the Caomhnóir from the beginning. The Code of Conduct clearly spells out that the Caomhnóir are a Brotherhood, and all the rules contained within it confirm that fact," Seamus said.

"The Code of Conduct was not the founding document of the Caomhnóir," Finn said. "It is the document to which we consistently refer in our training because it lays out the day to day regulations by which we must abide, but it only came about as a necessary part of organizing the Order of Caomhnóir, not in the formulation of the Order as a concept."

"But the Caomhnóir have always been male clan members. If the original proposition did not strictly mention it, it was because it was assumed."

"Do we really want the root of who we are—and therefore who we exclude from our ranks—to be based in an assumption, and an outdated one at that?" Finn countered.

Seamus threw up his hands in exasperation. He turned to Celeste. "Please, High Priestess, why are we entertaining this nonsense? They are predicating this request on a matter of semantics. If the original request to form the Brotherhood did not stipulate that the members must be men, the subsequent documents and process certainly did."

Celeste did not answer right away. She seemed lost in thought. I could practically see her mentally paging through every fact she had ever retained from her study of Durupinen history, sure that she could extract something that would contradict what Savvy and Finn had put forward, but as the moments stretched on, so did the weight of her silence.

It was Savvy who broke it. "Look, if you ask me—"

"I assure you, no one did," Seamus muttered, but Savvy ignored him.

"If you ask me," she repeated, talking over him, "that assumption Finn is talking about was a sign of the times. I've always been impressed with the way that women run things around here. It's refreshing, you know? I mean, all over the bloody world, women are still fighting just to get a seat at the table, and here we are, with women making every decision."

Seamus snorted again, although this time his disdain was met with a sharp look from Celeste, and he quickly assumed a more respectful demeanor.

"And it makes sense because women are the only ones who can be Gateways, so they should be the ones making the decisions about how we do it. But that doesn't mean we're immune to the bullshit assumptions people make about men and women and what we're all good for."

"What do you mean, Savannah?" Celeste asked.

It was Savvy's turn to look incredulous now. "Oh, come on, now," she said. "It's everywhere. The men are the strong ones, the ones who do the physical labor, the ones that carry weapons and do our fighting for us. The men drive the cars, the men open the doors, the men treat the women like getting too close to them might poison them. I mean honestly, that's not a result of believing women can be in charge. That's a result of believing that women can't look after themselves and need nursemaids to prevent them from falling off cliffs or seducing everything within snogging distance."

"The Caomhnóir have nothing but the highest respect for—" Seamus began but I had heard enough.

"The Caomhnóir and the Durupinen hate each other," I cut in. "Our dynamic is dysfunctional at best and dangerously antagonistic at worst. And it's no use pretending it's not true. For God's sake, you've spent the last month assessing the damage from the rebellion at Skye. That never could have happened if Caomhnóir and Durupinen weren't at such odds with each other. It's the entire reason we are trying to get the Code of Conduct changed."

Seamus looked as though he would have liked to say a thing or two about why I wanted the Code of Conduct changed, but surprisingly, he restrained himself.

Savvy continued, "Look, I think Hannah's bill will sort out all of that. But let's just say that it does. Let's say that it passes, and we can make those changes, and things get better. Where does that leave someone like me? I'm still in the same muddled mess as before. Where does it leave the next Bertie who comes along, groomed for a job which, sod all, he'll never be able to do properly? We've been lost in this system. We've been lost and no one is bothering to look for us."

No one, it seemed, had an answer to this. Savvy took full advantage of Celeste's inability to conjure comforting platitudes and plunged on.

"According to the very people who founded the concept, the Caomhnóir need two things—*just two things*: a connection to the spirit world and the proper training. I've got one in spades. I'm asking for a chance at the other. I'm ready and I'm willing. I've never felt a calling before in my life—not in school, not here at Fairhaven, never. Duty, sure, but never... *never* a calling. A *vocation*. But I feel it now. And before you suggest it, it's not just guilt over Bertie, and it's not recklessness over the damage to my Gateway. I considered all of that. Believe me, I tried to talk myself out of it, not least because I knew Seamus and his ilk would lose their bloody minds over it. It's a mad idea, and yet, it's not mad at all. I know I'm meant to do this. I don't know how I know it, but I know it just the same, so please. Please give me the chance."

I could hardly breathe, the lump in my throat was so constrictive. Never had I heard Savvy speak in this way before, this impassioned combination of pleading and absolute certainty. It was breathtaking in its power, and I was quite sure that Celeste had been struck equally dumb, because she, too, was simply staring at Savvy as though she had never seen anything quite like her before. And, indeed, she hadn't.

No one had ever seen a female Caomhnóir.

At last, Siobhán cleared her throat, as though to remind Celeste that someone needed to say something, and that person should probably be the High Priestess. Celeste gave her head a little shake, freeing her power of speech from the temporary shackles of shock.

"Savannah, I want to thank you for your honesty and forthrightness in coming to us with this request. It cannot have been easy to do, and I applaud you for it."

"Cheers, miss," Savvy mumbled. Now that she had finished speaking, she had dropped her eyes to the floor again and bowed her head, as though waiting for an ax to be dropped on it, and I realized that she absolutely believed all along that her request would be shot down. Finn, too, looked braced for the worst, his expression stoic and resigned. It was so demoralizing to see them both looking so sure they had failed that I found myself swallowing back protest after protest, searching frantically for just the right thing to say in support of them, and knowing that I could never make a better case for Savvy than she had made for herself.

"I must say," Celeste continued, "that it never occurred to me to question whether gender was essential to the role of a Caomhnóir. Nor, I imagine, has it occurred to any member of our leadership over hundreds of years. This is not surprising. We have never known anything different, and no one has ever challenged the status quo until this moment. I suppose this is not so much an excuse as an explanation. We have never had a reason to question the assumption until now."

"We *still* don't have a reason to question it now," Seamus said, in a voice so stilted with anger that I was impressed he could get any words out at all.

"I would venture that we do," Celeste said, weighing each word slowly and carefully, and Savvy's head shot up, her face full of

76

shock. Seamus looked as though Celeste had slapped him right across the face.

"These are new times for the clans. The world is not what it was when these laws and policies were written. We must acknowledge that, at the very least. In some ways, the Durupinen have done well at adapting to the ever-changing circumstances in which we must operate in secret. We have integrated technology and modern conveniences into ancient practices. We have insinuated ourselves into social circles and business environments that have kept us both influential and safe. We have taken great care to make any and all adjustments that ensure our security. Security—protection—has always been the greatest priority, has it not?"

Seamus nodded warily, as though afraid of what he might be agreeing to.

"And here we have a chance to do something else that may be in the interest of our safety. We have the chance to think about our Caomhnóir in a new way, a way that might indeed make us safer. What if we chose our Guardians not as a mere default, based on their gender, but on their merits and on both their desire and proclivities to handle the job?"

Seamus' face was turning red. I would not have been surprised to see steam start leaking from his ears. Milo, clearly thinking along the same lines, floated to my other side, putting several more feet between himself and Seamus in case of a violent outburst.

"And you think this would be wise?" Siobhán asked, her voice as incredulous as Seamus'. "To allow female clan members to become Caomhnóir?"

"To be honest, I'm not seeing a good reason to disallow it," Celeste said. "What reason do we have?"

"Here we go," Milo whispered.

"What reason? *What reason?!*" Seamus' voice rose nearly to a shriek. He looked quite mad. "Hundreds of years of tradition and brotherhood! A system of training and living and interacting that has been exclusively designed for and by male clan members! Our very identity and meaning of our role in the spirit world! In short, everything that the Caomhnóir have become and everything we stand for!"

Celeste shook her head sadly. "Seamus, I'm not trying to disrespect you or your men. You have served so selflessly, so bravely over the many years that you have devoted yourself to the protection of the Durupinen, and I know that you will continue to do so. This is in no way a questioning of that—of your fitness or your dedication or your aptitude. You serve because you know it is your role and your duty. Savannah has been dealt a unique hand that has left her in a very nebulous position. She has done some soul-searching and has found that very same sense of purpose and duty. So, we must ask ourselves, do we deny her the opportunity to fulfill that sense of purpose simply because 'that's the way it's always been?' Is there anything innate about a female clan member that would prevent her from performing the duties of a Caomhnóir effectively?"

Seamus froze, and it was obvious why. This last question was a trap and he knew it. If he said yes, he was essentially admitting he believed the women of the clans to be inferior to the men in this capacity. If he said no, then he was giving Celeste a green light to disregard nearly a millennium worth of tradition.

"I... I am sure there are Durupinen who are quite capable of handling training, but—"

This was all Celeste needed, apparently. "I am glad to hear you say it, because I happen to wholeheartedly agree. And I, for one, think that any clan member with the drive, dedication, and ability ought to have the chance to serve the clans in this capacity, especially given the current climate of hostility. We have allowed the politics of gender to weaken us. I think this might be an invaluable opportunity to learn from that mistake and begin to heal the rifts that have grown over the centuries between the Guardians and those they are sworn to protect."

"Blimey," Savvy whispered, the faintest suggestion of a hopeful smile tugging at the corners of her mouth.

Seamus stood aghast, unsure of how to proceed. He swallowed several responses before he said, "High Priestess, I beg you to consider the possibility that this break with tradition will do more harm than good to the relations between Durupinen and Caomhnóir. I believe the Guardians will see it as an affront to their time-honored role in the spirit world and an insult to hundreds of years' worth of valiant sacrifice. At a time when Guardians have proven themselves vulnerable to Necromancer propaganda, do we really want to further undercut their sense of worth and purpose by opening the door on the suggestion that they are expendable?"

"Allowing another clan member to stand beside them in their

SOUL OF THE SENTINEL

mission does not diminish them, and the suggestion says much more about how you feel about Durupinen and their abilities than it does about anything else," Celeste replied, and her tone had cooled, a frost settling upon the words as they fell from her lips.

The panic was clear in Seamus' eyes for a moment, and then it was as though I could see the lightbulb come on over his head. His expression relaxed, and something quenched the fire in his eyes. When he spoke, his tone was deferential, almost unconcerned. The shift was unnerving.

"Very well, High Priestess. There is certainly wisdom in what you say. Not every Novitiate that has come through my ranks has been well-suited to his job by virtue of his gender, that much is true. And I am willing to concede that it is possible for a female member of the clans to undertake the role of a Guardian and perform it admirably. That being said, I propose a compromise."

Celeste narrowed her eyes. "What compromise is that?"

"I propose that we allow Ms. Todd to commence with Caomhnóir training. Let us put her through the program and see how she fares. If at the end of her training period, she has passed all of her exams, her physical aptitude tests, and her combat sessions, and still desires to become a Guardian, we can take a formal vote on allowing her to join the Caomhnóir as a full-fledged member and give her an assignment."

It was Celeste's turn to look stunned. Indeed, it took a few seconds for her to regain her powers of speech, at which point she stammered and stuttered quite a bit over her words. "I—I—I must say, that was—unexpected, Seamus. If I'm honest, I was gearing myself up for quite a battle with you over this."

"So was I," Savvy whispered, so softly that only I knew she had spoken.

"I have no wish to battle with you, High Priestess," Seamus said with an ingratiating smile. "If Ms. Todd believes that she is called to the role of Guardian, then, by all means, let her prove that to be true. I am all too willing to give her that chance."

Savvy's eyes filled with tears which she immediately tried to mask with lots of blinking and throat-clearing. Finn, on the other hand, did not seem to share her relief. His eyes had narrowed with each word that Seamus spoke, and his posture was so stiff that he might have turned to stone.

Celeste clapped her hands together once and breathed a deep

79

sigh of relief. "Thank you, Seamus, for your cooperation in this matter. I feel that there will be much resistance coming our way, as is always the case when faced with monumental change. The more united the leadership can be in meeting that resistance, the better chance we all have of changing for the better. After all, this is about better serving the spirit world. There can be no more important cause. Surely it is worth some growing pains."

"Well said, High Priestess. No more important cause in the world," Seamus said, with a smile that did not reach his eyes.

"Very well, then. Savannah, how does this arrangement suit you?"

"It's... more than I dared hope for," Savvy managed hoarsely. "I... thank you for this opportunity. I won't let you down, Seamus."

Seamus pressed his lips into a tight smile and inclined his head toward her. "Don't thank me yet, Ms. Todd."

7

FALLOUT

CELESTE DISMISSED US and returned to the Grand Council Room to adjourn the meeting. We could tell from the level of noise that there was much confusion and concern surrounding the abrupt ending, and rather than filtering out quickly and in an orderly fashion, many people were lingering in the aisles and grouping around the outside of the room, discussing the day's events in hushed tones. It was hard to gauge what the overall tenor of the conversation was, given that everyone would break off their exchanges the moment they saw me approach, although that wasn't surprising, seeing as I was walking alongside the two people most likely to be the topic of those exchanges. Savvy was called back to Celeste's office to further discuss next steps, and so, after promising to meet us back at the room, she stumbled anxiously after Celeste through a side door and off to the North Tower.

I watched Karen ascend to the Council benches where Hannah was gathering up her things, and give her a long, bracing hug. They spoke quietly together for a few moments and then walked down to meet me. "I'm going to stay here for a while and try to get the lay of the land," Karen murmured into my ear. "There are a few people I want to talk to, to see if I can get a better sense of how the legislation was received, and what might be coming next, both in support and in opposition to it. I'll come find you girls when I've discovered all I can, alright?"

"Okay," I said, glad to have someone like Karen who knew how to play this game better than we did. Hannah didn't speak, but made a movement halfway between a shrug and a nod, which seemed to indicate that she, too, was fine with this arrangement.

Milo, high on the buzz of fresh scandal, also vowed to stay behind to see what snatches of gossip he could pick up. He was, after all, the least intrusive eavesdropper of our group, so he was more likely to overhear things that people might not be willing to say in front of Karen. Finn murmured that Seamus wanted to convene the Caomhnóir in the barracks, no doubt to fill them in on the developments that had transpired with Celeste's decision. His face as he leaned in to give me a quick peck on the cheek was at once tense and resigned. He was about to face a backlash the likes of which had likely never been felt amongst his Brotherhood, and there was nothing he could do but brace himself and take it.

"Good luck," I told him.

"I'll need it," he replied with a grim smile. "I'll come see you as soon as I can. Forgive me for not telling you about all of this."

I waved his apology away. "There's nothing to forgive. You promised Savvy. I totally understand."

Finn brought a hand tenderly to the side of my face, stroking my jawline with his thumb, before turning and joining the tail end of a column of Caomhnóir now marching out of the room.

Once we had made it back to our room and closed the door behind us, Hannah, whose pretense of confidence had been slipping, dropped all attempts at composure and fell into one of the chairs by the fire, dropping her face into her shaking hands.

"Hey," I said soothingly, folding myself into the chair with her and throwing my arms over her shoulders. "Are you alright?"

"Of course, I'm not alright!" I could just make out the muffled words that escaped from between her fingers. "I nearly worked myself to death putting that proposed legislation together and now I'll be lucky if it ever sees the light of day."

"That's not true," I said, in what I hoped was a good impersonation of a bracing, hearty tone. "They aren't going to just ignore all of that work and research just because Savvy sort of... um..."

"Sort of dropped a nuclear bomb in the middle of the Council Room?" Hannah suggested.

"Uh... okay, yeah, it was sort of like that," I admitted. Hannah let out another little whimpering groan. "But hey, look on the bright side. Maybe it will have the complete opposite effect."

"How?"

"Well, maybe, instead of souring the response to your proposal, Savvy's will seem so unreasonable and outlandish, that your legislation will look tame and reasonable by comparison."

Hannah finally lifted her face out of her hands, but it was only to glare at me. "Jess, don't be ridiculous. Don't you see? By me proposing to change the way Caomhnóir-Durupinen relations are regulated, I've opened the floodgates. It's the slippery-slope argument, the one I've been sure would be the death of this legislation from the start, and Savvy stood up and proved it within minutes of my finishing my proposal!"

"But Milo already told you, Celeste was totally onboard with it! Honestly, she hardly batted an eyelash, and she's the High Priestess! She's the one whose job it is to uphold our traditions and shape the entire trajectory of our future. If she's so willing to make these kinds of changes, what makes you think that others won't follow suit?"

Hannah actually threw back her head and laughed, though admittedly the sound was very bitter. "What makes me think the Durupinen won't fall in line to embrace change? You can't really be serious with that question."

"Okay, okay, every experience we've ever had as members of the Durupinen has proven that they cling to tradition like drowning people to life preservers. But Celeste used to be no exception! She toed the line flawlessly for decades—that's no doubt why Finvarra groomed her for the Head Priestess position. If she's willing to make these kinds of changes, with hundreds of years of tradition and responsibility resting on her shoulders, anything is possible."

A hasty knock, followed by a fumbling turn of the doorknob revealed Savvy, breathless and grinning, in the hallway.

"Bloody hell. I can't believe it. I can't bloody believe it. They're actually going through with it. I could start training as soon as Monday!"

She fell into the chair at my desk looking dazed. Then she got a good look at Hannah's face and her grin slipped sideways. "What's wrong, mate?"

Hannah hastily tried to rearrange her expression into something resembling excitement, but she couldn't quite manage it with tear tracks still visible on her cheeks. "Wrong? Nothing! Nothing's wrong. It's so great for you, Savvy, I just... I was a little shocked, that's all."

"We all were," I added. "We had no idea you wanted to be a Caomhnóir."

Savvy looked guilty. "Yeah, look, I'm sorry I didn't tell you. It wasn't that I didn't think I could trust you, or anything like that. I knew you'd keep the secret. It was more like I couldn't trust myself. I felt like, if I told someone, that would make it too real and I'd lose my nerve to go through with it. All it would have taken was just one of you to try to talk me out of it and I would have scrapped the whole plan. I wouldn't even have told Finn if I hadn't needed a Caomhnóir to help me sort it all out."

Hannah looked like she'd very much have appreciated the chance to talk Savvy out of it, but she did not reply. I jumped in instead, to cover the awkward moment.

"Why would we have tried to talk you out of it?" I asked.

Savvy chuckled. "Ah, come off it, mate! Because it's completely mad? Because I've never had enough self-discipline to heave my sorry arse out of bed for a nine o'clock lecture, let alone a five o'clock run? Because every single member of the leadership was sure to laugh right in my face? Let's be honest, I've got more reasons to forget this madness than I've got to go through with it."

"So then, why are you going through with it?" Hannah asked, unable to suppress a note of desperation in her voice. "And why did you have to go through with it today?"

Savvy raised her eyebrows in alarm at Hannah's tone. "I thought you'd be pleased. Isn't this what you're trying to do, change the rules for Caomhnóir and Durupinen?"

"Yes, of course, but not all at once!" Hannah said, trying and failing to keep a tremor out of her voice. "I... Savvy, I absolutely support you, but..."

"But?" Savvy prompted.

Hannah seemed unable to complete the thought, so I stepped in. "But it might have been a bit too much for the traditionalists to handle, two full-on frontal assaults in a single meeting."

Savvy looked horrified. "Oh bugger. I never thought... do you think I've cocked things up for you now?"

Hannah just sniffed.

"Look, mate, I never meant to... oh, bloody hell, I have, haven't I? They're all going to lose their minds and get cold feet about your changes, the whole lot of them, and all because I couldn't just wait my damn turn."

Hannah shook her head, all the frustration draining out of her. "I'm sorry, Savvy. This isn't fair to you. You did such a brave thing today, and the last thing I want to do is make you feel bad about it. I'm just exhausted and anxious and I'm taking it out on you when it's not your fault at all. After everything you've been through recently, with Bertie and Phoebe, then with your Gateway—I have no right to feel anything but joy and support for you right now."

"Yeah, well, you've been through the wringer yourself, mate. You can feel whatever you bloody well like," Savvy said, and then turned to me. "And you, as well. You and Finn. I'm so sorry. If I'd thought I was hurting your chances, I would never have—"

"Everyone stop apologizing and start hugging right now!" I shouted. Hannah and Savvy looked at me in alarm as I waved my hands violently at them until they obeyed me. I pulled them both into a hug. Judging by their muffled shrieks of pain, I may have banged their heads together in my enthusiasm, but I didn't care.

"Seriously. No more sorries. No more guilt. We're all trying to fix the same problem and the more people fighting for change, the better, you'll see."

There was a gentle knock on the door; so gentle, in fact, that neither Hannah nor Savvy, still hugging and crying, even looked up to acknowledge it. A second, more forceful knock followed the first, causing them to break apart, but I was already extricating myself from the embrace and crossing the room to answer it.

Kiernan stood on the other side of the door, his expression twisted into an anxious, miserable knot. "Please excuse me for disturbing you," he said, "but is Hannah here? I didn't have a chance to... I wanted to speak with her, but I was ordered back to the barracks with the other Caomhnóir."

"Of course," I said, pulling the door wide and beckoning him inside. "Come on in, she's right here."

Kiernan hesitated at the threshold for a moment, evidently weighing the chances of entering a Durupinen bedroom without being reprimanded for inappropriate socialization, and then deciding to risk whatever consequences he might face if caught. I closed the door behind him and gestured toward the chairs near the fire, but he continued to stand awkwardly by the door, twisting the strap of his wristwatch around and around his wrist.

Two bright, red spots had appeared on Hannah's cheeks, and she suddenly began tucking her hair obsessively behind her ears. "Kiernan! I didn't... what are you doing here?" she said breathlessly.

"I... I wanted to make sure you were alright," he said, barely flicking his eyes up to meet Hannah's face before dropping them to his watch again. "You looked rather upset when Celeste adjourned the meeting."

Hannah blinked, eyes wide, and tried to smile. "Oh. Thank you for checking on me. I'm fine. Just... um, worried, I guess. That whole process was a bit more... well... dramatic than I expected it to be."

"It was certainly the most extraordinary Council meeting I've attended in a very long time," Kiernan agreed.

"There's a euphemism if ever I heard one," I said with a snort.

"It... well, it didn't go as planned, that is for sure," Kiernan said.

He glanced almost involuntarily at Savvy, who shrugged dejectedly. "It's alright, mate. You can say it. I might as well have set fire to your legislation and danced around it watching it burn."

"We'll have to wait and see about that," Kiernan said, though he sounded nearly as dejected as Savvy. "I just... I wanted to make sure I told you, Hannah, that you did brilliantly in there."

The red spots on Hannah's cheeks were spreading now, creeping across her cheekbones and down to her neck. "Really? You think I did alright? I was so nervous, I thought I was going to pass out."

"You didn't sound nervous at all. You sounded very confident, and... and *commanding*," Kiernan insisted, still hardly able to look at her. "No one in the room could take their eyes off you."

Someone couldn't take his eyes off you, that's for sure, I thought to myself, but uncharacteristically kept the thought to myself. I must have been maturing, or something.

"You're just saying that to be nice," Hannah mumbled.

"I assure you, I'm not," Kiernan said earnestly. "You have that gift—the gift to make people listen to you. You had many of them swayed, I just know it. Don't forget, I had to get up in front of the Council and make a very similar argument. I still remember every detail of it like it was yesterday. I never once had a captive audience like you did today. Never once did they nod along or smile at me or look so transfixed."

"You're just trying to make me feel better," Hannah said, her face beet-red now from the roots of her hair to the collar of her shirt.

"No, that's not it at all," Kiernan insisted, taking an involuntary step toward her and then catching himself, and stepping back again so that he remained planted safely by the door. "I wouldn't lie to you, Hannah, not after all the hard work we put in together on this project. We've got a real chance for change at last, and it's all thanks to you. I don't think anyone else could have done it, truly, I don't."

Kiernan's body language was so rife with awkward embarrassment, it was a wonder he was still standing upright, as opposed to burying himself right through the floorboards. He seemed determined, though, to say everything that he had come there to say, regardless of how mortified he was to say it. I wondered if it might have been easier for him if Savvy and I hadn't been present, and found myself half-formulating an excuse for the two of us to leave so that he could talk to Hannah on his own, but I suppressed that idea at once. In the first place, Kiernan struck me as the kind of Caomhnóir who would never allow himself to be alone with a Durupinen in her bedroom, no matter how innocent the intentions. And secondly, it would be so obvious what I was trying to do, that I would probably just humiliate him further. So, I just hung back, trying to make myself as small and unobtrusive as possible, so that he could at least try to pretend he didn't have an audience. Savvy, on the other hand, was watching the exchange between Hannah and Kiernan like a spectator at a tennis match, her head bobbing back and forth ludicrously, her eyes wide with the realization that had just hit her. If I'd been closer to her, I would have kicked her in the shin to get her to stop staring, but that wasn't really an option from all the way across the room.

Meanwhile, Kiernan and Hannah had mumbled themselves into silence. It stretched on just a few seconds longer than was comfortable before I leapt in. "Well, I do see at least one potential upside to Savvy's request being accepted."

"What's that?" Savvy said, frowning.

"If they really are going to open the door for women to serve as Caomhnóir, then that door should swing both ways," I said, turning to Kiernan and smiling at him. "It would be illogical now for the Council to uphold their denial of your request from two years ago, when you were fighting to become a Scribe. After all, if women can fulfill traditionally male roles, then it stands to reason that the men of our clans may well have a multitude of career paths now open to them. You may just have the chance to pursue your ambition after all."

Kiernan gave me a tentative smile. "I cannot deny that the thought did cross my mind."

"So, why not renew your request?" I asked.

Kiernan put up a hand. "I think we've rocked the boat quite enough for a single day," he said. "But if Savannah is successful in her bid to join the Caomhnóir, I certainly intend to give it another go. That's actually the other reason why I... I don't suppose you'd be willing to help me with something, Hannah?"

Hannah's eyes went wide. "Are you kidding? After all the help you gave me on my proposal? What do you need?"

"Well, I just thought, since there's a good chance I'll be able to renew my request, I'd like to rewrite it, you know, in light of all the new information and arguments we made in your proposal. Do you... would you be willing to give me a hand with it?"

Hannah blushed again, though now she looked flattered rather than embarrassed. "Absolutely, Kiernan. When did you want to get started on it?"

Kiernan gave a sigh of relief. "I don't know, I hadn't thought that far, yet. Maybe... maybe we could go down to the dining hall and talk about it over tea?"

Hannah smiled. "Yes, alright. Let's go."

I opened my mouth to let loose a half-formed, teasing remark, but Hannah gave me a look that silenced me as effectively as a hearty slap in the face. I swallowed my taunt and gave a feeble wave instead, chastened. "I'll, uh... see you later, then."

Hannah flashed me a grateful smile and followed Kiernan out into the hallway. Savvy stared at the closed door, blinking rapidly, then turned an incredulous face on me.

"What was that, then?" she whispered.

I smirked. "All that time you spent working with them in the library and you never noticed?"

Savvy shook her head. "Not a clue. Well, I was a bit distracted, wasn't I? Blimey, what a total prat I am."

"Don't be too hard on yourself. Milo had to clue me in, too," I admitted. "I'm notoriously obtuse about this kind of stuff. It's kind of great, though, isn't it?"

"It's brilliant!" Savvy said. "I always hoped she'd poke far enough out of that little shell of hers to get a taste of romance. She deserves it after all she's been through."

"Yeah," I said softly. "Yeah, she sure as hell does."

Another knock on the door revealed Finn, looking grim.

"What's the good word, then?" Savvy asked, leaping to her feet

SOUL OF THE SENTINEL

at the sight of him and blanching at the look on his face. "Bollocks, they changed their minds, didn't they? Was it Seamus? Did he convince the others to—"

Finn shook his head and hoisted a smile onto his face, where it hung somewhat unwillingly. "No one's changed their minds. Seamus has agreed to allow you to join the training, as he promised. You'll start a week from Monday as an official Novitiate."

Savvy's eyes filled with tears. "Finn, mate, I don't know how I can ever repay you for this. I couldn't have done it without you standing alongside me."

"Don't thank me too soon," Finn said, and his smile became rather fixed. "As I've told you before, Caomhnóir training is not for the faint of heart."

"Oh, I get it," Savvy said swiftly. "I know I'll have to work my arse off, and I intend to, for maybe the first time in my life. But I'm not going to let you down, mate, I swear it."

Finn hesitated, and then smiled again. "I know you won't. I know you'll give it your best. Seamus has requested that you report to the barracks tomorrow morning at 8 AM to obtain a schedule and to be measured for your uniform."

Savvy whistled. "Blimey, it's getting real now. I've got to go call Phoebe and tell her all about it. I can't decide whether she'll be horrified or pleased. Reckon I'll go find out. Cheers again, mate," she said, slapping Finn on the back as she walked by him and out into the hall.

I closed the door behind her, and then turned to Finn, my arms crossed over my chest.

"Okay, out with it."

"Out with what?" Finn asked me, avoiding my gaze.

"You can bullshit Savvy all you want, Finn, but I know you better than that. I know something's wrong, so just tell me what it is."

Everything about Finn seemed to cave in. His careful expression crumbled, and his body collapsed in on itself as he sank into the chair at the foot of my bed. He gave a great, emptying sigh, and bent down wearily to begin the arduous process of unlacing his boots.

"I told her it wasn't going to be easy," Finn said, "and that was most certainly not a lie. Seamus is going to make this as difficult for her as is possible within his power to do so."

I crossed the room and perched myself on the edge of the bed

89

beside him, running my fingers through his hair as he continued to tug and pull at his laces. "Tell me everything," I said. "Start at the beginning."

"I told Savvy that I thought the entire scheme was impossible right from the off," Finn said. "I couldn't believe it when she first told me what she wanted to do. I thought she must be joking, or else she just felt the need to stir up some real trouble, after everything she's been through. You know, the way that people sometimes want to rage and storm against things that are out of their control, simply because they *are* out of their control."

I just nodded. I'd suffered enough loss to understand what he meant. Sometimes you just wanted to make trouble, to fuck things up just to siphon off some of the pain.

Finn didn't seem to need me to reply. He went on, "The more she talked, the more it became clear to me that she was dead serious. She really wanted to do it—I would even venture to say that she *needed* to do it, and not just for herself. There was such a mess of anger and loss and frustration and grief, but there was something deeper propping it all up. And I knew it wasn't just an emotional storm that would pass. It had the underpinnings of real determination, and the longer she talked, the clearer that became. I had to respect it because I understood where it was coming from. She needs to honor Bertie. She needs to find a way to right that wrong, and this was the only tangible way that she could find to do that. Once I realized that, that it was bigger than her own grief, I couldn't say no. I knew it was my duty to help her, and that I owed it as much to Bertie as I did to her."

I continued to stroke his hair. I knew that Finn still had his own, very complicated feelings of guilt to work out with regards to Bertie and what had happened to him. I also knew that process would be too personal, too private, for me to try to get involved in it. If he asked for my help or advice, I would give it. Otherwise, I would keep my mouth shut, and let him sift and sort through that pile of broken things in his own time and in his own way, just as I would've wished for him to allow me that same space.

"I am also ashamed to say that my reservations were not only based on the leadership's attitudes. They were also firmly entrenched in my own. I'm not proud of it, but my first thought was, *that's not your place.*" He looked up at me, straight into my eyes, probing my reaction. He spoke every word bluntly. "It's ugly, but there it is. I did not believe that she had the right to pursue the role of a Guardian. I believed that calling was reserved for men. I had never questioned it. What must you think of me?"

"I think you aren't immune to a lifetime of conditioning, and I'm glad that you're owning it," I said, truthfully. "I think that it's important to admit when we think or feel something we aren't proud of. I think it's important to examine it."

"Well, I did examine it. I asked myself why I felt that way, and it soon became clear that it was a gut reaction born of a lifetime of being force-fed a single damaging philosophy. It fell right to pieces at the most rudimentary of examinations. But it was strong, even in me, and I know that very few of the other Caomhnóir will bother with such examinations."

"This isn't the first time you've questioned the way things are, though," I reminded him. "Accepting your feelings for me wasn't exactly a walk in the park either, was it?"

"No, it certainly wasn't," Finn admitted. His face was growing darker and more brooding by the second. His expression softened, though, when he looked up and caught my eye. "I'm very glad I came to my senses, though."

"So am I," I said, and leaned forward to plant a kiss on his forehead. "What happened, then, after you got over your initial reaction?" I asked him. "Why did you decide to help Savvy?"

"It was the way she spoke about Bertie. What she said about him, about how he never should have been forced into such a role, about how there are probably a hundred Durupinen who would be better suited to be a Guardian, about how some of the Trackers' jobs are even more dangerous. It's all true. And once I allowed myself to admit that, what else could I say but yes? I didn't want to discourage her, because I could see how truly important it was to her, but I also didn't want to give her a false sense of hope. That didn't seem fair, either. And so, I was very honest, and I told her that it was very unlikely that we would succeed in securing her place among the Novitiates. She accepted that assessment right away, but she would not be dissuaded from trying. And so, I gave her my input on what I felt would be the most effective ways to argue her case, and she got to work."

"Thank you. Thank you for helping her, Finn," I told him.

"That gratitude is premature," Finn said grimly. "I've just spent the last hour amongst the Caomhnóir, and if one thing is clear, it is this: they will make this as difficult as they possibly can for Savvy, every blessed inch of the way."

"You'll be there to oversee things, though," I said. "You'll make sure they're fair to her."

Finn shook his head. "No, love, I won't be. I've been reassigned from Novitiate training to overseeing Fairhaven guard duties."

"They fired you?" I gasped, outraged.

Finn smirked at me. "Oh, not fired, no. Merely 'reassigned' to where I was more urgently needed," he said, complete with mocking air quotes. "Only lasted a week in my previous post. I expect that's some sort of record."

"So, who's going to be overseeing Savvy's training?" I asked.

"Seamus himself, of course," Finn said. "He couldn't allow such a momentous shift in his ranks to happen in his absence. He has engineered his transfer back to Fairhaven at once and has shifted responsibility for the Skye Príosún investigation onto several of his less qualified underlings."

"But that's ridiculous!" I cried. "What could possibly be more important than that investigation! It almost took down our entire social order!"

Finn laughed bitterly. "Jess, as far as Seamus is concerned, Savvy is trying to take down our entire social order. He honestly sees this as the real threat now."

"What happened to everything he said in there with Celeste? He agreed to allow Savvy to complete the training and then have a vote!"

"And if he makes it too difficult to complete that training, there will be no need for a vote," Finn said. "If Savvy fails, no one else is going to step forward to question this system. She's got to succeed. This is the only chance anyone will get. Seamus knows this."

"Do you think Savvy knows it?" I asked.

"I don't know," Finn said. "But if she doesn't, she's about to find out."

8

IN THE THREADS

T HE CASTLE WAS ABUZZ FOR DAYS as a result of the Council meeting, but it was hard to comprehend exactly what all of the buzzing meant. Karen returned from the Council Room to report that the reception to the legislation was hard to gauge—everyone was still talking about Savvy's request, which overshadowed most everything else. However, Karen still thought that things had gone as well as could be hoped for.

"It's possible that Savannah's acceptance into training may even bolster Hannah's argument," she said, thoughtfully. "If she can prove herself, there will be very little grounds to dismiss Hannah's proposal outright."

This direct tie between Savvy's success and Hannah's proposal did little to ease my nerves, given what Finn had told me. Did this mean that if Savvy failed, the proposal would fail, too? Would anyone even care that Savvy had been set up to fail, or would they be happy to have the excuse to put the entire uncomfortable business behind them? And what would happen to Finn and me if they decided to do that latter?

It was almost too gut-wrenching to think about, so I suppose it was good that I had a new project in Fiona's tower that promised to take up nearly every waking hour for the foreseeable future.

"Okay, I'm ready! Put me to work! What are we doing today?" I announced as I entered the studio the morning after the Council meeting.

"What have you got to be so bloody cheerful about?" Fiona grumbled from her chair by the window. I was glad to see that she had managed not only to dress herself, but also apply fresh bandages to her eyes, which Mrs. Mistlemoore had declared to be healing "as well as anyone could hope."

"The spirits who like to use me as their own personal Etch-A-

Sketch actually left me alone last night, so I got a decent night's sleep for once!" I said brightly. "And I've already had three cups of coffee this morning."

"I absolutely refuse to tolerate you in my presence on three cups of coffee, so if this is how it's going to be, clear out," Fiona snapped.

I fought back a laugh and adopted a somber tone. "Fine. Funereal airs only."

"That's better," Fiona said. Then, after a pause, added stiffly, "How's your sister holding up?"

I hesitated, surprised. "I... she's okay, I guess. Nervous."

Fiona nodded sagely. "She did well."

"I'm glad you think so," I said. "I only hope the rest of the Council agrees."

"Oh, it's not up for debate," Fiona said. "Even those who detest your clan and fear your sister's agenda have admitted it. She has rendered herself impossible to dismiss. That is a feat in itself."

"Thank you for saying that," I said. "She'll be happy to hear it."

"Be sure you also tell her not to rest on her laurels either," Fiona said sharply. "She's got a long road to travel yet."

"No one is resting, I promise you," I said. "And I don't think she even knows she has any laurels."

"Smart lass," Fiona said approvingly.

"What's on the schedule for this morning?" I asked, setting my bag down on a nearby chair, which defied convention by being both upright and not covered in an assortment of random art supplies.

"This," Fiona said, gesturing to the wall over her shoulder. I stepped a few feet out into the center of the room so that I could see what she was referencing and let out a gasp of surprise.

"What? What are you on about?" Fiona asked at once.

"I... nothing, I'm fine," I said, though truth be told, my heart was racing oddly. "I just didn't expect to see that face, that's all."

Agnes Isherwood was gazing serenely down over the room from her tapestry which usually hung in the Gallery of High Priestesses. Having taken a different route than I usually did, coming from the grounds where Finn had been taking Savvy through a practice of some basic training exercises, I hadn't realized that it was gone from its usual place.

"What about it? You've seen it plenty of times before, haven't you?" Fiona asked with an impatient wave of her hand.

"Yes, of course, I just... how in the world did you get it up here?" I asked, trying to regain my composure.

"I didn't get it up here, you daft thing. I ordered it moved. Six Caomhnóir delivered and rehung it here this morning. Never thought I'd be reduced to entrusting my work to such unpracticed hands, but that's where we are. It's probably a blessing I couldn't see what they were doing or you'd be stepping over their mangled bodies right now. I only hope they haven't destroyed it in the process."

"No, they... it looks pristine," I murmured, navigating around the desk for a closer look. As usual, the tapestry had a sort of magic to it—as though the fibers themselves were woven with the breath of life.

Fiona snorted. "Pristine she's certainly not. She's been in need of restoring for quite a while now, and her time has come at last."

I turned to Fiona, startled. "So, when you asked me to come down here to help you with a project, you meant... this?"

"Obviously."

I felt a stab of panic penetrate my lungs. "But... are you sure you don't want to start with something a bit... I don't know, simpler? Not quite so irreplaceable and priceless?"

"No," Fiona shot back. "I want to start with what I had planned. Unless, of course, you're telling me that you're not willing to help me?"

"No! I'm not saying that at all! Of course, I want to help you, it's just... aren't you worried I'll screw this up?" I asked, my voice a bit shrill.

"Absolutely," Fiona replied, hoisting a single eyebrow. "But I'd be worried about that no matter what project I gave you."

"Your confidence in me is truly overwhelming," I said dryly. "But seriously, Fiona..."

"Jess, everything in this castle is old and relatively priceless," Fiona yelled. "It all needs to be taken care of, and I've been rendered useless in that regard, possibly forever. Now, someone has to learn how to care for these relics, and it seems the only thing I can do right now is instruct someone else how to do that. So, are you going to be that person, or aren't you? Because if you don't want the responsibility, I'll find someone else who does."

Fiona's face was so fierce, so full of barely restrained grief, that I dared not say no to her. And honestly, I don't think the word was in my heart, not really. Was I terrified that I would irreparably damage historical artifacts? Hell, yes, I was. But then again, this kind of opportunity was what I had been hoping for, if not exactly in the way I expected it to happen. I was an art history major. My first job after college was at an art museum. I had never had the guts or motivation to put my own work out into the world to be scrutinized and deemed worthy or unworthy of notice. I was much too private and self-conscious a person to ever want my deepest, most personal expressions on display. But I did dearly love the chance to be around and a part of great art. I had wandered those museum halls and dreamed of the day that I could stop giving tours to field trips full of bored teenagers and actually make a real difference in the preservation and perpetuation of art. The people who discovered, restored, and curated great works of art were like modern-day explorers and treasure hunters. This was a chance that would take me decades to earn, if at all, in the traditional art world. But here at Fairhaven, it had fallen right into my lap. Was I really going to let a little fear prevent me from gaining skills that I could learn almost nowhere else—skills that could one day put me at the helm of one of the great museums of the world?

No, even I—Grand Champion of Shitty Decisions—wasn't foolish enough to pass this up.

"You don't need to find anyone else," I told Fiona, and was glad to hear the determination in my own voice. "Let's get started."

"Excellent," Fiona said, rubbing her hands together. "Get yourself a pencil and a blank notebook; there should be one in the bottom drawer of my desk, unless you've completely emptied that as well."

"No, I left the inside of your desk alone," I assured her as I hurried to collect the items she had instructed me to find. For all her complaining, it took me only seconds to find everything, thanks to my overhaul of the space. I cringed to think how long I might have searched through the artist carnage that used to litter every square inch of the place if I hadn't reorganized it.

"Okay, all set," I told her, coming and sitting down on a rickety stool she had pulled up alongside her chair.

"What do you know about tapestries?" Fiona asked.

"Not very much," I replied at once. No point in glossing over things. I wasn't going to do myself or the art any favors by pretending I was more knowledgeable than I was.

"I thought as much," Fiona grumbled. "What kind of rubbish education did they give you at that fancy college of yours, anyway?"

I rolled my eyes, and dug back through my memory to my courses that touched on medieval art. "The weavers hand-wove them on huge looms, I remember that," I said. "And they mostly used wool, and vegetable dyes to create the different colors. Very few were made here in England—it was France and Belgium that were known for them. The images were typically Biblical, although I know that doesn't really apply here. They were often produced in sets of multiple panels that told a story. And they took an incredible number of man hours to make—it would have required months and months to produce a single large tapestry like this."

Fiona looked impressed in spite of herself. "Right then, I take it back. You did a fair bit of studying, didn't you?"

I shrugged, but didn't respond. Yes, I had, but I knew most of it wasn't going to help me now, so there was no point in patting myself on the back. We were venturing into uncharted territory. I smirked as I thought about the way many of my professors would have salivated over the chance to study a piece like Agnes Isherwood's tapestry.

"What we've got in front of us are two layers that possibly need to be restored and repaired," Fiona said, her voice snapping into professional mode. "The weaver who created this tapestry started by stretching the plain warp threads on the loom—these were simple, undyed wool threads, meant to bear the load of the tapestry—if you were to think of the tapestry as a painting, the warp threads would be the canvas. Then the colored threads—called the weft—were woven onto the warp to create the image. The weft threads were sometimes simply dyed wool, it's true, but in the case of this tapestry and other more expensive tapestries like it, the weft is made partially from silk and even gilt-metal wrapped silk."

"They wove actual metal into the tapestry?" I asked, impressed. "Like, real gold and stuff?"

"Gold, silver, copper, only the finest for the High Priestesses of old," Fiona said, nodding. "Of course, that makes it a bugger to restore, but that was never a consideration when these pieces were created. It's only now that we've got to reckon with the excesses of our ancestors."

"The colors still look so vibrant, though," I murmured, gazing up at the tapestry. "How is that possible, when it's so old?"

"It wasn't looking so vibrant a few months ago," Fiona said. "I had to have it properly cleaned before I could begin to restore it. But I haven't got the facilities for that kind of thing, so I had it sent out to the Louvre."

"The Louvre?!" I gasped. "Like... the *actual* Louvre in Paris?"

Fiona clicked her tongue sharply. "What other Louvre would I be talking about, for Christ's sake? Only the best museums in the world have the equipment and staff to handle a job like this."

"But the code of secrecy!" I said. "How did you manage to get this cleaned without arousing the suspicions of the academics there?"

"Fairhaven has a long and prestigious false history as a very private, very exclusive University," Fiona said. "Surely you know that. How else do you think we avoid detection?"

I didn't reply. Karen had told us that Fairhaven used the façade of a University to facilitate the training of all the Apprentices and Novitiates, but I had never thought to ask too many questions about how exactly they pulled off such an elaborate charade.

Fiona went on, "Our art collection is well-known in the academic art world, even if the true history behind the art is not. We've had many of our tapestries, paintings, and sculptures loaned out to exhibitions and private art shows around the world. We turn down regular offers of millions of dollars from collectors. Each and every piece in our collection has a well-documented and entirely false cover story for such occasions. Their authenticity has never once been questioned."

I laughed at the look of pride on Fiona's face. This job was getting better and better. I felt less like a treasure hunter now and more like some kind of glamorous art thief, dazzling the world with my sleight of hand, passing Durupinen art off as the works of great masters.

"Okay, so no problems at the Louvre, then," I said, still laughing. "But if you trusted the Louvre to clean it, why not have them restore it as well? Surely, they've got the expert staff to do it?"

"An expert staff that's already overwhelmed with the upkeep and restoration of their own collections," Fiona pointed out. "Besides, a bit of cleaning is one thing, but the Louvre has never handled pieces like this onsite for months at a time. The effects could be... interesting."

"Interesting how?" I pressed.

Fiona smirked. "Well, the Louvre doesn't generally deal with Durupinen artifacts, do they? Not knowingly at least. The residual effects of Castings could make for an abundance of unexpected museum visitors, and I don't mean tourists."

"What... oh. Right," I said. "Probably best not to unleash the spirit realm on the world's most famous museum."

"Correct," Fiona said. "Thus, we are left to restore it ourselves. So, here we are."

I looked up at the massive tapestry and repressed the urge to start panicking again. "Okay. Where do we start?"

"There will likely be several different kinds of repairs to be made," Fiona said. "The first kind to identify are any tears in the weave. These can generally be stitched back together fairly easily. The second kind of damage is breakage and snagging of the threads. Some can be carefully tucked and pulled back into the weave, while others may need to be repaired or replaced altogether. The third type of repair is the most difficult and will require the most time. There will be areas of the tapestry that have worn down and faded so that the details of the image are no longer visible. Some of these areas are worn right down to the warp. In these areas, we will need to select replacement threads and recreate the image as best we can through restoration."

"Where do you want me to start?" I asked.

"There's a scaled-down image of the tapestry here," Fiona said, rapping her walking stick on the nearest filing cabinet, on top of which a manila file folder already lay open. "Use it to record any damage you find. This top drawer has a binder of thread swatches. When you find an area that will need new threads, do your best to match the colors and keep a list of what we'll need. I can order the fibers from an antiques specialist I know in Yorkshire. He's the absolute best, produces all his materials with period techniques."

I tried to imagine what it would be like to eschew all modern technology and advancements and spend my life pretending to be a medieval tapestry weaver on purpose, but I couldn't quite wrap my brain around it.

"And you actually trust me to do this?" I asked her.

"No," Fiona said. "But I haven't any bloody choice, have I? On we blindly stumble, as the saying goes," she added, pointing to her bandages.

I cringed as Fiona chuckled. It felt way too soon for jokes about any of this, but then again, Fiona didn't have a solitary damn to spare for what was appropriate or comfortable. I ignored the joke and set to work, deciding to climb the ladder and start at the top of the tapestry, working my way down.

The work probably should have been tedious, but it wasn't. It was fascinating. All I could think about, as I pored over the fibers from centuries ago, was how real human hands had created this piece from piles of thread. It was remarkable and impossible—almost like magic. The way that the threads came together in such finely wrought detail was like the disparate ingredients of a complex recipe, the resulting product of which was so much more than the sum of its parts. There was an alchemy to this art—that was the only way that I could think to describe it, and it was due in part, I knew, to the Castings that had been placed upon and around it over time. It felt as though the spirit world were keeping watch over this tapestry and its occupant, just as she had once been tasked with keeping watch over them.

When examined up close, however, the tapestry definitely showed some wear. Some areas showed signs of having been repaired previously, and with incredible skill—the stitches were so tiny and precise, they could surely only have been done by a machine. God help me if I found any further damage of the kind and was expected to repair it myself; I couldn't even sew a button.

The work, as it turned out, however, was far more physically taxing and exhausting that I ever would have imagined. In fact, the next time someone suggested that art wasn't a grueling profession, they would likely earn themselves a swift kick to the shins. Four hours later, my head was aching, my eyes were practically crossing, and there wasn't a single muscle left in my back, my arms, or my legs, that wasn't screaming for rest. And despite that, I'd only worked my way through examining about a third of the total height of the tapestry.

It's possible my progress would have been quicker, had Fiona not been present, demanding every few seconds that I describe exactly what it was I was looking at. Each time she did this, it became harder and harder to bite back my request that she kindly shut the hell up so that I could get something done. But I knew that that wasn't fair. Fiona had never relinquished even a modicum of control in her studio before this project, and it couldn't have been easy for her, sitting there, sure I was fucking everything up, but unable to confirm that for herself. And so the tedious process went on, ninety percent interruption and ten percent actual work, until the sun had sunk to the tree line and the light in the studio had faded to a rosy twilit orange that draped the tapestry's details in shadow and left me squinting hopelessly at the fibers less than an inch from the tip of my nose.

"It's time to call it a day," Fiona announced at last.

"Are you sure?" I asked, not wanting to sound too eager to be finished. "I can stay another hour if you need me to. I'm not supposed to meet Hannah for dinner until six."

"The details of my world may be a blur, but I can still tell light from dark. It's getting far too dim in here for you to do that job properly, and God only knows how badly you were cocking it up in broad daylight," Fiona snapped. "So, let's be done for the day. We can pick up where we left off tomorrow morning, bright and early."

"Bright and early," I muttered. "Three of my least favorite words in the English language."

Fiona made a sound that might've been a chuckle. I decided to allow myself to believe that it was one; it made the aching and the cramping just a bit more worth it to know that Fiona could actually find something to laugh about at the end of this day.

Fiona stood up from her chair and stretched her arms high above her head. Then she began to grope her way over to the wall and inch slowly along the shelves.

"What do you need, Fiona?" I asked. "Whatever it is, why don't you let me help you find—"

"Oh, shut your trap, and let me try it, would you?" Fiona shouted. "I got to figure out some of this for myself, or you'll be up here wiping my arse next."

"Actually, you'll be delighted to know that I draw the line at arse wiping," I said cheerfully.

Knowing she was determined to accomplish something on her own, I tried not to watch Fiona too closely as she made her way slowly down the room shelf by shelf. Instead, I took a straight pin from the work belt that hung around my waist and inserted it carefully to mark my place in the tapestry so that I would know where to pick up again the next day. But as I stepped down to climb off the ladder, something just below the pin caught my eye.

It was unlike any irregularity that I had yet spotted in the tapestry. The section in question depicted Agnes Isherwood's right hand, in which she was holding an open book. I had seen enough of the other tapestries and remembered enough of my Medieval Art seminar to know that the objects that appeared within the images were often symbolic. Figures wore crowns and held scepters, not because they were always kings or queens, but because those objects were symbols of power or righteousness. Books, it came as no surprise, were symbols of great wisdom and learning, especially given how few people of the time period were literate. So, it wasn't odd, in the likeness of a High Priestess, to see her clutching an object that suggested that she was wise. But what was unusual was the book itself, or rather, the way it had been woven.

"Hey, Fiona?" I asked, an unexpected tremor in my voice that I could not explain nor suppress.

"Can it wait?" Fiona barked. "I'm trying to count here, and I don't want to lose my place."

"I... sure," I said, my eyes still raking the details of the book. Every other section of the tapestry showed great wear and age in its fibers. The colors were still visible, but they had surely faded from the brighter hues that they had once been dyed with. The threads had a dull softness to them, the result of age, and having been handled likely hundreds of times since they had been woven together. But the fibers used to create the image of the book seemed newer, brighter, and thicker than the surrounding fibers, as though the book itself had been woven and then rewoven again, so that the shape of the book was raised above the rest of the surrounding imagery.

"Aha!" Fiona cried out, and I spun around in alarm to see her waving a tea kettle triumphantly over her head. "Found it at last!" she said, and she did not bother to disguise the pride in her voice at her accomplishment. "Now, what was that you were bothering me with?"

"I was just wondering, has this tapestry been repaired before?" I asked.

"Repaired? You mean by me?" Fiona asked. "No, it's never come down from the gallery of High Priestesses since I've been here."

"What about before you were alive?" I asked, grazing my fingers over the slightly raised outline of Agnes' book. Tingles of anticipation shot through my fingers, and my heart pumped itself into a gallop. I pulled my hand back, startled. What the hell was going on?

"Not that I'm aware of," Fiona said, now feeling around the shelves for her tin of loose-leaf tea. "There aren't any repairs listed in the record, but not every curator of the art around this place has been as meticulous as yours truly. Why do you ask?"

I opened my mouth to tell her exactly why I was asking, but something stopped me. I couldn't possibly have defined it, but some sort of energy, some sentient something that seemed to be vibrating in the very fibers under my fingers was suddenly telling me — shouting at me, really – not to say another word. Somehow, in that moment, I knew that what I had found had been meant to be found by me, and me alone. It frightened me, how utterly sure I was of this fact, but I couldn't unknow it, and I couldn't ignore it. So instead of answering her, all I managed to do was make a strange sound somewhere between an "um" and a "huh?"

"What's that, then?" Fiona barked. "Speak up! I didn't develop supersonic hearing the moment my eyes stopped working, you know!"

I swallowed and tried again. "No reason," I replied, and I felt the very fibers sing their approval of the words. "I was just wondering how often some other sorry bastard had to do this job, before us, I mean."

"If all the previous occupants of this tower had done their job properly, we wouldn't have to be doing it at all. You should've seen the state of things when I took over this place," Fiona scoffed, shaking her head. She had meandered her way over to the tiny kitchen area and was now fumbling about to fill the kettle with water from the tap. "And before you start coming at me with your sass, I'm not talking about the mess," she added, raising her tin of tea over her head as though she was going to throw it in my general direction, but then lowering it again and plunking it down with a bang on the counter. "I know I've never kept a tidy space, but there's nothing tidy about art. Never has been. No, I simply mean that so much of the work that needed to be done so desperately was completely neglected. The statues were dusty and falling into disrepair. The paintings all desperately needed to be professionally cleaned. Things had been loaned out to galleries, and never returned, or lost track of. There was no documentation to keep a proper record of it all, no schedule of restoration, nothing. It was as though they took care of the collection by whim. It was an unmitigated disaster, and it took me years to whip things back into shape. I don't want to knock my predecessor; she was a brilliant painter, and no doubt she inherited a mess, but she never should've had this job. She didn't have much respect for art that wasn't of her own creation, and that's the sad truth of it."

"Uh-huh," I muttered, hoping this would suffice for a reply. I wasn't really paying attention to Fiona's tale about her predecessor at all. I was now examining the lower left-hand corner of the book in Agnes' hand. There was a thread that had not been properly woven into the warp, but instead, one end of it stuck out from the others. About a quarter of an inch of emerald-colored thread, just... dangling there. As I stared at it, a tiny voice inside my head seemed to whisper to me:

Just give it a tug.

I reprimanded the voice at once. *I can't do that. Fiona would kill me. I can't just pull on a thread of the centuries-old tapestry. What if I unweave the whole damn thing? What if it just falls apart in my hands? This thing is priceless, you don't just tug on the thread.*

Go on, just give it a pull, the voice urged me again, immune to my protests.

I tried to decide if the voice was coming from me, or from someone else. Sometimes, because of the way that spirits chose to communicate through my own personal passion for art, it was difficult to make the separation. Was a spirit who was connected to the tapestry trying to guide my hand? Or was it my own intuition that continued to nag at me, urging me to just reach out and give the thread the tiniest of tugs. I realized that I couldn't make the distinction, and it was this more than anything that convinced me that this was a voice that could not be ignored.

Though caution and common sense were both screaming at me to resist, though I expected that Fiona would somehow sense my transgression, and swoop violently down upon me for what I was about to do, still my trembling hand reached out, took the fragile end of the errant thread between my finger and thumb, and pulled.

It shouldn't have come away so cleanly, as though it were only waiting for the slightest encouragement to flee the woven surface. But it did. And as it came away, as it ran back and forth, it began to reveal a second color beneath it, a deep, wine-soaked crimson. It was as though the artist had created a red-bound book first, and then covered it up with a green-bound one. I felt a thrill of fear as this hidden layer of the image was revealed, but the fear quickly morphed into excitement and curiosity. Why had the book been hidden? What if anything would it reveal?

The green thread dangled nearly to the floor, and now the color had changed, for the cover of the book had fallen completely away, and it was the open pages of the book that were unraveling now. The green had given way to a natural ivory color of the paper, identical to the hidden color beneath it. But as the thread continued to come away sliding through my fingers so readily, another detail became clear: while the pages of the green book were blank, the pages of the red book beneath contained text.

The hidden book had words. Words that no one had ever seen before. Except for me.

My heart was pounding so hard that it was hard to catch my breath. I clutched at the ladder with my left hand to steady myself as my right hand continued to pull back and forth, the thread sliding away with the slightest of effort. How many pairs of eyes had gazed up at Agnes and her book over the centuries, completely unaware that a message lay hidden beneath the fibers? At last, the end of the thread freed itself from the woven surface. The characters were crisp and clear, having been protected from the world for so many years by the secondary layer of threads. I read them over and over again, and as I did so, the excitement bubbling in my veins gave way to a sense of utter bewilderment.

CA-126B-1240-ISH

I blinked. I blinked again. I'm not sure what I expected to see, but it certainly wasn't this. My mind reeled. What in the world did it mean?

"Oi! Jessica! Earth to Jessica!"

"What?" I whirled around on the ladder and nearly lost my footing. Fiona was waving a teacup at me impatiently.

"I said, do you fancy a cuppa?"

"Oh... no. No, thanks," I said. Quickly, I turned back to the message of the hidden book and committed it to memory. Then I carefully descended the ladder, gathered up the pile of thread from where it had fallen to the floor, and stuffed it into my pocket. "I should probably get going. I need a shower before I head to dinner. I smell like old dust and mildew."

"Right then, off you go," Fiona said with an indifferent shrug.

The kettle began to whistle softly on the burner in front of her. She managed to take it off the heat and turn off the burner without further injury. She paused though, as she turned to fill her cup. She pressed her lips together as though she might cry, or scream, or both. Then she swallowed the sound back and asked softly, "Could you?"

"Of course," I said, and crossed the room to take the kettle from her hand. She relinquished it with a sigh.

"I'm effing useless," she grunted.

"You're doing great," I told her firmly. "Stop feeling sorry for yourself. We'll do this together once, then you'll never need me again."

I counted slowly aloud, until the teacup was filled, but not to the brim. "One, two, three, four. Count like that while you pour, from the moment you hear the water hit the porcelain, and you won't overfill it. Listen for the sound of the spout against the edge too, to make sure it's positioned correctly.

"Right. Got it. Cheers," Fiona said curtly.

"You want help with the milk or sugar?"

"No. I'll manage."

"Okay, then," I said. "There's a Caomhnóir outside the door if you need anything. Someone from the dining room staff will be by in an hour with your dinner. Don't throw anything at her, okay?"

"I make no promises," Fiona grumbled.

"I'll see you in the morning," I told her. "What time do you want me here?"

"Eight o'clock sharp," Fiona instructed. "I need my beauty sleep."

"Okay, then. Eleven it is," I agreed, but my last glance as I left the room was not at my mentor, struggling to sweeten her tea before it cooled. My eyes found Agnes Isherwood, and the book she had opened only for me.

How in the world was I going to figure out what she was trying to tell me?

9

ONE OF THE LADS

"WHAT CAN IT MEAN?" Hannah asked in a whisper, holding her hand out for the code of numbers and letters that I'd copied down onto my napkin for her to examine.

"If I had any idea, I wouldn't be asking you," I whispered back.

"How very strange. And you think they are original to the tapestry?"

"I suppose so," I said. "Of course I'm no expert, but they looked to be the same age as the rest of the tapestry. I couldn't find any signs that they had been added, or repaired, or sewn on afterward. Even the second layer of weaving that was used to cover it looked really, really old. I never would have realized there was anything underneath it if I hadn't seen that dangling bit of string." *And heard that strange voice in my head telling me to pull it,* I added silently. Hannah didn't need to know that particular detail.

"But who covered it up? And do you think that you're the first person to discover it?" Hannah pressed on, clearly intrigued.

"I don't know who hid it there—I suppose it could even have been the person who originally made the tapestry. But I do think that I'm the first person to discover it."

"What makes you think so?" Hannah asked.

"Just a feeling. A strong one," I replied, and Hannah nodded, her expression solemn. Basing such a conclusion on a mere feeling might have sounded ludicrous to the average person, but to another Durupinen, there was nothing "mere" about a feeling. Feelings ran our lives—they connected us to the spirit world and were often the only clues we had to guide our decisions. Feelings were everything, and we had learned by now to heed them very carefully indeed.

"Did you tell Fiona?" Hannah asked. "Surely she can help you figure it out?"

Here I shrugged sheepishly. "She might, but... well, that tapestry has been around for centuries. It's been in her care for decades. But the one moment that message chose to reveal itself was the first time that I ever touched the threads. I'm sorry, but that has to mean something."

Hannah tapped her fingers against her chin thoughtfully. "Yes. Yes, I think you're probably right about that," she said after a few moments. "But if you were meant to find it, you were certainly meant to interpret it as well."

"Yeah," I said. "I'm kind of failing at that part right now."

"It looks like a code or something," Hannah said. "I wonder what all the hyphens mean."

"The 'ISH' probably stands for Isherwood, wouldn't you think?" I asked.

"Yes, that's possible," Hannah said. "But I have no idea what any of the rest of it might mean. What's C.A.?"

"I have a feeling it's not California," I said. "I don't think Hollywood is Durupinen territory."

"Not to mention that California didn't exist when this tapestry was woven," Hannah pointed out.

"I know, Hannah, I know," I sighed. "I was kidding."

"Oh," Hannah said, grinning sheepishly. "Right."

"I guess I'm just not sure where to start," I admitted. "If I had any kind of reference at all—any clue..."

"Well, the only reference you have is Agnes," Hannah said. "I would start with her. Try to find everything you can on her, and see what you can come up with."

I looked down at the message again. "Yeah, I guess she really is the only connection I've got."

"Oh, um... sorry, Jess, but I've got to go," Hannah said, downing her glass of water in a single gulp and waving over my shoulder. Based on the radiant smile on her face, I knew who I'd see before I even turned around.

Kiernan stood in the doorway to the dining hall, his bag slung over his shoulder and his hands thrust deep into his pockets. He returned Hannah's wave awkwardly, then dropped his eyes to his feet.

"Where are you going?" I asked, as Hannah took one last, hurried bite of pizza.

"Kiernan is putting his final touches on the resubmission of his proposal. We're going to go through it tonight before he turns it in so it can be added to the next meeting's new business," Hannah explained.

I tried not to smile, but my face had a mind of its own. Hannah frowned at me.

"What are you smirking for?" she demanded.

"Smirking? Who's smirking?" I asked, trying to reign in the smile, but it only widened.

"You and Milo, you're ridiculous, the pair of you," she said huffily.

"Whatever do you mean?" I asked innocently.

"I know exactly what you're thinking, and you can just forget about it right now," Hannah said. "We are just friends. Colleagues, really. Working together on a project. That is all."

"Colleagues, huh?" I said, cocking my head back over my shoulder. "Someone better tell Kiernan, then. I don't think he's gotten the message."

Hannah grumbled something that sounded suspiciously like "mind your own business," and crossed the room to meet Kiernan. The two walked out together, leaving me to stare down at the two things in front of me: the hidden tapestry message and a slice of pepperoni pizza. I had no clue what to do about the tapestry. Luckily, I knew exactly what to do with the pizza.

§

For the rest of the week, every spare moment I wasn't in Fiona's studio helping her with the tapestry restoration, I was searching for any clue I could find that might shed even the tiniest beam of light on the hidden message. I combed through the biography section of the library for everything that had ever been written about Agnes Isherwood, but had no luck there. The closest I could find was a passing reference to an old proclamation that "Her Nobleness the High Priestess shalt be depicted in tapestry in accordance with our tradition," along with a few financial details about the purchasing of threads and metals for use by the artist. From there, I tried to trace the history of the tapestry itself, but there was no record of it ever being loaned out, displayed, or otherwise handled outside of the castle, other than its recent cleaning. In fact, based on written record, it was entirely plausible that it had hung in the same location since it had been woven on a loom. I might have had more luck if I'd asked some of the Scribes for help, but I didn't want to draw anyone else's attention to what I was researching—not yet, anyway. I supposed it wouldn't have seemed too suspicious, looking for information on a tapestry that it had literally become my job to restore, but I couldn't bring myself to do it. And so, most evenings that week, I sat alone poring over books or else haunted the stacks, wandering helplessly, unsure of where to search next. Sometimes, Finn was able to get away from Caomhnóir duty long enough to help me, but on most evenings my only company was Lucida, who, for some unknown reason, had taken up almost permanent residence in the library. Once or twice, I nearly walked up to her and asked what she was working on, but I refrained. If Lucida had managed to find something innocuous with which to occupy herself, who was I to interrupt her? Besides, if I had asked her, she'd likely give me the same answer that I would have given her: none of your damn business.

Fiona was of absolutely no help either. I asked what questions I thought I could without arousing her suspicions, pretending it was all simply out of intellectual curiosity as we worked. But as the process went on, she was becoming more and more bad-tempered about her limitations, and what few answers she gave me were terse at best, and downright insulting at worst.

"I am not a bloody encyclopedia!" she shouted one evening, when I had apparently posed one query too many. "Christ on a bike, were you always this annoying, or is it only now that I can't see you that I want to tape your mouth shut?"

"Sorry," I murmured, and let it go.

After that, I took to wandering the Gallery of High Priestesses, studying the other tapestries and paintings for patterns or further clues. Though several of the other High Priestesses had been depicted with books in their hands, all of the other books were closed, and no text was visible upon them. I could discover no other letters or numbers anywhere on any of the other works of art that compared with the strange arrangement of letters, numbers, and hyphens that appeared in Agnes' tapestry. I could find no obvious repairs that could be masking a secret pattern beneath, no dangling threads that screamed to be pulled. In my desperation, I even began placing my hands upon paintings and tapestries at random throughout the castle, closing my eyes and willing them to speak to me, to inspire me—*anything* to help me out of the complete dead end in which I found myself. Finally, after Seamus came through the gallery and happened upon me obsessively groping and whispering to tapestries, I gave up even this last resort. I finally had to resign myself to the theory that, if the message was really for me, then Agnes would find a way to send me another clue—to cosmically point me in the right direction. I had to trust that this was true—I had no other choice.

By the time the weekend rolled around, I had been so consumed with the search for Agnes' message that I had nearly forgotten that Savvy was to begin her Caomhnóir training the very next day. Naturally, this made me feel like the shittiest friend in the world, but Savvy herself was too preoccupied with preparations to notice that I was barely around. In fact, when Hannah, Milo, and I set out to wish her luck on the eve of her first day, it took her nearly five minutes to realize that anyone had arrived in the central courtyard where she and Finn were working together.

"Jolly good," Finn told her, closing a book and clapping her on the back. "Let's leave it there for tonight."

"Nah, mate, I want to go over that last page of the Code again," Savvy said, gnawing at a fingernail that had already been bitten to the quick.

"Absolutely not," Finn said firmly. "Studying is good. Preparation is good. But you can certainly have too much of a good thing, and that's the point at which we've arrived. You'll burn yourself out if you carry on like this."

Savvy pressed her palms to her eyes, as though she were trying to force information to stay in her brain that wanted to leak out of her eye sockets. "Yeah, you're right. Mustn't overdo it." She removed her hands, blinked around for a moment, and then caught sight of us at last. "Oi, you lot," she said, grinning. "Come to give me a proper send-off, have you?"

"We couldn't let you head off to training in the morning without wishing you luck," Hannah said.

"Well, let's have it, then," Savvy said, holding out her hand expectantly.

"Have... have what?" Hannah asked, nonplussed.

"The luck," Savvy said. "I need all of it I can get, so let's have it, then. Empty your pockets. Don't be stingy buggers."

I laughed. "What time does it all start?"

"Roll call at 5:30, and physical training starts at 6," Savvy said. "That's still the middle of the bloody night as far as I'm concerned."

"Not anymore," Finn said. "Set that alarm, and a backup one, too. And mind you heed what I told you about Seamus and tardiness. He'll not tolerate it from anyone, least of all you."

"Duly noted," Savvy said, giving him a salute.

"Are you nervous?" Milo asked. "I mean, I'm nervous *for* you, so I can't imagine how you must be feeling."

Savvy chuckled. "Oh, I'm nervous, sure, but I reckon I can take whatever nonsense they see fit to dish out. I grew up in the council flats, love. I don't scare easily, and Seamus would do well to remember it." She glanced down at her watch and clicked her tongue. "Well, if I'm meant to be up with the sun, I'd best turn in. Good night, then!"

She strode off through the courtyard. As she turned the corner into one of the cloisters, I could hear her whistling a cheery tune. I turned to Finn, who was watching her go with a strange expression—it was half-pitying, half-admiring.

"Tell me the truth," I said to him. "How do you really think it's going to go tomorrow?"

"Well, if she keeps up that attitude, she might just be alright," Finn said. "But I'm not taking any chances on that." He turned to Milo. "Are *you* ready for tomorrow?"

Milo nodded, a grim smile on his face. "Oh, you bet your boots I am."

Hannah and I both turned to Milo in confusion. "What are you talking about?" Hannah asked him, frowning. "What have you got to do with tomorrow?"

Milo turned to her and grinned a bit sheepishly. "Well, I was going to tell you about it, but you've been so busy with Council stuff and Kiernan's proposal, and Jess, you've been so busy with Fiona, that I just sort of... never really found the right time."

"So, tell us now," I urged him. "What's going on?"

Milo shrugged. "A couple of days after the Council meeting, when Savvy sort of imploded the entire Durupinen/Caomhnóir gender construct, I got summoned to Celeste's office."

"Celeste?" Hannah cried, looking terrified. "Why? Are you in trouble? Is it the blog? Do we have to shut it down before someone—"

"Relax, sweetness, it's nothing like that," Milo said at once. "Celeste just wanted my help."

"With what?" I asked impatiently. "Just come out with it, Milo!"

"Okay, okay," Milo sighed. "She said that she was worried about Savvy. She said that even though Seamus had seemed to acquiesce in that meeting, she believed he would do everything in his power to ensure that Savvy did not pass her training."

I turned to Finn, wide-eyed. "That's exactly what you told me that night, too."

Finn nodded. "Evidently, I wasn't the only one who noticed."

"Did you... did you go to Celeste to tell her?" I asked.

Finn shook his head. "I didn't need to. Celeste was shrewd enough to understand why Seamus caved so easily, and it was because he hadn't caved at all. He simply told her what she wanted to hear."

"Why didn't Celeste call him out on it?" I asked indignantly.

"Because it was pointless," Finn said. "Seamus would simply deny it. And she didn't want to speak to Savvy about it, first, because she didn't want to alarm her, and secondly, because she didn't want Savvy to be put in an awkward position."

"What awkward position?" I asked. "Doesn't she deserve a warning?"

"Yes, but you know Savvy. She's got too much pride to complain, and she's certainly not going to go running to Celeste if things get tough. And anyway, she'll learn pretty quickly that that kind of behavior is despised in Caomhnóir culture."

I rolled my eyes. "So, it's like the first rule of Caomhnóir training is don't talk about Caomhnóir training?"

"Sorry?" Finn asked, looking confused.

I sighed. "Never mind. I'll just add it to the list of American cultural references to catch you up on."

"Anyway, that's where I come in," Milo said, jumping in before Finn could keep asking questions. "Since she doesn't expect to get the real story of what's happening in training from Savvy or Seamus, Celeste wants me to get it for her."

"How?" Hannah asked.

Milo smiled. "I'm a spy now."

I laughed. "Are you serious?"

Milo looked mildly indignant. "Of course, I am. What, you don't think I can be a spy?"

"Well, no, it's just... you don't exactly fly under the radar, do you?" I said.

"I do enjoy drawing attention to myself on occasion, yes," Milo admitted. "But this will be different. I'm going to keep a low profile—wipe that smirk off your face, Jess—and report back to Celeste about what's happening at training. That way, if Seamus is abusing his position, Celeste can confront him about it."

"But how are you going to do that?" Hannah asked. "Won't the Caomhnóir get suspicious if you're hanging around all the time?"

"I'm not going to materialize," Milo said. "Besides, this place is constantly crawling with spirits of every description, but how often do you take note of them?"

This was a very good point. Spirits were a constant at Fairhaven, so much so that, for most of us, they had been relegated to little more than background noise. I gazed around the courtyard. Even at this moment, there were several spirits passing through, but not a single one of us had paid them the slightest attention. And I knew that there were even more of them that we couldn't see—the air was thick with their energy. Every Durupinen and Caomhnóir had learned over the years to compartmentalize the effects of spirit presences. We had all learned, in essence, to tune them out when we were otherwise engaged. If we hadn't, it would have been impossible to function.

"You'll be hiding in plain sight," I said, grinning. "It's actually completely brilliant."

"Exactly," Milo said.

"That's a huge responsibility," Hannah said to Milo. "Are you sure you want to take that on?"

"Excuse you, I am *very* responsible," Milo said, placing his hands on his hips and looking indignant.

Hannah rolled her eyes. "That's not what I mean," she insisted. "But that's going to be a twelve-hour-a-day job. What about your design stuff? This is a busy time for you."

"This is more important," Milo said, shrugging. "And anyway, it won't just be me. She's enlisted the help of several other spirits as well. We'll be taking shifts."

Hannah's furrowed brow relaxed. "Oh, okay. I guess that's fine, then."

"Sweetness, you know I love you for looking out for me, but I can handle this, I promise," Milo said. "It's what I signed on for, just like you."

Hannah's face fell into the sad smile it always wore when Milo spoke about his position as a Spirit Guide. No matter how often he insisted that he was happy and content in his role, she would always carry guilt about the way he chose to stay behind with her, and by so doing, Bound himself to her for the remainder of her life. Milo smiled back, because, of course, he knew exactly what she was thinking.

"Well, I've done all I can to prepare her," Finn said. "It will be up to Savvy now."

I took his hand and squeezed it. "I'm glad you've prepared Savvy for this," I whispered, "but I think someone really should have prepared the Caomhnóir ."

§

I spent the entire next day on edge. Both Hannah and I promised not to bother Milo while he was overseeing training so that he could concentrate, but it was not an easy promise to keep. By the end of classes for the day, at five o'clock, I was nearly beside myself with anxiety.

"Just a quick check in," I begged Hannah.

"No."

"But they're done! There's nothing else to see!"

"Jess, we promised," Hannah said, frowning at me like a schoolmarm with a ruler. "He'll be back any minute. We just have to be patient."

As though on cue, Milo sailed through the wall above the fireplace and floated down onto the couch like a feather. "What a day!" he announced.

Hannah and I descended on him like kids on the freshly spilled contents of a busted pinata.

"What happened?"

"Is she okay?"

"Were they awful to her?"

"What did they do?"

"Did they haze her?"

Milo held up a hand to silence us. "I think I'm going to let Savvy tell you herself. She's on her way up, I think. But don't tell her I was watching the training—Celeste doesn't want her to know."

"Are you serious? We've been waiting all day to find out what's been happening, and you aren't even going to spill?" I cried. "That's it, I'm going to Savvy's room so that I can meet her when she gets there." I jumped up from my seat.

"Jess, don't you dare pounce on her the moment she gets back!" Hannah admonished me, as though we both hadn't just done that very same thing to Milo. "She's no doubt had a long, hard day, and I'm sure she'll want to—"

Our bedroom door flew open, banging against the wall and making all three of us scream. Savvy stood in the doorway, covered from head to toe in mud and grinning from ear to ear.

"I did it! I bloody did it! It was incredible!" she announced, arms spread wide, as though expecting us to start applauding and throwing flowers at her.

"What... that's great, but... what *happened* to you?" I asked.

Savvy looked down, as though noticing the state of her clothes for the first time. "Aw, this? Just a bit of mud."

"A *bit* of mud?" Hannah squeaked. "Sav, you've brought an entire swamp with you!"

"Ah, well, Seamus thought he'd have a bit of sport today, setting up this massive obstacle course," Savvy said. "I think he was hoping I might not want to do it, or else that I'd get stuck somewhere in the middle. Well, laugh's on him, because I had one of the best times."

"What about the rest of the day? How did it go?" I asked.

"Well, the boys were trying to take the piss out of me most of the day, which is no more than I expected," she said, still smiling.

"Like what?" I asked. "What did they do?"

"Oh, let's see," Savvy said, and started ticking things off her fingers. "Put salt in my coffee, changed the due dates on the calendar, put bricks in my hiking pack, dulled my practice blade—you know, kid stuff. It was a lark."

"But that's... that's all awful!" Hannah cried.

"Ah, come off it, Hannah. They were just having a laugh. Well, except the one who tried to threaten me. He was pretty serious, I reckon."

"Someone threatened you?" I asked, rage boiling inside me. "Did you report it?"

Savvy shrugged. "Nah, I did him one better."

"What do you—"

"Got into a bit of a dust-up with him. Don't think he was expecting it, to be honest. Anyway, after I'd busted his nose and blackened his eye, I asked him if he'd like to head back to training and tell them a girl had beaten his arse. He wasn't too keen on it," Savvy said with a bit of a mischievous smirk.

Hannah looked horrified. "You got in a fight?! But Savvy, you're going to get in so much trouble!"

Savvy patted Hannah on the shoulder, depositing some mud on her shirt. "Novitiate training isn't grammar school, Hannah. The lads were getting into Barneys all over the place. The instructors expect it. I reckon it's how they maintain their social order, see? Anyhow, when it comes down to it, I don't think many of them are too keen on beating up a girl, which is fine by me, because I'll knock a bloke to the pavement for looking at me sideways. I don't think I'm going to have too much trouble with them after today."

I just stared. "That's... I guess that's... good?"

"Oh, yeah, it's brilliant!" Savvy said brightly. "Although, I'm total crap at running, because of all those damn fags I keep smoking, so I've got to work on that. And Seamus likes putting Novitiates on the spot to answer questions—just calls on you out of the blue, like, and barks a question at you. If you don't know the answer, he docks points, so I'll have to study my arse off because if today is any indication, he thinks I should answer most of the questions."

"Now, that's something we can help you with," I said.

"I'm so glad you had... well, I guess not a *good* day, but..." Hannah began, trying to find the right words to describe what to her probably sounded like a hellscape.

But Savvy didn't need to hear them. "Thanks," she said with another broad grin. "I'm going to shower off, and then eat. You fancy grabbing a bite with me in a bit?"

"Sure! Text us when you're heading down," I told her.

She agreed, then headed back out the door with a considerable swagger.

I waited until I could no longer hear her footsteps, and then turned to Milo. "Tell us the truth. Is she just pretending to be okay, or what?"

Milo shook his head and gave an incredulous laugh. "She's telling the truth. I wish you could have seen it, it was glorious. They had absolutely no idea what to make of her. When that creep poured the salt in her coffee, they all just sat around waiting for her to freak out. Instead, she took a sip, then swallowed the whole cup in one huge gulp. Then she smiled at them and said, 'Think I'll have another. Pass the salt, there's a chum.'"

He paused as Hannah and I had a good laugh.

"Then, when she found the bricks in her bag and the Novitiates all started laughing, she laughed right along with them, so loud and so long that she was the last one laughing," Milo said. "Then she picked up one of the bricks, chucked it at the nearest group of Novitiates so that they had to dive out of the way, and declared, 'I like having fun with bricks, too. Cor, we are going to have a swell time, ain't we, lads?'"

"Okay, well, she can definitely hold her own with the other Novitiates, but what about Seamus? How did she handle him?" I asked.

"You'd think she'd have flown off the handle at him, given the rest of the violence she committed throughout the day, but she didn't. Not even once. She was cool as a cucumber, and she knew the answer to nearly every question he asked her. I don't think he expected her to be this prepared," Milo said, and the relish in his voice was clear.

"Well, Savvy's reputation precedes her," Hannah said. "I'm sure Seamus thought she'd show up late and hungover so that he'd have a reason to kick her out on the first day. But if she keeps showing up prepared, he's going to have to come up with a different strategy."

"Yeah, he's not going to give up easily," I said. "We'll have to make sure she doesn't screw up. We'll have to try to keep her motivated and away from the bad habits that might trip her up."

"I don't think motivation is going to be a problem," Milo said. "But, yes, staying a step ahead of Seamus is going to be important. He was thrown today, but he will totally regroup."

"Well, you keep spying, and we'll keep adjusting," I said. "If there's one thing we can all agree on, it's this: if you come for Savvy, you come for all of us."

"Forever and ever, amen," Milo replied.

10

THE GLIMPSE

TO EVERYONE'S ASTONISHMENT—perhaps Savvy's more than anyone's—Savvy's first two weeks of Caomhnóir training were a success. We hardly had to help her at all, with the one exception of hiding a package of cigarettes toward the end of the second week, when she became too stressed out studying for her first test.

"Come on, Milo, be a chum," Savvy had groaned. "Just one fag and I'll be right as rain again."

"Uh-uh," Milo had said firmly, "You just told me this morning that running was already getting easier now that you'd quit them. We're not screwing that up."

"Come on, you still have three flashcards to memorize, and then I'm putting you to bed," Hannah told her. "You're getting bags under your eyes. No more staying up late cramming. I know you're nervous about this test, but you can't pass it if you sleep through it."

"Yes, mum," Savvy had grumbled.

It was the very next evening, on my way to Savvy's room to see how she'd done on the test, that a voice boomed out behind me in the corridor, making me yelp in surprise and nearly choke on a piece of gum.

"Jessica Ballard! There you are!" A red-faced Caomhnóir jogged up the hall, gasping for air, and pausing to clutch the nearest doorway with one hand, and a stitch in his side with the other.

I waited for him to catch his breath, as I coughed and spluttered trying to catch mine.

"Please come with me," the Caomhnóir wheezed at last.

"I don't go anywhere with anyone unless they explain to me exactly what—" I began, my voice sharp with both anger and fear.

"The tower... Fiona... she needs you..."

My heart seemed to freeze solid in my chest for a second before bursting like a thrashing animal from the ice. I didn't hesitate another moment, but instead sprinted toward the Caomhnóir who, seeing that I was heeding his request, turned on his heel in the doorway and pelted back down the hall, leaving me to stumble along in his wake.

"Why... does... Fiona...?" I tried to ask the obvious question, but I couldn't get my breath under me. It didn't matter anyway, for we had reached the spiral staircase to the tower, and the Caomhnóir had no breath left to waste on answering me. Instead, he collapsed to his knees at the top of the stairs and gestured wordlessly to the door, which was standing ajar.

Fear stabbed through me like a white-hot blade, and for a moment I was utterly incapable of moving, terrified of what I would find on the other side of the door. But then the Caomhnóir made an impatient grunting sound that jolted me out of my immobility.

I could not contain my gasp of horror as I looked around the room that I had so carefully and meticulously organized. Now, it looked as though a wild animal had been let loose in the place, the proverbial bull in the china shop. Paint cans and writing implements littered the floor, and an entire shelf of dyes and stains had been knocked over, creating a swirling multicolored pool that was spreading steadily across the floor. I was so horrified by the chaos, that I did not immediately see Fiona, who was hunched over in the corner by the window, her back to me. I swallowed back the urge to cry with frustration and called her name instead.

"Fiona!"

No answer. She did not turn, did not so much as acknowledge that she had even heard me. I took a moment to try to get my breath back and tried again.

"Fiona? Fiona, what's happened? What are you doing?" I managed a volume closer to a shout this time.

Again, Fiona did not respond. Again, she showed no sign that she had heard me at all.

She was not entirely still though. She was hunched over something and her arms seemed to be moving around, though I couldn't see what was occupying them. My heart, already hammering from the strenuous climb to the tower, continued to pound even harder, this time with fear.

"Fiona?" I said her name again, but more quietly this time.

Hesitantly, because now that she had failed to answer me a third time, something had become clear: Fiona, though she was sitting there in front of me, was not in the room.

I picked my way across the tower as quickly as I could, careful to avoid stepping in the debris that I knew would later be my job to clean up, until I reached the corner into which Fiona had tucked herself. I approached her cautiously, but still she seemed oblivious to my presence. I knelt down beside her and peered around her shoulder to see what it was that she was doing.

Fiona's hands were frantically molding a large lump of potter's clay. Her mouth was moving in a rapid, silent stream of mutterings. None of this actually worried me all that much. In fact, I felt relieved. After all, I had once witnessed Fiona collapse to the floor in the throes of a spirit-induced drawing. On that occasion too, she could neither see nor hear me, for the spirit in question had almost entirely overtaken her body. Unsure at that time of what had been happening, I had panicked and, thinking that she was having a seizure, doused her in a pitcher of icy water, which had instantly broken the trance. Naturally, she'd been furious with me, for I had severed the connection between her and the spirit, and therefore interrupted the message that she was being used to transmit. Several years later, and now intimately acquainted with the strange ways in which a Muse sometimes worked, I knew better than to interrupt Fiona in her current trance. When her work was complete, she would rouse naturally, and we could deal with both the disaster in the room, and the resultant artwork.

I turned to look over my shoulder at the Caomhnóir, who was still panting and wheezing, nearly bent double. "It's okay," I told him. "There's nothing wrong with her. She's in a spirit induced trance right now; it's part of being a Muse. A spirit is using her to create this art. She'll come out of it when it's finished.

"I'm not sensing any spirits in here," the Caomhnóir said, his face set in a stubborn expression of distrust.

"The spirit doesn't have to be physically present in the room to use a Muse. The connections often span miles," I explained.

The Caomhnóir still looked skeptical. "But I heard all this crashing," he said slowly. "I opened the door to find her turning the place upside down. Knocking things over, throwing things everywhere. And she wouldn't answer me when I spoke to her. Are you saying that's part of this Muse experience as well?"

"Yeah, I know it seems strange, but she doesn't actually have any control over what she's doing right now. She was probably searching for a medium that she could use to get the spirit's message across. Chances are that's why she trashed the place. I'll clean it up, don't worry. I've got this under control now. You can go."

Again, the Caomhnóir did not seem to want to take me at my word, and I was struck anew at how little trust existed between the Guardians and the Durupinen. How in the world had we co-existed for so long under such a cloud? He continued to hover in the doorway, eager to leave this strange and chaotic scene behind, no doubt, but also clearly hesitant to leave me here alone with Fiona in this state. "You're not worried she'll start hurling things about the place again?" he asked me.

I gave him a wry smile. "You haven't dealt much with Fiona before, have you?"

He frowned, evidently wondering if he was being insulted. "No, I... this is a new assignment for me. I'm usually working the borders of the grounds. Why?"

I laughed. "No, it's just... when you spend enough time around Fiona, projectiles become the norm." The Caomhnóir just looked confused now, so I waved him away with my hand. "Look, all I'm saying is that it certainly wouldn't be the first time that Fiona threw something at me in this room. I promise you, I can handle it. Thank you for coming to get me."

The Caomhnóir hesitated just one moment more, and then swallowed his doubts. He clicked his heels together and gave me a respectful nod, and then backed himself out of the door, closing it behind him.

I sighed a deep sigh of relief. Now that the panic was receding from my brain, now that I knew that Fiona was simply caught up in a trance, I was able to calmly process the details of the scene around her. From what I could tell, it looked as though she had attempted and then abandoned several different forms of artistic expression before she finally committed to the clay. A sketchbook lay open, pencils and charcoal scattered across the top of it, a few haphazard lines drawn upon the top page. A set of watercolors and the canvas lay abandoned on the ground beside a half-open package of oil pastels. Even a lump of granite seemed to have been dragged part way across the room, a pile of tools and a smattering of dust suggested that it, too, had been tried briefly before it was cast aside. I had never experienced this kind of indecisiveness in my trances. To a fault, I had found the nearest, most convenient medium that I could get my hands on and began using it immediately. I had even gotten in the habit of leaving a notepad beside my bed, and taping pieces of sketch paper up on the walls, so that I would not start using the wallpaper as a blank canvas. But then again, I had never been confronted with physical limitations such as Fiona was dealing with now. Perhaps it was crucial to the spirit that Fiona herself be able to examine and interpret the art when she had finished creating it. If that were the case, settling on a medium like clay made perfect sense.

I examined the beginnings of what would apparently become a sculpture, but could not yet discern what Fiona was creating. Her hands had molded the clay into two sections, one larger, and one smaller, and were now smoothing and shaping the larger lump of clay into something narrow and vaguely rounded on the top. I gave a long sigh. This was going to take a while. I looked around the room and decided I might as well make myself useful.

For the next six hours, I occupied myself in the tower room, waiting for Fiona to finish her work. I reorganized and cleaned up all evidence of the messy beginnings of her trance. When I had the place spotless again, I rummaged through her tiny kitchen and cobbled together a make-shift midnight snack of tea, two over-ripe bananas, and a tin of shortbread biscuits. Then I stoked the fire in the grate until the chill in the room began to dissipate a bit. After making sure that Fiona was still working, I settled into a threadbare armchair in the corner and stared at Agnes' tapestry, the tin of shortbread still in my hands.

I still had no idea what the message on the book was supposed to mean. I was starting to wonder if I was meant to ask Fiona about it. After all, she was the historical art expert in the castle. If anyone was likely to understand why such a random collection of numbers and letters were to appear in an ancient tapestry, it was her, wasn't it?

But then, that nagging voice piped up in the back of my head, that voice that raised the hairs on the back of my neck and tingled with prescience in my ears. If that message had been meant to Fiona, Fiona would have been the one to find it. All the stars have aligned for this message to be discovered just at the very moment when Fiona herself cannot receive it. No, that message is for you, and you must discover its meaning without dragging Fiona into it.

But why would someone send a message for me? A message like that has to have existed within the fibers of that tapestry for centuries. Why had it been covered up? And why was I so very sure that the message, given its age and the unlikelihood of my coming across it, was meant specifically for me? I couldn't understand it, but if I didn't figure it out soon, I was going to need another tin of shortbread.

A soft moaning sound issued from the corner in which Fiona was working. I turned to see her shifting her body uncomfortably, moving something other than her arms for the first time in hours. I shoved the cover back onto the tin of shortbread and hurried over to kneel beside her. I knew only too well the exhaustion and physical toll that a spirit-induced episode could cause, and this had been a particularly long one. I held out my arms, ready to support her when she was finally free of its control.

As I watched, her frantic, insistent hands began to slow. The movements became smaller and gentler. It was as though she were a music box approaching the end of her tune, each note sounding further and further apart until it fell silent. Her hands paused on either side of the clay, hovered for a moment, and then dropped to her sides. Her chin dropped to her chest, lolled about for a moment, and then jolted back up as though she had just awoken from sleepwalking to find herself in an unexpected place. Which I had to admit, having experienced it myself, was a pretty damn accurate analogy.

"What the devil?" she muttered to herself, her hands scrabbling around frantically to identify her location.

"Fiona, it's okay," I said quietly.

"Blast!" Fiona shouted, and her right hand flung upward toward me, so that I had to dive out of the way to avoid being backhanded. "Blimey Jess, don't sneak up on me like that!"

"I didn't sneak up on you," I said, trying to maintain my patience even as I clambered back up to a sitting position. "I've been sitting here for the better part of six hours. It's well past midnight now."

"Six hours? What the bloody hell are you..." But her voice trailed away. Her nostrils began to flair as the scent of the potter's clay reached her nose at last. She lifted her hands to her nose, sniffing again, and rubbed them together, feeling the wet, sticky residue of the clay all over her skin. She expelled a breath, and when she spoke, her voice was barely more than a whisper.

"It was a trance, wasn't it? I had a trance?"

"Yes."

"And I've been sculpting?"

"Yes."

"That's... *dogs*. I've never had a Muse episode take the form of a sculpture before. That was always me mam's territory."

"Things have changed," I said gently. "The spirit probably realized it would be easiest for you to work this way now that you..." I hesitated only a moment in completing the sentence but Fiona leapt onto my hesitation like a hungry dog onto a scrap of meat.

"Now that I'm blind as Tiresias," she snapped. "You can just come out with it and say the word, you know. It's not as though I'm not acutely aware of the fact that I can't bloody see."

"Who's Tiresias?"

"Blind soothsayer in Greek mythology. Told Oedipus a few things that made him decide he'd rather not see anymore either."

"Oh, yeah. Right." I shuddered. Oedipus was one character from Greek mythology I understood only too well. Running from prophecies? Finding out your parents weren't who you thought they were? Luckily, I'd managed to sort things out before the "gouging out my own eyes" section of the story. Gah.

"Christ on a bike, my bloody arms!" Fiona moaned, rubbing at the muscles and trying to repress a sob. "And my *hands*. They feel about ready to fall off! You say I've been at it for how long?"

"Six hours since I got here," I told her. "Probably six and a half, all told. The Caomhnóir heard a disturbance in here and came to investigate."

"A disturbance? What kind of disturbance?"

"You... made a bit of a mess looking for the right medium for the message. No worries, I've already cleaned it all up, good as new," I added before she could freak out.

"Well, what is it, then?" Fiona asked in an exasperated voice. "What have I made?" She reached out in front of her to where the sculpture sat upon the floor, but even this movement caused her to cry out in pain again.

I glanced at the sculpture, but honestly, I was much more concerned about Fiona's well-being at the moment. "It looks like someone standing in front of a door—or a Geatgrima, actually," I said. "But enough about that right now. It's nothing that can't wait a few minutes. Come on, let's get you cleaned up. We can examine it and talk about the details when you've recovered a bit."

Fiona made half of a feeble protest but submitted completely to my orders. We struggled for several minutes to get her to her feet; she had been kneeling for so long without moving that both of her legs had fallen asleep. I eased them out from under her and worked at the muscles with my hands to get the blood moving again. Together we hobbled over to the far corner, where a tiny bathroom was concealed behind an unmarked wooden door. I helped Fiona to a stool, which she collapsed onto, and drew her the hottest bath I could coax from the castle plumbing. She didn't offer a word of protest as I helped her out of her shoes and clay-spotted clothes and into the tub, where she sank neck-deep into the steaming water with a groan of contentment. Then I perched myself on the stool and sat patiently for a full five minutes, giving the water a chance to wash away both the discomfort and the clay. At last, when Fiona's exclamations of aches and stiffness had given way to silence, I ventured to speak.

"Tell me what you remember," I said to her.

She gave a long sigh. "I had only just gotten up from an afternoon nap. I had... well, I had a bugger of a headache, if you must know—a bit too much whiskey at my one-woman pity party last night. I couldn't stand the light coming in from the windows, so I was on my way over to close the curtains. I felt that funny ripple, you know, so I felt around for a pen and some paper, and then, next thing I knew, we were sitting in that corner together and you were telling me six hours had gone by."

"What do you mean, ripple?" I asked curiously.

"That's what I call that feeling, you know, the one you get right before you fall under the trance. It's like your reality is suddenly made of water, and a massive wave rolls right through it, throwing you off balance and carrying you somewhere new. My trances have always started that way, which is useful. Gives me a moment to sit myself down somewhere safe, or position myself near some art supplies."

"Oh, wow," I said. "I've never thought of it that way before... well, most of my episodes have happened while I was sleeping, so I'm not sure if I've ever noticed the ripple thing."

"Yes, well, I imagine it's different for every Muse," Fiona said. "You get massive headaches from your trances, don't you?"

"Yeah, a lot of the time," I admitted.

"Never a twinge for me," Fiona said with a shrug. "The Muse experience is as different as the Muses, I'd imagine. I knew a Muse who had to sleep for a full day after a trance. Couldn't keep her eyes open after the drain of it."

"Is this your first trance since you... since we got back from Skye Príosún?" I asked.

Fiona snorted derisively but otherwise ignored my slip-up. "Yes."

"Was it any different? Than before, I mean?"

Fiona did not snort this time. She seemed to seriously consider the question before she answered. "I don't think so. Why do you ask?"

"I just wasn't sure if you had ever abandoned one medium for another before this. From the mess down there, it looked as though you tried a few before settling on the clay. I wasn't sure if you had any memory of that."

Fiona shook her head. "No. That must have been the spirit's doing, not mine."

"But your own limitations wouldn't prevent you from painting or drawing whatever it was the spirit wanted to tell you, would they? I always thought the spirit itself was directing our hands."

"Yes and no," Fiona said, and her tone was thoughtful. "My eyes might not have been instrumental in creating an image, but they would be instrumental in examining that image afterward. I wouldn't be able to interpret a painting anymore, but these beauties work just fine." She lifted her hands out of the tub, revealing clean, white fingertips as wrinkled as raisins. "I'm no use as a Muse if I can't understand what it is a spirit is trying to tell me. I expect I will need to keep a lot more clay within arm's reach in the future." She sighed. "Right, then. Well, I'm clean and recovered now, I reckon. Let's see what all the fuss is about with this sculpture, eh?"

I handed Fiona a towel and turned to give her some privacy as she stepped out of the tub and dried herself. She shrugged into a long, white frock that looked like an old man's nightshirt and led the way back to the corner where her newly-created sculpture stood waiting for us like writing upon a wall.

Fiona reached her hands out until she found the base of the

sculpture and then silently ran her hands over every tiny detail. It was fascinating to watch, the way she instinctively knew how to explore it, though her sight had been damaged such a short time ago. There was no frustration, no cursing, no apparent urges to hurl things across the room. There was simply calm examination, because there was no other choice, if the art was to be understood. In this moment, I admired Fiona perhaps more than I had ever admired her before.

Even as I marveled at Fiona's process, I took in the sculpture for myself, expanding upon my first, cursory glance, allowing Fiona's hands to guide how I, too, took in each new detail. By the time we both had finished, my heart was thumping in my chest.

"It's a Geatgrima," I said, slowly. "Isn't it?"

"Yes," Fiona said. "The Geatgrima here at Fairhaven, I'm sure of it. The way the stones have shifted over time, and this one here, that is slightly larger and twisted out of alignment." Her fingers found the offending stone, tracing the way its protrusion marred the otherwise smooth column. Now that she pointed it out, I recognized it as well.

"And this figure here is obviously a Caomhnóir, right?" I asked pointing to the figure that stood facing the archway.

"That's what I thought at first, but..." Fiona's voice was hesitant.

"But he has the uniform on," I pointed out, wondering if Fiona's fingers weren't quite as sensitive as they had seemed. "The vest and the boots, and the staff is exactly like the ones our Caomhnóir carry on the grounds."

"I don't doubt any of that. It is certainly a Caomhnóir uniform, but..."

"But what?" I asked.

"But I wonder why a woman is wearing it."

I blinked, too stunned to answer for a moment. "Are... you sure?"

"Pretty damn sure," Fiona said. "The shape of the body is all wrong for a bloke. And the features of the face are too soft, too fine. Come on, Ballard, you've got eyes that still work. Use 'em!"

I shifted around to the other side of the sculpture where Fiona was sitting so that I could now see the figure's front, rather than its back. From this angle, it was much clearer that this Guardian had curves in all the wrong places for a man, even under the bulk of the Caomhnóir uniform. The hair was short, which had thrown me before, but it fell across a smooth and feminine face... a face that I knew...

"Savvy," I whispered.

"What's that?" Fiona snapped.

"I... I can't be sure, obviously, but... it looks like... it's my friend Savannah."

"What's that?"

"Savannah. Savannah Todd. It looks a lot like her."

Fiona frowned. "Hmm. Is that so, now? Well, that's interesting."

"Ya think?" I asked with an incredulous laugh. "What does it mean?"

"Damned if I know," Fiona said. "I'm just the Muse, aren't I? Just the conduit."

I examined the sculpture again, hoping a small detail would leap out at me, explaining what I was looking at. Savvy—if it really was Savvy, and it certainly appeared to be—stood facing the Geatgrima, chest thrown out, staff drawn, chin up. It would have been a completely uninteresting pose in which to find a Caomhnóir, were it not for the fact that it was a woman who happened to be doing it.

"Why would a spirit want to tell you that Savvy is trying to be a Caomhnóir?" I asked, as much to myself as to Fiona. "We already know that. It's all everyone in this castle is talking about at the moment."

"Maybe the spirit is concerned about it. Maybe they are expressing their disapproval, like most of the living people around here," Fiona suggested.

"But what about this looks disapproving?" I asked. "It doesn't look like she's messing up. I mean honestly, she just looks like a Caomhnóir doing their job. You know, except for the whole being-a-woman thing."

"And why would she be in front of the Geatgrima?" Fiona asked, parrying my question with another question. "We don't have Caomhnóir stationed there unless there's a ceremony happening."

"I don't know, but there must be a reason. Why would a spirit bother taking all that time, using you to create a sculpture of the Geatgrima if it weren't crucial to the message?"

"I've got no bloody—wait, now, what's this?" Fiona muttered. Her hands, which had been continuing to wander over the sculpture, had come to a stop on the base of the Geatgrima, her fingers probing at the stones of the dais upon which it stood.

"What's what? What did you find?" I asked her.

"There's... there's a rune here that I don't recall being carved on the Geatgrima. Or, at least... bugger it all, I *think* there is..."

I looked at the spot her fingers were tracing. It was one of the many runes on the dais stones of the Geatgrima.

"Are you sure?" I asked her, trying not to sound skeptical. "There are runes all around the bottom of the Geatgrima, from what I can recall. I don't remember what they all are, or what they mean, but they're carved all over it."

"Of course, I'm not sure. I've just told you that, haven't I?"

I nudged gently at Fiona's finger so that I could get a better look at the rune. It was one I did not recognize—I probably should have, but my early stubborn rejection of my Durupinen role meant that I didn't know the vast language of runes nearly as well as I should have. Hannah was much better at recognizing them on sight, but even she had to look them up once in a while. "I don't recognize this one," I admitted, preparing to be berated for my ignorance. To my surprise though, I was not met with scorn, but a frustrated shake of the head.

"Nor do I," Fiona said.

"You're kidding!" I said.

"Naturally, as I'm such a kidder," Fiona snapped. "This isn't a rune I've ever learned, which is saying something, as I've learned all of them. It feels like the rune for Durupinen, except for this bit here," she added, running her finger over a set of lines at the head of the rune, which looked like the feathered end of an arrow."

"Maybe the spirit was confused," I suggested. "I've gotten mixed and confused messages before when a spirit was disoriented, or misremembered something. Maybe something like that happened here?"

Fiona's lips were pursed into a tiny wrinkled prune of a shape as though quite unwilling to allow her reply to escape. "Maybe. And that's not the only thing that's nagging me about this sculpture."

I didn't press her to elaborate. I knew if she wanted to tell me, she would, in her own time. And after another minute of examining the statue with her fingertips, she told me at last.

"This hasn't happened yet," Fiona said.

"Huh?"

"This. Your friend Savannah, becoming a Caomhnóir. It hasn't happened yet."

SOUL OF THE SENTINEL

I blinked. "Oh. Oh, yeah, that's true. But she is training. She's got the uniform and..."

"But she hasn't got this yet," Fiona said, running her finger over a small decorative mark on Savvy's shoulder. It was a pin, like the one Finn wore. Savvy would not receive one until she passed her training. "She's barely scraped through with approval to enter the program. It'll be a bloody miracle if she completes it."

I stiffened. "Savvy is tough. She can more than handle the training."

"I don't deny she's got the ability, but don't be daft, Jess. She's a bloody disaster, that girl. I remember when she was a student here—sneaking out, missing class, or sleeping through it, drinking, dalliances. She'll have to stay well out of her own way if she's going to pull this out."

I just shrugged, pretending I hadn't expressed the very same doubts repeatedly with everyone from Finn to Hannah to Savvy herself.

"So that means this piece of artwork is either symbolic or..."

I looked up, shocked. "Or?"

"Or it's prophetic." Fiona's voice was barely more than a murmur.

My heart began to race. "Are... do you really think so?"

"I don't know what to think. I just know I don't understand it yet, and we have to consider the possibility."

"But... but you've never made a prophecy before! Wait, have you?" I asked. Was it possible Fiona had hidden such a revelation from me?

"No, of course I haven't," Fiona said. "But I don't know what to make of this yet, and until we can figure it out, we have to at least consider the possibility that it is prophetic in nature."

I looked down at the sculpture again, seeing it through an entirely different lens now. If it was prophetic, what was it trying to tell us? That Savvy would successfully become a Caomhnóir? It seemed unlikely that such a piece of information, in and of itself, would warrant the creation of a brand-new Seer. I mean, for heaven's sake, it wasn't telling us anything we couldn't discover for ourselves just by waiting out the next few months of training. No, there must be another message here, something more specific—something that connected Savvy, that rune, and the Geatgrima. But what was it?

"We're going to need some time to research this," Fiona said, tapping at the rune once again. "As if we didn't have enough to do around here. Well, I don't want anything to happen to it, what with all the restoration equipment we have to set up, and the buggery Caomhnóir in and out of here all the blasted time. So, until I can figure out what the hell it means, I need you to take this up to the archive for me," Fiona said.

"What archive?" I asked blankly. I couldn't pull myself away from the statue, still lost in contemplation of what it might mean.

Fiona snapped her fingers impatiently. "What do you mean, 'what archive?' The archive! The archive! The only archive we've got in this bloody castle for potentially prophetic art like this! Silly me, I thought you'd remember it, seeing as how it completely changed the trajectory of your life."

"Oh, right. Yeah, sorry," I said, shaking my head. Of course. Wow, I really was distracted. Otherwise, how could I explain forgetting the existence of the room in which I had been given the most life-altering piece of information I'd ever received. Well, okay, the *second* most life-altering piece of information. Let's face it, nothing would ever compare to Lucida climbing in my window in the middle of the night and informing me that I was a Durupinen and also that I had a long-lost twin sister. That was the mother of all bombshells.

But it was in the Fairhaven archives, up in the furthest neglected reaches of the castle, where Fiona had sat me down, and told me, in no uncertain terms, that I was a Seer. I'd rejected her words at first, and as long as it took my brain to accept them, it took even longer for my heart to accept them. I had no desire to be a Seer and even now, I did not welcome the gift. But I had made peace with the fact that it was part of who I was, and part of what I could contribute to this mad world into which I had been born. The archive itself, Fiona had explained, was a catalog, a record of every piece of prophetic art and language that had been produced by the Durupinen over the centuries. Some of them had been produced by known Seers, while others appeared to be anomalies, a single moment of strange inspiration, or perhaps even the occasional coincidence. Each and every one had been filed away up in the archives, so that their patterns could be studied and perhaps the phenomenon of Seeing could be better understood. Several of my own pieces of art had their place up in that room, and now it seemed that Fiona's latest work would join them there.

"Do you really want me to take it up now?" I asked her. "Isn't there anything else you want to do with it? Study it? See if there are any more details still to come?"

Fiona shook her head violently. "No. I need it out of here. I need to think, and it's almost as though I can feel its presence pressing in on me, forcing itself on me. No, I need a bit of space. Get it out of here so I can get my head on straight, and then you can take me up to study it again when I've had a bit of time to process."

"Okay, sure," I said, eyeing Fiona with concern. "Whatever you need, Fiona. Whatever you say."

I walked around the desk and picked up the sculpture. It was heavier than I expected, and I staggered a bit trying to keep it upright in my arms. It was not going to be easy to lug across the castle. I also had to be exceedingly careful to handle it as little as possible, as the clay had not dried, and any rough treatment could mar the details. I would've liked to ask someone for help, but I knew that Fiona would never allow it. If I had learned anything during my time as a Seer, it was that prophetic art was meant to be examined by as few people as possible.

I turned to go, but Fiona called out. "Oi! Hold up there, you. You've got to make sure you file it properly."

I turned around, puzzled. "I... was just going to put it on the table up there," I told her. "How am I supposed to file a sculpture?"

"You can't just leave something like that lying around without being properly cataloged!" Fiona said, her voice dripping with disdain. "It's got to be recorded! It's got to be organized! If it can't be found, it can't be connected. It can't be understood as a part of the whole, do you understand me?"

The truth was I didn't understand her at all. First of all, the irony of someone lecturing me about organization when her studio usually looked like someone had let an army of toddlers loose in it was so absurd that I had to swallow a laugh. And secondly, no one entered that archive except for Fiona and myself, and it wasn't as though either of us were likely to forget that the sculpture existed, seeing as she had produced it mere minutes ago. But her indignation was such that it didn't seem worth the frustration of starting an argument about it. "Whatever you say, Fiona," I said again in an effort to placate her.

"Damn right, whatever I say," Fiona muttered, as she rose to her feet and felt her way forward to her desk. She reached into the drawer and pulled out one of about a million pads of sticky notes.

Then she picked up a pencil from the cup on the corner of her desk, and jotted something down, before peeling off the topmost sticky note and holding it out for me to take.

I shifted the sculpture awkwardly in my arms so that I could free my hand to take the note from her. "What's this?" I asked her.

"That's the filing system," Fiona said. "This is how you know where to store it. It will make sense when you get up there. Be sure to record it in the register as well. It's the big black book in the corner by the window. Just write that information down under the last entry."

I looked down at the note and had to clamp my lips together to stifle a gasp. My arms began shaking, and for a moment, I was in real danger of dropping the sculpture in my shock. I stared down at the note and felt a heavy weight of knowledge drop into my head with all the subtlety of a cartoon anvil.

"FA – 387G – 2019AIN

I whipped my head over my shoulder so quickly that I cracked my neck. Agnes Isherwood was smiling serenely down on me, and it was as though I could feel the glow of her approval. *Yes,* she seemed to tell me. *That's right.*

The collection of numbers and letters in my hand and the collection of numbers and letters on Agnes' hidden book were formatted in precisely the same way. They were both catalog numbers, I just knew it. Like the coordinates on a map, the hidden numbers and letters in Agnes' book were not meant to be understood in and of themselves, but were meant to lead me to something, to guide me to whatever it was that I was meant to find. As much as I had been dreading the walk to the archive just moments before, I now felt as though my legs could not possibly carry me there fast enough.

"I'll take care of it right now, Fiona," I said, unable to completely conceal the breathless excitement in my voice. "I'll be back when I've finished, okay?"

"Don't bother," Fiona said, with a dismissive wave of her hand. "That visitation wore me out. I fancy a kip before I tried to sort it all out. It must be nearly one o'clock in the morning, and for all my bragging before about never experiencing headaches with trances, I can feel a bugger of a headache coming on me right now."

I was already halfway to the door. "All right," I said hastily. "I'll let you sleep then, and come back tomorrow."

"Mind you don't trip and drop that thing! If I wanted it broken I'd carry it myself!" Fiona replied and, in lieu of thanking me, slammed the door promptly in my face.

11

TRUST

BY THE TIME I REACHED THE HALLWAY where the archive was located, I was fighting a strange, almost overwhelming urge to throw the statue from me. It had become increasingly apparent, as I traversed hallway after hallway, that I was carrying something significant in both physical weight and spiritual weight—indeed, the longer I held it, the more conviction I felt that Fiona had wandered for the first time into true prophecy.

A sliver of light at the end of the hallway caught my eye, and I froze. The door to the archive was slightly ajar, and gold light was spilling out into the hallway, slicing the darkness and casting strange shadows on the ceiling.

Only two people in the castle had access to the keys to that archive, as far as I was aware: me and Fiona. And since Fiona was currently down in her studio nursing a Muse-induced headache, I knew that whoever had opened that door had either picked the lock or forced it. My heart hammering a rapid tattoo against my ribcage, I crept forward, closing the distance between myself and the open door, placing each footstep deliberately and clamping a hand down over my cardigan pocket to silence the quiet jingle of the keys.

As I drew closer, a quiet series of noises met my ears, emanating from inside the archive. A rustling sound, like papers being shuffled, punctuated by an occasional dull, muffled clunk. It sounded like whoever was on the other side of the door was searching through the artwork. I looked down at the statue in my arms and froze. Whoever was inside that archive, I knew I didn't want them to catch a glimpse of the sculpture—we didn't know what it meant, and so it would be dangerous to let anyone else see it. I spotted a niche in the wall where another statue stood, this one an innocuous rendering of two Durupinen girls holding hands. I pushed this statue aside, slid Fiona's sculpture behind it,

137

and pulled the niche statue in front of it again so that it was hidden from view. Satisfied, I crept closer to the archive.

Just outside the door, I stopped and, on sudden inspiration, started staring around wildly for something I could use as a weapon. I wasn't sure who at Fairhaven I would have to use a weapon against, but my time as a Tracker had taught me to take nothing for granted. Whoever was in that archive had broken in, which meant their motives were already suspect. I spotted a second niche in the wall, this one containing a large porcelain vase. It looked small enough that I could wield it in one hand, but when I grasped it and tried to pull it from its place, the weight of it nearly pulled me over right onto my face. I was barely able to muster the arm strength to keep it from hitting the ground. Gripping it tightly with both hands and trying to quiet my breathing, which could now more accurately be described as panting, I heaved the vase up onto my shoulder and prayed that, if I needed to use it, sheer adrenaline would give me enough strength to swing it.

I pressed my back up against the cold stone of the wall beside the door and tried to listen over the blood now rushing in my ears. If I could just get some kind of clue as to who was behind the door, or how many of them there might be...

A single word in a woman's voice drifted out into the hallway.

"Bollocks."

I knew that voice.

I pushed the door open, causing the woman behind it to drop a stack of papers all over the floor and erupt in a stream of curse words.

"Bugger, blast, bloody damn hell!" Lucida cried, clutching at her chest as though to prevent her heart from leaping out in fear.

"Lucida, what are you doing?" I asked.

"Getting the knickers scared off me, that's what," Lucida gasped, her shoulders heaving. "What are you doing here at this time of night?"

"What am *I* doing here?" I asked with an incredulous laugh. "What are *you* doing here? I happen to know that I've got the only set of keys to this room. What did you do, pick the lock?"

Lucida shrugged, still panting. "Locks are a minor and temporary inconvenience for anyone with a proper bit of determination and a spare hairpin. Are you going to bludgeon me with that thing, or what?" she added, pointing at the vase, which I still had raised over my shoulder like a baseball bat.

Shrugging a bit sheepishly, I heaved it down onto the table with a resounding clunk. "I don't take chances anymore. You can thank yourself for that."

Lucida gave herself a sarcastic pat on the back.

"You still haven't answered my question," I said. "What are you doing here?"

Lucida scooped a stack of papers up off the table and slipped them back into a standing file behind her. "Just having a look around, you know. Never been up here before. Smashing collection."

I hoisted one eyebrow. "You want me to believe that you just came up here in the dead of night, picked the lock, and started rummaging through the archive on a whim? Do you really think I'm stupid enough to believe that?"

"I don't give a damn whether you believe it or not," Lucida said, supremely unconcerned. "No skin off my nose."

"And you think it's a wise decision to break into restricted spaces at Fairhaven when half the Council still thinks you should be thrown back in jail?"

"Oh, come now, love," Lucida said. "If you've learned one thing about me, it's that I rarely make wise decisions. I'm a magnet for trouble, me."

"You made some pretty decent ones at Skye," I said quietly. "I think you can make the right decision, when you want to."

Lucida did not reply, but seemed suddenly quite fascinated with her own fingernails.

"So, why don't you tell me what you're really doing up here, and I'll consider not telling the Council that you broke in," I said, crossing my arms over my chest in an attempt to look authoritative.

Lucida looked up at me, and there was a spark of panic in her eyes. "Please don't tell anyone you saw me up here. Look, I... I'm sorry I was smart with you. But, please, it's... it's not what you think..."

I was too taken aback at the change in her tone to reply right away. Lucida had never, in all the time I'd known her, presented herself to me as anything other than the pinnacle of bravado and swagger. Even at her lowest point, rotting away in a cell in Skye, she had nothing but cheek to offer me. And now she stood before me, her excuses and confidence exhausted after a few measly questions, sounding as scared and contrite as I'd ever heard her. I mean, for fuck's sake, she'd never even apologized to me for her role in the Prophecy, and here she was, begging my pardon for snooping around the archive and pleading with me not to turn her in? Something was very off here, and it wasn't Lucida's usual mischief.

"Are you okay?" I asked her, my voice soft and tentative. "Do you need help?"

Lucida made a sound, a tremulous burst of laughter that was also half a sob. "I... no, I'm fine."

"Fine is the single shittiest word in the English language," I pointed out.

"Too right it is," Lucida agreed, with a sad shake of her head.

"Can you tell me what you're looking for?" I asked her again.

A strange, vulnerable look came into Lucida's eyes, and for a moment, I really thought she may just open her mouth and tell me everything. She seemed to think the very same thing, because she threw a hand up in front of her mouth, as though to stop the confession from parting company with her lips. When she lowered it again, she had gotten a grip on herself.

"I already told you. I'm not looking for anything. Well, unless you reckon one of these here sketches would look nice on my wall." She snatched up a paper from the work table and held it up, pretending to eye it speculatively. The whole performance was rather half-hearted.

"Okay. I'm not going to say anything. I'm trusting you right now. Consider it a thank you for saving my life in the *príosún*. But... I just want to say... well, you can trust me. You don't always have to do everything yourself. It doesn't always have to be Lucida versus the world, you know."

Lucida's face twitched. It was an odd expression, like she couldn't decide whether to laugh or cry or destroy me with an angry diatribe. In the end, she swallowed all of it and, with a jerky nod of acknowledgement, pushed past me and out of the archive without another word.

I turned and watched her over my shoulder until her form was swallowed by the shadows of the corridor, and even several minutes after she vanished, I envisioned her marching back up the hallway, having decided to confess everything to me. Once my imagination had exhausted this possibility, I fell into a chair, put my head on my arms, and sank into contemplation.

Was I an absolute idiot for letting her go? A part of me—the part that clung most fiercely to the pain and terror of the Prophecy—was screaming at me to go after her, to demand a full explanation, or else walk straight to Celeste's office and report exactly what I'd seen. I couldn't much blame this part of myself; after all, Lucida had betrayed me on almost every possible level, and her betrayal of Hannah ran even deeper. It was not easy to suppress that kind of trauma, and no matter how many prisons Lucida helped me escape from, I didn't believe that I could ever trust her completely. No, some part of me would always be waiting for her to turn around and stab me in the back: that was immutable. On the other hand, the Lucida who had climbed through my bedroom window five years ago and the Lucida who had just left the archive were two very different women. The first, riding an intoxicating high of rebellion and impending revenge. The second, a battered hull desperately trying to weather the storm and searching for a port that would have her.

Jesus. When did I get so sentimental? What good was emotional vulnerability if it meant I was going to walk right into a trap? I sighed. I would reexamine my decision not to rat on Lucida in the morning, when I'd had a bit of sleep. And more than a bit of coffee.

§

My search of the archive took most of the night and, after a measly four hours of restless sleep and an exhausting day of work with Fiona, all of the next evening. To my intense disappointment, there was not a single item there that matched the catalog number from Agnes' tapestry. After searching the entire registry book, which listed every item and its catalog number, I manually searched through all of the papers, paintings, and artifacts, just to be sure. Every item in the archive started with the letters "FA," which I took to be an abbreviation for "Fairhaven Archives." "CA" must refer to another collection, or perhaps another place altogether, but where?

By the time I'd given up and stumbled into the dining hall for dinner, I was so exhausted I could barely function. I dropped into a seat next to Hannah and Milo.

Hannah smiled at my disgruntled expression. "Let me guess. No luck?"

"No luck," I confirmed. "Whatever Agnes' number is referencing, it's not in that archive. I think I might try down in the basement next, where all the Necromancer stuff is, but I don't know when the hell I'll have time to do it, because now I have to help Fiona interpret that sculpture."

I'd told Hannah and Milo about the sculpture right away, of course. My rules about keeping prophecies secret didn't apply to them, especially seeing as we frequently shared the same headspace.

"Where does Fiona want you to start?" Milo asked.

"With that weird rune on the dais stone. She says the library has a big collection of rune encyclopedias that I could—" I broke off abruptly as Savvy stumbled toward us with her tray. None of us had told her about the sculpture yet.

With a grunt of acknowledgment in my direction, Savvy practically fell into her chair and started attacking her food. For all my complaining about exhaustion, I felt downright chipper when I looked over at Savvy, who began nodding off over her bowl of soup within minutes.

"Sav? Are you okay?" I asked, pulling the soup bowl away before her face could land in it.

"Huh?" Savvy jolted upright, her spoon clattering to the floor. "Oh, sorry, mate. I'm just so bloody..." she stifled a yawn, "...tired."

Hannah gave a sympathetic smile as she handed Savvy a napkin so that she could wipe up the soup now splattered across her sleeve. "I can't imagine. Kiernan says the physical training is incredibly intense."

"No, I don't think it's that," Savvy said, blotting at her sleeve. "I mean, I reckon I can handle the exercise, it's just... I'm not sleeping well."

"How come?" I asked.

"I don't rightly know. I've always been a hell of a sleeper. Mum used to say it would take a brass band on a freight train to wake me up. But I've been waking up even more exhausted than when I turned in!"

"Maybe you need to go to bed earlier?" Milo suggested. "All that physical training—you probably need a couple more hours than you're used to."

"I've tried that!" Savvy said with an exasperated chuckle. "Last night when I turned in, it was barely seven thirty! When me alarm went off at five o'clock, I ought to have felt damn good—that was nearly ten hours of sleep! Instead, I was aching from top to bottom and felt as though I'd just barely closed my eyes!"

"That's so weird!" I said, frowning. "Are you waking up a lot? Or having nightmares maybe?"

"Not that I can remember," Savvy said. "I expected to be sore, what with all the training, but I feel like I've gone and slept on a bare wooden plank all night long."

"I wouldn't worry too much about it, Savvy," I said, with an encouraging pat on the shoulder. "You've only been at this for a couple of weeks. It's bound to get easier. Your body is still adjusting to a complete lifestyle change."

"Yeah, I suppose you're right. I mean, blimey, if you'd told me three months ago that I'd give up fags and drinking for cardio and kung fu, I'd have said you were taking the mickey."

"Exactly. Who even are you, anyway?" I asked seriously.

"I dunno, mate," Savvy said, and though she cracked a smile, it faded quickly. "I just hope I'm the person I thought I was when I set out to do this."

I reached over and squeezed her hand. "You are."

"I reckon we'll find out," Savvy said. "But cheers, mate."

I replaced the bowl of soup and watched her tuck into it, fighting all the while to keep her eyes open, and teetered on the edge of a decision: Should I tell Savvy about the sculpture?

On first consideration, the idea seemed to make sense. Of course, Savvy knew much more about her own experiences in Caomhnóir training then I did, though admittedly I was being kept pretty well-informed by both Savvy and Milo. Even so, perhaps the image would make sense to her. Perhaps it was even something that she had experienced as part of a training exercise or something like that. She may even be able to clarify whether the piece was prophetic or not, just by looking at it. The entire mystery might be solved at a single glance.

But then, I considered the other possibility. What if I showed it to her, and it was not familiar? What if it made no sense at all and instead, I scared the shit out of her by making her realize that she was the subject of a prophecy that nobody yet understood? If my time in dealing with prophecies had taught me anything, it was that knowing about a prophecy only ever made things worse. The constant efforts to understand it, to decipher it, to avoid it, or to guide it along the path to realization could drive a person to madness, and sometimes did.

No. This was not the right moment to involve Savvy. She had more than enough to deal with, struggling to prove herself in Caomhnóir training day in and day out without the additional and pressing weight of a possible prophecy resting on her shoulders. No, I would do what I could to decipher the sculpture myself, starting with that mysterious rune.

And I knew exactly the person who might be able to help.

§

Flavia's tiny office was tucked down a narrow hallway that opened up behind the furthest corners of the stacks in the Fairhaven library. All the Scribes had offices back there in that tiny rabbit warren of rooms stuffed full of crowded bookshelves, battered desks, and so much ancient knowledge that the very dust motes inside them seemed to tingle with it. I had only been back in this area once, to retrieve a box of scrolls that one of the other Scribes had pulled for Hannah's research. But Flavia spent most of her time here now, having been taken on full-time by the staff of the library.

Flavia's hiring had been, in part, a benevolent gesture. After all, Flavia couldn't return to the Traveler camp, not after choosing her independence and education in London over a life of isolation tucked deep in the woods with her clan. Not even after her attack was the Traveler Council willing to consider lifting her banishment and allowing her to return. There were even those among the Travelers who felt that what had happened to Flavia was karma—demonstrable proof that leaving the safety and security of the Traveler encampment led inevitably to punishment and disaster. Poor Flavia had been reduced to a cautionary tale, a tragic figure to be forgotten except when it was convenient to take her out, dust her off, and parade her around in front of other young Travelers whose heads might otherwise fill with dangerous notions of venturing out into the world.

However, the Council at Fairhaven did not keep her on merely because they pitied her. Flavia was an incredibly knowledgeable and accomplished Scribe, especially for someone so young. It was obvious that she would be an enormous asset to Fairhaven's own staff of Scribes. Flavia had studied texts that the Fairhaven Scribes would likely have sacrificed limbs to have access to, and she had an almost encyclopedic knowledge of Durupinen history. From a brief snatch of conversation I overheard between the Head Scribe and Siobhán, I gathered that the Traveler Council would be irate if they knew that Flavia had accepted the position at Fairhaven. It would be seen as a further betrayal, a peddling of Traveler knowledge amongst outsiders. Whether that was an exaggeration, I didn't know, but Flavia had accepted the position and had been diligently working in the library ever since, whatever the Traveler Council might think. If she had any doubts as to whether she should be there, she kept them to herself.

I found her precisely where I expected her to be, tucked into the chair behind her desk, her arms wrapped around her knees, and her face bent low over a scroll that had been spread across the surface of her desk. Her eyes moved back and forth rapidly from behind her bifocals, and a well-chewed pencil was clamped tightly between her teeth.

"Knock, knock," I said in lieu of actual knocking.

Flavia looked up, pencil still in mouth, looking mildly surprised, as she often did when emerging from her work, to discover that the world had continued to exist around her. She plucked the pencil from her mouth and set it down on the desk and then lifted her arms above her head stretching her stiff muscles.

"Oh, Jess! Hello. I didn't hear you come in," she said dazedly.

"No worries," I told her, smiling. "Am I interrupting something important? I can come back later."

"No, no, not at all," Flavia said, stifling a yawn with the back of her hand. "I was just going through this box of acquisitions and trying to figure out which collections everything should be sorted into. I should take a break anyway, I've been at it for a few hours, and my eyes are beginning to cross." She gave them a fierce rub behind her glasses. "What can I do for you?"

"I've got something here that I wanted you to take a look at, if you've got some time," I told her. I held up a scrap of paper on which I had drawn the rune from Fiona's sculpture.

"Let's have it, then," she said brightly, gesturing to the chair that had been wedged in against the other side of her desk.

I felt like one object too many in the cramped little space as I folded myself into the chair and handed the piece of paper across to Flavia. "It's a rune. Or, at least, I *think* it's a rune. Have you ever seen it before?"

Flavia stared down at the paper in bewilderment for a few moments, before replying, "No. No, I'm afraid I haven't. Are you quite sure it's a rune?"

"I... well, it *looked* like one, so I kind of just assumed," I said, feeling the familiar sinking weight of disappointment. I had been so sure Flavia would recognize it.

"Where did you see it?" Flavia asked. "A bit of context might help."

I hesitated and then decided to tell only part of the truth. "It's... well, I didn't see it anywhere physical. It was part of a Visitation. A Muse thing."

Flavia just nodded, accepting my explanation. "Hmm, I see. So, a spirit provided the image, and you copied it down?"

"Yes, I suppose so," I said, glad I could at least answer this part truthfully.

"Right. Well, let's have a closer look," Flavia said. She rolled up the scroll she had been reading and tucked it neatly back into a box on the corner of her desk. She then heaved the box up off the desk and set it down heavily on the floor before twisting around to the bookshelf behind her desk. She ran a slender finger along the spines until she found what she was looking for, a faded red leather-bound book which she plucked from the shelf and opened onto the desktop between us. Her office was so small that she accomplished all of this without walking a single step. She sat back down, adjusted her glasses and began flipping through the book, which appeared to be a rune encyclopedia.

"It's amazing how many places runes can still be found, and how little is understood generally about them," Flavia said to herself, as she flipped through the pages. "So many cultures used runic alphabets at one time, before the introduction of the Latin alphabet, so it has been easier than one might expect to mask the long history of Durupinen rune use, helping us to keep it secret."

"You mean our runes aren't unique to the Durupinen?" I asked in surprise.

"Not at all. We have simply used them in unique ways," Flavia said. "We unlocked the power in them, in combination with natural elements, that have made our Castings possible."

"I probably should have known that," I said with a sheepish grin.

"Probably," Flavia agreed, with a wink. "But there is a downside to our having adopted a common set of symbols as well. When our own ancient relics or sites have been lost to us, it has been very difficult to definitively identify them centuries later by runes alone. It is thought, therefore, that many of our oldest experimentations with runes have been lost."

"So, there might be runes we don't know about?" I asked.

"I think it unlikely, although we have been known to combine runes, and that may be what has happened here," Flavia said, tapping her finger on a paragraph at the top of a page toward the end of the book. "Ancient Durupinen would sometimes layer runes one upon the other in an effort to unlock some combination of their affinities. Such experimentations, as with all Castings, could go very wrong. In the end, it was found that most Castings were most effective when runes were used individually. But a few obscure Castings do exist that require the layering of several runes, resulting in a symbol that looks unfamiliar."

"That's pretty cool," I remarked, wishing I had something more substantive to contribute that didn't make me sound like a delinquent student of Durupinen history. "So, is that what you think it is? A layered symbol?"

"It just might be, but if it is, it is not one that has been used in any Casting that we have a record of. There are nine known layered runes. This is not one of them," Flavia said. "And yet, if you look at it carefully..."

She snatched a notepad from the top drawer of her desk and tore off the top page, laying my rendering of the rune beside it. All of her drowsiness of a few moments before was gone now, burned away by the bright flame of her intellectual curiosity. She picked the mutilated pencil up off the desk and began to draw. "You see, here we have the rune for 'protection' which you probably recognize... or, I don't know, do you? It's one of the more common—"

"Yes, I've seen that one. I'm not completely useless," I grumbled. The rune was one of several used in Warding spaces against spirits, and so it was one of the very first runes that I had become familiar with.

"Right, sorry," Flavia said with a fleeting smirk. "Anyway, you can see how this rune has the same elements, but with additions here and here." She pointed out the markings, a small diamond with a circle inside it and a curved line with a triangle on its end like the point of an arrow. "It's possible that what you have here is a rune for protection with two other runes drawn on top of it." She drew two more runes, each consisting of the same vertical line up the center, a shared feature with the protection rune. Then to the first, she added the concentric circle and diamond to its center, and to the second, she added the curved line with the triangle tip. Next, she ripped the paper upon which she had drawn into three pieces, each containing one of the runes. Finally, she placed them one on top of the other, adjusting them so that each rune lined up perfectly with the one below it. "You see? What appears to be a single, unfamiliar rune is actually an amalgamation of three familiar runes."

"Oh, wow," I said, watching Flavia remove and then replace the layered papers one by one, constructing and deconstructing the rune as she did so. "Yeah, that would definitely explain it."

"So, if I'm correct that this is, in fact, a layered rune, then here are the components," Flavia said, and she laid the three pieces of paper side by side again, pointing to each one as she named them. "Protection. Connection. Open."

We both frowned down at the runes for a few seconds, taking them in. "What does it mean?"

"Your guess is as good as mine," Flavia replied.

I snorted. "Oh, come on. We both know *that's* not true."

Flavia giggled. "As you like. Well, the truth is that I'm not ready to venture a guess. Can you tell me anything else about how this symbol came to you? It might help."

I hesitated and, again, decided on part of the truth. "It... I got a flash of the Geatgrima as well. The one right down in the Fairhaven courtyard. The rune had been carved on it. And there was a Caomhnóir there as well."

Flavia's eyes narrowed behind her spectacles. "There are many runes carved into the Geatgrima. Is this one of them?"

"I haven't looked for myself, but I don't think so."

"Hmm. Well, let's make sure, shall we?" Flavia said, popping up from her seat and pulling an oversized cardigan off the back of it. She slid her arms into it and rolled up the ends of the sleeves, looking like a child playing dress-up in her father's clothes.

"Now?" I asked in surprise.

"Why not?" Flavia asked with a smile. "No time like the present."

§

I was concerned that the courtyard might be busy. After all, it was early in the evening and there were likely to still be a good many people out on the grounds. The last thing I needed was to attract attention and awkward questions about what we were doing. Luckily, however, the central courtyard was completely deserted as we stepped out into the last rosy moments before twilight set in.

The Geatgrima stood at the center of the courtyard, presiding over the space like a monarch on a throne. It rose up from a round stone dais into a graceful, almost gothic pointed archway. The stones were so old and worn that it seemed a miracle the whole thing had not crumbled to dust a century ago, and yet it exuded an air of permanence—an assurance that it was both eternal and ineffable. Vividly, I recalled the first time I had ever encountered it, nervous and trembling, clutching a candle, about to be sworn to its service for the rest of my life. Even I, as reluctant as I had been to be there, could not help but be drawn closer to it, to feel the lure of its awesome power. I had at once both feared and revered it, felt connected to and entirely within the grip of its energy. A Geatgrima, it had been explained to me, was a physical manifestation of the Gateway that lived inside every Durupinen. They were constructed to mark great seats of clan power, where Durupinen had lived for so long and performed so many Crossings that the fabric between the worlds of the living and the dead had become very thin. The Fairhaven Geatgrima had also been the site where Hannah had, after being manipulated by the Necromancers, reversed the Gateways and nearly brought about the end of the Durupinen. Even now, I had a hard time tearing my eyes from it to search the courtyard for observers who might have gone unnoticed.

Flavia, who no doubt had a much more thorough understanding of the Geatgrima and its powerful attractions, kept her eyes largely averted from the archway as she walked the perimeter of the courtyard, peering into the apses and niches until she was sure we were alone. "Right, then," she said. "Let's have a gander, shall we? Do you remember where you saw the rune in your vision?"

"Um... I'm not sure exactly," I hedged. "Somewhere around the dais on the bottom."

We approached the Geatgrima and, keeping our eyes cast down, began scanning the rounded stones for any sign of the mysterious layered rune. Many of the carvings were weathered and fading, so that several times we had to examine a marking carefully to be sure that it was not the symbol we were searching for. We located each of the marks individually, but not close enough to each other that they could possibly be meant to be interpreted together. Finally, after circling the dais twice, we were forced to conclude that the marking we were looking for was not there. Its absence left me with a fluttering feeling of anxiety in my chest.

Flavia pushed her glasses back up the bridge of her nose and pierced me with a stare from behind the windows of her lenses. "Well, that's that, I suppose," she said. "It's not here."

"No, it's not," I agreed.

"You don't look surprised about that," Flavia said.

I looked up at her and returned her penetrating gaze. "Neither do you."

Flavia sat down upon the edge of the stone dais and sighed. "Jess, you... of course you don't have to answer this question, but... this 'Muse thing' you experienced, where you saw this symbol... do you think it might have been another prophecy, like the one you had the last time you were with the Travelers?"

The last vestiges of my pretense dropped away. Why was I hesitating to share the truth with Flavia—Flavia, who had only ever proved herself to be trustworthy and invaluable to me? Flavia, who had once saved my life, and then helped to rescue Irina, all because I chose to confide in her about a prophecy?

I sank to my knees in the grass beside her. "I'm not sure. But I think it might be. The vision wasn't even mine, it was Fiona's. It came in the form of a sculpture. The rune should be somewhere around here," I said, placing my hand on a blank stretch of stone just to the left of where Flavia sat, "and the Caomhnóir who stood guarding it was Savvy."

Flavia's eyes widened to outlandish proportions behind her glasses. "And this sculpture... where is it now?"

"Up in the Fairhaven Archivess."

"And has Fiona ever created such a thing before?"

"No. Well, I mean, she's created spirit-induced art before. She's a Muse, but she's never showed any signs of being a Seer as well. Her mother created some prophetic art once, but the struggle to recreate and understand it drove her mad."

"Oh, my. That's dreadful," Flavia said in little more than a whisper.

"I'm sorry I didn't tell you all of that to begin with," I told her. "But I'm just not really sure what's going on yet. The sculpture might be prophetic, and it might not. And if it is, I have no idea what to make of it, and I just..."

Flavia held up a hand at once. "Don't apologize. Prophecies and visions are... delicate. You could negate their very existence just by sharing them with someone. I understand, Jess."

I exhaled, feeling the knot of anxiety loosen its hold slightly. "Thank you."

"You haven't told Savvy, have you?" Flavia asked.

"No, and I don't intend to," I said.

Flavia nodded solemnly. "That's wise. Yes, I think that's very wise, at least for the time being."

"What do you think I should do now?" I asked.

"Well, I think you should let me do some digging," Flavia said, waving her little collection of papers around. "Let me see if this truly is the first recording of such a symbol. If it has ever been used before, I'll find it, I promise."

I grinned. "Oh, I have no doubt about that. You're like a library wizard. No, wizards are way too obvious, you need to be much sneakier than a wizard. A library *ninja*. Is that a thing? It should be a thing."

"I'm going to have it put on a plaque and hung on my door," Flavia said firmly.

"That might spoil the whole 'sneaky' descriptor, but I'll allow it," I said.

12

VIGIL

ANOTHER WEEK PASSED, and still my two mysteries remained very much unsolved. After searching the Seer archive, I scoured the library, the Necromancer artifact collection in the dungeon, and even, with Mrs. Mistlemoore's permission, the medical archive in the back of the hospital ward. The result of each search was the same: a dead end. I began questioning myself. Was it ludicrous to believe my discovery in the tapestry had been a message? What if I was just deluding myself? Day by day, I could feel the conviction inside me ebbing away.

"Why do you doubt yourself, love?" Finn asked me one Saturday morning as we shared a rare hour together walking the grounds. The chill of fall had set in now, and the breeze that whipped my hair around my face carried fallen leaves in swirling patterns through the air.

"Because I'm making absolutely no sense? Because I've convinced myself a message has lain in wait for me for hundreds of years before I was born, and that's utterly insane?" I suggested.

"You're listening to your gut," Finn said, taking my hand. "That's one of the very first things we teach to Novitiates, and you would do well to remember it, too."

"It's not feeling like very good advice at the moment," I sighed.

"Jess, have you got a mo'?" I turned to see Savvy approaching us from across the lawn. Her voice was casual but her expression was strange—cheerful, but fragile, like one wrong word would shatter the illusion. "Sorry to interrupt," she added, nodding at Finn.

"Sure, what's up, Sav?" I asked.

"Can you... would you mind coming by my room right quick?"

"What—"

But Savvy shook her head just a fraction of an inch, widening her eyes and casting them in Finn's direction. I swallowed the rest of my question. My curiosity deepened, but I didn't press her for any more details. "Of course," I said. "I'm right behind you. Finn, come by after shift change, okay?"

"Of course, love," Finn replied, looking curious, but waving us off.

Savvy chatted all the way to her room about completely inane things. She talked so much that I didn't even get a chance to respond with more than an occasional "yeah" or "cool," and what was more, she barely seemed to be talking to me at all. Her entire monologue appeared to be for the benefit of the people, both living and dead, who were passing us in the halls. Savvy kept nodding her head and shouting greetings to everyone we passed, and even started whistling as we made our way past a large group of Novitiates in the front entrance hall.

When at last we arrived at her room and were safely on the other side of the door, Savvy's entire being seemed to sag. She let out a long sigh, and when she looked up at me, her eyes were dilated with fear.

"Jess, mate," she whispered. "I think I've gone 'round the twist."

"You mean, more than usual?" I said in a pathetic attempt to inject a little levity into this sudden and dark turn of the conversation.

Savvy shook her head. "Now's not the time for a lark, Jess. I'm dead serious."

I dropped the last pretense of humor. "Savvy, I'm sure you're not crazy. Tell me what's going on."

"Remember how I told you that I've been waking up knackered, no matter how early I turn in?" Savvy asked.

"Yeah."

"Well, it's still happening. I feel like a zombie. And then this morning, I noticed this." She pushed past me to her closet, where several pairs of shoes were lined up side by side, including her Caomhnóir boots. She picked up one of the boots and held it out toward my face, so that I was looking at the mud-caked sole of it.

"What am I supposed to be looking at?" I asked, perplexed.

"The mud! Look at all the mud! They're filthy!" Savvy cried.

"Well, yeah, but is that so surprising?" I asked. "It rained all day yesterday, Sav, and I saw you all, training in the downpour. It makes total sense that your boots would be covered in mud."

Savvy thrust the boot closer to my face so that I had to back away from it. "I cleaned and polished these boots before I went to sleep last night," she said in a slightly hysterical whisper. "They were spotless. We stand inspection every morning, and we get docked points on the day's work if our uniform doesn't start the day fit for tea with the Queen. When I turned in, you could have admired your reflection in the leather. And now look at it!"

I frowned. "Do you think someone stole them out of your room or something?"

"What sort of daft prick steals a pair of boots, wears them, and then puts them back?" Savvy snorted.

"I don't know, it was just a—"

"And anyway, my door was locked when I woke up—from the inside. I always lock it, in case some Novitiate decides he'd like to have another go at hazing me. And another thing. I took a long shower last night and dried my hair. But then, when I woke up, my hair was all tangled and wet again, and I found this." She gestured over to her bed. Even from halfway across the room, I could see that her pillow was smeared in dirt, and there were several small bits of leaf and twig lying on the pillowcase.

"I woke up filthy, damp, and stiff as a board!" Savvy cried. "I had to shower all over again. Remember I told you before, I woke up in the morning feeling like I'd been out all night? Well, here's the thing: I think I *have* been out all night. I think I might be sleepwalking."

I stared at her stricken face and tried to think of something to say to contradict the evidence in front of us, but I could think of nothing.

"That seems to make sense," I said. "But that doesn't mean you're crazy, Sav, it probably just means you're incredibly stressed out. I remember reading that about sleepwalking—that it can be a sign of stress. Have you ever done it before, like when you were a kid or anything?"

Savvy shook her head. "Nope. Not once, that I know of. I've always slept like the dead. Well, I guess that expression is bollocks, knowing what we know about the dead, eh?" she added with a half-hearted chuckle.

"Well, you've been through a lot in the past few months. What with Bertie and Phoebe, and now the Caomhnóir training—no wonder you're sleepwalking!"

"Sure, I get all that, but... where am I going? What am I doing? By the looks of things, I'm making it all the way out onto the grounds! What if I fall in the lake and drown myself? What if I wander all the way down the drive and get myself run over by a passing motorist? And how the bugger am I supposed to get any *rest*?" She dropped the boot, sending chunks of dried mud all over her floor, and sunk down onto her bed, succumbing to a storm of tears.

I crossed the room and slid onto the bed beside her, throwing my arm over her shaking shoulders and giving her a long squeeze. She continued to sob, her voice shuddering. "I'm sorry, Jess," she said, drawing her sleeve across her face and sniffing loudly. "I'm sorry to go all to pieces like this on you, but I don't know who else to talk to. Phoebe's still off at her mum's, and my family don't know enough about Fairhaven to help me sort this all out. And I can't complain to anyone in the Caomhnóir ranks, or they'll think I'm going soft and use it as an excuse to chuck me out of training. I haven't got anyone else and I'm going spare here."

"Savvy, you're one of my best friends. I *want* to be the person you come to when you're going spare," I told her. "Just tell me how I can help you."

"I dunno," Savvy said. "Unless... you wouldn't be willing to sleep in here tonight, would you?"

"Of course, I would!" I said. "Only, I don't think you're supposed to wake a sleepwalker. Isn't that something people say? Doesn't it make the sleepwalker freak out or something? I could just try to lead you back to your bed and get you to lie back down."

"I don't want you to wake me up or put me back to bed," Savvy said, lifting her red, blotchy face off her arms and looking right at me. "I want you to follow me."

"Follow you?" I asked, taken aback. "You mean just... just let you sleepwalk and see what happens?"

"Well, yeah," Savvy said. "I know it sounds a bit mad, but I'm dead curious now. I want to know where I'm going and what I'm doing! And I'd also like some reassurance that this is just a dream thing and not a... a... ghost thing."

"Why do you think it might be a ghost thing?" I asked.

Savvy raised one eyebrow at me. "Asks the girl who once woke up to find herself drawing pretty pictures on a narrow castle ledge three bloody floors up from the ground."

I grinned sheepishly. "Fair point," I said. "My sleeping brain has been a free-for-all for spirit activity hasn't it, even in a Warded bedroom."

"So, you'll do it?" Savvy asked.

"Of course, I will," I replied. "Tonight, the world's weirdest sleepover shall commence."

§

Fifteen minutes later, I opened my bedroom door only to be frightened back into the hallway by an ear-splitting shriek. I leapt backwards, tripped over my own pant leg, and fell to the floor.

"What the hell—" I shouted.

"Jess!" Hannah's face poked out into the hallway, where I was picking myself up off the floor. "Oh, I'm sorry! Here, let me help you up."

"Next time, you can just feel free to say 'hello,'" I grumbled as Hannah grabbed my arm and helped hoist me up.

"It's not you, it's my legislation! It's passed a committee vote and they are going to put it to the full clans!" Hannah cried. Still clutching tightly to my arm, she pulled me into our room, where Milo and Karen were both reading a piece of paper Karen had in her hand.

"It's a great achievement," Karen said, looking up from the paper and smiling. "A few short years ago, this would have been killed in committee and never seen the light of day, let alone a vote. I'm so proud of you, Hannah."

"You helped me so much, Karen," Hannah said breathlessly. "I never would have been able to phrase it properly without your edits."

Karen waved a hand dismissively. "All I did was close up a few loopholes. You did the real work. Take the credit for it!"

"I never thought I'd be so excited about something as très dull as the legislative process," Milo said. "Honestly, AP Gov had me wanting to claw my flawlessly-lined eyes out."

Hannah turned her glowing face on me. "We're one step closer, Jess! For you and Finn. For Mom and Carrick. For everyone whose life has ever been ruined by these stupid laws."

I smiled at her and pulled her into a fierce hug. "Thank you, Hannah. This is just awesome news."

"I can't wait to tell Kiernan!" Hannah said, breathless with excitement. "Do you think... is the library open yet, or is it too early?"

I checked my watch. "Nope, it's after nine. The library should be open now."

"He's going to be so excited!" Hannah cried. She was halfway to the door when Karen called out to her.

"Hannah, they've attached a list of questions and points of clarification," Karen said, flipping to the second page of the document. "They want us to answer them so that they can attach them as an addendum to the legislation before sending it out to the other clans to read. It all looks pretty standard, but we should get started on them right away. The sooner the Council has them, the sooner they can schedule a vote."

"What? Oh, okay. I'll take it down to the library with me and get to work on them," Hannah said, holding her hand out for the paper. "Can you meet me there?"

"Not today, I've got a meeting in the city and then a conference call, but I'll touch base with you tonight, and we can work out a game plan," Karen said, picking up her purse and glancing at her phone before dropping it inside. "I should be going. I'll walk you down."

She and Hannah disappeared into the hallway, Karen's arm thrown around Hannah's shoulders. I turned to Milo, sure he was thinking the very same thing I was thinking.

"She can't wait to tell Kiernan," I said, waggling my eyebrows like a middle-schooler.

"Hannah and Kiernan, sittin' in a tree..." Milo began.

"K-I-S-S-I-N-G!" we both finished with a snort of laughter.

"I will always have a deep appreciation for your willingness to sink to my level of immaturity," I told Milo.

Milo laughed. "Bitch, please. I am permanently seventeen, and an emotionally stunted seventeen at that—thanks, Dad!" He gave a sarcastic two-thumbs-up. "I am suspended in a permanent state of nonsense and immaturity. Someday you will be forty and I will still be fawning over boy bands and lamenting whether someone 'likes' me or '*like*-likes' me. It is both your blessing and your curse, sweetness."

"Well, I consider it a blessing for now. If you ever mention me being forty again, though, I'll Cage you," I said with a saccharine smile.

"Noted," Milo said with a wink.

The wink made me think of Savvy. "Hey! Kind of a weird question, but in your nighttime wanderings over the last couple of weeks, you haven't run into Savvy at all have you?"

Milo's eyebrows contracted in confusion. "Savvy? At night? No, why?"

"Well, it's just... she thinks she's been sleepwalking," I told him.

"Wow, really?" Milo said. "What makes her think that?"

"She's waking up exhausted, and her boots look like they've been worn outside."

"She thinks she's sleepwalking all the way out onto the grounds?" Milo asked, incredulous. "Don't sleepwalkers usually just wander around their rooms or raid their fridge or something?"

"Normally, yeah, I think so, but she's definitely been outside, and she has no memory of it."

Milo shook his head. "That's freaky."

"I know."

"But she should ask some of the other Caomhnóir," Milo said. "If she's walking all the way from her room out onto the grounds, some of them are bound to have seen her! They're stationed at all the entrances. I mean, how would she even get out of the castle without passing one of them?"

"Huh. I hadn't thought of that," I said. "But I know she doesn't want to draw any attention from the Caomhnóir... well, any more attention than she's already getting, I mean. She doesn't want them to think she's cracking under the pressure, you know?"

Milo nodded sagely. "Yeah, I get it. I was the king of that charade in my day."

"So, she asked me to sleep in her room tonight, just in case she does it again," I said.

"You want me to do it instead? I miss my old job of staring at you while you slept to ensure you didn't climb out the window onto the roof," Milo offered, batting his eyelashes.

I rolled my eyes. "No, I think I can handle it. But if I need back-up, you'll be my first call."

"Of course, I will," Milo said, grinning. "I'm on speed dial inside your head."

Twelve hours later, I was curled up in front of Savvy's crackling bedroom fireplace, sketching and drinking a cup of tea while she went through her nightly routine. Well, actually, I wasn't getting much sketching done, mostly because I couldn't stop watching Savvy as she worked diligently through an hour of drilling herself on Caomhnóir code phrases, meticulously polishing her boots and ironing and laying out her uniform for the next day. It was, frankly, bizarre to watch someone being so organized and responsible, knowing that just a few weeks ago, her bedtime routine had consisted of falling, fully clothed and made-up, into her bed immediately upon stumbling into her room at some ungodly hour after a night of drunken shenanigans. Honestly, she was lucky if she remembered to stub out her cigarette first.

Savvy looked up from creasing her collar and caught me staring. She smirked self-consciously. "What are you gawking at, then?"

"Nothing, sorry, it's just... I'm starting to wonder if Tia Vezga is somehow inhabiting your body."

Savvy threw back her head and roared with laughter. It was a wonderful sound—one she hadn't made very often recently. "Yeah, I bet I look a sight, don't I? I barely recognize myself these days."

"Is that what you wanted?" I asked her, my smile fading. "Not to recognize yourself?"

Savvy shrugged and dropped her eyes to the ironing board again. "I dunno, if I'm honest. Maybe? Being myself hasn't exactly been a lark recently, and I don't just mean since Bertie copped it. I ain't had a real direction or sense of purpose for ages. It helped a bit when I had Frankie to mentor, but she's really adjusted well now. I reckon she doesn't need me much anymore. And now, with no Gateway..." Her voice trailed off.

"I know it hasn't been easy," I said. "And I know this training is anything but easy. I just want to make sure it's worth it—that you aren't just punishing yourself."

Savvy looked up, and her eyes were wide with surprise. "Punishing myself? No! This is the best I've felt in a long time! Well, I mean, besides how bloody tired I am, but that's nothing to do with the training, not really. I'm motivated for the first time, maybe ever. I'm getting pushed to my limits and I've found out how rewarding that can feel. I'm not just proving myself to Seamus and the lads, sod 'em! I'm proving myself to me, and it feels brilliant! And when it's all over, I'm going to have a job that really matters. No more stumbling arse over tit through my life anymore. I'm going to wake up every day knowing that I'm making a real difference. That might sound like a load of sentimental waffle, but I mean it."

"Bet you want a cigarette and a beer right now though, huh?" I said with a wicked grin.

"Mate, you have no bloody idea," Savvy groaned.

We laughed, and Savvy, at last satisfied with the state of her uniform, unplugged the iron and folded up the table. Then she climbed into bed, tugging the blanket up over her chest.

"You sure you don't mind if I turn in now?" she asked, the words nearly lost in an enormous yawn.

"Not at all," I said. "You need the rest. Maybe you'll sleep better, just knowing there's someone here."

§

I had no memory of dozing off, so I had no idea how long I'd been asleep, but quite suddenly, something jolted me awake. My sketchpad had slipped to the floor along with my pencil, and my head had drooped at an awkward angle, leaving my neck feeling stiff and cramped. I massaged it, blinking the blurriness out of my eyes and staring around. The fire in the grate had burned out completely: it was nothing but a pile of glowing embers now, casting just enough light to make out the shapes in the room. I squinted over in the direction of Savvy's bed, but I couldn't tell if she was actually in it or not. I got up from the sofa, pulled my sweater more tightly around myself to ward off the chill, and tiptoed over to the edge of the bed.

It was empty.

A panicked feeling began in my stomach and rose like water up through my chest and into my throat, filling me up and making me feel as though I were drowning. *Calm down, Jess,* I told myself. *Maybe you haven't completely screwed this up. Maybe she's just in the bathroom or something.*

"Savvy?" I called out, turning on the spot and squinting into the dark corners of the room, as though expecting to find her inexplicably crouching in one of them, preparing to leap out and scare the shit out of me as a joke. Of course, she wasn't there. I ran over to the door, ready to pull it open and search the corridor, but I froze. The deadbolt was still secured. Just as Savvy had mentioned on previous occasions, the door was still locked from the inside.

So, where was she?

This question was still rocketing around inside my head when Milo's frantic voice broke through, making me jump so badly that I tripped over one of Savvy's discarded slippers and tumbled to the floor.

"Jess? Jess, are you there? Are you awake? Oh my God!"

I clamped my hands down over my ears to stop my head from ringing with the force of Milo's emotions. "Milo, for the love of God, stop shrieking! I'm awake! But I don't know where Savvy is! She's not in her bed, and I don't know where she's..."

"She's out here! She's out here, and I don't know how the hell she's... You've got to stop her, Jess!" Milo's shrieks bombarded my brain.

"Out where? Stop her from doing what? What are you talking about, Milo?"

"She's climbing down the side of the fucking building like she's Spider-Man or something!" Milo squealed, far beyond the point of being able to calm down.

"Climbing down the... *what?*" I asked, my voice weak with fear. "But how did she...?"

"She climbed out the window!" Milo cried. "She just heaved it open and thrust herself out of it and started climbing. It's still open, go over to the window!"

Heart hammering, I flew across the room, banging into several different pieces of furniture in the dark in my haste to get to the window, which was still wide open. The sash had been thrown wide, and the cool night air was whistling through it from the grounds. Throwing caution to the wind, I thrust my entire head and shoulders out of the window and looked down.

Sure enough, there was Savvy, some ten or so feet below me, scrambling her way down the rock face of the castle like a professional mountaineer. Each movement was swift and sure — there was no hesitation, no fear. It was, I realized, as if she had climbed down the face of the castle a hundred times before, as though her hands and feet knew exactly where to find each crevice and fissure that made her descent possible. She was wearing her full Caomhnóir uniform, as well as the boots that she had so carefully polished and left by her door. I opened my mouth to call out to her, but then quickly shut it again. Instead, I called out to Milo inside my head.

"I don't want to try to speak to her," I said, my fear making every word vibrate and shudder over the taut strings of our mental connection. "What if she's asleep again? What if I wake her up and she gets startled and loses her grip?"

"No, no you're right, you can't call out to her. It's too risky," Milo said, and I could feel waves of calming energy, washing through my head, forcing both of us to settle down with its steady rhythm. "Let's not panic," Milo went on, and at last his voice stopped making my ears ring. "Whether she's asleep or awake, she seems to know exactly what she's doing. She's halfway down as it is. Let's just let her get on with it, and keep watching her to make sure she gets safely to the ground."

"How in the world did you spot her?" I asked. "Was it just sheer chance that you were passing by or...?"

"Let's just say I decided to keep an eye on things, even though you said you didn't need my help," Milo said with just a hint of sheepishness. "No offense, but I just thought having two people on the look-out was better than one, especially if one of those two people had no desire or need for sleep."

"Thank you," I said earnestly. "Thank God you did, or I would have missed all of this completely." I could only imagine Savvy's face in the morning when she awoke to find her clothes and boots sodden and filthy, her body aching and exhausted and me, snoring away on the couch, unable to tell her anything about what had happened to her.

We watched the rest of Savvy's dissent in silence, aside from the occasional gasp of horror when she made a movement that looked especially precarious. At last, when she was about four feet from the grass, she sprang out from the wall and dropped as lightly as a cat to the ground below. Part of me wished I had thought to pull out my phone and video the whole thing; never in her wildest dreams would Savvy believe she was capable of what we had just witnessed her do. But Savvy wasn't pausing for a photo op. Immediately, she stood up, dusted herself off, and started jogging around the side of the castle.

"Milo, you've got to follow her!" I cried as the sudden realization struck me that I was about to lose her. There was no way I could follow her down the wall unless someone stood under me holding a mattress I could land on, and she was already halfway along the south side of the castle.

"Already on it," Milo replied at once, and down below I caught the barest glimpse of his form—a pale, ephemeral shimmer that darted from shadow to shadow off in the same direction.

"Try not to lose sight of her," I told him. "But if you do, make for the central courtyard."

"Why the central courtyard?" Milo asked.

"Just a hunch," I said. "I'll get down to the grounds as fast as I can."

I slid my feet hastily into my boots, thankful that I had opted the day before for some ankle boots rather than some of my more complicated knee-high footwear that required several minutes each to lace up. Then I grabbed Savvy's jacket, not having thought to bring my own, and pulled my arms into it as I began to sprint down the corridor and toward the front doors as quickly as I could. The sound of my boots pounding down the entrance hall staircase sent the Caomhnóir posted there into a flurry of panic. I saw them snapping to attention and placing their hands firmly upon their staffs as they saw me racing into view. One of them made a movement as though he might try to block my progress out the front doors. I practically pinned him to the wall with my glare.

"Excuse me, I'm going out," I said pointedly.

The Caomhnóir, who looked barely older than a Novitiate, turned and glanced at his partner, as though asking silently for advice on how to handle the obviously hysterical female before him. But he merely shrugged helplessly, and so the first Caomhnóir turned back to me. "What do you need to go out for at this time of night?" he asked lamely.

"Oh, I just thought I'd take a nice stroll down None-of-Your-Fucking-Business Lane," I told him. "There are no curfews in place, and I am a Tracker. I can go where I damn well please, whenever I damn well please, and I don't owe anyone any explanations. Now excuse you, you're in my way."

Looking like he just been slugged in the face, the Caomhnóir stepped aside with a dazed expression, and I pushed my shoulder against the massive front door, using all my weight to push it open just enough to slip through. The wind that met me on the other side was cold and clean smelling, with a frosty bite that tingled my nose with the promise of approaching winter. But the shiver that ran down my spine as I took off across the lawns had nothing to do with the chill. I don't think that I was scared that something was going to happen to Savvy — she seemed to be more than in control of herself, at least physically. But there was a creeping feeling nonetheless making its way up my spine, a feeling that I associated with the onset of my prophetic art. And it was as though my body knew exactly what I was about to see as I rounded the far corner of the castle, slipped through one of the archways, and skidded to a stop in the central courtyard.

And there it was, a familiar image, every detail of which I had studied and memorized even as it rose from formlessness at Fiona's deft and skillful hands. Savvy, her chest thrust out, stood at attention facing the great, mystic arch of the Geatgrima. Her eyes were wide open and yet, she was unseeing, for she did not flinch or turn around or in any way acknowledge my existence as I carefully stepped in a wide circle around her, taking her in from all angles. It was as though the Geatgrima had cast its spell over her, as though the rest of the world had fallen away and it was just Savvy and the Gateway, locked in an intimate contemplation of each other. It was not until I had walked half the circumference of the great Summoning Circle that I saw the final element that made Fiona's prophetic image complete. The mysterious rune, the one that Flavia and I had been diligently searching for through the pages of our history, had been carefully drawn upon the central dais stone with the dark ash of a half-burnt piece of wood, which had been discarded in the patchy grass nearby.

I expelled a breath I did not realize I had been holding and a strange sense of calm came over me. Although I still did not fully understand what I was seeing, although I knew the anxiety and the hundreds of questions would come, for a brief moment, I had a sense of completeness, knowing that an event that had once been prophecy was now reality. There was a relief in that, somehow. A sense of rhythm and rightness where once there had only been confusion. I let the feeling fill me up completely, and then seep out of me, relishing what brief relief it could give me. As the last of it drained away, Milo's voice filled up the void that it left behind, and I came back to a sense of this new reality.

"What the hell is she doing?" Milo asked, and though I knew he was trying to keep his voice quiet, it rose in an anxious squeak. "What's going on, Jess?"

I shook my head. "I don't know," I said.

"Well, you must have some idea!" Milo said, a bit impatiently. "That was more than just a hunch, wasn't it, that she was going to come to the courtyard? You knew she was coming here, didn't you?"

I looked at him, and I could see my own fear, my own stricken anxiety staring back at me. "It's the sculpture, Milo. The one Fiona made. The one I told you about."

Milo's eyes went wide as the realization hit him, too. "Oh my God," he whispered. "This is what you described. This was what Fiona saw."

"Yes."

"But... but what does it *mean?* What's happening?"

"I wish I knew, Milo. I really wish I knew."

We turned from each other and looked back at Savvy. Her expression was at odds with her stance. With her chin thrust up and her shoulders thrown back, a fierce expression would have looked at home on her face. It was strange and contrasting then, to see that an expression of utter tranquility had come to rest upon her features. She gazed at the Geatgrima with a deep serenity that was, quite frankly, unsettling. It felt like an expression that ought to be reserved for someone who understood something beyond the living realm. It was as though one of those deep, abiding questions that lives within all of us—human beings with no sense of security about our future—had spontaneously answered itself deep inside her. It terrified me to see that peace on her face. I suddenly found myself struggling against an almost overwhelming impulse to race forward, grab Savvy by the arm, and drag her away from the Geatgrima so that I could break whatever powerful grip it had on her.

"Do you feel that?" Milo whispered.

"Feel what?" I asked.

"There's something there... *between* them," Milo said.

I scanned the empty air between Savvy and the Geatgrima, but I didn't notice anything unusual. I turned back to Milo. "What are you talking about?"

"It's just a feeling," Milo said, sounding almost hypnotized.

"It's... I can't really describe it. It's like the Geatgrima is... *reaching* for her."

"What?" My voice was sharp, like a twig snap in a silent forest. "What do you mean, '*reaching for her?*'"

"Look, I told you it was hard to describe," Milo said, shaking off some of that hypnotized tone and replacing it with annoyance. "But you know that pull that the Geatgrima has, that connection to the Aether? I swear, I can feel it blossoming out from the Geatgrima into the space between them. Just focus on it, Jess. Just focus, and I think you'll feel it, too."

Alarmed, I turned back to stare at Savvy and the Geatgrima once more, searching for any sign or signal of what Milo had just described. Since Milo was a spirit, his connection to the Geatgrima was different than mine. It was purer—unhindered by the interference of a mortal body and all the distractions and filters that came with it. It may just have been the power of suggestion, but the longer I looked, the more I began to think that I understood what Milo meant.

Usually, being near the Geatgrima meant that you were almost unconsciously drawn to it. You couldn't help but inch toward it until you caught yourself and made a conscious effort to stand your ground. If you never came to your senses, it was quite possible that you could just follow its lure, step right up onto the dais, and walk straight through it. What would happen if you did, I had no idea. But I knew that no one at Fairhaven was foolish enough to test what such nearness to the Aether might do to you.

Now, although I could feel the Geatgrima's pull, I could also feel something else. It was as though a degree of its power was being focused, so that rather than simply drawing someone toward it, it seemed to be... *exhaling* towards Savvy, as though it had grown a ghostly finger and was beckoning her forward. I did not get the sense that Savvy had any intention of following that beckoning. Indeed, it could not have been clearer that she was solidly standing her ground. And yet, the connection between Savvy and the Geatgrima was new and unsettling.

"What do you think it means?" I whispered.

"I have no idea, sweetness, but I don't think it's good," he replied.

"Neither do I," I admitted. "What do you think we should do? Should we... should we go get someone? Some help, or...?"

"Who would we get?" Milo asked. "And what the hell would we tell them?" He took on a casual tone. "'Um, excuse me, but if you're not too busy, could you please follow us to the courtyard? Someone's out there just standing in front of the Geatgrima. It's obviously an emergency.' You've got to admit it sounds pretty stupid."

"She's not just standing there, Milo," I said. "Something else is going on."

"Yeah," Milo said. "And it looks like it's the same thing that's been going on for weeks now. This explains everything that Savvy explained to you, doesn't it? The dirty boots, the sore muscles, the exhaustion? She's been coming out here every night, hasn't she?"

"I think so, yeah," I said. "I don't know. I don't know what to do. I don't know if we should tell anyone or what to tell them if we did."

Milo and I looked at each other, and all we had to offer each other were more questions and more uncertainty. It was an awful feeling, this helplessness. Finally, Milo seemed to decide that somebody had to take control of the situation, and I had given no indication that it was going to be me. He took a deep breath, blew it out again, and looked me squarely in the eye.

"I think we should wait," he said at last.

"Wait for what?" I asked.

"Just wait. Wait for something. Right now, she's just standing there. She's been doing it for weeks, and it's not like anything bad has happened. In fact, other than being tired, everything seems to be fine. Maybe we just wait to see if something happens. Let's keep vigil with her. If we're patient, it might become clear why she's out here."

Taking my cue from Milo, I tried to calm myself with a deep breath. "Okay, you're right. Let's just wait and see."

I found the least uncomfortable bit of wall I could, and leaned my back against it, tucking my knees up against my chest to help keep myself warm. Milo floated to rest beside me, and together, we simply watched. I feared at first that I might not be able to keep my eyes open, just as I had been unable to keep myself awake upstairs. But all trace of fatigue was now completely absent from my body. I felt like a live wire, poised to spark at the first sign that something was happening. And as the hours crept by, I did not tire or grow bored watching Savvy standing there. It was at once the most static and most dynamic thing I had ever seen. The connection that had formed between Savvy and the Geatgrima was mesmerizing, and I found that I really could not have torn my eyes from it even if I'd wanted to. Even Milo, notorious for his almost constant need for social interaction and entertainment, made not a sound of complaint or boredom, but simply occupied the space beside me, focusing all his concentration on Savvy.

The courtyard remained deserted, which was a blessing, given that we could neither hide nor explain what Savvy was doing. Only once did a sound give us pause—a shuffling noise near the cloisters gave the impression for a moment that someone might be approaching the courtyard. But the sound died away almost as soon as it began, and a quick search of the area by Milo revealed no onlookers.

At long last, the fiery orange edge of the sun peeked over the tops of the trees of the forest beyond. It was this first glimpse of daylight that broke the spell between Savvy and the Geatgrima. The moment the flame of the sun touched the flame of her hair, Savvy shifted her position. She clicked her heels together formally and placed her fist over her heart before bowing her head once in deference to the Geatgrima. Then she turned and began to jog toward the edge of the courtyard. Startled by the sudden change after hours and hours of stillness, I struggled to my feet in an effort to follow her. Milo sailed on ahead of me as I rubbed at my stiff muscles and numb extremities, forcing life and feeling back into them as quickly as I could. By the time I was able to stumble awkwardly back to the grass below Savvy's bedroom window, she had already ascended nearly the entire expanse of stone wall that separated her window from the ground. I watched nervously as she pulled herself through the window, and then turned and ran for the front door.

I arrived back at Savvy's room out of breath, having completely ignored the questions of the baffled young Caomhnóir who were still finishing their shift by the front doors. My cold fingers fumbled with the key that Savvy had given me, and it took several tries to undo the locks. By the time I had opened the door and stepped inside, Savvy was already back in her bed, snoring peacefully, her muddy boots carefully replaced by the door, and her uniform hung over the back of her chair. I looked at the clock; she had only twenty minutes before her alarm would go off to rouse her for her morning run.

Despite my exhaustion, I did not fall asleep when I took my place once again on her sofa. Instead, I waited until the moment that her alarm would wake her. Those precious few minutes ticked by remarkably fast. Each blaring beep from the alarm clock felt like a blow directly to my skull. From the look on Savvy's face when she sat up, she felt the same way.

"What fresh hell is this?" Savvy groaned. She clutched her hands to either side of her head as though she could force the throbbing pain back down inside. She continued to groan as she sat up, bringing her hands next to her neck, her shoulders, her back, and her legs. "I feel like absolute shite again," she grumbled, and then looked up to see me staring at her. Whatever she saw on my face caused all of her aggravation to drain away, replacing it with a palpable fear. She threw the covers back from her bed and stood up, folding her arms across her chest as though she were preparing herself for a physical blow rather than a mental one. "What happened, Jess?" she asked in a voice that was little more than a whisper. "What happened last night? Come on, out with it, I can tell from the look on your face that something's wrong."

"If I were you, I would sit back down," I told her. "This is gonna take a while."

By the time I had finished explaining what had happened the previous night, Savvy had pulled her knees up under her chin, compressing herself into a ball on the foot of her bed. It seemed as though she were trying to make herself as tiny as she could, perhaps trying to present as small a target as possible for each new terrifying detail to land.

"Wish you'd gotten a video of me climbing up and down that wall," she said at last with a weak chuckle. "Then I could show it to some of those other Novitiates and tell them to get stuffed. They won't quit getting at me because I can't get myself over that training wall Seamus put up on Thursday."

I answered her joke with half a smile, but it was the best I could do.

"Well," she said, "at least I know I'm not crazy. Something is happening while I'm sleeping, that's dead certain."

"Sure," I conceded, "but it opens up a whole new world of questions."

"Too right it does," Savvy agreed, nodding. "Do you... do you think I was asleep? Or do you think it was... something else?"

"I *think* you were sleeping," I told her. "I'm not a hundred percent sure, but I didn't sense any other kind of spirit presence. I didn't actually see you get up out of bed — I had dozed off for that part, unfortunately, – but when you came back up to the room, you climbed right back into the bed and laid down as though it were all just part of the routine. It didn't seem like you had to fall back to sleep. It was like your brain was already in that sleeping space, you know? All you had to do was close your eyes. It was all kind of... seamless."

"I don't remember anything," Savvy said, her brow furrowed as she dug back through her memory. "If you hadn't told me all this, I'd have been sure that I just slept straight through the night. Well, until I felt how sore I was, anyway."

"I'm sorry," I told her. "I'm sure you must be exhausted. But I didn't want to mess with anything, you know? I wasn't sure what would happen if I woke you up or tried to get your attention. I felt like, for this first time anyway, it seemed best just to watch and try to figure out what was going on."

"No, don't apologize," Savvy said, waving my words away. "You did exactly what I asked you to do. I wanted to know what was going on while I slept, and now we know. Now I've just got to figure out why."

"Do you... have you ever felt any sort of special connection to the Geatgrima? I mean, have you ever felt drawn to it or have you had any other strange experiences with it that you can remember?" I asked.

Savvy shook her head, looking bewildered. "No, mate. I can't make heads or tails of it. I don't think I've ever given the Geatgrima much thought, if I'm honest. I've passed by it plenty of times, of course, just like everyone else, but it's just a part of Fairhaven, you know? I can sense the Aether when I'm near it, but that's true for all of us, isn't it?"

I sighed. "Yeah, that sounds like my experience with it, too. Well, except that time I actually went through it to stop the reversal of the Gateways, but we all know that was an anomaly. What about the rune? Do you have any idea what that's about?"

"What rune?" Savvy asked, rubbing her temples again and giving a massive yawn. "Oh, you mean the one I drew on the dais?"

"I *think* you drew it," I reminded her. "I didn't actually see you do it."

"What did it look like?" Savvy asked.

I snatched my sketchpad up from the floor and drew a quick replica of the rune. I held it up so that Savvy could study it, but within moments she was shaking her head.

"I've got no bloody idea, mate," she said. "I don't recognize it."

"Yeah, I didn't expect that you would," I told her, feeling disappointment flood through me nevertheless. "It's what Flavia calls a layered rune, but I haven't been able to find its meaning."

"Wait," Savvy said, narrowing her eyes at me. "So, are you telling me that you've seen it before?"

I sighed again. "Yeah, I have. In fact, I've seen that entire scene from the courtyard before."

"If you're hiding something from me, Jess, now would be a brilliant time to let me know," Savvy said with a nervous laugh.

And she was right, of course, so I told her. I told her the entire story of how Fiona had created the sculpture, and how Flavia and I had been trying to shed light on its meaning. "And I'm sorry I didn't mention this to you before," I told her. "But you just had so much going on, trying to tackle this Novitiate training, and I didn't want to freak you out over something that I didn't even understand. I just thought if I could get more answers..."

But again, Savvy was already waving my apology away. "I understand, mate. You spent enough time dealing with prophecies to know that there's a right time and a wrong time to talk about them. And you're right; if you'd explained this to me a few weeks ago, I'd only have obsessed about it for no reason."

"So you're not mad at me?" I asked, my voice skeptical.

"Not a jot," Savvy assured me. "The only thing I'm mad about is that I've got to polish these bloody boots again."

"Here, I'll help you," I told her. "Why don't you lay back down and try to get a little more sleep."

"Nah, if I go back to sleep now, I'll never get up," Savvy said, nevertheless looking a bit wistfully at her pillow. "I'm going to jump in the shower, and hope that rouses me a bit. Chuck us that bathrobe, would you?"

I pulled a pink terrycloth bathrobe down off the hook on the wall behind my head and threw it over to Savvy. "Look, Savvy? I'm going to figure this out. Just try to focus on your training, and I'll keep working on it."

"Yeah, well, you'd better figure it out, and right quick, because if

I don't start getting some decent sleep soon, it won't matter how focused I am. I'll be too blasted tired to keep up." She glanced down at her watch. "Bugger, I'd best hurry or I'm going to be late. Seamus will skin me alive if I miss the start of the run."

And with that, she hurried out of the room, leaving me to brood, completely over my head in shoe polish and unanswered questions.

13

A RETURN TRIP

B Y THE TIME SAVVY HAD SCRAMBLED into her re-polished boots and bolted out the door to join the other Novitiates on the morning run, and by the time I had arrived back to my room, Milo had already filled Hannah in on everything that had happened during the night. Her face, as I crumpled like a marionette with the strings cut into the chair by the fire, was very grave.

"Is Savvy all right?" Hannah asked at once. "Have you told her everything?"

"Yep," I said, the word distorted around a wide yawn. "She's okay, I think. Weirdly relieved at this point."

Hannah's eyes widened in disbelief. "Relieved? Why would she be relieved?"

"I think she's just glad that she's not crazy," I explained. "At least now she has an explanation."

Hannah let out a derisive snort of laughter. "Jess, I'd hardly called that an explanation. She's got to have more questions than ever, hasn't she?"

"Undoubtedly," I said, and pulled a pillow down on top of my face. "Ugh, what a nightmare. Can't we just have, like, one decent stretch without another prophecy rearing its ugly head? Why does there always have to be another mysterious puzzle looming on the horizon? Why can't it just be boring around here? I would kill for some good old-fashioned boredom right now."

"I don't think Fairhaven and boredom have ever met, do you?" Milo asked.

I sighed. "No. Probably not."

"So, now what do we do?" Hannah asked. "We've got to tell someone, haven't we?"

"Why would we need to tell someone?" I asked.

175

Hannah rolled her eyes. "Well, no, you're right. I guess we don't have to tell anyone. We just have to wait another night or two until somebody happens to glance down into the courtyard and sees her standing there. Then they'll figure it out for themselves. Don't you think it would be a good idea to control that narrative before someone can take it and run with it?"

"I get what you're saying," I said. "But you can't really control the narrative when you've got no idea what the story's about. We need more time to flesh this out. If we start telling people now, we're going to start a panic. You know how well everyone around here deals with prophecies."

Hannah bit her lip. "I just think it's too much to hope that no one's going to discover what she's doing. It's only a matter of time."

"And we are going to use every bit of that time to find out what we can," I said. "What other choice do we have? Look, let's just say, for the sake of argument, that we tell someone. That we tell everyone. That we just go to the Council and come clean. So, then what? They start asking us a million questions, none of which we have the answer to. Then they drag Savvy into it and interrogate her endlessly. And with the same result. Savvy has absolutely no idea what's going on. Then the Council panics, Savvy loses her place with the Novitiates, and still no one knows what the hell is happening. It's only going to make things worse."

Hannah looked unconvinced, but she didn't try to argue with me. The truth was, we had no good options, and she knew it.

"Well, if we're going to start trying to find answers, where do we go first?" Hannah asked. "Surely some of the most knowledgeable people in this castle are sitting members of the Council."

"Flavia," I said at once. "She's better at finding answers than probably anyone we know. And like I said, she's already in on it. Let's give her a little bit of time to see what else she can develop."

"And in the meantime, what about Savvy?" Hannah asked. "There's no way that she can go on like this. She must be on the verge of collapse."

"Yeah, she's in rough shape," I said and even in my own ears, my voice sounded bleak. "But we can't give Seamus the opportunity to kick her out of the ranks. Savvy is tough, she'll keep soldiering on until we get this sorted out."

"I really don't like this at all," Hannah said, biting her lip.

"There's something... *significant* about it, Jess. I have a feeling this is a hell of a lot bigger than a few stress-induced dreams."

"I agree with you," I told her earnestly. "This *is* bigger than Savvy. And like any prophecy, we have to take it seriously. But that doesn't mean we need to shout it from the rooftops. In fact, it means that we probably shouldn't. We have to keep this close, Hannah, I'm sure of it.

Hannah let out a long sigh. "Okay," she said at last. "I trust you, Jess, you know I do. But you have to promise me that if we learn something big, something that takes this entirely out of our control, that you will let me take this to the rest of the Council."

"I promise," I said, and I almost meant it. "When the time is right."

§

I tried to use the rest of the morning to catch up on the sleep I'd lost in the courtyard the previous night, but my mind was racing and my body felt spring-loaded, as though I were just anticipating the moment when I would have to leap from the bed. Finally, I gave up around 11 AM, deciding that some sleep is not meant to be caught up on. Some sleep is just lost. I woke myself up as best I could with a long, hot shower, threw on some clothes, and swung by the dining room to grab half a sandwich on my way over to the library.

When I entered the library, I glanced automatically at the research table in the back corner. As she had been nearly every time I'd entered the library over the last few weeks, Lucida was there, her halo of dark curls just visible over several stacks of books. As I watched, she muttered something in a frustrated hiss, pulled a book down from the nearest stack, opened it up, and continued to read. The Tracker in me wanted to head over to the reference desk, pull all the call slips for every book on Lucida's table, and figure out what the hell she was researching. But the Tracker in me would have to wait. This business with Savvy felt far more pressing at the moment than anything Lucida might be up to.

"Hey Flavia," I said as I poked my head around her office door and found her hard at work as usual. "You got a minute?"

"Hey Jess," Flavia said, closing the book in front of her with a sigh. "I was just about to take a break, actually. Good timing."

I entered the room, dropped my bag onto the corner of her desk, and sank into the only other chair. My whole body ached from having spent most of the night leaning up against a stone wall.

My discomfort must've shown on my face, because Flavia's eyebrows drew together in concern. "Are you quite all right? You don't look very well."

"Rough night all around," I said vaguely. "I don't suppose you've had any luck tracking down that layered rune, have you?"

Flavia shook her head sadly. "I'm so sorry, Jess. I've absolutely scoured the records, gone through nearly the entire runic collection, and I just can't find it anywhere. It doesn't seem to exist outside of Fiona's sculpture."

"Actually, it *does* exist outside a Fiona sculpture," I said with a sigh. "That's why I'm here." And as quickly as I could, I explained to her all that had transpired the previous night with Savvy and the Geatgrima. When I had finished, Flavia's eyes were so wide that she looked as though she may never blink again.

"What in the world can it mean?" she asked when she had, at last, managed to find her voice.

"I have absolutely no idea," I admitted. "Nor does Savvy. But from what she told me, it's been happening every night for a couple of weeks now. I didn't actually see her draw the rune, but she must've, because there was no one else in the courtyard, and I think she may have pulled the charred wood right from her fireplace and brought it down with her."

"Did you see anything else out of place?" Flavia asked, her academic interest sparking in spite of her shock. "Any other signs of a casting, maybe? Any stones or herbs? Any chalk circles or candles? Anything else that she might've used or set up that might shed some light on what she was trying to do?"

I shook my head. "Milo and I scoured the entire courtyard," I told her. "We wanted to make sure we weren't being watched, obviously, but also we were looking for clues to help us understand what was going on. We didn't find anything. I'm not even sure if Savvy had her casting bag with her."

"It's all so mysterious," Flavia whispered. "And what about Savannah? Is she all right? Does she remember anything?"

"Not a thing," I told her. "If she weren't waking up filthy and exhausted, she'd have absolutely no idea this was even going on."

Flavia sighed and ran her hands through her hair, which had

grown quite a bit longer in the months since her attack and was now bright purple. "Well, I'll tell you the truth, Jess. I'm flummoxed. Absolutely flummoxed, and I don't like admitting it."

"Yeah, well I'm flummoxed right along with you," I said stifling a yawn. "Do you suppose I could steal a cup of that coffee?" I asked, pointing over my shoulder at the coffee maker sitting up on one of her shelves.

"Of course you can," she said with a smile. "I'm not surprised it's a two cup day, with the night that you've had."

"A two cup day?" I asked with a snort. "I feel a two pot day coming on, to be honest." I rose gingerly from the chair, every muscle aching, and poured myself a steaming cup of coffee into one of the large, blue chipped mugs that rested on the shelf beside the coffee maker.

"I don't suppose you sketched the sculpture, did you?" Flavia asked. "As I recall, your artwork was very helpful the last time we were trying to decode a prophecy."

"I did, actually," I said, nodding my head toward my bag. "My sketchbook's right in there. I'm not sure how much it will help. After all, it's just a sketch, not spirit-induced art, like last time. I should probably take you up to see the sculpture in person. You have any sugar up here?"

"There should be some packets left in that red jar," Flavia said as she reached for my bag. "The next shelf up."

I emptied two little white paper packets of sugar into my coffee and turned back to Flavia, who was now examining my sketchpad. A smarter person than me would have waited for the coffee to cool down a bit before drinking it, but I was too impatient and tired for smart choices. The coffee burned all the way down and I loved it.

"What's this, then?" Flavia asked, flipping through the sketchbook pages, but stopping mid-flip.

I leaned forward to see what she was looking at and my heart skipped a beat. She was looking down not at my sketch of Savvy and the Geatgrima, but at the page upon which I had scrawled down the mysterious combination of numbers and letters that had appeared on the hidden layer of Agnes Isherwood's tapestry. For a moment, I could conjure nothing to say. But then Flavia went on, rendering my reply absolutely unnecessary.

"Are you part of the Tracker team that's going to the catacomb archives?"

I blinked. "Huh?"

"The catacomb archives," Flavia repeated, with the curious half smile. "You know, at Skye Príosún? Are you one of the Trackers who's going over there this week?"

"Why are you asking me that?" I asked blankly.

Flavia gave a confused little chuckle. "Because you've got a call number from the catacomb archives written in your notebook," she said, pointing to it. When I still appeared confused, she added, "Surely you knew that?"

"Are you sure?" I asked, my heart now endeavoring to make up for that skipped beat by racing into overdrive.

"Yes, of course," Flavia said. "The catacomb archives have the same system of organizing our documents and artwork as all the rest of our libraries and collections. See here?" She reached down and pointed to the "CA" at the beginning of the string of characters. "Each call number begins with the letters that referred to the collection in which the piece is held. This is a call number from the catacomb archives." Flavia looked up at me, her expression still bemused. "Didn't you know what you'd written down? Where did you find it?"

"Oh, um," I stammered, fighting against my shock and excitement to concoct a convincing lie. "Fiona just asked me to write it down for her, and I did. I kind of forgot about it."

"Oh," Flavia said, and her expression fell. "I thought maybe you might be coming to the archives. I've been assigned as one of the Scribes to help sort through the collection and make sure that nothing is missing after the rebellion."

"I... yeah, actually, I am going," I said, deciding on the spot. "I didn't realize you were going, too. That's great!"

Flavia's eyes shone with excitement. "I was absolutely thrilled to have been chosen," she said. "I've never been to the catacomb archives before, but I've always dreamed of having a glimpse of the place. It contains some of our most coveted documents and historical artifacts. I'm giddy just thinking about it."

I tried to smile. "Yeah, me too. It was really cool just to get a glimpse of it the last time I was there. Not that it was under ideal circumstances but –"

Flavia began rambling on in an academic fervor about the many splendors of the catacomb archives. I nodded along, trying to seem as though I were paying attention, when inside, my mind was absolutely racing. Question after question came bubbling up, filling my head to capacity and leaving no room for answers. Who had hidden an archival call number in an ancient tapestry? Did Skye Príosún – and hence the archive — even exist back when that tapestry was woven? And even if it did exist, surely it was not already in possession of a modern organizational system to keep track of everything in it? It made almost no sense at all that the call number was part of the original tapestry, so it must have been added later, and then the additional layer of the book placed over it to hide the addition. Yes, that made sense, but then who added it, and why? And was it really meant specifically for me to find? Or had someone else already found it, and that was why it had been concealed? And then of course, regardless of who found it, what was waiting at the other end of that number? It was possible I might never be able to discover the answers to all of the previous questions, but this last one, at least, was within my grasp to answer. But there was only one way to get to Skye Príosún now, and only one person who could grant me permission.

§

"I need to get to Skye Príosún as soon as possible."

Catriona stared at me as though I had just announced my intention to land the first manned mission on Neptune. "Come again?" she asked me.

"I need to go to Skye Príosún. I need to get into the catacomb archives there," I said very slowly. "I want you to send me with the group of Trackers that are leaving in a couple of days."

Catriona closed her eyes and pinched the bridge of her nose with an expression on her face that suggested that she was praying for the patience not to murder me where I stood. "And why would I add you to a Tracker mission when you've already forced me to put you on a leave of absence so that you can assist Fiona?" she asked.

"This *is* to assist Fiona," I clarified. "I'm basically taking over her job, helping to organize and take care of the artwork. There's something in the catacomb archives that she needs me to check out, but I figured I probably needed your permission to go there, given that it's still the site of an ongoing investigation."

"Well, you're right about one thing, anyway," Catriona said. "You do need my permission. And I'm not going to give it to you, not right now. There's too much going on at the site, too much to organize. I can't have people sauntering over there for extraneous reasons when the place is still on lockdown. I'm sorry, but it's going to have to wait." And she looked back down at her work as though the matter was now closed.

I was not about to be dismissed.

"No, I'm sorry, Catriona," I said firmly. "But it can't wait."

Catriona looked up at me, raising one eyebrow in response to what I could only assume she perceived as insolence on my part. "Excuse me?"

"Look, this isn't just some frivolous trip," I said, endeavoring to keep my voice respectful, lest I blow my only chance to get into the archive simply because Catriona thought I was being rude. "It's really important. There's information in the archive that Fiona needs – that I need – urgently. I need to get in there, and you're the only one who can help me."

Catriona's expression changed. Her annoyance melted away as she registered the urgency in my voice. "More than a little art project, is it, then?" she asked.

I nodded.

"Well, what is it she needs so badly in the archive? Can you at least tell me that?" Catriona asked me.

"No," I said. "I'm sorry, but I can't."

"So, I'm supposed to send you into the site of a sensitive, ongoing investigation, with absolutely no idea why you're going, or what you intend to do when you get there? Catriona asked, her voice dripping with incredulity.

"That pretty much sums it up, yes," I said.

Catriona narrowed her eyes at me, and I sighed.

"Catriona, you know I wouldn't ask you if it wasn't important. You should also know by now that if I'm keeping something to myself, it's for damn good reason. I wouldn't be delusional enough to call us friends, but we've worked together for a while now, and we've been through some pretty heavy stuff together. I trust you at this point, and that's not a sentence I ever thought I'd say. I'm asking you to trust me. I need to get into that archive, and it can't wait."

If it were possible to extract information from a person purely by ferocity of glare, then Catriona shortly would've known every detail of why I wanted to get into the archive. Luckily, Catriona's gaze held no such mystical powers, and so her answer, when it finally came grudgingly out of her mouth, was a testament to that same trust. "Fine," she said abruptly. "I will add your name to the roster. But I'm going to have to give you an official duty while you're there, some reason to excuse your presence. And you're going to have to find a way to execute that duty while also finding whatever it is that you're looking for in that archive. Do you understand?"

"Yes," I said, my voice a grateful sigh. "Yes, whatever you need me to do. Thank you, Catriona. I really appreciate this."

Catriona flipped her hand dismissively, as though my thanks were nothing more than an irksome fly buzzing about her head. "Also you should know," she added, "we're not leaving in two days, we're leaving in three. There's been a delay in transporting the prisoners over for their hearing before the Council, and all our plans have been pushed back accordingly. However, in three days' time, when the prisoners have all given their testimony, I will add you to the contingent of Trackers tasked with returning them to the *príosún*. Once there, you'll only have about forty-eight hours to find what you need. That's going to have to be enough time. I'll include a clearance for the archives in your file. That should get you through the doors without a problem. But for God's sake, don't get in the way of the Scribes. Their work is crucial to this investigation."

"Thank you," I said. "Forty-eight hours will be enough." I said it with as much confidence as I could gather, even though I had absolutely no idea whether forty-eight hours would be long enough to discover what I was looking for, or to interpret it even if I did manage to find it. However, it looked like this was the only chance I was going to get, and so I was going to take it and be grateful. As for the rest of it, I would have to figure it out on the fly. Well, all my carefully laid plans usually went to shit, so maybe it was better this way.

"Oh, we may need you to answer some questions during the process of the prisoner testimony," Catriona said. "I'm warning you now so that you can prepare yourself."

"You haven't tracked down Charlie Wright, have you?" I asked, my breathing suddenly unsteady. "He isn't among the prisoners coming to the castle, is he?"

"No, I promise you I would've alerted you if we found him,"

Catriona said, barely moving her lips as she spoke. "Believe you me, I can't wait to get my hands on that little maggot."

"Do you have any new leads?" I asked her.

"No," she said grudgingly. "He managed that escape tidily, I'll grant him that. No word on your Caomhnóir either. Still, I'm hoping that the testimony in the next few days may shed some light on those who escaped."

I knew I shouldn't have been relieved that I wasn't going to have to face Charlie in a courtroom yet, but I was. My real concern should have been that he was still out there, unaccounted for, and planning God knew what else to further the Necromancers' ultimate goal of dismantling the Durupinen hierarchy. However, it was hard to conjure fear about vague theoreticals when placed up against the very real possibility of having to look at his face again, of having to hear that snide voice mocking me again. I should have been hoping for his capture, and instead, I'd found myself selfishly hoping that he would never be found.

"Is there anything else?" Catriona asked, a bite of impatience in her voice.

"No, I don't think so. Thanks, Cat."

14

AMBUSH

FINN LISTENED INTENTLY to every detail of the previous night. He sat so still that he might've been carved from stone, save for the occasional deepening of the furrow between his eyebrows. When I had finally finished, it was several long seconds before he spoke.

"Someone's got to watch her tonight," he said. "She can't be left alone. I'll do it for tonight, and then we need to figure out some sort of..."

"Hello, there," I said, grabbing his arm as he made to stand. "No need to shift into Guardian overdrive here. Milo is watching her. He's agreed to do it every night until we have this all sorted out."

Finn looked skeptical. "Milo? By himself? Do you think he's up to—"

"He's the only one of us who doesn't require sleep," I pointed out. "He's more than capable of keeping an eye on her, and if anything new happens, he's got a direct line to us right here." I tapped myself on the forehead to indicate our connection. "You can't be up day and night keeping an eye on Savvy, that makes no sense. None of us can. This is the perfect job for Milo, and he's willing to take it on."

Finn's expression cleared. "Yes. Yes, of course. That makes much more sense. I'll try to arrange patrol routes for the Caomhnóir that steer them clear of that area, at least for the present. That ought to help us maintain the secrecy while we figure out what's going on."

"That's a great idea, thank you," I said.

"And Flavia has no idea what that rune means?" Finn asked.

I shook my head. "She's looked everywhere, and she's run out of resources here at the castle. She thinks she needs to dig deeper into Durupinen records to find what she's looking for. Which brings me to the other thing I have to tell you."

Finn looked at me, eyes narrowed. "The other thing? Wasn't the first thing you had to tell me bombshell enough for one evening?"

"Well, they're sort of... related bombshells," I said hesitantly. I took a deep breath. He was going to hate this whether I told him now or two days from now, so I might as well get it over with. "I asked Catriona for permission to go back to Sky Príosún. I'm going to take Flavia with me, and we're going to search the catacomb archives for more information about this rune. And there's also this." I pulled the torn piece of sketch paper from my pocket, unfolded it, and held it out to him.

He looked down at it, puzzled for a moment, and then looked back up at me. "This is what you found concealed in the Isherwood tapestry, isn't it?" he asked.

"Yes," I said. "And today I found out what it means. Or rather, I think I know what it means."

Finn's eyes widened. "Well, what is it then?"

"It's an archival call number," I said. "Flavia recognized it right away because she knows the codes for all of the different Durupinen archives and collections. These first two letters are an abbreviation for the catacomb archives. So, whatever that tapestry is referring to, whatever message it's trying to get across, I think it can be found if I follow this number there."

Finn looked completely stunned. "Why would a call number be sewn into a tapestry that old?" he muttered. "Surely, the tapestry itself predates that sort of modern system of archiving our artifacts?"

"I know. It's strange," I said. "But I'm not going to understand it unless I go, so I asked Catriona to give me permission, and she's agreed to add me to the contingent of Trackers that are headed back there in three days."

Finn nodded. "Yes," he said. "Yes, that's the perfect cover. No one will question why you're headed back there, and it gives you the perfect opportunity to try to solve two mysteries at once."

I blinked, totally lost for a response. Finally, Finn looked up at me, frowning. "What is it?" he asked. "Why are you looking at me like that?"

"I'm waiting for the freak out," I said.

"Freak out?" Finn asked. "What are you on about?"

I gave an incredulous laugh. "This is usually the part of the conversation where you have a meltdown because I just told you that I'm going to do something dangerous, and you either try to find a way to talk me out of it, or you concoct some overprotective scheme that you think is going to keep me safe while I do whatever dangerous thing I decided that I'm going to do."

Finn stared at me open-mouthed for a moment, then he let out a chuckle, shaking his head. "My God. How you have endeavored to put up with me is a mystery."

"What do you mean?" I asked.

"If that's really how you thought this conversation was going to go, then I've been quite the ass. It would seem that I really do have some work to do to reverse that macho Caomhnóir conditioning, haven't I?"

"Well," I said, smiling sheepishly, "You're just a bit... you know... *protective,* that's all."

Finn's chuckle broke into a much longer, louder peal of laughter. "It's all right, Jess. You can say it, love. In the past, there have been times where I have been more guard dog than boyfriend, haven't I?"

"You said it, not me," I muttered.

"Well, please allow me to apologize for that," Finn said. "If there's one thing that I've learned over and over and over again, it's that you do not need anyone to take care of you. You are clever and competent and brave, and I'd do much better to stay out of your way than to plant myself in it. I will always do whatever is in my power to keep you safe, not because it is my job but because I love you. Besides, you are the one who's been doing all of the rescuing lately."

"We rescued each other," I said with a shrug. "Wow, so you're not even going to try to come with me or anything?"

Finn looked amused now. "Do you want me to come with you?" he asked.

"No," I said quickly, rolling my eyes. "God, you're so clingy."

He laughed again. "I would, of course, be glad to accompany you. I'd certainly feel better if we were together, given how much time we were forced to be apart. But I've got the entire defenses of Fairhaven to organize, and I'm not sure that walking out on that responsibility so soon after it's been handed to me would be wise. I'm sure you understand. And anyway, I'm sure Flavia will be much more help in the catacomb archives than I will."

"Yes, you're absolutely right," I said. "Look at you, being all reasonable."

Finn shrugged and stretched out his legs in front of him. "I suppose I must be mellowing out in my old age."

"Yeah, well, don't get too mellow," I told him. "I am going to need your help keeping an eye on Savvy while I'm gone."

Finn's smile faded away, and he nodded solemnly at me. "You have my word, Jess. I'll do everything I can to make sure Savvy is safe, and that these late-night vigils stay secret, at least for the present."

"Thank you," I told him. "I just hope the archive holds some answers, for Savvy and for me."

§

The day of the prisoner testimony dawned, and I was so anxious I could barely function. Between my worries about Savvy and her continued sleepwalking, preparing to go back to the *príosún* to search the archive, and the fact that Fairhaven was now housing half a dozen of our most dangerous enemies, my breakfast that morning consisted of staring down at my toast as though unsure what to do with it. I was sitting alone at the table, Hannah having been called to an early Council meeting and Finn swamped with Caomhnóir security concerns. I had been summoned to the Grand Council Room as Catriona had warned I might, and even though they would be in chains, the thought of having to look any one of those Necromancers in the face made the bile rise in my throat.

One day, I told myself. *I just have to get through this one, awful day, and then I will finally be able to find the answers I need.*

And if the catacomb archives were another dead end? Well, I wasn't mentally prepared to consider that possibility. Not this morning, when I couldn't even remember how to eat toast.

I was so distracted as I exited the dining room that I walked right into Catriona.

"Oh God, sorry," I said stepping back. "I wasn't looking where I was... Catriona? Are you all right?"

Catriona's face was stricken. Her eyes were wild with panic, and her usually pale complexion was chalky white. She looked at me for a moment as though she was barely registering who I was, and had not a single snide remark about the fact that I had just clumsily barreled right into her.

"Catriona?" I repeated. "Are you okay? Did I hurt you?"

This second use of her name got her attention at last. She grabbed me by the arm and murmured, "Have you seen Lucida?"

I looked down at her fingers, which were digging into my arm, and then back up into her face. "No, I haven't seen Lucida. Why?"

"Because she's bloody *missing*, that's why," Catriona hissed at me. "I left her up in the library – she's always up in that bloody library now. I have no idea why—she's never given a damn about books in her whole life. I told her I'd come to fetch her when the Caomhnóir arrived at the castle with the prisoners. You know how she's been banging on about how she's not safe while they're here. I promised her I would get her set up with some extra security when they arrived, but now I can't find her anywhere."

"Did you ask the Scribes? Did they see her leave?"

"Of course I've asked the Scribes. I'm not completely daft," Catriona snapped. "She didn't exit through the main doors, which means she could only have gotten out through a window. I don't want to alert the Caomhnóir because the last thing we need is to throw the castle into chaos the moment that everyone needs to be on high alert for the prisoners. But I've got to find her."

"I'll help you," I said at once. "And I can get Milo to help too, if you want."

"Yes, all right," Catriona said. "I think we need to search the grounds. I don't like to think of what the Council will do if she's tried to make a break for it."

"Surely, they'll understand if you explain how paranoid she was about the Necromancers coming here?" I asked.

Catriona shook her head. "She asked me to go to the Council, remember? I asked them to take her off house arrest, to transfer her somewhere else, but they flatly refused, which was exactly what I expected, of course. It was such an unpopular decision to keep her here in the first place. No one wanted to make it seem as though we were now just catering to the whims of a traitor. If we can't find her, and quickly, she may very well have landed herself right back in the *príosún*."

We moved through the entrance hall swiftly, trying to keep our expressions blank and businesslike, to draw as little attention from the Caomhnóir guarding the entrance doors as possible. Once out on the grounds, we made our way around to the east side of the castle, where the many windows of the library looked out over the gardens. It only took a few moments of scanning the castle walls before we spotted the open window.

"There," Catriona said, pointing. "If I'm not very much mistaken, that window there leads right into the rear reading room. It's private back there. She could've closed the door and snuck out the window without drawing anyone's notice."

"Yeah, but how the hell did she get down?" I asked. From where we stood, the dissent looked impossible. There was no ivy clinging to this part of the castle, no thick vines or turret edges to grab hold of.

Catriona laughed mirthlessly. "Jess, she's easily the best Tracker we've ever had. She makes Houdini look like a two-bit grifter doing card tricks in a pub. She'd have no trouble making that climb, I'm dead sure of it." Catriona turned and scanned the grounds. "Let's head over to the wooded grove, it's the closest place to seek shelter." And she took off at a jog.

I followed, realizing as I did that this was the second time in a week that I had chased someone across the castle grounds after they made a nearly impossible climb down the castle exterior. I sincerely hoped that it was not going to become the new normal.

"How long have we got?" I asked Catriona, panting slightly. "Before we have to be in the Grand Council Room for the hearing?"

"Not long," Catriona said shortly. "And I don't like to think what will happen if they realize that I've gone. If we can just find Lucida and get her back into the castle, no one need ever know what a near miss we had."

I reached through the connection until I found both Milo and Hannah's energies waiting for me. It took only the briefest of moments for me to convey to them what was happening.

"What can I do?" Hannah asked at once. "Do you want me to stall the proceedings? I could call a recess, or—"

"Don't do anything yet," I insisted. "We don't want to draw attention to the situation unless absolutely necessary. I just wanted to alert you, in case anyone in the Grand Council Room realized that something is wrong."

"What about me?" Milo asked.

"I need you out here," I told him. "Can you get some height and help us scan the grounds?"

"Sweetness, I'm on it. Aerial views from your favorite floater, coming right up," Milo replied without the slightest hesitation.

"Brilliant, thank you, Milo," I said. "Concentrate on the borders of the grounds, if you can. Catriona is afraid Lucida might not be content to hide, and that she might actually make a break for it."

"Border patrol. Got it," Milo answered swiftly, and I felt him pull out of the connection so that he could focus all of his energy on manifesting as a lookout.

"Jess, be careful," Hannah warned, her anxiety sliding along the connection like a bow over violin strings. The resultant music was harsh and discordant.

"Of course, I'll be careful," I replied. "Lucida's not out to get us, Hannah, she's just scared."

"Scared people do stupid things," Hannah countered, and she was right, as usual. "Just remember that before you start trying to reason with her."

I pulled out of the connection to find Catriona groaning with frustration beside me. "I don't even know why the hell I'm bothering to do this," she grumbled. "This is an exercise in futility. We have acres of grounds and she could be anywhere. I should just go back inside and alert the Caomhnóir, so they can start the manhunt. I'm just delaying the inevitable here."

"You don't know that," I said, even though I knew it was probably true.

"I know that I spent half my life covering for her when I shouldn't have," Catriona said. "I know that almost every spot of trouble I've ever been in was because I said 'yes' to something she proposed. I don't know what it is about her, but she's always been able to strip away every ounce of my common sense. I always think I know better, but in the end, I fall under her spell every time."

"She's your cousin," I said quietly. "You love her. Sometimes we do stupid stuff because we love people."

"Sometimes I wonder if I knew," Catriona said coming to a stop and turning to look me squarely in the eye. "Sometimes I wonder if some part of me knew that something was very wrong with Lucida, and that she was betraying us right under our noses. But the bigger part of me—the part that Lucida has always held sway over—took that sensible little part and just crushed it underfoot. I never once considered asking her the hard question. If I had, it would have felt like an unbearable betrayal. So instead, I betrayed myself and everyone else."

I didn't know what to say. How do you listen to somebody confess something so personal, so hard to admit, knowing that the only thing you can say to them is that they're right?

"You know, once I had read her confession, once she'd actually admitted all of it to me and she was behind bars, even then I couldn't close the door. I told myself I would stay away and forget about her, that I would never visit, never forgive her for what she'd done. But I still couldn't do it. When you're bound together by the Gateway, there's no such thing as letting go."

"Yeah," I said. "I understand that much of it, anyway. Look, you're the one who knows her best, whether you like it or not. Put yourself in her shoes. She scared. Even if we don't really understand why, we know she's scared of being in the castle at the same time as those Necromancers. So just ask yourself, where would she go? What would she do?"

Catriona bit her lip. After a moment, she said, "She sure as hell wouldn't trust the Caomhnóir to protect her. She never trusted anyone to look out for her but herself. Well, and me. No, she'd find a way to protect herself."

"How? How would she protect herself? What would she do? What would she use?" I pressed.

Catriona shook her head for a moment and then suddenly, the proverbial lightbulb went on over her head. She looked up at me, eyes wide, and said, "The barracks. That's where she'd go. It's full of weapons, and she could commandeer a vehicle."

"Let's go," I said, and we took off at a sprint in the direction of the barracks.

My breath seared in my chest by the time we rounded the far side of the grove and the barracks came into view. I struggled to keep up with Catriona, whose long golden hair flew out behind her like a battle flag. The barracks were nearly deserted, save for two Novitiates, barely older than kids, who were playing a game of cards on the front steps. They both looked up in alarm to see us running toward them and scrambled to their feet.

"We need to get inside," Catriona said. "Move."

Neither one of the Novitiates displayed even the slightest hesitation in obeying her command. They stumbled over each other to get out of her way, and she pushed through the door, staring frantically around.

I'd never been inside the barracks before. The interior looked like a military bunk, or else the sleeping quarters of an incredibly depressing summer camp. Row after row of metal-framed beds, their mattresses tucked neatly with olive green blankets and starched white pillows, interspersed with wooden benches and straight-backed metal chairs pushed in at small, square wooden desks. There was barely a personal belonging in sight because signs of personal attachment or frivolity were frowned upon. A quick glance at the nearest bed revealed the corner of a magazine peeking out from underneath a pillow. No doubt the owner of said magazine would find himself subject to some kind of punishment when he returned from his shift. Rows of staves and knives hung on hooks on the walls, along with overcoats and pairs of gloves and sets of pads for sparring. There were only two rooms off the main sleeping quarters. The first was a sort of locker room, but a quick search found it to be deserted. The second appeared to be an administrative office, but the door was locked. Catriona, of course, made quick work of the lock.

The door swung open, revealing a large office space with two desks, a row of gray filing cabinets, and an oversized bulletin board upon which a large number of maps, lists, and schedules were posted. It certainly looked more lived-in than the main room of the barracks — a coffee cup on the desktop, a photo in a frame, a casually abandoned paperback book. However, it was also clear that the room had been disturbed.

Catriona pointed to the window, which had been left wide open, and then to a filing cabinet drawer, which had not quite been properly shut. "She's been here," she said quietly.

"Do you think it's too late then? Do you think we've missed her?"

Catriona shook her head. "No, she's only just left. If that window had been open for any length of time, these papers would be all over the floor. The breeze is too strong. I think we should try the garage. If she's managed to get her hands on a set of keys, that's where she'll have to go next."

"Do you think there's any chance she might –"

But the rest of my question was swallowed as a piercing shriek rang out, assaulting my eardrums and sending my heart thundering up into my throat.

"Lucida!" Catriona cried, and fled for the door. I followed her, shoving past the two Novitiates who were now on their feet and staring around in bewilderment for the source of the scream. A second cry rang out, echoing clearly over from behind the garage.

"Fetch your superiors!" Catriona shouted over her shoulder at the Novitiates, already sprinting at full speed toward the garage. "Get reinforcements, go!"

The two boys took off at once for the castle, and I struggled to stay close on Catriona's heels. As we drew closer to the garage, we could hear more grunts and cries and sounds of a clear struggle.

One of the many garage doors had been jacked halfway open. Catriona ducked her head inside, but it was deserted. The sound seems to be coming from the other side of the garage. We took off along the side, leaping over abandon tires, carjacks, and toolboxes, turned the corner, and skidded to a stop.

"Oh my God," Catriona muttered. "Oh my God, Lucida."

There Lucida stood, her shirt half torn from her shoulders, her face bloodied, her hand pressed against her ribs, where the blood was steadily spreading across what remained of the white fabric of her shirt. Her other hand hung limply at her side, still clutching a long, viciously curved Caomhnóir blade. And at her feet, with eyes wide and staring, his throat cut like a gruesome smile, was Ambrose. The three of us watched him twitching and gurgling for a moment, before he fell utterly still. Something behind his eyes went out like an extinguished candle. I felt a sudden tingling rush in my veins, a passing flash of nearness to the Aether, and then it—and he—was gone. It was not until Lucida let the knife drop with a clunk into the grass that I could tear my horrified eyes away from Ambrose's body.

"Oh, my God, Lucida," Catriona said again. "What... what have you done?"

Lucida swayed. For a moment I thought she might collapse. Then inexplicably, she grinned. "I told you, Cat. I told you I wasn't safe here."

15

TRAITOR BETRAYED

IT WAS ALL LUCIDA HAD A CHANCE TO SAY before the shouts began to echo across the field. Before the Caomhnóir descended upon her, handcuffing her hands behind her back in spite of Catriona's shouts that she was injured, and to leave her alone. Before the body with its grinning neck and empty eyes could be covered up from public view. Before she was dragged roughly away across the grass and into the castle, cursing and crying out in pain.

The agonized sound of her voice had not yet faded from my ears before I found myself sitting on a bench outside the Trackers office, Finn on one side of me and Hannah on the other. Milo floated back and forth in front of us in his own ghostly version of pacing, which made him look like a faintly glowing pendulum.

"Are you okay?" Finn asked me, frowning down at me in concern. "You still look peaky."

"I'm fine," I said, unconcerned whether it was the truth or not. "It was just a shock. It's Lucida we should be worried about."

"At least they had the sense to bring her to the hospital ward instead of the dungeons," Finn said darkly.

"They nearly didn't," I replied, my teeth gritted against my anger. "If Catriona hadn't been there, they would have let her bleed out down in one of those cells, no doubt."

"I still don't understand what happened," Hannah said. "How did Ambrose get on the grounds? What was he doing here?"

"He was a Fairhaven Caomhnóir," said Finn shortly. "He knew the details of all of our defenses, and no doubt how to circumvent them. A thorough investigation will reveal how he managed to slip into the grounds."

"And as to why he was here, Lucida seemed pretty clear on that matter," I said. "He was here for her. She was convinced that the

Necromancers were going to make a move to silence her. She's been begging Catriona to be granted leave from the castle for weeks."

"And we wouldn't give it to her," Hannah said, her voice hollow with guilt. "The Council voted against it."

"You can't blame yourself for this," Milo said, pausing in his pacing to glare at Hannah like a disapproving parent. "That woman is a convicted traitor. No one knows whether they can trust what comes out of her mouth from one minute to the next."

"She was telling the truth this time," Hannah pointed out.

"And next time she'll be lying through her teeth," Milo insisted. "Sweetness, if you think I'm going to stand here and listen to you accept even a second's guilt over anything that happens to that woman, you have got a rude awakening in your immediate future."

His expression was so fierce that Hannah shrugged and dropped it.

"What I don't understand is why Ambrose would take on a suicide mission like that," Finn said. "It's a miracle he even managed to cross paths with Lucida in the first place. I expect if she'd just stayed in her room, he would have been caught by the Caomhnóir before he even reached her."

"You know Lucida," I said. "There was no chance in hell she was going to be a sitting duck. If she'd stayed in her room, she would have been in the first place in the castle anyone would look for her."

"You think it was just luck then, that Ambrose happened to bump into her on the grounds?" Milo asked, his tone dripping with skepticism.

"Not entirely luck, no," Finn said. "If he weren't already armed, the barracks would have been the perfect place to come to arm himself. If he was still working with the Necromancers, he would have known that the hearings were today, and that the vast majority of the security would be inside, where the prisoners are. He would also have known that there would be extra patrols everywhere, and that the barracks would therefore likely be nearly deserted. No doubt he would have made very short work of those two Novitiates left behind to guard the place if he hadn't run into Lucida first."

"So, you think he was here to kill her?" I asked.

"I haven't a clue," Finn said. "But whether that was his mission or not, he certainly had a good go at it once he encountered her. Ambrose was an excellent fighter. Lucida's combat skills must be formidable indeed if she survived a hand-to-hand encounter with him."

"I can't believe he's dead," Hannah whispered.

Neither could I. And it was probably a good thing that I couldn't actually process his death, because if I did, I'd also have to process my feelings about it, which, to be quite honest, would probably have been complicated enough to land me in therapy for the rest of my natural life and well into the Aether. Did Aether-therapists exist? Or did all of the human shit we repressed while alive just become miraculously clear the moment we reached a heightened spirit form? Either way, I had no intention of digging into the cesspool of guilt and judgment over whether I should have the warm fuzzies that another human being was dead.

Nope. Hard pass on that one.

It was several hours before Catriona shoved the Tracker office door open with a violent push and stalked past us in the direction of the hospital ward, muttering darkly to herself.

"Catriona?" I called after her tentatively.

She whirled around in alarm. "Jess! I... didn't see you there."

"Yeah, well, I'd say you've got enough to worry about without keeping tabs on me," I pointed out.

"You're not wrong there," Catriona said. She ran her hands through her hair and gave a long sigh. "I suppose you want an update, then?"

"I can get it from someone else if you—"

"No, you can't," Catriona snapped. "No one else has been briefed yet." She sighed, and her whole body seemed to sag. "She's refusing to speak about the attack. Unless I can get her to tell them what happened, they're going to send her back to Skye Príosún tomorrow."

"But why?" I asked, my mouth falling open in horror. "Why would she want to go back to that place? She spent years there, she knows how horrific it is. What could possibly make her risk being locked up there again?"

"I have no idea," Catriona said, and she sounded close to tears. "And I tell you this, she won't get another chance to get out. It was a miracle they didn't throw her right back in there after the rebellion. If she goes back now, she's back in there for life."

"Someone needs to talk to her!" I said. "To convince her to—"

"What do you think I've been doing in there for the last ninety minutes?" Catriona shouted, anger flaring and dying in a single moment, leaving her slumped and defeated again. "I've begged. I've pleaded. I've offered to cut her deals I could never swing in a hundred years. I've appealed to every weakness, exploited every detail of forty years of a friendship as close as sisters. She will not be swayed."

"So, we have no idea why Ambrose attacked her, then?" Finn asked, standing up from the bench to join us, Hannah and Milo right on his heels.

"Only speculation," Catriona said. "It seems logical that they don't want Lucida to reveal something she might know about the Necromancers, something she found out either while she was working for them or while she was locked up alongside them."

"If it was something she learned while she was working for them, wouldn't they have just killed her in the *príosún* when they had the chance?" Hannah asked.

"Perhaps. Perhaps they thought they didn't need to. She was locked up and disgraced, after all," Finn said. "No stock would have been put in anything a traitor had to say, even if she was given the opportunity to say it."

"But now that she's been released and is living amongst the Durupinen again," Milo added, "Now that she's helped the Durupinen defeat the Necromancers, maybe they were afraid people might start listening to her?"

"It's possible," Catriona said. "But all of it is just a load of speculation unless Lucida agrees to talk. And she won't."

"This is bullshit!" I said. "They're going to lock her back up just for defending herself?"

"No, they're going to lock her back up for refusing to testify about why she had to defend herself," Catriona said. "It doesn't feel like an important difference, but there it is. And so, Lucida's freedom is a memory again before it was ever allowed to be a reality, and all because she's still being targeted by the Necromancers."

"This just isn't fair," Hannah said.

"Fairness is a fairy tale," Catriona said, turning and striding off down the hallway. "If you haven't learned that by now, love, you've been walking through life with your eyes shut."

§

As it turned out, Lucida's refusal to cooperate was merely the first in a long string of frustrations for the day. The hearings with the Necromancer and Caomhnóir prisoners were a complete waste of time. Not a single one of them would utter a word about their involvement in the rebellion, the inner workings of how the rebellion was planned, nor any details about any of the others involved. Necromancers were notoriously tight-lipped under questioning, but there had been many amongst the Council and the Caomhnóir leadership who thought that the Caomhnóir who had been turned might, out of a lingering sense of guilt or duty, provide some crucial information, even if only to save themselves. These hopes were thoroughly dashed by the end of the day's hearings. With nothing to say in their defense and nothing helpful to offer, the prisoners would be returned to the *príosún*, which was now being staffed with help from distant clans from other parts of the world. And when they went the next morning, Lucida would go with them. And so would I.

"I hate the idea of you going back to that place," Hannah said anxiously, watching me pack a duffel bag with several days' worth of clothes.

"I'm not exactly jumping for joy about it myself," I said. "But on the bright side, this trip comes with several upgrades, including a room without bars on the windows and a distinct lack of danger of imminent death."

"I don't know how you can joke when you're so stressed out," Hannah said.

"Oh, Hannah, you know by now it's one of my unhealthy, emotionally-stunted coping mechanisms. Plus, it's charming," I said, grinning at her.

Hannah tried and failed not to smile back. It was a brief smile, though, like a camera flash. "What if you don't find what you're looking for?"

"I'm choosing not to think about that possibility," I said firmly. "Flavia is a brilliant researcher. If anyone can unearth a reference to that rune, she can. And once she does, we should have a better idea of what's happening to Savvy. As to the call number in the tapestry, well, even I can follow directions that simple. And when I do, I can finally put these ridiculous questions to rest."

"I don't think they're ridiculous," Hannah said.

I turned and narrowed my eyes at her. "Hannah, I'm traveling in a helicopter despite being aviophobic to revisit one of the most traumatizing experiences of my life in order to search a library made out of human bones for a number I found woven into a dirty old rug because somehow, I've convinced myself that it's actually a message for me."

Hannah stifled a giggle. "Okay, I take it back. It's one of the most insane things I've ever heard in my life."

I gave an elaborate bow with lots of hand flourishes. "Thank you very much. I take great pride in my seemingly endless ability to entertain you with my poor decision-making."

"Sweetness, I feel like I need a bucket of popcorn just to be in your presence," Milo added.

"I wish you could go with her. I'd feel so much better if you could go with her," Hannah said, pouting again.

"Hannah, it's pointless to drag Milo along for this," I told her. "The *príosún* is so full of Wards and protective castings that Milo would be lucky to last five minutes inside before he was too disoriented to function, let alone sass me. Besides, as long as I don't Walk—which I have absolutely no intention of doing—then you've got a direct line of access to me the whole time I'm there. You can check in on me every five seconds if you want to, although it's likely to be the most boring spying you've ever done in your life. What are you so worried about, anyway? I was expecting this kind of nail-biting from Finn, not from you."

"I don't know," Hannah said. "I'm just so on edge, between waiting for the vote on my legislation, to worrying about Savvy, and now you're going back to that creepy old prison. It just feels like too much to have to handle at once."

"I know, but there's a good chance this visit to the creepy old prison might just solve a few of these questions we've got hanging over our heads. By the time I come back, half of our worries could be completely resolved," I said.

"I guess so," Hannah said, sounding unconvinced.

"And as to the legislation," Milo added, a wicked gleam in his eye, "You could always spend a little more time in the library with Kiernan to take your mind off things."

Hannah picked up the pillow beside her and threw it directly at

Milo, who pirouetted gracefully out of the way. "I told you, we're just friends."

"Sure, sweetness, and this ghost thing is just a phase," Milo sang, rolling his eyes. "And anyway, I think Kiernan's the one you need to tell."

"You're impossible," Hannah grumbled.

"I know. It's one of my most endearing qualities," Milo replied, batting his lashes.

"I'm not sure if endearing is the most appropriate word in this instance," Finn said, pushing the door open and poking his head in.

Milo gasped. "Are... are you *sassing* me?"

Finn grinned. "Yes, I suppose I am, rather."

Milo grinned back. "Well, well, well. Look who came back from exile with a sense of humor!"

Finn shrugged. "Let's just say I've got much more to laugh about now that I'm outside of those walls than I had when I was inside them." He turned to me and pointed to my bag. "Are you nearly ready, love? They're bringing the cars around."

"Yeah, I'm almost done," I said, grabbing a pair of grey sweats off the top of my laundry basket and shoving them into the bag along with an oversized St. Matt's sweatshirt.

"Oh, you aren't packing that, are you?" Milo asked, wrinkling his nose in distaste.

I rolled my eyes. My St. Matt's sweatshirt was among Milo's least favorite items in my wardrobe, both because I wore it so frequently and because it was so full of holes. I called it "well-loved." He called it "an affront to his senses."

"Milo, I'm going to a dank underground library constructed of human skeletons, not a movie premiere, remember?"

"Oh, right," Milo said, brightening up. "Well, on second thought, bring it. And also, you know, leave it there."

I shoved my toothbrush, toothpaste, hairbrush, and a handful of hair elastics into a toiletry bag, tossed it on top of the sweatshirt, and zipped the bag closed. "I'm all set. Let's go."

Finn held his hand out for my bag. I put my hand in it. "Hold this instead."

Hannah gave me a fierce hug that had just a whiff of panic, and Finn and I set off for the front drive.

"I'll continue to ensure Savannah's safety in the courtyard while you're gone," Finn said under his breath. "The shift routes and changes have left her undiscovered at least for now, but I have no control over who may look out a window or venture out at night."

"Thank you. And Mrs. Mistlemoore's staff will help Fiona." I said. "I only hope Flavia and I can figure this all out."

"You'll do your very best, I have no doubt," Finn said. "And I know I don't have to say this, but—"

"I know. Be careful."

He squeezed my hand. "I'm sending you off to that place with my dearest treasure. You'd best take care of her for me."

I returned the squeeze. "You should be a poet or something."

Down in the entrance hall, I found Savvy shadowing a door guard along with another Novitiate. Her attentive posture slipped for only a second when she spotted me—long enough to tip me a wink and the shadow of a smile. I met her eyes and nodded at her, and I knew she understood me: I would, as Finn had said, do my very best.

Two SUVs and two prisoner vans stood idling on the gravel drive outside the castle. I was struck at how very out of place they looked in the otherwise bucolic setting of this castle in the English countryside; a jarring, out-of-tune note in a symphony. One of the drivers opened the back door of the second SUV and looked at me pointedly. I planted a quick kiss on Finn's cheek and walked toward the car. Just as I handed my bag to the Caomhnóir to climb inside, two guards crunched up the driveway, leading Lucida between them.

She looked terrible. Her face was swollen and she moved gingerly, her midsection heavily bandaged. As she waited for the back of the van to be opened, she looked up and saw me standing there staring at her.

"Jess! What are you doing here?" she asked. "You're not... are you going to the *príosún*?"

"Yes," I told her, even as the Caomhnóir shot me filthy looks for deigning to speak to a prisoner. "I'm part of the Tracker team heading back for the conclusion of the investigation."

Lucida's expression shifted from surprise to something else—it was hard to interpret. Her eyes looked at once hopeful and panicked, and her mouth was trembling.

"Well, don't forget, I paid you a little visit in your cell last time," she said, her tone casual, even snide, and yet her voice was trembling. "Mind you return the favor. It's only polite."

She vanished through the back doors of the van, which slammed shut behind her, effectively ending our conversation.

I stood with my hand on the car door, staring at the place where she had disappeared. What the hell was that? Why had Lucida been so shocked to see me? Surely it wasn't so strange for a Tracker to join in on a Tracker mission—I was central to the case, after all. And then there was that last bit—about returning the favor by visiting her cell. It sounded casual enough—one of those snarky, off-the-cuff quips that were trademark Lucida. Except Lucida hadn't simply visited me in my cell in Skye. She had stolen a set of keys and broken me out of my cell. Was she actually hinting that I do the same? The idea was ludicrous, even laughable... and yet that gleam in her eyes had bordered on manic...

"Jess? Are you getting in?"

I turned and peered into the car to see Flavia sitting there, staring curiously at me. I slid onto the seat beside her, doing my best to push Lucida's words out of my mind. "Hi, Flavia," I said, managing to conjure a smile. "How are you?"

"I'm a nervous wreck!" Flavia replied, bouncing up and down in her seat. "I can't believe I'm really going to research inside the catacomb archive!"

I smiled at her, amused. "This is, like, the Scribe version of fangirling, isn't it?"

"Huh?" Flavia asked, barely listening.

"Nevermind," I laughed, shaking my head. "I'm glad you're excited. At least one of us is."

Flavia's face fell. "I imagine you aren't very keen on being back inside that place," she said. "Forgive me. I'm so thrilled about the collection itself that I'm not even considering this might be traumatic for you."

"Stop apologizing!" I told her. "Honestly, I'm fine. So, what's your job going to be while you're there, professionally speaking?"

"Cataloguing. We'll be ensuring that nothing is missing from the collection. It's entirely possible that the Necromancers used their influence over the Caomhnóir to gain access to the archive. While we may never be sure if they simply read or studied materials there, we can at least be sure that they didn't manage to abscond with any of them. A thorough cataloguing will ensure that we are able to keep track of everything. But, of course, the archive has thousands of items, so that's why so many Scribes are assisting in the process."

"How many of you are there?" I asked.

"At least fifty, I understand," Flavia said. "Scribes are coming from all over the world to assist. It's going to be quite exciting, to work with so many."

"I'll try to stay out of everyone's way," I promised. "Are you sure you'll have time to look for... the other thing?" I asked. The Caomhnóir had just slid into the driver's seat, and I was uncomfortably aware of the way he kept glancing into the rearview mirror at us.

"Oh, yes," Flavia said, following my lead and tossing a quick glance toward the front seat before continuing. "I've already made a list of texts to start with."

"Right," I said, taking a deep breath. "Well, here we go then."

16

A WARNING

THE THIRD HELICOPTER RIDE OF MY LIFE confirmed what I already knew from the first two helicopter rides: that I never wanted to ride in a goddamn helicopter ever again for the rest of my corporeal existence, and that, even as a ghost, I would be likely to keep my spectral feet firmly on the ground. When we finally touched down on the rocky, salt-sprayed shores of the cliffs of Skye, I exhaled for what felt like the first time in ten years and finally allowed myself to take in my surroundings.

And honestly, the anxiety I'd felt at seeing the place again was gone. I was knocked breathless for a moment by the absence of it, for I had been so sure that it would consume me from the first glance. Instead, I was able to appreciate for the first time the staggering natural beauty of the place—the mist that threaded through the rocks, the lonely loveliness of the stark cliff faces, and the ancient, almost mystic air of a greenness so deep and rich as to defy possibility. I had taken all of this in before, but had been unable to truly appreciate it.

When first I had gazed upon the Skye Príosún, I could only view it through the lens of captivity. I was going to be trapped in that place, a place where unknown danger lurked, and a prophecy pulled all the strings, leaving my very life hanging in the balance. I was sick with the fear that Finn would be mixed up in the chaos threatening to boil over and breach the battlements. And worst of all, I was afraid that my vision—the one that eventually came to pass upon the towers and ramparts of that very fortress—would signal a triumph for the Necromancers and an end to centuries of Durupinen guardianship of the Gateways. Given all that had been resting on my shoulders during my last journey, it was a miracle that I had taken in even a single detail of the place. Now, as I stepped from the helicopter and gazed up at the great stone fortress, I felt only curiosity and relief.

With the Necromancers gone and the rebellion quashed, staring up at the hulking outline of the Skye Príosún was like looking up at an animal that had been killed and stuffed. The eyes empty, the claws stilled, the jaws frozen in an empty echo of danger that had long since been rendered harmless. The love of my life was no longer trapped inside the place, no earth-shattering disasters lurked in its shadows, ready to pounce, and I was walking in, knowing that I was free to walk out whenever I wished. And so, when Flavia stood there, intimidated into silence and seemingly unable to move forward, it was me who took her hand and pulled her along, and it was my voice, sounding calm and determined, that said, "Come on. Let's go."

Both Flavia and I, along with the other Scribes and Trackers, had been given laminated badges to wear around our necks. They displayed our photos as proof of identification, and also had designations printed on them, which determined which areas of the *príosún* we were to have access. Thanks to Catriona, my Tracker designation meant that I could move completely freely about the castle, with access to both cell blocks and the archives. Both Flavia and I showed our badges to the Caomhnóir at the gates, who examined them carefully before returning them. It was like showing a VIP ticket to a bouncer at a concert venue, except instead of listening to music, like normal people, we were going to dig through old ghost relics in a prison.

My God, my life was so weird.

We dropped our belongings in a large bunk room, not unlike the barracks at Fairhaven, and Flavia went off at once with the other Scribes to be briefed on their work in the archive, while I headed to the Tracker office where they would likely saddle me with hundreds of pages of paperwork. We had agreed it did not make sense for me to come down to the archive until the next morning, when everyone would be busy with their assignments and unlikely to notice a random Tracker hanging around.

"What are you going to do in the meantime?" Flavia asked. "Besides all the paperwork, I mean?"

"I've got a social call to pay," I said, and when Flavia looked confused, I simply laughed. "I've got Tracker business on one of the cell blocks that should prove to be... interesting."

SOUL OF THE SENTINEL

It was much simpler than I ever would have imagined to get onto Lucida's cellblock that night without interference. I suspected that it would not have been so easy even a few short weeks ago, when the Caomhnóir were fully in charge of all access and clearance within the walls of the great fortress. I still remembered how Catriona had been accompanied through the halls by a pair of Caomhnóir. It had been difficult to get even a few moments together in my cell on my last visit—the Caomhnóir had been breathing down our necks from the second we had entered the front gates. But now, with the advent of the rebellion and its accompanying fallout, Trackers had officially taken over the management of the *príosún*, with the Caomhnóir guards answering to them instead of their own leadership. I knew this—I knew that my ID ought to allow me access anywhere, but I still held my breath as the stone-faced Caomhnóir examined it at the entrance to the system of prison blocks.

Of course, I thought as I was waved through the doors, I would have been satisfied never to look upon a single cellblock in that place again, but Lucida's cryptic invitation was much too intriguing to ignore. In some regards, I felt like a fool. What the hell was I doing, answering some vague summons by the woman who had nearly destroyed my entire life? I owed her nothing, even if she had helped me escape the *príosún* last month. At best, we were even. She had no reasonable claim on my time or my energy. Despite this, I found that I could not ignore the nagging voice in my own head that insisted I discover what it was that Lucida wanted. And so there I was, well after 11 o'clock, when the vast majority of the Scribes and the Trackers had turned in for the night, walking along the third-floor cellblock—the very cellblock, in fact, that had been my home sweet home while I was posing as an undercover prisoner. I cursed myself under my breath. If I met trouble on this outing, I had no one to blame but myself.

The cellblock was nearly deserted. Many of the prisoners who had been kept inside it had since been transferred while the *príosún* was being investigated, and had not yet been returned. A single Caomhnóir was patrolling the cellblock, but he offered me no resistance, no awkward questions. A single flash of my clearance badge and he had given me a surly nod and continued on his way. I knew it did not matter who heard me coming, that I was completely within my rights to stroll down this particular corridor, but it did not stop me from making a conscious effort to quiet my footfalls. The confidence I'd had walking back in the doors of the *príosún* seemed to evaporate upon entering this hall. Whatever privileges I had since been granted, my recent memories of this place left me feeling as much of a prisoner as I had when I had first been locked into one of these cells. My palms began to sweat and my breathing became unsteady. By the time I had arrived in front of Lucida's cell, I was on the verge of a full-fledged panic attack. I pressed my hands and forehead to the cool metal of the door, willing myself to calm down, to master myself.

There were only two places through which I might be able to glimpse Lucida within the cell. The first was a small window, slatted with iron bars, in the very top of the door. The second was a small opening at the base of the door, through which trays of food could be delivered to the prisoner within. Not wishing to crouch upon the cold, grime-covered floor, I pulled myself up onto the very tips of my toes and peered into the gloom of the cell.

Before my eyes had even begun to adjust, a languid voice drifted out of the shadows. "You came," it said, shock evident in its tone.

"You told me to," I said. "You needn't sound so surprised."

"But I *am* surprised," Lucida admitted. "I'm gobsmacked, in fact. It was a spur of the moment request, and I wasn't even sure at the time if you understood me. I honestly didn't expect to see you here."

"I honestly don't know what I'm *doing* here," I admitted. "But don't get your hopes up. I wasn't sure what you meant when you spoke to me in front of Fairhaven, but if you think I'm here to bust you out with a stolen ring of keys, I'm afraid I'm going to disappoint you."

Lucida laughed. The sound was hollow. "My expectations were not quite that high," she said, still laughing that awful, empty laugh. "You might've spent a bit of time in the clink, but I know you're still a goody-two-shoes at heart."

I snorted. "What do you want, Lucida? Why am I here? Actually, I think the better question to ask is, why are *you* here?"

Lucida shifted on the bed, swinging her legs down over the side and sitting up. "Why am I here?" she asked. "Well, I would have thought that was fairly obvious. As I remember it, you were the one who found me covered in blood after I did in a former Caomhnóir on

208

Fairhaven grounds. We hardened criminal types call that 'murder,' and you'll find it's generally frowned upon."

"That's not a reason to lock you up," I said. "You were defending yourself. Anyone with half a brain could see that he'd attacked you, and that you'd done what you needed to do to survive. So, let me pose a new question: why was killing Ambrose the *end* of you defending yourself instead of the *beginning*?"

An odd shiver ran through Lucida's body. Her teeth chattered. "I don't follow."

"You just rolled over! You refused to speak a word in your own defense! You had a real chance of getting out for good, and you blew it on purpose. I want to know why."

Lucida looked up, and if her laugh had been hollow, it was nothing compared to the well-deep emptiness in her eyes. "I realized that it was safer for me on the inside than it was on the outside," she replied. She turned and looked out the window, where a bright half-moon was rising. Its light leeched the color from everything, leaving the cell looking like a black and white photograph. "I told Cat that I couldn't stay at Fairhaven, not with so many Necromancers on the loose. I knew they would come for me, and they did. And they'll keep coming for me."

"Yes, but why?" I asked. "Look, I believe you, okay? You're in danger. Ambrose's attack made that very clear. What I don't understand is why they're after you. What threat could you possibly pose to them now?"

Lucida didn't answer right away. One of her legs was bouncing violently, and she seemed unable to look away from the moon. "The last time you visited me in a cell like this, I told you that both the Durupinen and the Necromancers had decided that I was worthless, no longer of any use to them. They also knew that there was no chance I would ever be free again. And as a result, they didn't think twice about speaking freely, even when I was within earshot."

"So, you did hear something?" I asked. "Something about their future plans?"

"Not about their future plans, no," Lucida said. "But this *príosún* holds a lot more than just prisoners. There are many secrets locked away here as well, and I think the Necromancers might've discovered one of them."

"Go on."

"Deep in the bowels of this fortress, there's a spirit block. It's reserved for the most dangerous of spirit prisoners."

"I've heard of it," I said, my pulse quickening. "But it's empty, isn't it? Didn't the Necromancers empty all of the spirit cells so that they could use the spirits as Blind Summoners to inhabit the Caomhnóir?"

"Not all of them. Not this cell block," Lucida said, shaking her head forcefully. "Not even the Necromancers would dare unleash these prisoners. They're too unstable... too unpredictable. The Necromancers may be mad, but they're not fools."

"Okay, so what about it, then?" I asked.

"There's a spirit down there known only as the Tansy Hag. No one knows who she was or what she's been imprisoned for. Her history is naught but lore. Some even claim that she was never alive at all, but that she was a spirit form, cast off from an Elemental as it was destroyed. Some say that she was imprisoned on this spot even before the *príosún* itself was built—that it was, in fact, built to contain her. It used to be a game the new Caomhnóir recruits would play during their training, daring each other to go down into the bowels of the castle and touch the cell of the Tansy Hag. The legend is that if you whisper a truth to the Tansy Hag, she'll tell you a secret of the Aether. And if you tell her a lie, she'll curse you."

"And this Tansy Hag is real?" I asked. "It sounds like folklore to me. A story made up to frighten kids into behaving themselves."

Lucida shrugged. "Ask any Durupinen child who grew up steeped in the lore of our clans, and they'll sing you the song of the Tansy Hag—just a little rhyme they learned spinning circles in the dandelions. All folklore has got a bit of truth in it somewhere, though. Every fairytale is sprouted from a seed of reality."

"I suppose so. So, you're saying this spirit—or whatever it is—is real? And it's still here in the *príosún*?"

"Yes. Or at least she was, until the rebellion. I don't know what became of her after that."

"And why exactly are you telling me all this?"

"In the days leading up to the rebellion, I heard her name again and again, whispered between the Caomhnóir and the Necromancers. It was strange enough to catch my attention. Why suddenly all this talk of childhood monsters from grown men? I wondered if they might be thinking of releasing her, that perhaps they wanted to unleash a dangerous spirit just to see what havoc she could wreak. Perhaps they thought they could weaponize her and the other most dangerous spirits against the Durupinen. And then the day of the rebellion came, and the place was in chaos. Well, I don't have to tell you that, do I? You were caught up in it yourself. The Necromancer prisoners were all freed, and most of the spirit prisoners as well. I was left to rot, naturally, but then a guard decided to pay me a little visit."

I could feel the bile rising in my throat. Lucida had mentioned this attack to me once before. She also told me she had snapped the neck of her assailant.

"I was asleep when he snuck in, so by the time I woke, he had already pinned me to the ground," Lucida said. Her voice was flat, monotone, like she was reading the details of the event off a piece of paper. Perhaps detachment was the only way she could bear to relive them. "His foul breath was in my ear as he tore at my clothes. 'Not so high and mighty now, are you, girlie?' he said. 'We're going to teach you your place now, we are. You won't lord it over us any longer, with your stolen gifts. You're thieves, that's what you are. Nothing but a pack of dirty thieves.' And then he pulled a knife from his belt. I was getting my bearings by now, gathering my strength to fight him off, searching the cell for something I could use, a manner of escape or a weapon. That's when he started carving something into the skin on my back."

"He... he *what?*" I gasped, a shudder of horror running through me.

"I was weak from years of imprisonment, I couldn't stop him," Lucida snapped, as though my horror stemmed from her being unable to defend herself from the attack rather than from the attack itself. "When he finished, he said, 'There. A mark of your crime. The mark of the Tansy Hag. They'll find it with your body and they'll know. They'll know that we discovered their secret at last.' I went limp, hoping he would believe I had passed out from the pain. It worked. He loosened his grip on me as he began removing my clothes, and that's when I struck back. A few seconds later it was over. I never gave him a chance to explain. Once I had killed the bastard, my only thought was that I had to get out of the castle. I had to get away. I didn't give another thought to the mark—or what it might mean—until I arrived back at Fairhaven. When at last I was able to catch my breath and have a wash, that's when I laid eyes on it for the first time. If it weren't for the pain,

I might have forgotten it altogether in the absolute bedlam of the escape."

"What... what did he mark you with? What is the mark of the Tansy Hag?" I whispered.

Pressing her lips together in a grim expression, Lucida turned and lifted her shirt. There in the middle of her back, still scabbed and not yet fully healed, was a familiar mark.

A very familiar mark.

"Oh my God."

Lucida let her shirt drop and turned, staring at me with a shared understanding. "You've seen it before, haven't you?" she asked me.

"Yes," I breathed.

"I'd been trying to understand it, what it meant, where it came from. I'd read through damn near every book in that bloody library, searched every piece of artwork. I knew I needed to find some proof of it before I could tell anyone at Fairhaven."

"But you have the proof!" I said. "It's carved into your flesh, for God's sake!"

"And what would I say? 'Some half-crazy Caomhnóir did me a nice prison tattoo of a nonsense fairytale witch's mark. Please take this very seriously, because I've got a cracking reputation for telling the truth,'" Lucida replied, her voice full of false brightness. "Sod off, Jess. They'd have laughed me right out of the place."

I didn't reply. I didn't need to. We both knew it was true.

"And then one day, I got the idea to check the old family plots in the burial grounds. Those tombs and stones are some of the oldest relics on the property. I knew it was a longshot, but I was desperate. I decided to wait for nightfall to avoid awkward questions about what I was doing skulking around a bloody graveyard. I cut through the central courtyard, and that's when I realized I wasn't the only person wandering the grounds at night."

She gave me a pointed look, and I gasped. "You saw Savvy."

"Too right I did," Lucida murmured. "There she was, standing like a statue before the Geatgrima. And there on the dais stones, she'd drawn the mark—the very same mark still aching in the flesh of my back."

"What did you do?" I asked.

"Nothing!" Lucida cried. "What could I do? Your friend was clearly in some kind of trance. I didn't know what the hell was happening, but I knew I couldn't bloody well interfere with it! So

I watched her for a few hours until she stepped down, rubbed the mark from the stones with a handkerchief, and left. She never spoke a word, never looked at me. It was as though she were—"

"Sleepwalking," I supplied. "Because she was. At least, that's what we think she's been doing."

"I kept watching for her and realized she was keeping that vigil every night. And then, less than a week later, you and your Spirit Guide turned up as well."

"That was you in the courtyard, then?" I asked. "We thought we heard someone, but Milo did a sweep and couldn't find anyone."

"Yeah, that was me," Lucida said. "How did you find out she was coming to the courtyard at night?"

"She asked me to help her figure out what was happening—she kept waking up exhausted and dirty, with no memory of where she'd been. So, I stayed the night in her room, and when she got up, we followed her."

"Have you shown her the mark?" Lucida asked eagerly.

"Yes. She has no idea what it means, and has no memory of ever seeing it before, let alone drawing it on the Geatgrima."

Lucida's face fell. "Another dead end."

"It's not the only place I've seen it," I said slowly, and Lucida's head snapped up like a predator scenting prey.

"Do you know what it means?" Lucida asked eagerly. "Have you found documentation of it? If we had that, I could go to the Council and tell them what I—"

"No," I shook my head. "No, I haven't been able to find any other instances of that mark."

Lucida's brow furrowed. "Well, if you haven't been able to find it, what do you mean when you say it's not the only place you've seen it?"

I hesitated. Lucida was the last person I would ever imagine trusting with a secret, especially one concerning a prophecy, of all things. But I looked into her eyes and the words were out of my mouth before I could stop them.

"Fiona created a sculpture. We believe it was spirit-induced—maybe even prophetic. It depicts Savvy standing in front of the Geatgrima, and it includes that mark, right on the dais where Savvy drew it."

It was Lucida's turn to sit in stunned disbelief. She looked fragile in that moment, a delicate thing made of glass, a light breeze away from shattering to pieces.

"Something is happening here, Jess," Lucida whispered. "Something massive. What do we do?"

I was able to register, for the tiniest fraction of a second, the oddness of Lucida asking *me* what to do, but then my anxiety swept the moment away in its current almost instantly. "It's one of the reasons I'm here," I told her. "I thought I might be able to find a record of the mark if I could get into the catacomb archives."

Lucida's expression cleared. "That's a jolly good idea. Some of our oldest records are down there."

"That's what I've been told," I said. "I enlisted the help of one of the Scribes."

"What?" Lucida gasped. "You... you told someone? How can you be sure you can trust—"

I raised one eyebrow. "You aren't seriously going to lecture me about trustworthiness, are you?" I asked.

Lucida made an impatient noise. "Look, fair enough, but if the wrong person gets wind of this at the wrong time..."

"I trust this woman," I said, my expression fierce. "She saved my life when the Necromancers attacked the Traveler camp, an attack they carried out in part thanks to your betrayal. I trust her more than I'll ever trust you, so I don't want to hear another fucking word about it."

Lucida's face went rigid for a moment. Then, in a stiffer voice than before. "There is something else you could do while you're here, if you want to get to the bottom of this."

I took a deep breath, working to calm the sudden defensiveness that Lucida had kindled. It wasn't easy, but I managed it. "And what's that?" I asked.

"Go down into the spirit wards and talk to the Tansy Hag."

I blinked. I laughed. I laughed again. "Go... what?"

"Look, I don't know how much of her legend is true, and how much of it is complete bollocks," Lucida said, and there was a note of desperation in her voice now. "But there's something down in the spirit ward, yeah, and the Necromancers made contact with it. I don't know if they stumbled upon her, or if they knew she was there, but she told them something, something about a "crime" that we've supposedly committed, and this mark is supposed to be a symbol of that crime. The Necromancers aren't talking, and neither are the Caomhnóir who joined them. And now that mark has shown up at Fairhaven, and your friend is making nightly vigils at the Geatgrima in her sleep. What choice have we got? We have to figure this out. Something big is brewing here, love, you've got to know that."

I swallowed down something sharp and acidic—it tasted like fear. "Yeah. Yeah, I know."

"Right, then. So, will you do it?"

"How do I get down there? And will they even let me near that cell block if I can find it?" I hedged.

"It's in the second basement level, as far down as you can go before you reach the tunnel for the catacomb archives," Lucida said. "They don't patrol it. All the cells have been sealed and Warded, some of them for centuries. There's no need for guards. I don't think anyone will stop you."

I gave a harsh laugh and shook my head.

"What's so funny?" Lucida asked.

"Nothing. I just can't believe that I'm going to try something like this on nothing but your information," I said. "I'm either the bravest fucking person alive or the dumbest, and I'm afraid of the answer."

17

THE TANSY HAG

"**T**HE ANSWER IS THE DUMBEST," Milo practically shouted. "You are the dumbest person alive!"

"Milo! That's enough! You're not helping the situation!" Hannah snapped.

Both of their voices were as loud as gongs in the echo chamber of my skull. I pulled my pillow up on either side of my face, which of course did nothing to muffle sounds, but did stifle my moan of discomfort.

"Please, you two, try to tone it down," I replied. "And for the record, I'm not disagreeing with you on the dumb thing. Is Finn there yet?"

"No, but he'll be here any minute. I just texted him." Hannah replied, making a conscious effort to calm her energy.

"All I'm trying to say," Milo began, his tone calm but his energy still jumping with tension, "is that this whole plan sounds way too sketchy. I know that you had no choice but to team up with Lucida to escape the *príosún* last month, and I totally get that. But things are different now! She's behind bars and you're free! You've got a whole team of Trackers in the *príosún* with you, and dozens of Scribes as well. This alliance makes literally no sense at all!"

"I realize it's not ideal," I began.

"Not ideal?!" Milo gasped, fully worked up again. "Not ideal?! Jess, that's, like, the understatement of the century!"

"Milo, if we can't discuss this rationally, then I'm going to have to close the connection."

"Okay, sure, *I'm* the one being irrational," Milo cried, but I felt him working to reign in his energy nonetheless.

"I've never heard of this Tansy Hag before," Hannah said. "Are you sure Lucida's telling the truth?"

"Of course, I'm not," I said. "I'm never sure of anything with

Lucida. But I can't imagine what reason she would have to lie about it. I mean, if it were just a plot to lure me into a dangerous situation, why would she have rescued me last month? If she wanted to hurt me, all she had to do was leave me in that cell. Why would she go to all that trouble to rescue me only to throw me to the wolves a few weeks later? It's not logical."

"I'm not sure someone like Lucida operates on the plane of 'logical,'" Milo muttered, the thought a mere ripple, which I decided to ignore.

"The one thing I'm sure she's not lying about is that mark on her back." The memory flashed through my head, making all three of us shudder as we experienced it. "She can lie to me all she likes, but that mark is real. It's at least a few weeks old, based on the way it's scabbed over, and she sure as hell didn't put it there herself."

"But why didn't she tell someone? Why didn't she confide in Catriona or go right to the Council?" Milo demanded.

"I told you, she didn't think they would believe her," I said. "And anyway, Lucida has even less reason to trust the Council than we have to trust Lucida. She was never going to approach anyone on that Council, even her cousin, until she had indisputable proof."

"Sure, and now she wants to sacrifice you to get it," Milo said.

"No one is sacrificing anyone!" Hannah snapped. "We just need to... hang on, I think Finn is here."

I felt Hannah pull back from the connection, tautening the string but not releasing it, and then relax back into it. "Okay, I'm going to explain to him what's going on. Hang tight."

Waiting for Hannah to finish explaining the situation to Finn was almost worse than if I had to explain it to him myself. My imagination went mad envisioning the intensity of his reactions. At last Hannah's thoughts floated back to me once more. "Okay, he's caught up. What do you want me to ask him?"

"Ask him what he knows about the Tansy Hag. Is she real? What am I getting myself into if I venture down into that spirit block?"

I waited for a few loaded moments, and then Finn's words began dropping into my head, as dictated by Hannah. "I can't speak to the existence of the Tansy Hag. To my knowledge, it is nothing but a children's story—the Durupinen version of a fairytale. Anything I could tell you about her would likely be nothing but fiction. As to the deepest spirit block, there are several highly dangerous and very ancient spirits imprisoned down there. Their confines are so secure that they have held for centuries. I do not think any of them could hurt you if you simply entered the place. I have never ventured down there myself, so I cannot describe it to you: as Lucida told you, the nature of the prisoners means that the block requires no regular patrolling, and so I never had the pleasure."

I took a deep breath. "Oh yes, I'm sure it's going to be a delight. So, you have no idea if one of the spirits down there is really the Tansy Hag?"

"No, I don't," came the reply. "But let's just say, for the sake of argument, that the spirit in that cell is the spirit on which the Tansy Hag myth is based. It is highly unlikely that the spirit itself would bear any real resemblance, in form or substance, to what has become, over the years, a villainous witch in a cautionary tale. I highly doubt that if you walk down there and announce loudly that you won't eat your vegetables and won't go to bed, the spirit will jump out and curse you like the naughty little whipper you are."

Milo snorted. "Is that really what Durupinen parents tell their kids? Man, that's fucked up."

"Not all that different than telling them that Santa will fill their stockings with coal unless they behave themselves," Hannah pointed out. "Myths have always been used to teach lessons to kids."

Milo laughed incredulously. "There's a big difference between jolly old Saint Nick and a demon witch from the depths of hell, that's my point."

"Okay, okay, let's have the shitty parenting argument later, you guys!" I cried. "Focus, please!"

"Right. Sorry," Hannah replied.

"So, what you're saying is, it should be safe for me to go down there?" I asked.

"As long as you don't undo any Castings or open any cell doors, I can't see what danger those spirits could pose to you," came Finn's reply. "And believe me, I'm really trying to think of one, because Castings or no Castings, I don't like the idea of you down there alone in the least. Isn't there anyone you could bring with you?"

I considered for a moment. "I suppose I could ask Flavia to come," I said. "But I'm not going to force her. It's bound to be creepy as fuck down there, so she may not want to."

"That's a brilliant idea," Hannah said, and I wasn't sure if the relief I heard in the words was hers or Finn's.

"Okay," I said. "I'll ask her in the morning. Now, as unlikely as this scenario is, I'm going to try to get a little bit of sleep tonight. If I'm coming face to face with a childhood bogeyman in the morning, I'd at least like to be well-rested."

My head sang with a chorus of "good nights" before I sealed off the connection. I lay awake for a long time, staring at the patches of moonlight on the ceiling of the dormitory and both wishing for and dreading the onset of sleep.

Sure enough, when it came, it leapt and danced with monsters under bridges and witches in candy houses, an endless parade of nightmare villains straight out of a storybook, camped out in the dark recesses of my brain until the sun crept up over the cliffs outside.

§

"So, let me see if I've got this right," Flavia said, setting her coffee cup down on the table and fixing me with a bewildered stare. "You want me to go with you down into the deepest part of the *príosún* where the oldest, most dangerous spirit prisoners are kept and try to get the truth about this rune from a spirit that may or may not be someone called the Tansy Hag?"

"Yes," I said.

"And you're asking me this before I've even finished my first cup of coffee?"

"Okay, yes, I realize my timing is off. I should have waited until after the first cup of coffee," I admitted.

"I think you should have waited until after the first dram of whiskey, actually," Flavia muttered, shaking her head.

"I know it sounds a bit odd..."

"It sounds *mad*," Flavia corrected me.

"But I don't think we can ignore this lead."

"The Tansy Hag? It sounds vaguely familiar but I can't think where I've heard it. The Travelers will sometimes use tansy flowers in castings, of course, but this sounds like something different," Flavia said, sounding positively baffled. "You say it's a common children's tale in the Northern Clans?"

"Evidently," I replied with a shrug. "I'd never heard of it before, but then again, I'd never even heard of the Durupinen until someone told me I was one. But Finn said it's a familiar cautionary tale that most any clan children would have heard mention of growing up."

"Fascinating," Flavia said. "But he didn't recognize the rune as part of the story?"

I shook my head. "No. The story itself seems to be well-known, but the idea of the Tansy Hag's 'mark' does not."

"I wonder... let's check one thing before we head down there," Flavia said, downing the rest of her coffee in a single swig and jumping to her feet.

"Before we head down?" I asked, hardly daring to believe my ears. "Does that mean you're coming with me?"

"Certainly, I'm coming with you," Flavia said briskly. "You don't think I'm going to let you go down into that creepy cell block by yourself, do you?"

"I don't know," I said with a laugh. "I mean, *I'd* probably let me go down there by myself."

Flavia joined in the laughter. "Look, I might be just a crusty academic, but I'm tougher than I look."

I grinned at her. "I don't doubt that for a second."

We made the long walk down to the catacomb archives, which was already crawling with Scribes even at so early an hour. Flavia led me into a row of stacks and dropped to her knees in front of a small, shabby looking set of books on a bottom shelf.

"I've been so absorbed in searching for that mark in runic histories and Casting compendiums that it hadn't occurred to me that we might be looking in entirely the wrong place. If, as you say, this mark is part of a story, then perhaps we ought to be looking in storybooks."

"Does this library have storybooks?" I asked in amazement. "This is hardly the place I'd come if I wanted to check out a bedtime story for my kids."

"This library has everything," Flavia said, running her forefinger along the spines as she searched. "Even Durupinen fiction must be documented, more so perhaps because we have a responsibility to understand how our mythology is disseminated."

"What, we're afraid we're going to turn into popular ghost stories?" I asked, amused.

"Something like that, yes," Flavia replied. "And even popular fiction can be too close to discovery for us. We must take precautions."

"Oh, God, you're not going to tell me we're book burners, are you?" I asked. "Because I seriously don't think I could deal with that type of stigma on top of everything else."

"Here we go," Flavia said, ignoring my question, pulling a tattered book from the shelf, and handing it to me. "Have a look in here and see what you can find. We're looking for a reference to the Tansy Hag."

It took forty minutes and six volumes of children's stories and rhymes before we found what we were looking for. Flavia's cry of triumph was so loud that several other Scribes turned to grill us with disapproving glares. "Here it is! Look!"

The book lay open in her lap to a beautifully detailed picture, the caption for which was written in an old form of Gaelic I could hardly make out, let alone translate. In it, a pair of young girls, clad in long white dresses, sat amongst a patch of yellow flowers, holding hands, one whispering into the other's ear. They both had long golden hair, on which they had placed delicate crowns of the flowers. And just behind them, lurking in the shadows of the encroaching forest, a stooped and menacing old woman leered at them. She was draped in a long black hooded cloak, and one gnarled old hand clutched at a tall walking staff. The other hand was stretched out before her, and there, clearly visible on the wrinkled palm of her hand...

"The mark of the Tansy Hag," I whispered. "Holy shit, Lucida was telling the truth."

"I'm going to have to work to translate this story," Flavia said. "The Gaelic is antiquated. But that's it! That is undeniably the mark we've been searching for!"

"I can't believe it," I whispered. "Just sitting here in a book of fairy tales, where anyone could have found it. If it was the mark of some great secret, why would anyone allow it in a book of children's stories?"

"What better way to dispel the belief in something than to turn it into a fairy tale?" Flavia pointed out. "No one wanders the woods with cameras to search for gingerbread houses belonging to witches, or dives into the sea intent on proving the existence of mermaids or kelpies."

"Well, sure, some people do stuff like that," I said.

"And how are such people perceived?" Flavia asked shrewdly.

I nodded, understanding her meaning. "Wackos. Crazy people."

"Exactly," Flavia said. "If the story is mythologized, and those who would seek to prove it are cast as delusional, then it is easy to make such a truth disappear in plain sight. And it has worked. The mark has faded into obscurity, and the Tansy Hag is nothing more than a bedtime tale."

"Unless, of course, she's actually here in this castle, locked away and forgotten," I pointed out.

"Indeed," Flavia said solemnly, closing the book and returning it to the shelf. "And I think it's time to find out.

§

Flavia and I arrived at the base of the staircase that led to the catacomb archives, but rather than climbing up them, we approached the guard who kept watch at the bottommost step.

"Hi," I said awkwardly. "We, uh... need to visit the spirit block. On, um... Tracker business."

I held up my badge, and the Caomhnóir gave it a cursory glance. He pointed up the stairs. "Next level up, first landing you come to, but I take it you know it's empty. All those spirits were released during the Necromancer takeover, and none have been recaptured." His speech had a slight lilt to it—the accent might have been French, but it was hard to tell.

"Actually, that's not the spirit block we're talking about," I said. "We need to visit the, um... other one."

The Caomhnóir looked me in the face properly for the first time; it seemed I'd finally gotten his full attention. "The other one? You don't mean the old spirit block?"

"I do, actually," I said, my voice full of false brightness. "Is it this way, or...?"

"What business do you have down there?" the Caomhnóir asked, narrowing his eyes at me.

"Tracker business," I repeated. "Otherwise known as none of your business. Now I didn't ask for an interrogation, I asked for directions. Are you going to give them to me, or should I ask someone more competent at following basic instructions?"

The man's eyebrows drew together and he took a moment to swallow whatever retort he was planning on throwing at me. Then he turned and pointed wordlessly at the yawning black mouth of a hallway across from the staircase.

223

"Thank you," I said, and walked past him toward the archway. I kept my pace brisk and my chin up until we had entered into the tunnel beyond. As soon as we were out of his sight, however, I stopped dead in my tracks and took an unsteady breath.

"Are you okay?" Flavia asked, nearly walking into me.

"Yeah. I just... can you feel that?"

We'd barely entered the hallway and already there was a heavy, palpable dread thick in the air. It was as though someone had draped a wet woolen blanket over my face—it was hard to breathe, and the air itself tasted strange and sour.

"What... what is that?" Flavia whispered as the sensation hit her, too.

"I'm not exactly sure," I admitted. "It's... awful."

It was as though the spirits' suffering had changed the very nature of the atmosphere here, as though someone had taken hundreds of years of solitary confinement, rolled it up, and hit me over the head with it, bludgeoning me with misery. If it felt this oppressively awful to me, I couldn't imagine what it would have done to an Empath like my friend Mackie. She probably would have been driven mad within a matter of seconds and been forced to flee. Personally, I would have liked nothing better than to flee, which was why, of course, I started walking deeper into the cell block.

It certainly didn't look like the other cell blocks. Bars and locks were not required to keep the prisoners trapped, and so there were none. Rather than cells, there was a series of caverns dug into the walls on either side of the hallway. Some of them had crumbling stone walls, while others seemed to have simply been hollowed out of the earth. Nearly every square inch of the place was covered in runes—the walls, the floor, even the ceiling, set with a row of feebly flickering yellow bulbs, was a tapestry of carved symbols. My skin was tingling, and my blood rushed in my veins. Every nerve screamed at me to turn around, all flight and no fight.

"I'm not sure how long I can stay down here." Flavia's voice was sharp and panicked in my ear.

"Neither am I," I murmured. "Let's try to be quick."

We peered into each cell one by one, looking for any sign of a spirit who might be the Tansy Hag. Most of the cells appeared completely deserted, however.

"Are... are they empty?" I asked. "Did the Necromancers free them, do you think?"

Flavia shook her head, her breathing ragged. "No. Some of these runes sap spirit energy, so that they can't affect their environment. Some of them probably don't have the will or ability to manifest. But... my God, I can still *feel* them, can't you?"

We'd passed maybe a dozen cells before we saw a spirit at all. Then on the right, the spirit of a young woman appeared. Her cell had been hung with dozens of mirrors, and the walls inlaid with hundreds of jagged mirror shards. She did not acknowledge our presence, but stood gazing into a hand mirror, stroking her own cheek over and over again, and singing softly to herself. She did not appear to have any eyes.

A few cells down, the spirit of a man crouched in the corner of his cell. He opened his mouth and began shouting at us the moment we came into view. Though no sound penetrated the walls of his cave, the air around us began to vibrate with the force of his silent screams. I recognized the symptoms of a spirit who had been Caged.

In another cell, a spirit flickered back and forth between different versions of herself, first a round-faced child, then a young woman, then a shriveled old crone. Each iteration of herself simply stood and cried, blooming and withering in rapid succession for eternity.

"What could they have done?" Flavia whispered. "What could any of them have done that was so terrible that they earned themselves an eternity in a place like this?"

"I can't imagine," I whispered. "Surely there couldn't be a crime that fits this level of punishment."

We rounded a corner, past a spirit curled in the topmost corner of her cell like a sleeping spider in a web, and found ourselves face to face with the last cell in the block.

"Oh, my God," I whispered. "This is it. Look."

The cell was little more than a cave, so crudely and roughly formed that it might have been gouged from the earth with someone's bare hands. It appeared completely empty—its occupant either tucked away in its darkest recesses or else they had not materialized. Crumbling stone beams stood on either side of the opening, which was obscured with cobwebs and roots. The runes carved into the stones around the opening were so old that they had worn nearly smooth, and the musty stench was nothing to the overwhelming sense of dread and misery that hung over it like a death shroud. But what truly took my breath away was none of this.

No, what truly sucked the very air from my lungs, what paralyzed me where I stood with crippling fear was the mark.

The mark of the Tansy Hag. The mark we'd been searching for. It was *everywhere*.

Hacked into the floor, scrawled onto the stones, pressed into the dirt, arranged out of twigs and pebbles like little talismans: there was not a square inch of the cell from which that mark did not stare out at us like an eye.

"*Miri Devel!*" Flavia murmured, slipping into her native Traveler tongue in her shock.

At the sound of her words, there was a shifting and stirring in the deepest shadows of the cave. A shape that was little more than shadow itself peeled away from the darkness and floated, like the darkest feather, toward us.

Flavia and I nearly fell over in our haste to back up, but the shape did not approach us. It couldn't leave the confines of the cavern, Finn had promised me that. I reminded myself of this fact silently in my head about a dozen times before I found my voice again.

"Should I speak to it?" I breathed over my shoulder to Flavia, whose hands were gripping my shoulders so tightly that they were beginning to ache.

"I d-don't know," she stammered back.

The shape floated a few inches closer to the edge of the cavern. Then, the darkness receded from the place where its head might have been, concentrating itself into what was unmistakably a pair of eyes. The eyes stared at us. And then a voice—no, a ghost of a voice—whispered in our heads, as though the shape had pressed its mouth to our ears to speak.

"*Romni?*" it sighed.

Behind me, Flavia let out such a gasp that I spun on the spot, sure she had been injured or attacked. "What?" I asked her, taking in her milk-white face, her mouth hanging open. "What is it? Flavia? Are you okay? Speak to me!"

Flavia tried to tear her eyes from the spirit behind me, but managed only a flicker of a look before it drew her gaze once more. "It's... Jess, I think it's speaking Romany."

"Are... are you sure?" I asked, my own mouth hanging open now. "Do you mean... is that thing... did she used to be a *Traveler?!*"

"I don't know. I don't know what to think. But how else would she know the language, unless..." a light of recognition sparked in

226

Flavia's eyes, and when she spoke again, her voice was stronger. "Unless Tansy isn't a fictional moniker at all, but a real name."

"You've lost me," I admitted. I glanced nervously over my shoulder. The spirit continued to stare with its gathered shadow eyes.

"Tansy isn't just the name of a flowering plant. It's also a name—a surname in Traveler history. That's why it rang a bell for me, not because I'd heard of the Tansy Hag before, but because I had heard the name 'Tansy.' I've come across it in old genealogies and the like. And the word 'hag' is synonymous with the word 'witch' which is a stigma that has plagued Traveler women for all our history."

"There's... there's a Traveler ghost locked up in our *príosún?*" I asked.

"She must be! She only came out when I spoke Romany. She must have recognized it! And just now, *'Romni.'* She's asking if we are Romany, that's what that word means. She's trying to find out if we're Travelers!"

I turned back around. The spirit was still staring at us, waiting for us to reply. "Can you answer her?" I asked Flavia.

Flavia closed her eyes for a moment as though she were fighting the urge to be physically ill. Then she nodded once and opened her eyes again. She cleared her throat and replied in a trembling voice, pointing to herself. "Yes. *Romni.*"

"Come," the spirit's voice resounded inside my ear again, and I shuddered. Flavia gave a whimper and we both moved a few steps closer to the Tansy Hag's cell. As we closed the distance between us, her shape seemed to settle and resolve into a more human form. The shadows wrapped and twisted themselves into arms, a hunched back, a pair of gnarled hands, and the suggestion of a face obscured beneath the hood of a black cloak.

A tiny portion of my fear trickled away as I appreciated, for perhaps the first time since entering the cellblock, that the creature before me was not a creature at all. She had, at one time, been a human being. And whatever she had become in the many hundreds of years since, she was still, at her core, a human being. A terrifying human being, yes, but still. Forcing myself to hold tight to that piece of information helped me to calm down and think rationally.

When we stood a mere yard or so from the entrance of the cavern, the Tansy Hag narrowed her eyes at me, studying me. Then she pointed a gnarled finger at me, and whispered, "*Djan rakli.*"

Flavia stepped out from behind me to stand beside me now. "She says she knows you," she whispered to me.

I turned to look at Flavia in shock. "She knows me? How could she possibly know me?"

"I don't know. I'm just telling you what she said," Flavia replied, her voice still shaking.

I turned back to the Tansy Hag and asked, "You know me?"

I waited for a moment while Flavia translated in a breathless voice. The Tansy Hag nodded her head once.

My chest seemed to be filling with icy water. "How do you know me?" I asked.

The old woman raised her hand to point at me again. "*Dook rakli.*"

Flavia gasped. "She... she says you're the girl with the Sight."

"The Sight? What does that mean?"

"She's... she's talking about your gift. About being a Seer."

"But how? How can she know that I'm..."

But the old woman cut me off, leaning so close to the edge of the cavern that I felt the crackle and buzz of the Castings that held her in place as she met their boundary. Almost involuntarily, I leaned in, too. Then she opened her mouth and whispered, "Jessica."

I shuddered, breathless and terrified. "How do you know my name?"

Flavia translated in a squeak of a voice but the Tansy Hag did not answer. She merely continued to stare at me, as though my face were a familiar book and she was simply reading the text upon it for the hundredth time.

"Ask her about the mark," I whispered to Flavia. "Ask her what the mark means."

Flavia translated my question, pointing with a violently trembling hand at the many iterations of the rune all over the cell. The Tansy Hag followed the direction of her gesture, looking all around the room at the mark as though she had only just realized it was there, as though she herself hadn't been creating it over and over again for centuries trapped in this tiny space.

The Tansy Hag floated over to one of the marks, this one formed from tiny pebbles lined up upon the ground. She gazed down at it for a moment, then looked up at me, pointing to the mark and whispering, "*Mule-vi tshor!*" Then she threw back her head and shrieked, so that her voice echoed and shattered against the walls and echoed again. "*MULE-VI TSHOR!*"

I flung myself back from the cavern's edge in fear, crashing into Flavia and sending us both tumbling to the floor in a heap. "W-what is she saying?" I asked her as I helped her back to her feet. "What does it mean?"

Flavia didn't seem to want to answer at first. Her face was twitching, as she fought the urge to cry. Finally, she choked out, "She... she said... 'Durupinen thieves.'"

I spun around to face the Tansy Hag again. She was still huddled over the mark, and now she seemed to be singing a little song to it. My voice, when I spoke again, was harsh in the aftermath of my fright. "What are you talking about? Why are you calling us thieves? What does that mean?"

"*Lavash vortimo,*" the old woman sang, over and over again.

Flavia whispered to me, "She says it's the shameful truth."

"But what does that mean?" I asked, frustration creeping in now. "How do I find out more about this shameful truth?"

The Tansy Hag stopped singing. She met my eyes, and I watched as her shadowy face clarified into real features for the first time. Her eyes were so deeply, unendurably full of sorrow that a lump rose instantly in my throat. Then she passed her hands over the pebbles at her feet and they began to roll around the ground, rearranging themselves into another pattern and disturbing the ancient dust in which they lay. When the dust settled again, the mark was gone, replaced by another familiar sight:

CA-126B-1240-ISH

Behind me, Flavia cursed in Romany again, but all I could do was stare. I felt no shock, although that would have been the natural response. I felt only a settling deep in the pit of my stomach, a rightness as things fell into place because, of course. Of course, it was all connected. My time as a Seer still hadn't taught me all there was to know about prophecies and the interconnectedness of causes and effects, but I ought to have known by now that when the universe was screaming at me from all sides, it was probably screaming about the same thing. I wasn't trying to solve two mysteries at Skye Príosún. I was trying to solve one.

I locked eyes with the Tansy Hag. It was as though she had looked right into my head with those ancient, miserable eyes and read every single thought as it materialized in my brain. She nodded her head, as though agreeing with my silent assessment of what was before me.

Then, in broken, heavily-accented English, she whispered to me, "You must go back. Deep. Deep through the door that will not open. I find you there, Jessica. There you find answer, yes? There you find *vortimo.*"

Then the Tansy Hag melted away into shadow and spoke no more.

18

PORTRAIT

"**S**HE KNEW YOUR NAME," Flavia muttered as we traversed the tunnel back toward the catacomb archives. "How could she have known your name?"

"I don't know," I said. "I just don't know. But she didn't just know my name, Flavia. She *recognized* me."

"But that doesn't make sense," Flavia hissed. She was clearly still very shaken from the encounter, perhaps even more so now that she understood the ancient spirit to be one of her own people. "A Traveler in a Northern *príosún*? What is she doing there? Why would she know who you are? And how does a spirit trapped for hundreds of years know something as modern as a library call number? That archive wasn't updated with that organizational system until centuries after she was imprisoned, and it's not as though they granted their oldest and most dangerous prisoner research privileges to have a look around the place!"

"That's true. Unless someone told her? One of the Necromancers, maybe?"

"But how in the world would the Necromancers know the significance of this call number? And how would they even speak to her?" Flavia asked. "She wouldn't even materialize until I accidentally spoke Romany, and even then, she barely seemed to trust us! Unless there is a Necromancer who speaks Romany, which I highly doubt, how did they even make contact?"

I didn't reply. No, it didn't make sense at all. It made no sense for the Tansy Hag to know that call number. It made no sense for that call number to exist woven into a centuries-old tapestry either. But one thing was clear: both the Tansy Hag and the creator of the tapestry had found a way to put that call number into my hands. It was time to discover what was hidden there.

After a swift and whispered conversation outside the doors of the archive, Flavia and I agreed that we couldn't possibly risk searching the library while it was so full of other people. The call number had been passed along to me not once, but twice in the most mysterious, most clandestine of ways—it would be absurd to lay its discoveries on display where any passing scholar could glance at it. Instead, we agreed that we would meet again at 8 o'clock that night, by which time Flavia assured me that the archives would be nearly empty.

"The work starts and ends early around here," she told me. "I'll wait for one of the smaller reading rooms to free up, and then wait for you there. It won't be guaranteed privacy, but we'll at least be able to head off anyone who tries to come in while we're working."

The idea of waiting all day to unravel the mystery of the call number was nearly unbearable. I considered visiting Lucida again, to let her know what I had discovered, but I dismissed the idea almost as quickly as it popped into my head. All I had to offer were more questions. Until I discovered what was waiting in the archive for me, there was really nothing to tell Lucida and, in any case, I wanted to fully understand the Tansy Hag's cryptic message before I decided whether or not I even wanted to share it with her. I didn't owe her anything, I reminded myself. Whether she was working to redeem herself or not, I definitely did not need to feel any obligation whatsoever toward Lucida. So, I shoved my weirdly conflicted, guilty feelings about her out of the way and chose instead to update the other people I knew were waiting anxiously for news.

Hannah was as full of questions as Flavia had been. "Jess, I just can't believe that she knew who you were! Why would she know you?"

"I still can't believe you went down there," Milo said, and I could feel the force of his shudder vibrate through the connection. "It sounds terrifying. I mean, I'm a ghost and you still couldn't bribe me enough to set foot in that block."

"Yeah, well, it wasn't pleasant, I'll give you that," I said. "I can't believe we keep spirits trapped down there like that. It doesn't seem right. Maybe that should be our next policy to tackle, once the Code of Conduct gets overhauled."

"Don't, don't, you'll jinx it!" Hannah squealed, and I winced. "Sorry," she said at once. "I'm just... I'm really nervous about the legislation. Let's not talk about it right now, okay?"

"Yeah, let's talk about the prescient ghost in the bowels of the medieval prison instead. That's much less nerve-wracking," Milo replied, his voice dripping with sarcasm.

"Tell me again what she told you, about the door?" Hannah prompted me, ignoring Milo's sass.

"She said, 'You must go back. Deep. Deep through the door that will not open. I find you there, Jessica. There you find answer, yes? There you find *vortimo*.'"

"And '*vortimo*' means truth?" Milo asked.

"Yeah. That's what Flavia said when she translated it."

"What do you think she's talking about? What door?"

"I have no idea," I admitted glumly. "I'm hoping that whatever we find in the archive will help to explain it. If all goes well tonight—if I find what I'm looking for—then I'll catch the first chopper out of here in the morning back to Fairhaven."

"Listen to you," Milo said with a laugh. "Talking about 'catching choppers' like it's all casual."

"Yeah, you should see how casual I look when I'm all strapped in, breathing in a paper bag and begging for someone to knock me unconscious until we're on the ground again," I said. "Totally unbothered. Super cool."

Milo snorted. Hannah shushed him.

"Just do me a favor," I said, "and let Finn know what happened with the Tansy Hag, okay? And tell him I'll touch base tonight, to let you guys know what I find."

"Okay," Hannah assured me. "I'll text him now. He wanted to wait for you to contact us, but he was called down to the barracks, and couldn't stay."

"It's fine," I said. "Just let him know. And wish me luck!"

"Good luck," Milo and Hannah said together.

"And be careful in the archive," Hannah added, her voice pulsing with anxiety again. "I know it's just a library, but at this point, I don't trust anything in the Durupinen world to be harmless, even a bunch of old books."

"I will. I'll let you know when I find something," I told them and, savoring one last warm zing of affection and support, I closed the connection.

§

At last, after what felt like one of the longest days of my life—though, admittedly, not as long as the day I'd spent actually locked up as a prisoner in the same castle—8 o'clock arrived and I made my way back down from the dormitory to the catacomb archives. The *príosún* was quiet—admittedly, there were far fewer prisoners than the last time I'd been there, but even the prisoners who had since been returned to their captivity seemed unusually calm. No moans or cries for mercy rang out as I traversed the long hallways. No bangs or shrieks startled me as I descended the long staircase. In fact, on the entire journey down to the Archive, I saw only four people: a Scribe, yawning and rubbing her eyes on her way back to the dormitory for bed, and three Caomhnóir guards, none of whom even spared me a look, let alone spoke to me. When I finally entered the archive itself and saw Flavia's friendly face smile up at me, I felt an overwhelming sense of relief.

"Thank goodness," I said. "Would it be weird if I said I missed you?"

Flavia laughed. "What are you talking about?"

"Nothing. I'm just really glad you're here. I don't think I could have done this by myself. So, I guess what I'm trying to say is, thanks."

Flavia smiled. "You're welcome."

"Are we ready?" I asked, scanning the room. Flavia had been right; a single Scribe remained in the archive now, tucked in a far corner of the room and ignoring us completely as she organized scrolls into several cardboard boxes and sealed them with tape.

"Yes," Flavia said, giving a satisfied nod. "Let's do it. I confess I had a hard time refraining from just looking up the damn call number myself while I was in here today. I've been an anxious wreck since we left the spirit block."

"So have I."

Flavia picked up her backpack, a notebook on a clipboard, and a stack of pencils. "I've checked the private reading rooms, and they're all empty. Let's dump our things and then we can figure out where to start looking."

We staked our claim on the reading room at the far end of the archive, as private as we could manage given that it had neither a door we could close nor a lock we could fasten. From our seats at the table, we had a clear view of the entrance to the archive, so that we would be forewarned if anyone entered the archive while we were working. Then, call number in hand, we set off through the stacks.

"All right, let's see what we've got here," Flavia said, adjusting her bifocals on the end of her nose and examining the paper. "This first number here means we are headed not for the books or the preserved documents, but for the art and artifact collection. That's right through here," she said, setting off at a brisk pace for a second large chamber off of the first one. This room was full, not of bookshelves, but of glass cases, massive wooden chests full of drawers, and great closets which, when opened, operated like oversized filing cabinets. A cursory glance around the room revealed such disparate artifacts as suits of armor, walls crowded with gilt-framed paintings, an assortment of tattered old flags and tapestries behind glass, and a collection of glittering, gem-encrusted jewelry that made the crown jewels look shabby.

"This... is incredible," I breathed, taking it all in. "I can't believe this is all just hidden away down here. It should be on display somewhere—a museum or something!"

"I imagine they would be, if we weren't trying so desperately to keep it all a deep and impenetrable secret," Flavia said. "Hmmm... it looks like the reference numbers start over here..."

Each item in the collection was meticulously marked with a call number similar to the one clutched in my sweaty hand. We slowly circled the room, watching the numbers tick up until we reached one of the very last large wooden chests. It resembled an old library card catalogue desk, or an apothecary chest, but instead of many small, square drawers, it was divided into a dozen long drawers.

"You see the dates?" Flavia asked, pointing to the numbers on the drawers. "These are some of the oldest artifacts in the entire library. And the ones we're looking for should be right..." she slid her finger down the drawers, "here." She placed her hand upon the handle and turned to me.

"Are you ready?" she asked.

"I have no idea. Just open it," I whispered.

Flavia grasped the handle and slid the drawer open. It squeaked and jerked along the track, an indication that it was not often disturbed. I held my breath, my heart in my throat, as the inside of the drawer slid into the glow of the lamplight.

It was empty.

All my excitement drained from me, leaving me hollow with disbelief. Beside me, Flavia let out a quiet exclamation of shock. It couldn't be true. After all of the clues, the hints, the strange coincidences—it couldn't be a dead end. It just couldn't.

Desperately, I began wrenching open the other drawers, unsure of what I was looking for, but sure I would know it when I saw it. Every other drawer contained something—tattered maps, botanical sketches, journals bound in animal hide, letters with broken wax seals, a lethal-looking set of daggers with rusted blades and carved ivory handles. I scoured each item for a sign of something—anything—familiar. Finally, I opened the empty drawer again, as though it were a magician's trick, and something would appear out of thin air. It remained, of course, stubbornly empty.

"I don't understand," Flavia whispered. "It should be here. Whatever it is, it should be right here, unless... Jess, do you think someone might have taken it? The Necromancers or someone? Do you think they got to it before we did?"

I shook my head. "No. This can't be right. They can't have found it—the tapestry and the Tansy Hag—they wouldn't have led me here for an empty drawer. They just can't have!" I slammed my hand down into the empty drawer in frustration. With a hollow thunk, the bottom of the drawer came loose.

"What the hell...?" I whispered. One corner of the wooden panel that comprised the bottom of the drawer had pulled free of the little groove into which it fitted. A tiny puff of dust was expelled from the gap now visible between the drawer bottom and the side.

"It's false!" Flavia hissed. "It's a false bottom!"

My heart thundering, I wedged my finger into the gap and wiggled it back and forth. Slowly, bit by bit, the gap widened. At last, I was able to slide all four fingers into the gap, grip the edge, and pull. The panel came away in my hand.

Flavia and I peered into the newly revealed depths of the drawer. The bottom of it was lined with once-red velvet, now faded to a brownish mauve. And there lying upon it, was a black leather portfolio, tied closed with a strap. My hand shaking, I reached down to pick it up. The moment my fingers brushed the leather, I experienced a sense of Déjà vu so strong that it flooded every sense. My nostrils filled with a pungent, herbal smell. My ears echoed with a snatch of music, played on a lute. And—so quickly that it was gone by the time I blinked my eyes—I saw that same portfolio lying on another surface in another place—a wooden desk, a guttering candle, a pile of crudely sharpened quills beside an upended bottle of ink.

I pulled my hand away, my breathing coming hard and fast.

"What is it?" Flavia asked. "What's wrong?"

"Nothing, I... it's just..." I swallowed hard, all traces of the vision fading like a dream upon waking. "This is it, Flavia. I recognize it. I can't explain how, but... I just know this is it."

"Someone certainly went to great lengths to conceal it, even in a place as secure as this. If anyone else tried to find it, even if they knew where to look, they would have been met with the same empty drawer," Flavia said.

I lifted the leather folder gingerly from its resting place and held it to my chest, as though afraid it would fly away from me if I didn't hold it tightly enough. Flavia carefully replaced the false bottom in the drawer, and then slid it shut. "Come on," she said, and we hurried back to the reading room. A quick glance into the far corner confirmed that the only other Scribe was still absorbed in her own project. She did not even bother to look up from her boxes as we passed, but stifled a yawn and wearily crossed something off of the paper lying in front of her.

Back in the reading room, Flavia and I pulled two chairs as close together as we could in front of the portfolio now lying on the tabletop between us.

"After all of this, I'm afraid to open it," I admitted to her.

"If you don't, I will," Flavia said impatiently.

Fingers trembling, I fumbled with the leather tie until it fell open, and then gently peeled the top cover of the portfolio back from its contents.

My own face stared back up at me.

Flavia was gasping, exclaiming, asking me questions—it was nothing but meaningless roaring in my ears. Everything else in the room fell away as I stared down, impossibly, at myself. The sketch had been rendered in ink with smooth, expert strokes. My hair tumbled in its typical mess of curls around my face, which had been drawn in three-quarter profile. My eyes stared at the artist, and my mouth was cocked into the suggestion of a smile—I felt the muscles of my face tug familiarly into it, mimicking the image before me.

Flavia's voice cut through at last, sharp with fear. "Maybe it's not you," she said. "Maybe it's just someone that looks like you—a distant Durupinen relative?"

I shook my head and pointed to the artist's rendering of the curve of my neck. "It has to be me. She's even drawn my tattoo on here. Look." The flock of little black birds trailed from my shoulder and up my neck to just behind my right ear. The artist had drawn each and every one, exactly as I'd had it inked onto my skin.

"She? How do you know the artist is a she?" Flavia murmured.

How *did* I know? How did I know that, if I followed the curve of my arm, I would find a signature scrawled at the bottom of the drawing, and how did I know whose name it would be before my eyes had even found it?

Agnes Isherwood.

There it was. My own ancestor had drawn a portrait of me hundreds of years before I was born, including details as specific as my tattoo and the little scar beside my left eyebrow from where I'd burned myself with a hair straightener when I was twelve. It was impossible—unfathomable—and yet, here it was. But what did it mean?

"Jess? Are you okay? You look really pale," Flavia said, placing a tentative hand on my shoulder. "Do you... do you want me to get you some water, or something?"

"No, thank you, Flavia," I said. "I'm fine, really. I just... I'm trying to take it in. I just... what do you think?"

"I'm flabbergasted, to be honest," Flavia admitted, leaning closer to the drawing and pushing her bifocals further up the narrow bridge of her nose. "I'm not sure how this is even possible, but it looks authentic. The quality of the paper is consistent with the time period, and so is the condition of the leather wrappings. I handle old documents all the time, and I like to think that I can spot the real thing."

"Okay," I said, taking a deep breath and trying to dig deep down into my confusion to find a thread of logic. "One of the first things I ever learned about Agnes Isherwood is that she was a Seer. She was notorious for her Sight because she made the Prophecy about Hannah and me, and the reversal of the Gateways."

Flavia bit her lip, still deep in thought. "So, you're saying that this drawing may be a vision of Agnes Isherwood's? Another prophecy of sorts?"

"Yes," I said, trying to convince myself as much as Flavia. "Maybe

238

when she was having her visions about the Prophecy, she also had a vision of... me?"

"But the Prophecy was so carefully documented, given its gravity," Flavia said. "Every tiny hint of it was meticulously recorded and analyzed. I find it hard to believe that this sketch wouldn't have been treated with the same attention."

"Unless no one else knew about it. Unless Agnes Isherwood found a way to keep it hidden," I pointed out.

"But why? Why would she tell the Durupinen world about the Prophecy, but keep your image a secret?" Flavia asked.

I shook my head, rubbing at my temples. "I don't know. I just don't know. And aside from all of that, what does any of this have to do with Savvy, or the Tansy Hag or that mark that keeps popping up everywhere?"

The question hung like a fog in the air over us. We sat in silence for several minutes before Flavia, who was continuing to pore over the drawing, suddenly said, "You don't have a tattoo on your hand, do you?"

"Do I... what? No, why?" I asked, holding my hand up so that she could see the unmarked skin.

"Because there seems to be something drawn on your hand here, look," Flavia said, pointing.

I leaned down so close to the sketch that Flavia's head and mine were touching each other. She was right; the sketch revealed just a glimpse of the underside of my hand, well-darkened by shadow, but within that shadow, there was a pattern of markings, almost too faint to make out and yet, most definitely *there*.

"I... I can't tell what it is," I said. "There's like a swirl here, and... maybe a rune, but it's all too dark..."

Cursing in frustration under her breath, Flavia picked the sketch up delicately between her fingers and lifted it up in front of us, adjusting it so that the light from the lamp fell across it more brightly. Then she gasped so violently that she almost dropped the paper. I gasped with her. The light streaming across and through the paper revealed that there was a second image drawn upon its other side. Flavia rotated the paper in her hands and placed it flat on the table top once again so that we could examine it.

It was an image of the palm of someone's hand—*my* hand, I could only suppose, and yet it was not bare, but covered in a delicate pattern of vines and flowers and runes, blossoming like a garden over the fingers and palm, creeping up the wrist. And there, right in the center of the palm, the seed from which the rest of the artwork seemed to spring and bloom and flourish in all directions was the mark of the Tansy Hag.

"It's... it's beautiful," I breathed. "But I still don't understand. Is this supposed to be me? My hand doesn't look like this."

"No," Flavia said in a trembling voice. "No, but it could."

I turned to her, and she was almost smiling, for she had understood something that I had not yet grasped.

"What do you mean, it could?" I asked.

Flavia turned to me. "Don't you remember, when you visited the Traveler camp? That night by the fire, when we all decided to have a little fun—take a little journey a bit closer to the Aether?"

And at last, the final puzzle piece dropped into place in my head. The Tansy Hag's words echoed back to me, and now they finally made sense.

"You must go back. Deep. Deep through the door that will not open. I find you there, Jessica. There you find answer, yes? There you find vortimo."

"Flavia," I cried, "You have to help me again. I have to Rift!"

19

THE SENTINEL

THAT LAST NIGHT at Skye Príosún passed in a strange haze of half-sleep, of dreams of darkened woods and Traveler wagons and sentient shadows that whispered and beckoned. I woke up feeling as though I had not slept at all, as though I really had been wandering a forest all night, chasing the sound of my own name. As I stumbled out of bed and into my clothes, I thought I might just have a taste of what it had been like for Savvy these past weeks, my body heavy and aching with a crippling exhaustion that ought not to have been possible after arising from a night in bed.

I joined Flavia at a small table for breakfast. She looked nearly as unrested as I did—deep dark circles had nestled in under her eyes, and her complexion was pale. In contrast to her appearance, though, she was full of a jumpy, jittery energy, which I knew was a direct result of nerves. After all, she had a priceless stolen artifact in her bag, and she was about to smuggle it out of the *príosún*.

We had agreed the previous night that it was not a good idea to attempt Rifting at the *príosún*. In the first place, we had no way of procuring the herbs and other items we would need to complete the Casting without attracting awkward questions and, even if we did manage to find everything we needed, where would we perform the ritual? Caomhnóir patrolled the entire place, and Scribes and Trackers were everywhere. No, it made much more sense to wait until we arrived back at Fairhaven, where we could at least find some privacy, and count on Hannah, Milo, and Finn to help us.

"I can't believe I'm doing this," Flavia was whispering into her teacup. "I can't believe the Northern Clans actually let me into the most remarkable library in our world, and I'm going to steal from it. This is insane." She took a shaky sip, which dribbled down onto her sweater.

"I already told you, you don't have to do it," I murmured back. "Give it to me, I'll carry it out."

"And I already told you that I'm the expert in handling and transporting ancient documents, thank you very much," Flavia snapped. "One wrong move and we could damage it beyond repair, and then we'd be in real trouble. I made up my mind, I'm the only one who's going to be handling it. And then, somehow, I will find a way to put it back where we found it. End of discussion."

"Wow, I never knew librarians could get so testy," I muttered. "I thought you were all supposed to be, like, mild-mannered and scholarly."

Flavia's face twitched into a momentary smile. "A common misconception. Mess with our collections, and we are a fearsome sight to behold."

"What's your weapon of choice, in such a battle?" I asked.

"Devastating wit. And sometimes a book cart. Scared?"

"I'm shaking in my boots," I assured her. I looked down at my nearly untouched plate of eggs and toast. "Are you about ready to go?"

She nodded, pushing her own plate away with a groan. "Yes. Let's get this over with."

"I'll meet you outside," I told her. "I've got one little detour to take first."

§

Lucida was curled up on the corner of her bed when I arrived outside her cell, gazing out of her barred window with a vacant expression. When I spoke, I startled her out of her reverie.

"You were right."

She jumped and stared over at me. It seemed to take a moment for my words to penetrate her consciousness. "Right? About what?"

"About the Tansy Hag. That symbol. It was all over her cell."

Lucida's eyes went as round as coins. "You... you never went down there?" she whispered, awestruck.

"Of course, I did. You told me to."

"I know I did, but I hardly expected you to listen to me," Lucida admitted.

"Ah, come on, you know me, Lucida," I said. "I can't resist the opportunity to make an epically bad decision. You and I are basically soulmates, in that regard."

"Out with it, then! Were you able to figure out what it means, or...?"

"Not exactly," I said carefully, unsure of how much I wanted to reveal to her, but still wanting to ease her mind. "She was very... cryptic. But I gleaned a few clues from what she said, and I think I'm on the right track. I have to go back to Fairhaven, though, to figure it out."

Lucida nodded. "I underestimated you. Again. I ought to know better by now."

I shrugged. "I never thought I'd be able to trust a single word that came out of your mouth, but here we are. I guess we both have more to learn about each other."

Lucida's face twitched into an odd expression. I couldn't decide whether it was a prelude to laughter or tears. "There was a time I wanted to burn it all to the ground, you know. Burn it all to the ground and dance in the ashes. All I managed was to light my own bloody self on fire. Now I'd just be content to walk away from it all, but..." she gestured around the cell. "Precious little ways I can walk now that I'm here."

"You never know, you might get released again," I said, without any real conviction in my voice.

Lucida laughed bitterly. "You never know," she said. "Look, the point I'm trying to make is, I may have put my matches away, but the Necromancers, they never will. They do not give up. They don't go away, they just go to ground and regroup and try again. Now, I don't know what this symbol means, but the Necromancers certainly seem to. And they're going to weaponize that knowledge if you don't disarm it first. If you give a damn for the life you've built with the Durupinen, you can't rest a single bloody minute until you figure this out."

"I know," I said. "I promise you, I won't."

It was such a strange moment, making a promise to this woman, vowing to protect the very thing she was once hellbent on destroying. I was starting to wonder if there were even such black and white things in the world as good and evil, heroes and villains, or if we all just lived and died in a sea of gray, all the good and the bad mixed up together, and doing our best not to drown in it.

She looked up at me. "You off, then?"

"Yeah. The helicopter takes off in about twenty minutes."

"Right. Well. Best of luck to you."

"Thanks," I said. It didn't seem like the right sentiment to return to her. Who needed good luck to rot away in prison? Luck had already abandoned the situation, let's be honest. So instead I said, "I'll let them know. When I've got this all figured out, when we come to the end of it, whatever it is—I'll find a way to let them know that you tried to help."

Lucida smiled sadly. "Won't make a bit of difference to any of 'em. But... tell Cat for me, would you? I want her to know why I'm here, even if there's not a thing she can do about it."

"Okay," I said. "I'll make sure she knows."

"Thanks, mate," Lucida said.

I wasn't her mate, that was for damn sure. But I allowed the word to hang in the air between us as I walked away.

§

For all of Flavia's nervousness, our exit from the *príosún* was completely uneventful. No one searched our possessions or interrogated us. The Caomhnóir couldn't have cared less whether we stayed or left, and the other Trackers seemed equally ambivalent. Only one of them returned with us—Elin, who had to file a report on a search of the grounds, and she had barely a word to spare for us. Nevertheless, Flavia clutched her backpack tightly in her lap, white-knuckled with anxiety, until we landed. I was white-knuckled, too, though for entirely different reasons. We were both exceptionally relieved when the helicopter touched down.

Finn walked out of the castle doors as the SUV crunched up the gravel drive. The instant I had closed the door behind me, he caught me up in a fierce embrace and kissed me. I was swept up in the moment, all the more wonderful because he had chosen to greet me in this way while half a dozen Caomhnóir stood looking on disapprovingly.

"Hi," I said, a little breathlessly as he set me back down.

"Hello, love," he said. "I'm glad you're back."

"So am I, as delightful as Skye Príosún is," I said. "Where's Hannah? I really want to show her—"

Finn held up a hand. "There will be time for that. There's something I need to tell you first."

244

"What?" I asked, feeling my anxiety kick back in at once. "What is it?"

"It's about Savannah," he said, and the brief flare of warmth at my arrival had settled into a very sober expression. "She's... well, perhaps I'd better just show you."

I glanced at Flavia, whose face reflected my fear, and the three of us set off across the lawn toward the castle. I didn't ask Finn where we were going, or what was happening. Once I knew the answer, I couldn't unknow it, and a very loud, very insistent voice inside me was already screaming that I didn't want the burden of this knowledge. My curiosity got the better of me, however, when we passed Savvy's mentee Frankie, huddled on a stone bench and sobbing unrestrainedly into her hands, her sister bent over her and attempting to soothe her with comforting words.

"Finn, you're scaring me," I muttered, jogging a few extra steps so that I was walking right alongside him. "Just tell me what's going on."

"I'm afraid telling you isn't going to alleviate your fears at all, love," he said. "And anyway, here we are."

We ducked through an ivy-covered archway that opened up into the central courtyard. It was crowded with people, and so all I could see at first was a sea of backs turned to me, as everyone whispered and craned their necks at something in the center of the courtyard. Finn was important enough in the Caomhnóir ranks that the crowd parted for him when it saw him coming, and at last the spectacle that had drawn such a crowd lay revealed before me.

There stood Savvy at attention, clad in her full Caomhnóir attire, unmoving and unblinking, her gaze fixed intently upon the Geatgrima. It was the very same scene as the night I had followed her out to the courtyard—her staff upon her back, the mark of the Tansy Hag drawn in ash upon the dais stone—and yet, it was different.

When we had watched her that night, there had been a hint of a connection between Savvy and the Geatgrima—Milo had described it as "a reaching"—as though the Geatgrima itself was reaching out toward her. Now, the reaching was not only tangible; it was visible. A shimmering glow, like a cloud or a thick, creeping fog, had billowed out and filled the space between Savvy and the Geatgrima. It swirled around Savvy's head, enveloping her in its iridescence, pulsing and caressing, swirling and elongating into tendrils that wrapped her in an ethereal embrace. It should have been beautiful.

It was not.

"What the hell? When did this happen? How long has she been like this?"

"She came out here and started her vigil in the middle of the night, as usual. But then, when the sun came up, when she normally would have left, she lingered instead and then..." Finn gestured helplessly toward Savvy. "I wasn't here to see it, but Milo was keeping watch over her, and he saw the whole thing."

"Where is M—" I began, but saw him floating toward me, around the outside perimeter of the courtyard, skirting the ring of spectators. Hannah and Kiernan hurried along behind him.

"I'm sorry," Milo said, his face stricken. "I'm so sorry, Jess! I promised I'd watch out for her while you were gone, and I did, every night, but there was nothing I could do!"

"It's okay, Milo," I said, and I leaned into him, giving him the closest approximation to a hug that we could muster in his current state. "It's not your fault. Just tell me what happened."

"She... well, nothing much, all night long," Milo said, his form crackling and blinking with the intensity of his emotions. "It was just like every other night, really, until the sun started to come up and, instead of wiping that rune away and leaving, like she usually did, she stayed where she was. And then, right when the sun hit the top of the Geatgrima, she raised her hand toward the Geatgrima, and then that shiny cloud thing blossomed out of it and drifted toward her. Then it touched her hand, and..." Milo broke down into sobs. It took several minutes for him to calm down enough to continue. "It latched onto her, that's the only way I can describe it. It touched her outstretched hand and made some kind of connection, and then it crept up her arm and surrounded her, just like you see it now. Then Savvy slowly lowered her arm and... and she hasn't moved since."

"Why didn't anyone tell me?" I asked, trying not to sound accusatory. "Why didn't you guys come through the connection to let me know what was going on?"

Hannah reached out and squeezed my hand. "There wasn't anything you could do, Jess. Freaking out about Savvy wasn't going to get you here any faster, and we knew that helicopter flight was going to be harrowing enough. We just needed you here in one piece, so we could figure this out."

I scanned the courtyard. I saw many Council members there, but the High Priestess was nowhere to be found.

"Where's Celeste?" I asked.

"She's away, meeting with the International High Council," Hannah said, biting her lip. "It's my fault she's not here—the High Council got wind of my proposed changes to the Code of Conduct and asked Celeste to come and testify about it before the vote. I offered to go, but she insisted that the matter would be taken much more seriously if she presented it herself. She left yesterday afternoon. Seamus has already gotten word to her about what's happened to Savvy, and she's on her way back, but she hasn't arrived yet."

"The Caomhnóir are in absolute upheaval," Finn said. "The leadership has been at each other's throats, arguing about how to proceed. Seamus wants to attempt an expelling Casting to try to break the connection, but others fear that it might do more harm than good. Meanwhile, spirits have been flooding the boundaries of the grounds, drawn by—whatever this is that's happening—and it's all we can do to keep the courtyard clear of them. Right now, they're discussing the logistics of cordoning off the courtyard to protect people, but no one wants to leave until they know what's going on."

"People are panicking," Hannah said in a murmur. "Just like they always do when faced with something they don't understand."

I looked back at Savvy, and every well of strength in me that had held up and held fast over the last few weeks felt ready to dry up and crumble to dust. What was happening to Savvy? Was she in pain? Was she going to be okay? What happened if the Geatgrima didn't release its hold on her? What happened if it *did*? Why did the Geatgrima choose Savvy? And what the hell did it all mean?

I watched her, the girl who dared to give up the life she knew not once, but *twice* in service to the spirit world, a lone sentinel standing guard in a vigil that none of us could understand.

Or maybe we could. And there was only one way to find out.

"All of you come with me," I said quietly, tearing my eyes from Savvy and looking to Flavia, who wiped the tears from her eyes and nodded once. "Up to the room, now."

"I'll... I'll see you later then, Hannah," Kiernan said awkwardly, and turned to leave.

"No, Kiernan, come with us. It would be helpful to have another Caomhnóir. Unless..." I turned to Hannah and locked eyes with her. "We're going to need help. Do you trust him?"

Hannah did not hesitate even a moment. "Yes, I trust him." She turned to Kiernan who flushed, but nodded solemnly at her.

"Your trust is not misplaced, I promise you," he told her.

"Good. If we want to help Savvy, then there's something I've got to do, and I'm going to need as much help as we can get."

§

Back up in my bedroom, Flavia and I told our story to our captive audience: Finn, his expression stony, Hannah and Milo, full of questions they could hardly contain long enough to let us speak, and Kiernan, who shifted from one foot to the other, looking unsure whether or not he was meant to be included in this gathering at all, but rapt all the same. We described our encounter with the Tansy Hag and our search of the archives. Then Flavia carefully extracted the leather portfolio from her bag and revealed the sketch to a chorus of gasps and sighs. Then she turned the sketch over, revealing the second image on the back.

"That's definitely the same mark," Hannah whispered, bending low over the sketch and poring over the details in awe.

"But you don't have any markings like that," Milo said, frowning at me. "Are we supposed to be looking for someone else who has tattoos like this?"

"No," Finn said. I looked up to see that he had made the same realization that I did. "That's the same kind of temporary artwork that Jeta painted on you in the Traveler camp. I recognize the style."

"That's right," I told him. "The Tansy Hag was a Traveler. She would know all about Rifting. And so, when she told me to "go through the door," she wasn't talking about a building or any other physical place. She was telling me to go Rifting to fully understand what's happening, and this sketch has provided the artwork I need to do it."

"But I don't understand," Milo said, gripping his head on either side and shaking it back and forth, as though he could somehow reorganize his thoughts into a pattern that made sense. "These

248

drawings were made by Agnes Isherwood, right? But how are she and the Tansy Hag connected?"

"I haven't figured that part out yet," I admitted. "But the Tansy Hag knew where this sketch was, and she knew I needed it to go Rifting. We have to trust that we'll find answers if I do."

"Why do we have to trust that?" Hannah asked, looking worried. "The last time you went Rifting, you had a difficult time coming out of it, didn't you?"

"I... was in it a little longer than Flavia expected, yeah," I admitted.

"So why do you want to risk that again?" Hannah asked. "There's got to be another way to figure this out."

My bark of incredulous laughter echoed around the room. "Hannah, I love you, and I know you're just looking out for me, but the time for caution is past. This artwork didn't survive in secret for hundreds of years for me to find just so I could turn around and ignore it! The Tansy Hag knew me! Agnes Isherwood drew me centuries before I was born! And they both seem to have left an elaborate series of clues to lead me to this moment. Even if nothing else about this clusterfuck of a situation is clear, their instructions for me are. I have to Rift. That's how we figure this out."

Hannah opened her mouth, no doubt to argue, but Finn cut her off.

"Flavia," he said, addressing her for the first time, "You understand more about Rifting than anyone else in this room. What do you think?"

Flavia flushed at being put on the spot, but she cleared her throat and answered in a strong, clear voice. "Rifting is not dangerous. People occasionally dive a bit deeper than others, but that's no cause for alarm. Jess was able to come out of her trance last year without any lasting negative effects, and the knowledge she gained was crucial to understanding the prophecy she had made. Rifting has always been used by the Travelers to help us more clearly understand what the spirit world was trying to tell us. I can think of no more important moment than the current one for Jess to seek that kind of understanding."

"I agree with Flavia," Milo said, floating forward from the corner, where he'd silently been taking in the conversation. "The potential benefits far outweigh the risks."

"But..." Hannah began, but my patience was at an end.

"I don't understand why we're still talking about this!" I cried. "Do I seriously need to remind anyone here about what is happening down in that courtyard? Savvy needs me, and I'm done discussing the pros and cons. Only one thing matters, and that's figuring out how to help her!"

"I... okay, okay," Hannah sighed finally. "This... this is all just happening much faster than I can process it."

"I know, but I need you to trust me," I said to her. "This is the right thing to do, I know it."

Hannah crossed her arms over her chest, a defiant posture, but she nodded just the same. "You're right. I know you're right. That's doesn't mean I have to like it."

I kissed her on the cheek. "I know. I don't like it either. But I'll be careful."

"Alright then," said Flavia, climbing to her feet. "If we are really going to do this, and do it now, we have some preparations to make. Kiernan, is it?"

Kiernan started and leapt automatically to attention. "Yes."

Flavia paused, narrowing her eyes at him. "I know you, don't I? Do you often work down by the library?"

"Yes, indeed I do," he said, bowing his head.

"I thought so. Well, it's nice to meet you. Would you please start a fire in the grate?"

"Of course," Kiernan said, looking taken aback but going right to work.

"Hannah, would you be willing to go down to the dining room and ask to borrow a small bowl or a teacup? It has to be sturdy, something that can withstand being heated from beneath."

"Yes, of course," Hannah said at once. "Milo, come with me?"

"Stuck to you like glue, sweetness," Milo said, and the two of them left, closing the door behind them.

"I'll go down to the Casting supply closet and gather the herbs we need for the Casting," Flavia said.

"I can do that, if you like," Finn said. "If there are other things you need to prepare."

"Thank you, but I think it will be quicker if I go," Flavia said. "By the time I'd finished making you the list, I could have been there and back myself."

Finn simply nodded. "As you wish."

"Now, Jess, we've got a challenge, and I'm not sure how we're

SOUL OF THE SENTINEL

going to solve it," Flavia said, turning to me with a puzzled expression. "We've got a drawing of the artwork as it needs to be painted on your arms, but I have a feeling you may be the only artist skilled enough to recreate it, and I can't see how you're going to be able to paint it on yourself. On your left arm, perhaps, but certainly not on your right, unless you happen to be ambidextrous?"

I shook my head. "My control is shit with my left hand."

"And I don't suppose...?" Flavia looked hopefully around at Finn and Kiernan who both shook their heads.

"I can't draw to save my life," Kiernan said at once.

"Nor can I," Finn said.

Flavia turned to me. "I could try it, but I fear my artistic skills are rather poor as well."

A sudden idea occurred to me, and I jumped to my feet and ran to my desk. "I may have a solution to this problem," I said as I dug through my drawer, pulling out stacks of paper and drawing pads and supplies. "Yes, I've got some!" I said, holding up a pad of tracing paper and a stencil marker. "If I trace the design onto this tracing paper with this marker, apply it to my skin, and then peel it off, the ink will transfer to my skin, leaving the design!"

Flavia blinked. "But... that's brilliant!" she cried. "And you just have things like that sitting around in your drawers?"

I shrugged. "I'd been working on some new artwork to add to my tattoo. I wanted to test it out, to see how it looked before I committed it to permanent ink."

"Well, get drawing," Flavia ordered. "And I'll be right back with the Casting ingredients."

Finn sat with me while I carefully turned Agnes' sketch of my arm upside down so that when I traced and applied it, the image would not be reversed. Then I taped the tracing paper to the ancient drawing and set to work. It was easier than it should have been, tracing the design. The strokes felt so natural, so familiar. The hairs on the back of my neck began to stand up, and my arms broke out in goosebumps, despite the considerable heat now emanating from the fireplace beside us, where Kiernan had successfully kindled a roaring fire. Several times I found myself adding to the design without consciously following the image underneath, and then stopping in panic to check and make sure that what I had drawn and what Agnes had drawn matched up. It always did. Perfectly.

When I had nearly finished, Hannah and Milo returned with an

251

assortment of bowls and cups so that Flavia could choose which would work best. Flavia slipped into the room a few minutes later, carrying a mortar and pestle, a small linen bag full of herbs, and a little metal tea strainer. She set to work grinding the herbs and instructing Kiernan to stoke the fire so that some embers would break away from the bottommost logs.

When the herbs were ready, Hannah helped me transfer the artwork from the tracing paper to my skin. The moment the paper was peeled away, the ink lines began to glow, just as they had when Jeta prepared me for Rifting, and so I knew at once that I had copied the design successfully.

"Well done," Flavia said, smiling encouragingly. "You've done it."

"I have a feeling that was the easy part," I said, taking a deep calming breath.

"Are you ready?" Flavia asked.

"Yes," I replied, hoping very much that it wasn't a lie.

A knock resounded against the door, causing us all to jump and Flavia to nearly spill the bowl of herbs. We all froze, looking around at each other, silently panicking.

"No one say anything," Finn said. "I'll handle it."

He walked swiftly to the door, opened it, and stepped out into the hallway, closing it behind him. We all held our breath, listening to the muffled conversation of which I could not make out a single word, although I thought the other voice might be male. Finally, after a tense minute or so, Finn stepped back into the room.

"That was one of the Novitiates, sent to fetch Hannah and me," he explained.

Hannah jumped up, looking frightened. "Why? What's going on?" she asked.

Finn held up a hand. "Take a breath. Everything's alright. You have been summoned to the Council Room. The Council is convening to discuss the situation with Savannah."

Hannah flapped her hands frantically. "But what am I supposed to say? What should I tell them?"

"Nothing," I said swiftly. "Tell them nothing. You knew that Savvy had been complaining about waking up exhausted and finding her boots muddy. That's all you know."

Hannah groaned. "Jess, I am a terrible liar, you know that!"

"Just do your best," I told her. "With any luck, this Rifting will provide us with the answers we need, and I will go straight to the

Council with them. But they can't know that you've been hiding all this from them, or you'll get reprimanded, and we can't have a stain like that on your membership, not with your legislation hanging in the balance."

"Okay, okay," Hannah intoned to herself, closing her eyes and taking several long, slow breaths to calm herself. Then she turned back to me. "Are you *sure* you'll be—"

"I will be absolutely fine," I assured her. "You won't do any good sitting around here fussing over me anyway. Go find out what's happening."

"Fine," Hannah said, still looking thoroughly unconvinced, but realizing she had no choice. She looked up at Finn. "What about you? Have you been summoned to the Council Room, too?"

"No, to the barracks," Finn said. "We need to organize the security of the courtyard."

Kiernan stood up, looking anxious. "Shall... shall I come with you?" he asked.

"No," said Finn. "I'm ordering you here, to keep watch over Jess while she attempts this Casting. If anything goes awry, come and fetch me at once."

"I'll stay, too," Milo said. "That way I can keep Hannah updated through the connection."

Hannah looked slightly more reassured at this, and with one last whispered demand that I keep myself safe, she slipped from the room.

Finn knelt down and kissed me, then took my face into his cupped hands. "Stay safe, love," he said.

"I will," I told him.

"I will make sure of it," Flavia said, meeting Finn's eyes and nodding once, fiercely. "Upon my honor as a Traveler, I will see she comes to no harm."

Finn returned the nod gratefully, and left, closing the door firmly behind him. Kiernan stood up, crossed the room, and fastened the deadbolt.

"We don't want any unannounced visitors while this is going on, do we?" he asked, and then planted himself in front of the door for good measure.

"Well, then," Flavia said. "It's time."

She scooped a small glowing ember into the tea strainer and

handed it to me, still smoking. Then she gave me the bowl of herbs and said, "Do you remember what to do?"

"Repeat the incantation, inhale, and then lay down before I fall over," I said. "That sound about right?"

Flavia smiled. "That's it. And do you remember how to come out of it, when you're ready?"

"Find the door," I repeated. "There's always a door, and it will always be open. I walk through it to wake up." I didn't ask the question out loud that I wanted to ask—about the Tansy Hag's words, telling me I needed to go "deep through the door that will not open." It would do no good to ask a question to which I knew she had no answer. Flavia assured me that there would always be a way out of the Rifting, and I had to trust that I would be able to find it.

"You're ready," Flavia said. "I'll watch over you. Good luck, Northern Girl."

I smiled at the use of my old nickname and closed my eyes.

Here goes everything.

A whispered incantation. A deep, floral breath. And I fell.

20

THE SECOND DOOR

G RASS TICKLED MY CHEEK. The air in my nose still smelled of foxglove and sage and smoke. My body felt light and weightless, and for a few moments, I had no desire at all to open my eyes. It was bliss, lying here with the sun on my face. I could see the great yellow curve of it from behind my eyelids. I was the carefree girl in the flowers once more.

But open my eyes I did, for my curiosity got the better of me at last. What I saw made me blink with confusion. It was not the golden curve of the sun that hung over me, but a great round yellow flower towering above me on a stalk that stood at least twenty feet high. I sat up at once and looked around. I was surrounded by flower stalks as large as tree trunks, each blossom waving in the breeze over my head like a dirigible. And there I sat, like Alice after partaking of dubious tea party snacks, no larger than an insect.

"What the hell..." I began, feeling my panic begin to rise, but I stopped myself, forcing myself to take a slow, deep breath and calm down. Nothing in the Rift was real, I reminded myself. It was all just a dream—a hallucination. It had been disorienting and strange last time, and it was likely to be that way again. I needed to stop thinking about how I felt and start paying attention to the world of the dream, because that was where I would find the clarity I sought.

Just as I had convinced myself to calm down, my heart leapt into my throat again and I let out an earsplitting shriek. A face loomed down at me from above the flowers, parting the blooms with a massive hand and peering down at me. It was a face I knew, although I'd never seen it except in spectral form.

"Well, well," said Eleanora Larkin in a booming voice. "What have you gotten yourself into now, Jessica Ballard?"

"I... I'm not quite sure," I confessed. "I'm still getting my bearings."

"Here, let me help you," she replied, and extended a great hulking hand down toward me.

As I reached toward her hand, I suddenly found that I could grasp her fingers easily within mine, that her hand was indeed no bigger than my own. And as I sat up, I found the flowers no larger than dandelions. Eleanora no longer towered over me either, but sat beside me in the flower patch, looking contented and serene in a long white dress, with a crown of the yellow flowers in her hair. It all looked vaguely familiar.

"Thank you," I said. "For a second there I felt like I was only about an inch tall."

Eleanora wasn't listening. She was picking more of the yellow flowers and weaving them into a second crown. As she worked, she sang a lilting little song under her breath.

"For boys and girls who will not mind,
Who trouble court and mischief find,
The Tansy Hag, she lies in wait
To leave her mark upon your gate."

"What did you say?" I asked.

"Hmm?"

"That song. What are you singing?" I asked again.

"Was I singing?" Eleanora asked with a shrug.

And then I remembered why I was here, the answer I needed. "Eleanora, do you know what this symbol means?"

And I held my palm up to face her so that she could see it clearly.

She paused in her flower weaving and stared at it for one bewildered moment, before saying, "Why, no. Should I?"

I laughed and dropped my hand back to my lap. "No, apparently not."

Eleanora tucked one last bloom into the crown and held it up in triumph. "Here you are, Jessica. I've made you one as well. Now we can both be queens. Queens of the tansy patch!"

She reached out and placed the crown upon my head. I reached up to straighten it and caught a glimpse of my own sleeve. I was wearing a white dress identical to Eleanora's, rather like a nightgown, and it was at that moment I realized where I was. It was the drawing in the storybook, the one that Flavia and I had found upon the shelf in the catacomb archives.

Two little girls, playing in the flower patch. And behind them, lurking in the shadows...

I knew what I would see when I turned around, but it didn't lessen my shock upon seeing it. As Eleanora continued to hum her nursery rhyme, oblivious to everything but her own childish enjoyment, I looked over my shoulders into the deep and murky woods that were materializing behind us. I watched as a great invisible hand created each tree, each branch, each deep and shadowy recess, stroke by stroke, until the painting was complete. And at last, two shining eyes appeared, and the darkness around them deepened and condensed into a human form, shrouded in a cloak.

A hand reached out from under the folds of the cloak and beckoned to me.

As I wondered whether I ought to follow her, I spotted a door, carved right into the trunk of a tree beside the Tansy Hag. A dim glow issued from all around it, indicating that it was indeed open, ready for me to pull it wide and return to reality any moment I chose. I would not choose it yet, I knew—there was still too much to understand—but it gave me a sense of relief to see it was there, just as Flavia had promised it would be.

Eleanora took no notice of either the door or the stooped and menacing figure watching us. She stood up and stretched her arms, stifling a yawn. Then she reached up, up, into the sky toward the sun. She plucked it like a flower, and it came away in her hand, a little golden orb. She tucked it delightedly into her crown and turned to me. "We must be getting home. It's growing dark."

Indeed, it was. In the absence of the sun, a twilight blue was streaking over the sky above us like watercolor. I stood up and followed Eleanora who turned to enter the woods. The Tansy Hag had faded back into the shadows and disappeared. Even though I knew it was all a dream, I still didn't like the idea of traipsing off into those woods.

"Are... are you sure that's the right way?" I asked Eleanora.

She laughed at me. "Of course, I am. Don't you remember how to get home? Come on, Jessica!"

And she skipped off down the path, leaving me little choice but to stumble along after her in my overly-long frock. The crown slipped sideways on my head, and I tried to straighten it. The tiny sun tucked into Eleanora's crown bounced along ahead of me like a lantern, lighting our way.

Brambles and thorns tugged at our skirts, but Eleanora seemed not to notice. She simply skipped on, running her hands over tree trunks and hopping over roots and puddles. Although I could not see the Tansy Hag, I could feel her eyes upon me, raising the hairs on the back of my neck. Once or twice, I even felt a breeze on my cheek that could have been a breath. I knew I needed not to wander too far, for as scared as I was to see the Tansy Hag again, I knew I needed to follow her, because she had promised that she would find me here.

At last, the trees began to space out and we reached a clearing. Eleanora danced out into it. Overhead, the sky was scattered with stars. With a sparkling laugh, Eleanora reached for the tiny sun in her crown and tossed it into the sky as high as she could. It sailed up amongst the stars and hung there, having transformed into the moon.

"Time for bed!" Eleanora sang. "Come along, or mother will be terribly cross!"

I tore my eyes from the newly hung moon that had once been the sun, and all the awe I felt curdled at once into shock. Eleanora was dancing around a small structure rather like a bed, and at first glance, a girl seemed to be lying on top of it asleep, like a fairytale princess awaiting true love's kiss. As I walked across the clearing toward it, however, I realized it was not a girl, but a carved stone statue, and that the structure was not a bed, but a tomb.

Smiling contentedly, Eleanora slid the cover of the tomb aside as easily as if it were a blanket and swung her legs over the side. She looked up at me, and the shadows cast by the moonlight transformed her friendly smile into a sinister leer.

"Come along, Jessica. It's bedtime. I'll tuck you in."

Eleanora slipped down out of sight into the tomb. I was dizzy with fear, remembering my foray into the Larkin mausoleum—the claustrophobia, the dust of decay, the overpowering smell of death. Just as I decided not to follow her, a gnarled hand reached up out of the tomb and beckoned me forward before slipping back down again. I took a deep, unsteady breath, and approached the tomb.

I peered down into it, expecting to see Eleanora lying inside, or else the Tansy Hag staring up at me, pointing her finger at me like a malediction. Instead, I saw only blackness, a deep and gaping hole in the earth.

"Eleanora?" I called. My voice echoed in the depths and my call went unanswered. "Just great. Really great," I muttered to myself, climbing up to swing my legs off the side of the tomb and letting them dangle down into the darkness.

One of the Travelers had once told me, "Remember, you can't get hurt in the Rift, so do whatever the fuck you want!"

Well, this didn't exactly qualify as something I *wanted* to do, but...

I jumped, enveloped in the rushing sensation of the fall and, unexpectedly, wonderfully free from the fear of it. I knew a brief moment of glorious freedom, and then my feet hit solid earth.

In the real world, it would have broken my legs, but here in the Rift, I landed as lightly as a feather. It was, I argued to myself, the most graceful I would ever be. I laughed, but the laughter died away almost at once; I knew the place in which I had landed.

Eleanora was nowhere to be found, but this did not surprise me—the people that populated a trip into the Rift were as transient as the journey itself. I did not call for her, nor seek her out, but instead looked around the place in which I now found myself: the forgotten spirit block in the depths of Skye Príosún.

It was familiar and yet it was different. It had the same musty smell, the same flickering, dim light. Cells lined the walls and rats scurried unseen in the shadows. But the inhabitants of the cells were decidedly different than during my foray into reality's version of the spirit block.

In the first cell: Hannah, in a straight jacket, with padded walls.

In the second cell: Mackie, beating her bleeding fists against the stones.

In the third cell: Flavia scribbling in tiny writing from floor to ceiling, whimpering to herself.

In the fourth cell: Karen, sitting in an armchair, in a posture identical to her father all those years ago, lips moving rapidly and silently, clutching at the armrests and looking ready to spring from the seat and into the sky if someone would only release her.

I tore my eyes from these distressing sights to glance behind me. There was the door, partially open, through which I could make my escape any time I chose, but I firmly turned my back on it. I couldn't leave, not yet. I still had so many questions.

I yelped. Just ahead of me, a figure had appeared, dressed in Caomhnóir attire, standing at attention with their back to me. I may not have been able to see her face, but I knew that figure, that hair...

Savvy.

I approached her cautiously, walking around her until I could see her face. It was just as I had seen it up in the courtyard: serene and determined, eyes fixed on something I could not see.

"Sav?" I asked, with no real hope that she would answer me. Which is why, I suppose, that I jumped and shrieked when she did.

"*Vortimo*," she said, in a voice that was decidedly not her own, but ancient and cracked. She still did not look at me, but the Romany word for "truth" hung in the air between us.

"Where?" I asked her at last, when I had finally found my voice. "Where is *vortimo*? Where do I find it?"

Savvy raised one arm and pointed straight ahead of her. I followed the direction of her gesture. The cell of the Tansy Hag, that deep earthen cavern, lay straight ahead of us, but it had changed. Through the curtain of roots and cobwebs, I could see, not a cave, but a path, and at the end of the path, a great stone archway upon a dais...

The Geatgrima.

Leaving Savvy behind standing guard, I crept into the cavern and onto the path. The moment I did so, the entirety of the spirit block fell away, dissolved like a morning mist, and I found myself in the central courtyard of Fairhaven walking toward our own Geatgrima.

And yet, it wasn't our own Geatgrima. Large sections of the stones had fallen away from both the archway and the dais upon which it stood, and a small figure was struggling to shift the rock piles. As I drew closer, I realized that it was Irina.

"Irina!" I cried out, and she looked up from her work. Her expression was frantic.

"Don't just stand there, Northern Girl! Help me!" she snapped and continued her struggle.

I knelt down beside her and together, we managed to lift one of the smaller stones back onto the plinth.

"What's happened to the Geatgrima?" I asked.

"Destruction," Irina replied through gritted teeth. "They were never meant to withstand this. And now it may be too late."

"Too late for what?"

"Too late, too late," Irina repeated, heaving another stone into place on the dais.

I groaned. Even the imaginary Rift version of Irina was enigmatic. I couldn't get a straight answer out of her in the real world either. "Irina, do you know what this symbol means?" I asked her, raising my palm so that she could look at it.

Irina gazed at my markings for a moment and then shook her head sadly. "That was the mark. That was the mark that started it all. The deception. The thievery. The lies."

"So, you've seen it before?" I cried. "You know what it means?"

"Lies upon lies," Irina said. "A sisterhood built on lies. And now look," she gestured sadly toward the pile of stones. "It crumbles."

"What are you talking about?" I asked excitedly. "What lies?"

Irina shook her head more forcefully now. "No. I cannot tell you. I do not know the whole story."

"Then who? Who can tell me? Please, Irina, I have to know. My friend Savvy's life might depend on it!"

Irina stared into my eyes with such piercing intensity that I shrank back from her. Then she said, "You will have to be brave. You will have to choose the other door—the one that will not open."

"What other door? What do you mean?" I looked around and saw a single door set into the wall of the courtyard, and it was partially open, just like every door I'd seen since I'd entered the Rifting. It was the way back out, to reality and to consciousness. So then, where was this second door?

"Irina, I don't see a—" I began, but the rest of my sentence was swallowed in a scream. Irina was gone, and in her place, huddled right beside me, was the Tansy Hag. She no longer looked like a spirit at all—in this place of otherness, I was able to see her in a human form, but it was not much less frightening. Her features were ancient, so folded in wrinkles and creases that it looked as though she had found a much larger person's skin and crawled into it. Her eyes were small and beady and black, just like a raven's eyes, and they bore into me with an intensity that made me long to turn away and yet rendered me completely unable to do so. When she spoke, her toothless mouth expelled a breath that reeked of the same tomb-dust stench as the mausoleum.

"*Dook Rakli*," she whispered, pointing at me.

"Yes," I choked out, dragging the meaning of the Romany words from my memory. "Yes, I am a Seer. Please, can you tell me what this symbol means?"

I showed her the artwork upon my arms and palms. Her face broke into a black-gummed grin when she saw it.

"You are ready," she whispered, in English this time.

"Ready for what?" I asked.

"*Vortimo*," she replied, and then pointed behind her, "Deeper. Through the second door."

I looked where she was pointing and discovered that the Geatgrima had gone. In its place now upon the dais was a rough planed wooden door, curved like the stone archway had been, with no handle at all. And unlike every other door I had seen since sinking down into the Rift, this door appeared to be firmly closed.

I whirled around and looked behind me again. The first door was still there, warm and inviting light spilling out from around it. If I listened closely, I could almost hear Hannah and Milo's voices, laughing and talking together, urging me to join them.

I glanced back at the new door again only to discover that the Tansy Hag had vanished. I was alone, kneeling by the edge of the dais, a door behind me and a door in front of me, and wishing I did not have to make the choice between them, that someone would arrive and shove me through one of them instead.

No such helpful individual appeared. I knew they wouldn't. I knew I had to make this choice myself. And I also knew I'd already made it.

I stood up, brushing the dust from my white dress, and stepped up onto the dais. I examined the door carefully, but this closer inspection revealed no handle, no keyhole, no knocker, nothing at all that would indicate how I was meant to get through the door. Nothing Flavia or the other Travelers had taught me had prepared me for this.

Tentatively, I brushed a single fingertip against the door. Nothing at all remarkable happened. It felt, in all respects, like an ordinary old door. I pressed all five of my fingertips to the door and pushed against it, first gently, them more forcefully. It did not budge. I tried pressing my shoulder against the door and leaning my full weight against it. Still, the door would not move. I curled my hand into a fist and knocked, and then pounded. Nothing.

I looked around me in desperation, looking for some kind of clue, but the world of the Rift had left no such hints for me. Feeling defeated, I leaned against the door, resting my hand and my forehead against the wood.

Immediately a tingling sensation began in my hand. It startled me so much that I pulled it away, and the tingling faded. I looked down at my hand and saw the last glimmers of a glow recede from the artwork on my palm. Gasping, I glanced up at the door just in time to see the very same artwork, golden and glistening, fading from the planks, leaving the door bare and unremarkable once more.

I looked down at both of my hands and inspiration dawned at last. I pushed both of my sleeves up past my elbows, revealing the full extent of the artwork. Then, with a silent prayer, I pressed both of my forearms and palms flat against the door.

The effect was instantaneous. Curling golden tendrils of vines and flowers and runes blossomed from the place where my skin had touched the wood and spread over the entire surface of the door until it was aglow from top to bottom. I stepped back, watching it in wonder, feeling the rushing, tingling magic racing over my skin, lighting up the markings I had drawn there until both the door and my arms were beaming like the sun.

The last of the symbols to appear, right in the very center of the door, was the mysterious mark of the Tansy Hag. The moment it materialized, drawn by some invisible hand, the door creaked and swung open. All fear and doubt burned away, I stepped through it without hesitation. It slammed shut behind me, leaving me in darkness.

A flicker. A tiny flame. A candle lit and held aloft.

A figure approached me out of the darkness, the candle clutched in her hand. Her face was as familiar as home, her voice, when it spoke, as soothing as a lullaby. She smiled at me, and I smiled back.

"I have been waiting a very long time for you," said Agnes Isherwood.

E.E. Holmes is a writer, teacher, and actor living in central Massachusetts with her husband, two children, and a small, but surprisingly loud dog. When not writing, she enjoys performing, watching unhealthy amounts of British television, and reading with her children. Please visit www.eeholmes.com to learn more about E.E. Holmes and *The World of The Gateway*.